MURDER ON THE DANUBE

Dear Guest,

We hope you enjoy our selection of
itinerary-related books. This book is part
of our ship library and you are more than
welcome to take it to your stateroom.
Please return when you are finished so
that other guests may also enjoy it.

Thank you for your cooperation,
Your Hotel Manager

MURDER ON THE DANUBE

▼

A Robbie Cutler Diplomatic Mystery

William S. Shepard

Writers Club Press

New York   Lincoln   Shanghai

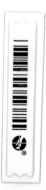

Murder On The Danube
A Robbie Cutler Diplomatic Mystery

Writers Club Press
an imprint of iUniverse, Inc.

iUniverse books may be ordered through booksellers or by contacting:

iUniverse
2021 Pine Lake Road, Suite 100
Lincoln, NE 68512
www.iuniverse.com
1-800-Authors (1-800-288-4677)

The wine label on the front cover is used with the kind permission of Mr. Laszlo Meszaros, General Manager, Domaine Disznoko, Tokaj, Hungary.

ISBN: 0-595-20740-5

Printed in the United States of America

DEDICATION

▼

As the 50th anniversary of their courageous exploits nears, this book is gratefully dedicated to the Hungarian Freedom Fighters of 1956. Their courage in the epic days October 23—November 4 made it possible to advance the cause of liberty everywhere. The eventual victory for their heroism was the downfall of the Berlin Wall, the implosion of the Soviet Union, and the end of the Cold War.

And it all started on a Tuesday in October, when a proud people heard poetry recited, and started their march into history across the Danube bridge.

CONTENTS

PROLOGUE

▼

BUDAPEST, NOVEMBER, 1956

Eva Molnar had held out as long as she dared. In the rubble Janos Magassy, the last man alive, had told her to save herself now. The Russian tanks and their guns had systematically reduced the areas in Pest still held by the Freedom Fighters, one by one. Even Radio Budapest had fallen, which meant that no help would come from the West after all.

Soon the infantry would come. Rumor had it that the Russians were now using Mongolian infantry, so that Russian troops would not be able to return home and tell what they had done here, or indeed what they had seen here. Even in the worst days of 1953 under Rakosi, the Hungarian Stalinist, Hungary had been materially better off than the Soviet Union. That remained true even today, three years later. And in the early days of this uprising, just two weeks ago, Russian-speaking Hungarians had argued with Russian troops.

No more of that. Csaba Kovacs had said that using Mongolian troops was a nice historic touch. It was the Khan's hordes that had devastated Hungary centuries ago.

Their resistance pocket was an apartment building in a narrow street that allowed concentrated fire on approaching Russian tanks. A nearby gas station had supplied the gasoline needed for Molotov cocktails, and the quarter's police station had yielded its guns a week ago, when the winning side had seemed to be the Freedom Fighters.

Time and again during the previous few weeks Csaba, Eva and their young comrades had emerged, darted between the tanks like Drake's squadrons amongst the Armada, and destroyed them with their Molotov cocktails.

But now time was running out. Csaba, who had left to reconnoiter the quarter three days ago, had not returned. Was he really dead? There were rumors that the Imre Nagy ministers, and Nagy himself, had taken refuge in the Yugoslav Embassy on Dozsa Gyorgy *utca* (street) facing *Hosok Tere* (Heroes Square). Nobody knew the fate of General Pal Maleter and other leaders of the Hungarian armed forces who had gone —when was it, she tried to remember—a week or so ago under a safe conduct to negotiate with the Russians.

Outside their pocket, there had seemed to be a lull. Eva went into the street, shivering in the cold November early morning sunlight. The few who still had some heating coal burned it, adding another layer of residue to the buildings, many of which were still scarred from 1945. Eva was appalled by the destruction that she saw, in street after street. What had happened to the beautiful Budapest of her art books, the Budapest of the Parliament, the *Matyas Templom* (Matthias Church), the *Halaszbastya* (Fishermen's Bastion), and the Opera?

Suddenly, she just wanted to escape. It was too much. But where? Then she remembered what Csaba had said. Everyone knew that Jozsef Cardinal Mindszenty had sought asylum at the American Legation on *Szabadsag ter* (Freedom Square). She had even visited the Legation once, and talked with a nice American in the cultural affairs section, a Mr. Cutler. He had learned some Hungarian, and had been highly amused when, using her most polite voice, she had addressed him as *"Konzul Elvtars"* ("Comrade Consul").

Their laughter and his concern at her embarrassment were nice memories, even now.

*   *   *

Swarms of people waited outside the Legation, which was a lonely, fortified place. Ever since the November 4 cable from Washington granting asylum to Cardinal Mindszenty, other Hungarians had flocked to Freedom Square. But the Legation had only taken in American press representatives. After the evacuation by car of all Legation dependents on October 28, now only key staff remained. Classified messages had already been destroyed, in anticipation of a possible military attack on the Legation. Anything seemed possible, and the mission's diplomatic status was thin protection against artillery or tank guns.

Minister Wailes gave Trip Cutler the task of posting a notice that nobody else would be admitted. He was told to do so early in the morning, before the daily crowds had formed. Shivering in the early morning air, Trip left the Legation for the first time in four days and tacked up the sign on the Legation door. Most of the people already waiting started to disperse. Others waited. One never knew.

Then he turned to look into the square, Freedom Square, named for the fact that a Hapsburg prison that once had stood here had been demolished. A nearby plaque reminded the passerby that here, in that prison, leaders of Hungary's 1848 rebellion against Austria had been martyred. Was it going to happen again, this time from the East?

Trip shook his head and turned to open the Legation door. He was stopped by a voice, calling faintly across the square. It sounded somehow familiar, girlish and cultivated. Then came the sound of tanks and infantry entering Freedom Square, from the eastern outskirts, pouring down through the broad boulevards and infiltrating the public squares, one by one. Those who had been waiting outside the Legation now began to run in the opposite direction, towards the Danube.

The girl started running across the square towards the Legation door. *"Konzul Elvtars!"* she shouted.

Trip spun around, and saw the girl one hundred feet away, running towards him. But the soldiers streaming across the square from his right removed any possibility that she could beat them to the Legation. Trip started to run towards her, but she was cut off by the wave of soldiers clearing the square.

Trip stood alone in the silent square. He listened hard, but all that could be heard was the sound of small arms fire in the distance, and the approaching clank clank clank of the tanks.

He turned, entered the Legation and closed the door.

ACKNOWLEDGEMENTS

▼

I have many to thank. First and foremost, I would like to acknowledge my teacher of Hungarian at the Foreign Service Institute, Mrs. Eva Eszenyi. At a time when her native Hungary was beset by darkness, her personal example, and that of her family, showed by contrast a Hungary that was cultivated, and rich in history and the quest for freedom.

In the same vein I would like to thank my friend of many years, Istvan B. "Steve" Gereben, former Executive Secretary of the Coordinating Committee of Hungarian Organizations in North America. Steve is a nationally respected Freedom Fighter, and an American who has always sought that his adopted nation should live up to her own ideals.

In specific preparation for this book, I would like to thank Ambassador Gyorgy Banlaki and Dr. Zoltan Banyasz, Consul of the Hungarian Embassy in Washington. They arranged my very useful interviews in Budapest with Dr. Miklos Jordan, Head of the International Department, Budapest Chief Prosecutor's Office, his legal colleague Dr. Sandor Csordas, and Colonel Laszlo Mezo of the Prison Service.

I am grateful to Political Counselor David C. Summers of the American Embassy in Budapest, and to his wife Beatrice Camp, the Embassy's Cultural and Educational Attache, for their helpful insights into contemporary

Hungary. The recollections of my friend Gaza A. Katona, who served as Assistant Political Attache at the American Legation in Budapest in 1956, were invaluable. So was the personal testimony of Endre Marton, whose book *The Forbidden Sky* remains a classic first-hand account of the events of 1956.

Particular appreciation is due to the officials and staff of the Institute for the History of the 1956 Hungarian Revolution, 74 Dohany utca, Budapest. Executive Director Andras Hegedus and Research Coordinator Csaba Bekes were helpful hosts, opening many doors. I am very grateful to the Institute's authority on the streetfighting in 1956, Laszlo Eorsi, and to media associate Reka Sarkozi for their practical and painstaking help in guiding me through the various phases of the 1956 fighting.

I am grateful to Mr. Laszlo Meszaros, General Manager, Domaine Disznoko, Tokaj, Hungary, for the privilege of using their famed Tokaj *Eszencia* label for the front cover of this book.

CHARACTERS

▼

Hungarian Freedom Fighters, 1956:

Eva Molnar		Laszlo
Csaba Kovacs		Pista
Janos Magassy		Red
Attila Nemzeti	(Margit)	Magda
Imre Mohacsi	(Magda)	Jozsef
Istvan Szepvaros	(Maria)	Karoly

Robbie's Family:

Samuel Lawrence "Trip" Cutler III. Lucille Cutler. Robbie's parents
"Uncle Seth" Cutler, great uncle
Evalyn Cutler, sister
Sylvie Marceau, girl friend
Minouette, a Siamese cat

American Embassy Budapest:

Ambassador Eleanor Horton. Sam Horton
Deputy Chief of Mission Arnold Johnson. Charlotte Johnson
Colonel Joshua Tidings USA, Defense Attache
John Robinson "Robbie" Cutler, Political Officer
Arpad Novotny, Cultural and Information Officer
Julia Broadbent, Economic and Commercial Officer
Randolph Davis, Consul
Gunnery Sergeant Lemuel Shiflett, USMC

Budapest Diplomatic Corps:

Eduardo Dos Campos, Spanish Ambassador. Elena Dos Campos
Alexander Kovatch, Australian Ambassador. Julie Kovatch
Charles Lauricette, Political Officer French Embassy. Marie Lauricette
Eleni Papadopoulos, Consul Greek Embassy
Iliu Monescu, Consul Romanian Embassy
Jorge Angelos. Political Officer Brazilian Embassy. Ana Angelos

Hungarian Officials:

Imre Racz, Inspector, Central Police Station, Budapest
Janos Horvath, FIDESZ Deputy from Eger. Ilona Horvath
Ferenc Esztergondos, Socialist Deputy from Sarospatak

CHAPTER ONE

▼

THIRTEEN FOR DINNER

Robbie Cutler looked around his Castle Hill apartment with satisfaction. He seemed to have thought of everything Two vases of fresh cut flowers added splashes of color. Dishes of cold *hors d'oeuvres* had been set out by the waiter, a college student who was now placing wine and ale glasses on the bar. There was a choice of Czech Pilsener beer or Hungarian wines, either the rich red *Egri Bikaver* ("Bull's Blood of Eger") or a white wine from the shores of Lake Balaton south of Budapest.

Erzsi, Robbie's occasional cook, was making her specialty, *paprikas csirke galuskaval*. She bustled around the small kitchen sniffing the spicy chicken *paprikas* while she formed the homemade dumplings for cooking. Her chocolate desserts were already stashed away in Robbie's small china cupboard, whose wooden front was painted with colorful Hungarian folk designs. Erzsi was an absolute ruler in charge of a very small domain.

Embassy lodgings were now allocated by family size, not responsibility. As a bachelor Robbie therefore didn't rate that house on Roskovits Street in the Buda hills where the Political Officer at the American Embassy in

Budapest had always lived. Size of family was everything now, not the job you had to do.

That was why Robbie was packing a dozen or so people into his apartment, where six would have been a crowd. Still, on this mild evening his guests would spill out onto his small patio, which had a nice view over the Danube. Come to think of it, in the old Cold War days when his father had served in the Legation here, the waiter and the cook would have been spies supplied by the official Diplomatic Service Bureau, not private hires. But back then, there would have been no Hungarian private citizens to entertain, either. It wouldn't have been safe for them or allowed by the state.

Minouette, his Siamese cat, brushed his ankles. She had probably slept the afternoon away, during Robbie's afternoon excursion to Eger. Now it was time for her dinner. As a sign to Minouette that company was expected, Robbie picked her up, patted her once or twice, and then deposited her and her supper dish in the small study upstairs in the duplex apartment, and closed the door. No sense taking chances with so many people expected. It would only take a moment for Minouette to run out the door, and become lost in the *Varhegy*, the Castle Hill district of Buda.

Robbie was pleased with the afternoon's excursion. The whole thing had been his idea, really. Lithe and athletic, he liked getting out of the office, and there was a great deal to see and do in Hungary. Some of his colleagues liked hiking, or jogging. Some even combined the two and had formed a local Hash House Harriers group, setting out markers along a predetermined route. If you liked that sort of thing, it was all right. But you didn't see much of Hungary that way.

And so, Robbie had had the idea, one evening while dining with diplomatic colleagues, to form the Goulash and Touring Club. When you weren't stuck as duty officer, or showing some visiting fireman around Budapest, his plan was to visit a different city or region in the Hungarian countryside on the first Saturday of each month. The organizer would be responsible for the day's excursion, including dinner either in the countryside, or in Budapest if they hadn't had a long trip. It would be even better if Hungarians from the region being visited joined the group for the day.

Of course, since the Goulash and Touring Club had been Robbie's idea in the first place, it was up to him to organize the first Saturday outing. He had decided on Eger, a town in the northeast about 80 miles from Budapest. Janos Horvath, a young Deputy from the conservative *FIDESZ* Party in the Hungarian Parliament who represented Eger, had joined them for the day. Since he was needed for some votes on Monday morning, and had to work Sunday in his parliamentary office to catch up on pending legislation and party business, he and Mrs. Horvath also planned to return to Budapest that evening and join them for dinner.

The Horvaths had met the ten diplomats in Eger, and had also arranged for a local historian, and for the curator of the arts and crafts shop, to join the group for the afternoon. The Mayor of Eger even greeted them briefly on their arrival in town, and a stringer for the local press accompanied the group around Eger, taking pictures from time to time.

It had been a fine outing, Robbie reflected. Eger was chiefly known in Hungarian history and legend for the desperate and successful stand of a few thousand Hungarians against overwhelming odds during the sixteenth century Turkish invasion.

As they toured Eger Castle, they could almost sense the ghosts of its gallant defenders. They had even prepared primitive noisemakers, drums with small pebbles, which would rattle slightly if miners were tunneling under the castle walls. Robbie could imagine the hush in the dark corridors as the defenders listened, and watched the drums. He had wondered whether similar devices were used during the trench warfare centuries later on the Western Front in World War One.

The guests began to arrive. "You seem pensive, Robbie," said a smiling Eduardo Dos Campos, as he and his wife Elena entered the apartment. "Not solving another mystery, are you?"

Robbie greeted the rotond Spanish Ambassador and his wife. They were friends from his previous assignment at the Consulate General in

Bordeaux. Robbie was pleased that Dos Campos had now been assigned by Madrid to head the Spanish Embassy here.

"I was just thinking about our excursion to Eger today," Robbie said. "Sorry you couldn't join us. That desperate seige the Hungarians withstood so long ago. I'm reminded somehow of 1956. Gallantry seems a recurrent theme in their history. Anyway, enough of all that. Come and have a glass of wine. The others will be joining us shortly."

Next came Charles and Marie Lauricette. They were elegant, modish Parisians, and Charles was Robbie's counterpart, Political Officer at the French Embassy. "Nice start today for the Goulash and Touring Club, Robbie. We enjoyed it. What's the program for next month?"

"That's up to you, Charles. This organization is young enough to make up its own rules. One of them is going to be that after each excursion, the organizer for the following month's outing will be named at dinner. I have the distinct feeling that you'll be our organizer for next month." He caught himself. "That is, if Marie agrees. It would be fun if you and Marie would plan it for us. Maybe we could even work in a real French picnic for luncheon along the way." Marie Lauricette smiled her agreement. Back to business. "By the way, what did you make of Janos Horvath? He and his wife will be joining us tonight."

"He seems impressive. It's interesting to see a teacher in politics, particularly one who isn't on the left. He is also young enough to represent something new. So many of the people that you and I meet at the Parliament have something to hide, or to explain. They seem to be part of the past."

The waiter appeared with a tray of glasses of wine. It was just warm enough so that his guests wouldn't be wearing topcoats, Robbie realized. That was a good thing. It would save lots of turning around in his apartment, and also, reduce the chances of Minouette getting loose, since coats were usually put in his study upstairs.

A dazzling youthful smile from Julie Kovatch next greeted Robbie, as she strode boldly into the apartment, leaving her husband, Australian Ambassador Alexander Kovatch, in her wake. "Such a successful afternoon,

Robbie! I really enjoyed myself. Too bad Alexander was stuck at the Embassy again with visitors. He misses all the fun."

"I'll bet," Robbie thought, returning her smile while extending his hand to the Ambassador in greeting.

There was only time to grin a hello and thank you when Robbie's boss, Deputy Chief of Mission Arnold Johnson, arrived with his wife Charlotte. Johnson, perhaps edgy because he would have to refrain from smoking his trademark cigars in the small apartment, managed a somber grin. Charlotte, as usual, made up for her husband with genuine charm. They hadn't been on the excursion, but it was always a good idea to invite the person who wrote your annual efficiency report when you were showing some initiative. Now seemed to be such an occasion.

The waiter, and now Erzsi festive in her red and green hand embroidered apron, passed the wine and *hors d'oeuvres*. The Consul of Greece, Eleni Papadopoulos, had just arrived along with her counterpart from the Romanian Embassy, Iliu Monescu. Her appearance was dramatic. "Callas without the voice," Robbie thought. Monescu on the other hand was a methodical person. Robbie had been curious to see how he would enjoy these excursions. Romania and Hungary had been so often at odds.

Too bad the German and Brazilian Political Officers had been unable to come this evening. Hans and Jorge and their wives had been good company that afternoon, but they had other obligations for the evening. That often happened. Good thing Robbie had foreseen that possibility, and filled in with Eduardo and Eleni Dos Campos and the Johnsons.

Janos and Ilona Horvath arrived next. Perfect timing, Robbie conceded. Not late at all, and not too early either. Their timing silently said that they were the Hungarians who mattered. *"Jo eszakat kivanok"* ("Good evening"), Robbie greeted them. He might translate where necessary for Ilona, whose English was unsteady, but Janos was an English teacher by profession, who had also put in a graduate year at the University of Wisconsin.

Except of course for Australian Ambassador Kovatch, a native speaker, Robbie was the only diplomat there who spoke Hungarian. Only the

United States routinely trained her diplomats in esoteric foreign languages. Maybe the Romanian, Monescu, spoke some Hungarian. Robbie wasn't sure. But the evening would be in English, testimony to Hungary's defining isolation even in peaceful times.

For the Hungarian language was devilishly hard to learn, a barrier that most never crossed. For those who did, there were compensations of culture and understanding. One could begin to dig beyond the surface. And who knows, Robbie sometimes wondered, perhaps his membership in that small band of career diplomats who had learned Hungarian might someday result in his being named Ambassador here. He hoped so. The future would sort that out.

It wasn't that Americans were always in favor here, Robbie realized. It was easy to think so now, when things had eased in this country. Freedom, democracy, the beginnings of trade and substantial foreign investment crowned now with NATO membership, that was all to the good.

But there had been a disturbing reminder of other times that very afternoon. Robbie had overheard his Brazilian colleague, Jorge Angelos, talking about the 1956 Revolution with their guide at Eger Castle. Swept away by the legendary stand of the outnumbered defenders, Jorge had simply made a graceful remark about Hungarian courage over the years, citing the 1956 Hungarian Revolution.

The guide's reply had been bitter and immediate.

"Yes, it was brave, all the more so because so many of us believed that the Americans would come. Our people heard their broadcasts which encouraged the uprising. We fought in the streets against an army. Then nobody came to help. We were left alone, as usual. That has happened often in our history."

The embarrassed Jorge fell silent. After an awkward pause, the tour had continued. Robbie had studied the events of 1956 at Brown. Now that he was in Budapest, he could have a closer look at that history. Perhaps Uncle Seth would comment as well.

The evening was going well. Erzsi's trademark chicken *paprikas* with dumplings was excellent, and so were her chocolate desserts. Janos and Ilona Horvath were good company, anxious to share both tidbits of parliamentary gossip and information about Eger. Yes, *Egri Bikaver* wine was finally up to prewar quality. No, Janos didn't foresee any further prosecutions based on 1956, nor even any parliamentary commission to publicize what had happened then. He personally favored it, you understand, but as a backbencher he lacked the clout to force a decision on the matter. He was mulling things over, arguing with himself on the principles involved, not fully decided.

Robbie thought that Horvath had left unsaid what many knew, that many members of the Hungarian Socialist Workers (Communist) Party, had been politically reborn as Socialist deputies. There were also conservative pressures to let bygones be bygones, and to turn towards the future, a democratic impulse to move on. He made a note to gauge the matter at the reception in Parliament later that week.

"It's a dangerous matter not to expose the past," ventured Australian Ambassador Kovatch, almost to himself. "Bottle it up, and something festers. Better to make everything public, and let the chips fall where they may."

"What a gloomy thing to say," his wife Julie cut in. "You should have been with us at Eger today. It was delightful. Would have lightened your mood." She leavened this with a quick, darting smile at her husband. "Where are we headed for next month, Robbie?"

"That will be up to our colleague from the French Embassy, Charles Lauricette. He and Marie will plan the day and let us know later on." The Lauricettes nodded their agreement.

"I'm not superstitious," Eleni Papadopoulos murmured to Robbie as the evening ended, "but I couldn't help noticing that we were thirteen for dinner. Did you plan it that way?"

*　　　　*　　　　*

As Eleni left, Robbie smiled and shrugged it off. But she was right, after all. They had been ten diplomats in Eger that afternoon, not including their hosts. Minus the Brazilians and the Germans, that made six. Plus the Johnsons and the Horvaths, Ambassador Kovatch, and Eduardo and Elena Dos Campos. That did make thirteen. Well, what of it? Robbie liberated Minouette from the upstairs study and patted her absentmindedly as Erzsi and the waiter completed the cleaning up, and then left.

It was at times like this that Robbie thought about Sylvie Marceau. She was stylish, and like Marie Lauricette had a good fashion sense, but at the same time she was very real and down to earth, like a 'thirties film star. Robbie put that quality down to her background as a working print journalist, which she had been before her current television career had started.

It had been months since he had seen her, far too long really. Too bad he had been yanked out of Bordeaux, but given his role in unearthing the Basque ETA terrorist leadership, that had been unavoidable. One's private life just couldn't be put in a nice time capsule, all loose ends neatly tied up when one finished an assignment.

He couldn't say that he and Sylvie were engaged. They weren't. But it was far more than casual and, he grinned, she also had his sister Evalyn's seal of approval.

Robbie would have liked to talk with Sylvie now. They would go over the day's excursion to Eger, and she would tell him what she had thought of his new friends. He hoped she would like Budapest.

They had shared a beautiful weekend together in the late summer last year in Reims, at the Boyer resort, *Les Crayeres*. The former private champagne millionaire's mansion, now worth three stars in Michelin, was a peak of French elegance. Sylvie had been lovely, tailored perfection in the home of champagne. After some initial awkwardness, they were once again at home together. It had been wonderful to be with her.

He wished they could have gotten together over Christmas, but her feature television news schedule was too demanding for her to leave Paris. Since Robbie was the most recently arrived substantive officer at the

Embassy in Budapest, he had gone to the end of the line as far as vacation plans were concerned. So neither had much freedom to travel. And here it was May.

They tried to compensate with a spirited e-mail correspondence, phone calls laden with meaning, and occasional postcards. Robbie felt some relief that at least, they had settled on their next meeting. How nice it would be, and how elegant. There was no city like Vienna for New Year's Eve. And that was just across the border.

He looked across the Danube, towards the Pest side of the city. Here on the hilly Buda side, the residential bank, one had the best views. There were for example the bridges. Could he remember their names? Let's see. The *Erzsebet hid* (Elizabeth Bridge) was named for the Queen of Hungary, beloved of her subjects as her husband, Hapsburg Emperor Franz Joseph, had not been. Lights from the *Lanchid* (Chain Bridge) which led to Castle Hill, the *Margit Hid* (Margaret Bridge) connecting Pest and Buda with Margaret Island in the middle, and other bridges glistened below. They were grand now, but all had been destroyed by the Nazis in the closing days of World War II in Hungary. The Margaret Bridge had even been blown up when it was crowded with people.

There across the Danube was the gothic *Orszaghaz* (Hungarian Parliament), built as had been many of Budapest's public monuments and buildings at the end of the nineteenth century to mark the millennium of the Magyar tribes' arrival here, led by the legendary Arpad. The lights were still on in the Parliament, and one could even see beyond it the Pest boulevards that cradled the Opera and many theaters. Great public squares, including of course Freedom Square, where the American Embassy was located, gave Pest a feeling of space and urbanity.

The broad Andrassy Avenue was a quick lesson in politics. Once Stalin Avenue, after 1956 it became *Nepkoztarsasag ut* (People's Republic Avenue). Now once again it was named for Count Gyula Andrassy, the statesman who placed the Crown of St. Stephen on the head of Emperor Franz Joseph, inaugurating Hungarian prosperity under the Dual Monarchy.

Andrassy Avenue contained the Opera and led to Heroes Square and its statues of celebrated Magyars.

Heroes Square in turn led to Hungary's most famous restaurant, Gundel's. Near the neighboring *Varosliget* Park was Robbie's favorite statue, a shadowy depiction of Anonymous, the medieval monk who first wrote in Hungarian, his face forever hidden in his monk's cowl. The statue was near the *Vajdahunyad Vara* (Vajdahunyad Castle), the copy of a famous castle in Transylvania, now Romania, connected with the celebrated Hunyadi dynasty. Robbie tried hard, but not successfully, not to think of the original as Dracula's Castle.

Just before leaving home, Robbie had finally asked his father about his own service here, over forty years ago. It had not been an easy matter to raise, and their conversation was unsettling. Those had been very different times, of course. His father had been assigned to the Legation as Cultural Officer in 1956. Robbie gathered that his father's great disappointment that the United States had done nothing to help the desperate Hungarian Freedom Fighters then had affected him deeply, with a kind of lingering permanent melancholy. That must have been it. His father had taken it all personally.

It was therefore an open question whether his parents would accept his invitation to visit him in Budapest. But Robbie was certain that his sister Evalyn would do so. They had been FSBs, Foreign Service slang for "Foreign Service brats," raised at several overseas posts, but Budapest had not been one of them. It was all new and challenging for Robbie, and he was sure that Evalyn, with her great enthusiasm for travel, would enjoy it too. He very much looked forward to her visit in the fall. The weather should be perfect then for some quiet sightseeing, after the summer tourists had all left. And by that time, he should also have absorbed a fair amount about the countryside outside of Budapest.

Robbie thought that Evalyn should have joined the Foreign Service. She sized up people well, and had a real empathy for other cultures. Evalyn didn't share Robbie's opinion because, as she put it, her enthusiasm stifled any halfhearted attempts at diplomatic reserve. "You're the diplomat in the family, Big Brother," she would say. They looked alike and sometimes were even taken for twins. But Robbie couldn't help being too serious, and his merry younger sister was quite the opposite.

Robbie checked the downstairs of his apartment before switching off the lights. The kitchen was clean and orderly. Good old Erzsi. He really depended on her. The living room, which doubled as dining room and downstairs study, had been straightened out. His bookshelves were crammed full of books about France from his last assignment, books that now remained unread and shifted to other shelves as touring books on Hungary and the Central European region were placed within easy reach. A Laszlo Orszagh Hungarian-English dictionary, and some basic Hungarian literary texts, for when Robbie felt ambitious, completed the collection. There was so much to learn and absorb.

Most of his pictures and prints from France were in informal storage at his parents' home. But there was a nice print of the illuminated Chain Bridge over the Danube at night, with the gothic Parliament Building in the background. It looked rather like the view from his small patio, which was why he had bought the print and then had it framed.

Robbie's family photographs, including one of his parents, Evalyn and Uncle Seth, were placed on a shelf of his bookcase at eye level when one was sitting down on the sofa.

On the wall he had framed his membership certificate in the wine society, the *Jurade de St. Emilion*, a scroll in old French framed with the *Jurade's* crimson neck sash. In a silver frame next to it was a picture of Sylvie and himself smiling at the door of the Cathedral of Reims. A passerby had obliged them by taking the picture, and by luck it had turned out just right, capturing the mood of the elegant and relaxed afternoon they had spent there.

Robbie turned off the lights and went upstairs. There seemed to be even less room here, with a bathroom directly over the kitchen, his own bedroom with its window overlooking the patio below and its perspective of the Danube and Pest beyond.

On the other side of the small hall were his study and a spare bedroom with an outsized armoire. Heaven only knows how the packers had managed to get it here from storage, let alone how the Hungarian unloaders had managed to get this massive piece of furniture up his tiny staircase. But they had done so. The armoire had been Robbie's one important furniture purchase in Bordeaux. It was probably out of place, but he was fond of it. It also contained his CD and cassette player, so Robbie had arranged discreet wiring to separate speakers in his living room area. It had been a little tricky to arrange, but it worked.

Both the study and the spare bedroom had nice views, a little cut off perhaps, of his picturesque Buda street. And a nice picture of Nantucket hung over the bed, a memory of college vacations spent there.

Damn. There, hanging over the chair in the second bedroom was a scarf, a discordant element in his orderly bachelor world. Robbie didn't remember who had worn it, so he wouldn't know to whom it should be returned. But the owner would contact him soon enough. He was sure of that.

*   *   *

Robbie liked going to church. Here on Castle Hill it was a particular privilege. He had his juice, warmed up some milk for the *cafe au lait*, and enjoyed a breakfast of fresh pastries. Then he strode out of the townhouse and ambled towards *Szentharomsag Ter* (Holy Trinity Square) in the morning sunshine.

This was Robbie's favorite location in Budapest. His opinion was shared by many. Facing the Danube was the ornate Fishermen's Bastion, all towers and crevices carved from white stone. Robbie recalled one glorious afternoon the previous fall when a red caped hunting horn ensemble from Burgundy had played their hunting calls from the Fishermen's Bastion ramparts.

A fine statue of St. Stephen on horseback, first King of Hungary and the great great great grandson of the Magyar invader Arpad, stood in the square. A few steps beyond, and Robbie entered the Matthias Church. Churches had stood in this location for centuries. This one, with layers of architectural renewal that Robbie couldn't trace, was named after King Matthias the Just, a medieval ruler from the Hunyadi family whose court was said to be a beacon of culture for all Europe.

It was also called the Coronation Church because the last Hapsburg Emperors, also Kings of Hungary, had been crowned here. Robbie had been intrigued to hear that during the 1916 ceremony for Karl IV, the Holy Crown of St. Stephen had slipped from his head. Two years later, the Hapsburg empire had ceased to exist.

Robbie entered the church and sat down. He was in luck. As often happened, the services of the Coronation Church featured superb music. "I'll sit through a sermon any day to hear Liszt's Coronation Mass," Robbie thought. And so he did. He remembered that his father had also enjoyed the music here. In those days, the communist rulers had allowed such music in an attempt to attract tourists, and probably as an alternative to worship. At least, that is what Cardinal Mindszenty had told his father. He should write home about the church. That would encourage his parents to visit him in Budapest now.

For Sunday dinner there was a choice of superb restaurants, many with period furnishings, in this historic quarter. At this time of the year they were beginning to be crowded, but not to the point where reservations were necessary. The headwaiters knew Robbie by sight anyway, and he could usually manage a good table with a minimum of fuss. A carafe of *Egri Bikaver*, which he would appreciate even more now, having seen Eger, would go nicely with his *toltott kaposzta* (Hungarian stuffed cabbage), boiled potatoes and salad.

After his hearty Sunday dinner, Robbie ambled around Castle Hill for an hour, and once again resolved to visit the Castle museums in more depth one day. He had admired the medieval exhibits during a visit to the

Castle museum the previous fall, but there was still much to be seen. It had struck him that the fine arts displayed in these exhibits corresponded exactly to periods of national creativity when Hungary had not been occupied by a foreign military power.

He looked into an antiques shop, in a side street that paralleled *Orszaghaz utca* (Parliament Street). That was the nice thing about Buda's Castle Hill. There were all sorts of colorful little side streets and shops to poke around in. He almost wished that he were hungry, which he most definitely was not, in order to justify a visit to Ruszwurm's Cafe, for some cake and coffee.

In a halfhearted sort of way Robbie looked for possible additions to his cane collection. During a tourist visit to Budapest when he had been a student at Brown, he had bought a fine silver-tipped cane at the flea market. Now he was rather tempted by a cane with an antler handle. But he wasn't in the buying mood. For the real collector, half the fun of buying was the looking that went before any purchase.

Anyway, his cane collection had just been replenished. Unexpectedly through the mails had come two carefully packaged canes, his sword cane and a Basque sharp pointed *makhila*, which had been sent by Commissioner Jacques Moineau of the Bordeaux police. They were no longer required for evidence there, and Moineau, with a graceful little note, had returned them to Robbie. In the case of the *makhila*, Moineau assured him that his experts had removed every bit of the poison that had been intended by a Basque terrorist for Robbie.

Robbie wondered whether it was safe to return to the French southwest now. He rather hoped so. Perhaps Moineau's note indicated that. It would be easier to see Sylvie then.

*　　　　　*　　　　　*

He returned to his townhouse and checked for messages. There was no e-mail, and his fax machine showed no activity. There was one message on his telephone answering machine, from Julie Kovatch. "Robbie," she purred, "I seem to have left my scarf there yesterday. Silly of me. I'll stop by in an hour or two, to see if you are home, and pick it up. 'Bye."

She had probably already been there and gone, when nobody had answered the door. Well, he could always bring the scarf to the reception at Parliament later that week. She would be sure to be there. What was Henry Higgins's line in "My Fair Lady" about woman always losing things, anyway?

As Robbie put down the receiver, the phone rang. There was no mistaking the gruff voice of Gunnery Sergeant Lemuel Shiflett, the marine guard on duty at the Embassy.

"Sir! This is Gunnery Sergeant Shiflett. We had a Hungarian-American visitor this afternoon at the Embassy. He wanted to drop off a package of some sort for you. He asked for you by name. He wouldn't tell me his business. Just said that he would be calling you in a week or so to make an appointment. The man's name is Magassy. Janos Magassy. Of course, I've taken all the usual precautions, x-rayed the package and all that. The Duty Officer is leaving the office now, and he'll drop the package off shortly. Hope that's all right. Have a nice Sunday, Sir!"

Good old Gunny. His handling of the matter was textbook perfect. And his concluding sentence made the banal "Have a nice day" sound like an order straight from Quantico!

Let's see, given the time difference it was probably all right to call Uncle Seth now. He would probably be just back from church himself. Uncle Seth's OSS career during the Second World War had been legendary, but he had not accepted Allen Dulles's offer to help found the CIA after the war had ended.

Retired now, Uncle Seth's Washington connections had remained first rate. His intelligence exploits were the stuff of legend, but his national reputation had been made as an educator. In fact many of today's Washington insiders had been his students.

It wasn't often that *Time Magazine* had made a New England preparatory school headmaster its Man Of The Year, but Seth Cutler's early and groundbreaking educational curriculum reforms, and his opening of his famous national school across lines of gender and race, had made that choice both logical and well deserved. It had also, some said, inspired the extension of his principles into the public arena when the Warren Supreme Court a few years later had ruled segregation in public education illegal in *Brown v. Board of Public Education.* On the cover, Uncle Seth had looked like a twinkly professor, all shrewd grey eyes, tweed jacket and a trim moustache, but behind him, the artist had sketched a suggestion of parachute drops behind enemy lines.

The call went through immediately. "Hello, Uncle Seth. This is Robbie calling. I hope that everything is going well at home."

"Good to hear from you Robbie. Yes, I'm fine, and your parents seem to be in good spirits. The Red Sox lost a heartbreaker series, but the season is young. We're reserving tickets for another World Series at Fenway Park!" Robbie chuckled, "I took an outing to the countryside yesterday, to Eger. It was interesting." Robbie could see Uncle Seth nodding agreement, and he picked up the softspoken comment, "Yes. Picturesque town. Nice wine too, as I recall."

"While we were there, there was a comment about 1956 and the broadcasts. You know, the old assertion that the Hungarians were encouraged to rise up against the Soviets because of American official encouragement, relayed through the broadcasts. I was just wondering if there was any new scholarship on that."

There was a moment's silence. It didn't have to be emphasized that the radio was Radio Free Europe, and that it had been an official American voice, regardless of disclaimers made at the time. The allegation was not a new one, but it remained a serious moral issue. Had we encouraged the uprising, and then, having done so, left the Hungarian Freedom Fighters in the lurch, to face the Russian tanks by themselves?

Uncle Seth's reply came in a rush, as though he had just remembered something. "Look into what came out of Budapest last year. There was a seminar organized by the 1956 Institute just before you arrived there that looked into the issue of the 1956 uprising and the effect of the Radio Free Europe broadcasts rather closely. I remember reading about it in the *Times*." He paused and went on, more deliberately."That is part of the story, and relates to your specific question. But remember, Robbie, what people believe to be true carries its own consequences. It's always that way. Sometimes the results are elusive. That may prove to be true in Budapest. There are a lot of unsettled scores there, I'm sure.

"It may be more dangerous for some if people act on what they believe to be true, rather than on what actually happened, if that cannot be known. It's an interesting problem. Some people may have a great deal to hide. It's a bit like the French Resistance.We know what happened, but it's not so clear knowing who was on what side, at precisely what time. History is written backwards, as you know. And there is something to be said for not disturbing the past, for letting old wounds heal. Add to that the fact that some people will always have their own reasons for not wanting the events of 1956 to be reopened. History is not fixed. It's a moving target."

Uncle Seth paused for a moment, then added, "I'll cast my net around and see what can be found. Meanwhile, keep up with your reading. I'm an old schoolmaster, and I know that reading is good for you. You can't be a gourmet and tourist all the time, you know."

So Uncle Seth had heard something. And if he could piece it together, he had just indirectly told Robbie that he would let him know using their old book code. Well, time enough for that later. He patted Minouette, who purred in pleasure at the lazy evening to come. After all there were prospects for supper soon, and it looked like Robbie would be spending the evening at home.

*   *   *   *   *   *   *   *   *   *

The First Day—October 23, 1956 (afternoon)

Eva Molnar's heart was pounding so fast that she could barely hear. The excitement of the crowd, first made up of students but now swelling with other people, was catching. For the first time in her life she was caught up in something, and a demonstration that the government had tried to forbid, at that. To hell with them, she thought.

Eva had intended to spend the afternoon sketching, but the noises of the swelling crowd had soon stopped that. She walked out of the Faculty of Arts Building of Budapest University half a block to the statue of the national poet, Sandor Petofi, near the Danube. Often her mere appearance was enough to cause a stir, her step was that graceful, with her flaxen hair, slim figure and an elegant face that Botticelli might have painted. Other students often supposed she was a model.

Today, however, the excited crowd was paying exclusive and rapt attention to the speaker near the Petofi Statue. As she drew near, Eva drew one appreciative smile, from a distinguished woman, a flower seller who gazed thoughtfully at the young people filling the open square.

Eva could just hear what was being said. She listened intently. Some of the words were drowned out by the noises of the crowd. That didn't make any difference. Everyone knew them by heart anyway. The actor Imre Sinkovits was reciting Petofi's stirring national poem *"Talpra Magyar"* ("Arise Hungarians"), which the poet had written in 1848. The words of the "Hungarian *Marseillaise*" were so thrilling that they had helped ignite the 1848 Revolution against the Hapsburgs. They still stirred. "Now or never…shall we remain slaves?" Petofi could have written that this morning about today's Hungary.

Eva looked straight ahead past the Petofi Statue towards the Danube and the Chain Bridge that crossed it, leading up to Castle Hill, the Matthias Church and the Fisherman's Bastion, all stone symbols of the Hungarian nation. The aptness of Petofi's words brought forth tears here and there, tears of lost pride and present determination.

Everyone knew that Poland under Gomulka had just made the Russians blink. Stalin was dead at last and with him, Stalinism. That was all gone now, discredited openly. It was time for the people at last, speaker after speaker had been saying for months at the Petofi Circle. Eva was not political, but she had attended one meeting, with hundreds of her fellow students from every faculty. And they were not reactionary firebrands, Eva nodded with conviction. They were students like herself. Many were even members of *DISZ*, the Communist Youth Organization.

The actor's recitation heightened the crowd's excitement. This was an event to pour over and savor, Eva told herself. Things were going to change now. There would be more attention paid to the people's needs, the way it should be, not just heavy machinery, most of which was exported to the Soviet Union anyway, at bargain prices it was rumored.

The crowd, sensing its new authority, didn't want matters to end there. "On to Bem Square!" someone shouted. And the crowd, feeling its powers like a great cat awakening and flexing its claws, murmured its assent, stretched and started to move.

The Bem Square symbolism was perfect, Eva knew. The Polish hero General Bem had fought on the Hungarian side against the Hapsburgs in 1848. And now, Warsaw had made the Russians back down. Something fine was in the air. This time Hungary would not be isolated. History was on her side.

A tall, good-looking fellow, ruddy faced and scrubbed, wearing a worker's blue coveralls, stepped in beside her.

"Exciting, isn't it?" he said. His pleasant voice, resonant, manly and confident, attracted her, and she nodded in agreement. For a moment she was amused by what her very proper mother would think. Well, you couldn't very well tell someone not to walk beside you in a demonstration now, could you?

Eva won the silent and onesided argument with her absent mother, and the two young people walked along together, crossing the bridge. Once a wedge of people coming from the roadside threatened to sweep them aside. He made an arc with his muscled arms, protecting her from the crowd. "All part of the friendly service," he said with an engaging grin. "Count on me."

After that, they stayed together all the way to Bem Square.

The crowd swelled with more students from the Technological University and the Agricultural College. The mood was festive. An army unit appeared. They were also friendly, waving to the crowd. As they all reached Bem Square, the hundreds became thousands.

The speakers saluted Poland, and called for an independent socialist Hungary. They wanted equality with the Soviet Union, but no more bullying. The mood was relaxed and positive. Nobody cared that this meeting also had been banned. It didn't seem to make the least difference. A rumor went around the crowd that the government had just approved their holding the demonstration that had taken place at the Petofi Statue. That provoked grins and sardonic laughter. "We'll do it, then they'll approve it afterwards," said Eva's companion.

The speakers finished, and the demonstration started to melt away. Eva and her companion, who introduced himself as Csaba Kovacs, crossed the Margaret Bridge towards *Szent Istvan korut* (St. Stephen's Boulevard) on the Pest side of the city. They passed the *AVH* Building, a headquarters of the hated Hungarian Secret Police. "Dirty swine," Csaba glowered. Eva let the comment pass in silence. She was not political, but everyone hated the *AVH*.

Csaba suggested a glass of beer, and that sounded good after their long walk. They found a table at an outdoor cafe near Parliament Square. It felt good to sit down after all that. Too bad it was overcast. Some afternoon sun would have been perfect. The beer was cool and refreshing, and they made some exploratory small talk. Csaba had no illusions. She was a university student and he was a factory worker. This was going nowhere. But he didn't very often have the chance to sit and have a glass of beer with a pretty young woman. Might as well enjoy it, then see her home safely.

With the second beer they realized they were hungry. Eva found some forint notes and they pooled their money. They found just enough to splurge on sandwiches and coffee. It was easy talking with this Csaba Kovacs, Eva realized. Now, though, it was time to go back to the dormitory. There wasn't any harm in letting him see her home. She rather enjoyed his company.

To their surprise, the crowd hadn't melted away. It seemed instead to be growing in size. They paid their bill and joined the crowd in *Kossuth ter* (Kossuth Square), facing Parliament. Now it was more than university students, intellectuals and curious onlookers. The Tuesday workday was over, and the crowd now seemed as varied as the nation itself. There were factory workers, shop people, soldiers, all sorts of people. Clearly they hadn't gone home after work, dispersing as usual through the bus network on Marx Square. They had gathered here instead, in the vast open space outside Hungary's large Gothic style Parliament. This was a substantial crowd, in every sense.

It also seemed to require something more than oratory, an accomplishment or at least a promise from someone who could deliver, something concrete that would make the day memorable. In fact they soon got even less. Radios, placed in windows at Parliament, were on high volume. Soon the crowd could hear Party leader Erno Gero on the radio, speaking in a cold and condescending way, condemning those who would destroy socialist Hungary. The crowd's restive reaction showed growing impatience. Not yet unruly, they muttered in anger.

Then Gero said that it wasn't true that Hungary was sending food and supplies to the Soviet Union that were needed at home. "Since he said it, it must be a lie. Well, at least they seem to know what we want!" Csaba said to Eva. Several people nearby heard him and nodded approvingly. "That's right!" Others added their own embellishments. "We ought to feed ourselves first. We need it here in Hungary!"

Then Imre Nagy spoke. He tried to make the crowd quiet, but didn't succeed. "Comrades!" he began. "We are not comrades!" the crowd muttered. As Prime Minister three years earlier Nagy had tried to make things easier, with more consumer goods for the people, easing up on police control. But everyone knew that Moscow had ordered his ouster. Now he seemed out of touch. He began again. "My dear young friends," he began. The crowd was silent, in rapt attention. It seemed to understand that something important was beginning. This was new. Nagy cut his remarks short. He almost seemed to be a prisoner. But there had been a spark.

As Nagy finished speaking, a young man lit a torch from newspapers. "Good idea, Csicsa!" his friends called. "Let's all do it!" Everyone, it seemed, made torches from newspapers. It was a gesture, and a spontaneous one, the first spontaneous gesture anyone could remember for years. It felt good, adventurous, liberating, to stand there torches glowing. "What's going on now, do you think?" Eva asked. There was no question of her returning to her dormitory now. Events were unfolding too fast, and she wanted to see everything, and be part of it all.

Csaba waded into the nearby crowd, talking excitedly with people around them, including some factory workers that he seemed to know. Or maybe it was just his friendly manner and air of authority that made them open up and respond. Csaba shouted something to those near him. Then he came back to Eva's side and told her what had just happened.

"A list of reform demands had been prepared, but nobody would receive it," he told Eva. "So they were going to give up. Typical defeatist attitude," he added. They both knew that there were no presses, no independent radio, and in short no way to make the reform demands known. "So I just said," Csaba went on, "'Let's go to the Radio Station. Then we'll get them to broadcast what we have to say.' Everyone seemed to think that was a good idea. Let's go."

Csaba and Eva started walking hurriedly towards the Radio Station.

CHAPTER TWO

▼

CSABA'S LIST

On Sunday evening, the day after Robbie's dinner, Ambassador Alexander Kovatch realized with satisfaction that he had finally crossed the line from brooding to action. That had to happen, of course, at some point. He had to find out what had happened to Csaba. Even now, he owed his brother that much.

His mind went back over forty years. By some miracle, Csaba had returned to the family apartment in Buda just before the collapse. His parents had been frantic with worry, and now were overjoyed to see him. But their elation had not lasted long.

His eyes were dull and his body seemed wracked with the superhuman efforts of the past several weeks. He gave his brother some advice. "You must get out of here. Out of Hungary, I mean. Start somewhere else. Here there is no hope."

Csaba took a few hours of rest, and changed clothes before leaving his family. He had to get back to the others, he said. He seemed to feel guilty about coming home for even a few hours. He had left the resistance pocket in Pest to find help. But it hadn't taken long to realize that there would be no help. The Russians had overrun every pocket, and now were mopping up whatever areas still resisted, such as the Csepel Iron Works.

Now he was a marked man, and his presence here would endanger his family. Better not to tell them where he was headed. It would protect them if they didn't know.

Csaba had stared at his younger brother before saying goodbye. "We've lost this fight," he said. Then he had murmured almost inaudibly to himself, "I've got to get back to her."

That was the last time that Sandor had seen Csaba.

He had taken his brother's advice, and his parents had understood and approved. They only had the two boys. Perhaps one of them could make it to a better life.

A better life it had been, in many ways. He had been lucky, just making it to the Austrian border before it was sealed so tightly that one had to brave machine gun fire in the winter to cross into safety. Sandor had always been a good student, and he knew enough German to get by, and could even make out simple English. He practiced both, and when the refugee camps were set up, he was already favorably known to the disaster relief staff workers, who hired him as a translator.

For a year, he had his own questions of the refugees, after the official ones had been asked, answered and translated. But nobody seemed to know anything certain about Csaba. He once heard a rumor that Csaba had been betrayed by a member of his own resistance group, and was being held by the AVH, the Hungarian secret police. That was about all.

He had jotted down at the time the names that Csaba had mentioned to him...Janos Magassy, Eva Molnar, Attila Nemzeti, Imre Mohacsi, Istvan Szepvaros. They were, so far as Csaba had been aware, the last members of his resistance pocket still alive when he talked with his brother. And so if there had been any betrayal, one of these people might know about it.

During that year there were a number of opportunities to emigrate. Sandor had weighed his options carefully. It was the decision of a lifetime. Most went from the refugee camps to the United States, or to Canada. Some went to England, or even to West Germany or to the Low Countries.

But several of his superiors in the camp had talked to him of another world, where he could make his own way, a place like America used to be, they said. There a man could still rise, based on his own efforts. That country was Australia.

And so Sandor Kovacs had emigrated to Australia. His sponsors there were vindicated in their judgment of his character and capacity for hard work. He did well in the construction business, but grew tired of working for others. And so after ten years in Australia he had founded his own construction company. Gradually, but surely, it had prospered.

His marriage did not. Divorce was probably inevitable for a wife that he never saw, and Kovacs ungrudgingly blamed himself. He was never home. She was almost right in howling at him that she wished that he had a mistress. That, she could at least understand and fight against, woman to woman. But this lust for material success was too hard to fight against.

He was sorry that she felt that way, but the uncontested divorce was a relief. Sandor redoubled his efforts at the company. In an expanding economy, it had flourished. So did his backing for several provincial politicians on the way up. His luck was good. They prospered, and rarer still, they remembered who their friend had been. Along the way, Sandor got tired of explaining his name, and having it misspelled anyway. Sandor Kovacs became Alexander Kovatch.

The return to Hungary was smoother than he had thought. There had of course been for years a book kept by the AVH of those who had been Freedom Fighters in 1956, who would not be allowed to return. He was not in that category, but had decided to return only when he was ready. No, when he returned, it would be a personal and financial success story, beholden to nobody. Then he could trace what had happened to Csaba more surely.

His second wife Julie was ecstatic at his appointment as Ambassador to Hungary. All of the ceremony, and her chance to begin a reputation as a diplomatic hostess, charmed her. Well, let her take care of that side of things. It was all harmless enough. She might even turn out to be an asset, after all.

It would be so much easier if the records of the period were unsealed. He had sounded out the Foreign Ministry on that topic more than once. But they were not, and there seemed to be no realistic prospect that they would ever be opened. There should be enough time, during his several years in Hungary, to find out what had happened. The key was to control his anger, and be sufficiently patient That was also the hardest part.

Of the names on Csaba's list, he had decided to start with Janos Magassy. That was logical. Over the years, Magassy had been an easy person to keep tabs on, for he had busied himself with emigre politics, and issues concerning the United States and Hungary. He had also occasionally been in the news, particularly when he had led Hungarian-American opposition to the return of the Crown of St. Stephen some over twenty years ago.

When he had learned through a journalist friend that Magassy was back in Budapest, an introduction had been easy to arrange. Magassy had been rather flattered by the invitation to have coffee with the Australian Ambassador.

Meanwhile, the Hungarian Government itself now actively courted former 1956 Freedom Fighters, with recognition and occasionally, decorations. Some of that was conviction, but there was also a healthy self-interest involved. Hungary's future security was with the West. Making friends of former enemies was a sound strategy in pursuit of that goal. And so, former Freedom Fighters could return to their homeland. Let bygones be bygones. Well, that might do for a government, Kovatch thought.

His meeting wth Magassy that Saturday afternoon had been a good start. Magassy had not guessed that he was Csaba's brother. That was not surprising. Kovacs was one of the most common Hungarian surnames, and their family resemblance was not close.

Waiting for Magassy in the New York *Kavehaz*, Kovatch had wondered how Julie was enjoying her afternoon with the younger diplomatic set in Eger. Well, he hoped. He didn't need her well tuned feminine intuition aimed in his direction anyway, not just now. If need be, he could tighten the leash later.

The atmosphere at the New York *Kavehaz* pleased him. Larger than Ruszwurm's on Castle Hill, and less public than Gerbeaud's with its nev-erending stream of tourists, the New York was a traditional coffee house in Pest. As the Hungaria it had once been Budapest's greatest literary cafe, where Molnar composed his plays while having coffee in the afternoons, and the mail of famous writers was held for them as a matter of course.

During the communist years, the New York had shut its doors for some time. For a while, the premises had even been used to sell sporting goods. Now it seemed to be coming back. Surveying the rich dark wood of his sur-roundings, the discreet waiters, and fingering a copy of the newspaper *Magyar Nemzet* while he waited, Kovatch hoped it would once again prosper.

He had displayed correct interest in Magassy's latest project, a memo-rial for the 1956 Revolution. That might indeed be something in which the Hungarian-Australian community could take an interest. For the time being, Kovatch deflected Magassy's tentative inquiry whether he would be interested in an honorary chairmanship in the committee he would be forming.

Kovatch then steered the conversation around to the ebbing resistance at the end of November, 1956. He said that that was when he had himself left Hungary, and had asked what Magassy had done then. Magassy told his own account of those days. It was the familiar story of the uprising, and the heady moments when a military victory hadn't seemed out of the question.

Then, he said, the tide had turned. Hungary's military and government leadership had been betrayed. Fresh Soviet troops had poured into the country. The struggle seemed increasingly hopeless. Their own command post became less a strongpoint than a potential deathtrap. It had been time to get out, although resistance sputtered on for several months.

Kovatch poured some Tokay wine for his guest, and listened.

His guest coughed and continued. "The others had all been killed, you know. Towards the end, there were six of us left. I had no family. Nobody would miss me, so I decided to stay as long as I could, and cover the others.

"We were running out of ammunition. So I ordered people out, one by one, to look for some. If they couldn't get any supplies, they were to save themselves. First Attila Nemzeti left, then Istvan Szepvaros and Csaba Kovacs. Nemzeti returned later with supplies and stayed with me. We hoped the others had made it, but we didn't know." He was saluting the ghosts of old friends.

"Imre Mohacsi left next just before Nemzeti returned. That left Attila, Eva Molnar and me. Then shrapnel hit Attila.

"At that point, resistance was suicidal. I told Eva Molnar that she must leave. What happened to her, I don't know, although I had always thought that she might try to make it to America. She had a contact of sorts at the American Legation. But I never saw her in the United States, and I don't know where she went after she left us.

"I was the last to leave, after Eva."

Kovatch sighed. According to Magassy, Csaba had disappeared after his visit home. There was no betrayal. He had not made it back to the fighting group. Well, that was always a possibility. But Kovatch couldn't stop there, not after all this time.

"When did you leave Hungary?"

"That was in January of 1957, across the bridge at Andau."

Kovatch didn't remember Magassy from that period. But that was not unusual. There were thousands upon thousands of such refugees at that time, and by then, he was far from being the only translator that was employed by the relief services.

"Did you ever run across anyone who had been with you?"

"Yes, Imre Mohacsi. You'll meet him soon if you haven't already. A fine man, my right hand in many ways. He never left Hungary. He was wounded, then was caught and spent some time in prison, but he was one of the lucky ones who got released. He's in Parliament now, with the Smallholders Party."

"Does he believe your group was betrayed?"

"You'd better ask him about that."

Kovatch made a mental note to do so.

*   *   *

Imre Mohacsi smiled at the telephone call. So after all these years, there was again interest in the events of 1956. That wouldn't bring anybody back, after all. What was the use? He had kept in touch with the others informally, from time to time, and he would call them next. Istvan Szepvaros and Attila Nemzeti were also prominent men in different fields. Then we were fighters. Now here we are, the politician, the banker and the bureaucrat. He smiled at the evolution.

Magassy had not specifically asked to see them, but it had struck Mohacsi as an appropriate gesture to make. He himself had been aware of Magassy's activities from time to time. They had even bumped into each other once or twice in Washington. Mohacsi smiled and made the calls to Szepvaros and Nemzeti. Both would be able to attend, and would bring their wives as well.

Magassy's call reawakened a tumble of memories from 1956. Those were the days of idealism and hope, too much hope and trust perhaps, but it remained a source of pride. For a brief period loyalties were no longer confused, with parents saying one thing, and the party something else. Mohacsi remembered cases of children informing on their parents out of a sense of misplaced duty, and ending up in orphanages. Those were terrible days, when people had little and were cold, hungry and afraid most of the time.

For a brief period, people had really thought that things would get better. Everyone heard of Khruschev's denunciation of Stalin and his methods. That had come like a shock wave to Hungary, where people remembered the Hungarian Stalin, Rakosi. Under Imre Nagy, reform communism had seemed possible. It hadn't lasted very long, but for a while, it had been possible to be proud once again of being Hungarian. Then came Revolution.

His own group had done their best, time and again. "The Friends," they called themselves. Magassy had stayed until the end, he had heard, taking advantage of confused, sporadic fighting and then leaving only when the position was about to be overrun. Eva, dear pretty Eva, had left a day or so before that. His own foray for food and supplies had not ended well. A bullet that shattered his arm had destroyed his military usefulness. When he awakened, in a sort of military hospital, he had known that it was just a question of time before he was picked up.

Several years of imprisonment had followed, after a sham trial. Since he had not been caught actually fighting, the evidence against him was circumstantial only. He was lucky. If you were caught with a gun, you got ten years in prison, minimum. But what was the crime in looking for food, in a city of starving people?

Imre was released from prison in one of Kadar's periodic amnesties to impress the West. All in all, he knew that he had been very lucky to escape with his life.

The years that followed had been confused, while he sought to build some sort of career. At first, it was very hard. He did whatever odd jobs he could. His education had been good, but without the party's blessing, most doors that actually led somewhere worth going were shut. Early on, he had decided that he had better leave Budapest, and take his chances elsewhere in the country, where his slim chances of being spotted by a police informer would be lessened, and where his background would not be of consuming interest. After a while, the newcomer became a well regarded worker, who was generally known in his community.

Then, a turnaround of sorts took place fifteen years after the Revolution. Bright people were needed to infuse some commercial sense into Hungary's New Economic Mechanism or NEM, Hungary's attempt to combine market economics with the one party state. Finally, Kadar's statement that "He who is not against us is with us" provided cover for those who had learned to put rebellion aside. Imre was a leader with common sense who could run things and enjoyed doing so. He fit in well with the times.

Modest success began to come his way. He married a fine young woman, an unwilling collective farm resident, whom he had met during his travels around the countryside seeking to boost sales orders of machinery for his company. It wasn't strictly according to the five year plan, but some leeway in production allocation was permitted, increasing production for both his state machinery company and for the collective farm workers, who leased the machinery for their own plots, which they worked in what spare time they had.

The results of their labors could be seen on any market day in stalls throughout Budapest and the larger provincial cities. At least now we are feeding our own people, Mohacsi thought.

He and Magda had had no children. The future was so uncertain. Also, he could not help but remember those young faces from 1956. He could not raise children who might have to face those tanks once again.

Gradually, their economic situation eased. They could manage a small house in Szeged, in southern Hungary where they lived. On rare visits to Budapest, they looked forward to the theater or the opera. For a bit of daring, there was even some satirical theater, allowed by the party as a sort of safety valve. The *Microszkop Szinpad* (Microscope Theater) was clever, and Imre and Magda enjoyed themselves there, even if they nervously looked around at the audience to see if the authorities were shadowing them.

Those days seemed far past now. Their home in Szeged was substantial, as was Imre's reputation in the community. When multiparty politics became possible in 1989, Imre was called on by a regional deputation trying to jump start the conservative Smallholders Party. He was flattered by the idea, which appealed to his sense of fitness. Now he could put political substance to the ideas for which "The Friends" had fought.

To nobody's surprise, Mohacsi had won that election and the ones that followed, even as his party's fortunes had declined. He became a parliamentary leader of the Smallholders Party.

Mohacsi was generally optimistic about his nation's future, but did not overrate his own Smallholders Party, whose history went back to the interwar period. Of course it, like other political parties, had long been suppressed during the communist period. Now it was again a factor on the parliamentary scene.

Mohacsi's tactical problem was to continue to wean his party away from any extreme nationalism, and to temper its economic conservatism with good governing sense. If he could do that, there might be a national future for him. For a respected, hard working man like Imre Mohacsi, with a scandal free past, the political future in a political coalition might be very bright indeed. An eventual Cabinet Minister position was not beyond the realm of possibility.

Enough of that. For now, he enjoyed life in their apartment on the *Rozsadomb* (Rose Hill) in Buda, where he and Magda lived while Parliament was in session. She was calling him now for dinner, and a good substantial dinner it was, too. The pork roast, stuffed cabbage and dumplings smelled very tempting indeed. As the Hungarian phrase went, Magda was a *"szep kover asszony"* (a "pretty chubby lady"), and he was gaining a few welcome pounds himself. As long as nobody made the mistake of underrating him because of his growing heft, that was just fine with him.

*   *   *

Robbie was intrigued by the package that the Duty Officer had just delivered to him. Then he remembered who John Magassy was, and opened the package. He had not met him, but Magassy was well known to the Embassy, and favorably at that.

The letter was short, a sort of introduction. His business was quickly stated. Magassy wanted a memorial to 1956, in Budapest, to celebrate his resistance group.

Well, why not? Robbie thought. Now there were a number of memorials to the Freedom Fighters around the city.

Magassy seemed to want something less ceremonial. His letter mentioned some recent memorials in the United States. There was a clipping showing the Korean War Memorial in Washington near the Mall. Robbie had seen it and liked it, infantrymen advancing, their statues making an imposing total structure.

Magassy's idea was to picture the 1956 Freedom Fighters as a statuary group. It was an evocative notion. He wanted to show a group of resistance fighters in their pocket. The statues could be either free standing, or a sort of three dimensional frieze protruding from a stone wall or fence, on the actual location of a resistance group. His own Freedom Fighters group location on *Barat utca* (Barat Street) would be a fine location.

It might even be possible to sculpt the actual faces involved in several cases.

His note ended mournfully. Magassy's own pocket of Freedom Fighters, "The Friends," had been decimated over the weeks of fighting. Half of them had been killed, and Magassy was not even sure how many of the final six were still alive. But he was haunted by his memories, and thought that a memorial to their courage would be appropriate. It was a sort of benevolent exorcism, Robbie thought.

Enclosed with his letter was a yellowing clipping of the interview he had had with the Washington *Post* over twenty years ago, when he had opposed the return by the Carter Administration of the Crown of St. Stephen to communist Hungary. Robbie glanced at the article, which told of the final heroic days of Magassy's resistance group. He would read it in detail later.

At first consideration, Robbie liked the idea. It would also take advantage of the tradition of superior Hungarian public sculptures. There hadn't been anything that he really liked since the statues of Zsigmond Kisfaludy-Strobl, executed years earlier, and visible in several prominent areas around the city.

He remembered with a smile that the Kisfaludy-Strobl Liberation Memorial on the Citadella Fortress atop *Gellert hegy* (Gellert Hill) had somehow lost its Red Army statues in recent years. Like some monstrous wandering *golem*, these soldiers and other Stalinist relics were now in a statuary park in another part of the city.

Not that this was the first time that this statuary had been altered. Robbie knew that originally the same statue had been intended as a mourning group to commemorate the death of the son of the right wing Regent of Hungary, Admiral Horthy. Not completed during the war, it had then been adapted to please the Soviet Russian occupiers of Budapest as the *Felszabadulasi Emlekmu* (Liberation Memorial).

Magassy had the idea, and then the enthusiasm to see it through. That was evident from his letter. His target date, a few years in the future, Robbie found realistic. That would give enough time to raise the funds, and to commission the work, not to mention the permits and other official headaches that would have to be worked through. Magassy intended to finish and dedicate the statuary memorial on October 23, 2006, the fiftieth anniversary of the 1956 Hungarian Revolution.

He would call and make an appointment to see Mr. Cutler next week after his return from a few days in Sarospatak in northeast Hungary to see friends. He hoped that, with this introduction, Robbie would see to a brief introductory meeting with Ambassador Horton as well. Magassy added that he did not want official American involvement. But he did want to touch base as the project got underway, and keep American diplomatic officials informed as it went forward.

Robbie admired Magassy's skill in dealing with public officials. That had clearly served the man well in the past, during commemorations of the events of 1956, when Magassy had raised funds for refugee work. This was now surely his last hurrah for the generation that had been teenagers in those days.

Robbie put down the letter and its enclosures.

He looked forward to meeting Magassy in a week or so, as the letter had said. Probably he had some other former Freedom Fighters to meet in the provinces. That would be interesting to hear about too. Perhaps his father would be interested as well.

*   *   *

It was early afternoon in Massachusetts. Samuel Lawrence "Trip" Cutler III had just received a FAX transmission from his son Robbie in Budapest. "Thought this might interest you, Dad. A man named John Magassy will be coming to see me in a week. This is his story of 1956. He plans to raise funds for a memorial statue. It looks like an intriguing idea. Love to Mother."

Robbie had sent a copy of Magassy's cover letter, and the clipping. Trip hadn't consciously thought of those days in some time. He wasn't entirely happy that Robbie's assignment in Hungary had brought it all up again, the heroic uprising and American failure to help. It still gnawed at him, sometimes even in the early hours of the morning. Not that it still awakened him, but sometimes when his wife Lucille hadn't slept well, he could tell that his shouted dreams had kept her awake again.

Lucille looked over at him as he read the material, frowned and replaced his reading glasses. "What is it, Trip?"

No longer young, they communicated often without speaking. He wordlessly passed her Robbie's message. For years they had avoided discussing the specific incidents of Trip's assignment at the Legation in Budapest. And now, Robbie had forced this matter on their attention.

The Magassy article held their attention. Like most Foreign Service Officers at the time, Trip had been aware of the Carter Administration's plan to return the Crown of St. Stephen to Hungary. He approved of the idea in principle, although by that time he had no official connection with Hungarian-American relations. Trip was serving at the Embassy in Manila then, watching matters Hungarian from afar. But then, service in Hungary was a small club. You always were interested.

This article from the Washington *Post* brought that period back. John Magassy opposed the return of the Crown of St. Stephen to communist Hungary, and his article, which detailed the two weeks of a resistance cell of Freedom Fighters in Pest, gave the reason. Magassy had been the last to leave, just before the final mopping up. Nobody else was left alive. It seemed that from time to time people, mostly teenagers, had come and gone during the course of the fighting. Magassy was the continuity. He knew everybody who had fought there, it seemed, from start to finish. He wrote elegantly of the youngsters who had died.

Written a quarter of a century ago, and twenty years after 1956, there were still a number of unanswered questions that preyed upon Magassy's mind. He wanted specifically to know what had happened to those who had survived those days, if in fact some had survived. He gave four nicknames. What made Trip's heart race was Magassy's mention of the next to last person to leave the resistance pocket.

It was Eva Molnar.

Unlike the other persons mentioned, Magassy had given a few details about her, and her name in full. Perhaps they had been close. Or rather, just the knowledge of the end, and the fact that they were the last two had led them to exchange some personal information.

Even in this context, Magassy was guarded. Hungary was still in communist hands then, after all. But he did refer to her as an art student, a gifted one at the university. She was from the Hungarian region of Transylvania, in Romania, and had had the rare luck to receive permission to study in Hungary.

Trip vaguely remembered that Romanian connection, mentioned during their brief interview at the Legation so long ago. What had she said? She was from Cluj (the Hungarian Kolozsvar), or somewhere near there.

So she would have had someplace to return to, possibly. Perhaps she had made it through the aftermath of the repression that had followed 1956 in Hungary after all.

The memories came flooding back. Trip had tried, but failed to find any trace of Eva Molnar after he had seen her outside the Legation. He had looked up his earlier notes, and found her local address. It seemed wiser not to look too closely. That, after all, could get her in trouble. But his discreet inquiries, and those of trusted Hungarian friends, resulted in nothing.

She had disappeared completely. He fervently hoped that she had not been killed in the final days of fighting, as so many had been. And her final cry to him had haunted him for years. Well, before he had left Hungary, he had done his best. He could take some comfort in that.

Official contacts with the Foreign Ministry were rare, but he had paid a special, unauthorized farewell call. With stationery taken from the Legation, he had written a formal diplomatic note inquiring about Eva Molnar. He wrote that she had been abducted just before an official, scheduled meeting at the American Legation. The note officially demanded an accounting of her whereabouts. Trip then had initialed it himself.

Trip knew they would never answer it. If they did, he had clued in the Consul, who would file the reply without telling the front office. It couldn't do Eva Molnar any harm. He hoped it might help her in some way.

Trip opened up and shared some memories with his wife Lucille. For the first time in many years, he talked about those days in Budapest, before they had met. He did not mention Eva.

Evalyn, stopping by to see her parents later that afternoon, caught them in that reflective mood. They shared the clipping with her without comment. That whetted her appetite, which hardly needed any encouragement, to visit Robbie in Budapest when her finances and vacation schedule from the publishing house permitted.

* * * * * * * * * *

The First Day—October 23, 1956 (evening)

It used to be called Andrassy Avenue, Attila Nemzeti remembered, for a Hungarian statesman of the Austro-Hungarian Empire. Then Hungary had been part of a world power, and this avenue had been the *Champs Elysees* of Budapest.

Now this broad, imposing avenue was called Stalin Avenue. Attila shuddered as he passed numbers 60, 62 and 64. That had been Gestapo Headquarters. Now it was an AVH prison and interrogation center. When the Communists had first come to power the prison was expanded by Gabor Peter, a former tailor turned Hungarian Beria, now himself imprisoned.

This was just one of many prisons.

There was the *Marko utca* (Marko Street) interrogation center and adjacent transit prison near Parliament. There was the *Fo utca* (Main Street) prison across the Danube, between the Margaret and Chain bridges in Buda. There was the *Gyujto* Prison on the outskirts of Budapest near the airport, with the convenient cemetery across the street. It went on and on.

What a country to be studying law in, Attila thought, not for the first time. He was beginning to feel out of place wearing his suit. It was his only suit, to be sure, but he was the only person in this crowd of workers wearing a suit. He had just come from a meeting with a law professor, and was starting to stroll home when the excited crowds had caught his attention.

The avenue led from near the Danube east to Heroes' Square, with its Millennium Monument statues of traditional Hungarian leaders, the real ones, starting with Arpad and his chieftains. Attila turned right on Dozsa Gyorgy Street and joined the crowds milling around a colossal statue of Stalin. It stood on a pedestal, twenty-six feet high. A church had been destroyed to make room for it.

"It's time the swine came down," somebody yelled, and Attila found himself nodding agreement. Ropes were found, and the statue was lassooed around the head. "Just like in the Western movies," said a grinning young professional man in a suit standing on the sidewalk not far from Attila.

They seemed to share a sardonic sense of humor. On an impulse Attila strolled over and shook hands. They swapped the traditional Hungarian greeting. *"Szervusz!"* Attila and Istvan Szepvaros introduced themselves and walked towards the statue.

Now, as the skies darkened, the crowds gave way to make an open space for the statue to fall, like a malignant, gigantic metal sequoia. Several workmen were cutting the statue with acetylene torches, while others pulled on the ropes. Finally it crashed down. The workmen started to cut up the statue, first at the neck, leaving its enormous head glaring at the intersection.

Attila laughed at the remnants of the statue. It stood now just up to the knees. "Let's call this place 'Knee Square' from now on," he yelled with delight. The crowd roared its approval, and the name stuck.

*   *   *

Eva and Csaba reached the Radio Station. It was already guarded, they saw, by masses of heavily armed AVH men. They had been in place for some time, it seemed. "They are anticipating our movements," Csaba said. It was not a comforting thought.

There were also a few men in Army uniforms, but they didn't seem threatening. Eva noticed this too. "Well, everyone hates the AVH," she said. "Time for them to go, like Stalin."

Time passed. Several students in the crowd had been allowed inside the Radio Building and were negotiating to have their demands broadcast. An Army officer volunteered to help, and asking to speak with the head of broadcasting, went inside.

More time passed. The crowd became anxious. Why was this taking so long? What was happening inside the building? Were the young people who had gone inside safe? Had they been arrested? The crowd began to press closer to the building and to the cordon of AVH men guarding it.

"Shame on you!" someone said to an AVH man, and others in the crowd took up the chorus. "All we want is for Hungary to be left alone." Then a nervous AVH man fired his weapon above the crowd. Tear gas cannisters followed, thrown into the crowd from an upper window of the Radio Building. Then there were shots into the crowd. Several people were killed. Many were wounded.

Their blood turned the crowd's panic into resolution. People took cover, but did not disperse. A Hungarian Army unit, ordered to the scene, refused to join the AVH, in firing into the crowd. Instead, the soldiers made no resistance when the crowd took their weapons. Reinforcements arriving by truck also turned their weapons over to the civilians. Then a special police unit, hastily called to reinforce the AVH, refused to do so.

The scene at the Radio Station had become an armed siege. Very gradually the now armed crowd took the initiative, pouring fire wherever they could find AVH men.

Csaba Kovacs grabbed one of the newly liberated submachine guns and joined the fighting. "This is our chance to get the bastards," he said. Assuming an authority that felt natural he fired off a clip, then showed Eva how the clips reloaded. Without thinking she organized the reloading of the weapons.

*   *   *

In the Eighth and Ninth Districts of Pest, the southeastern parts of the city, factory workers were exhilarated by the news. "Serves the goddamned AVH right!" was everyone's opinion. They didn't care about politics. There wasn't any leisure time to consider such things, and who had the energy anyway? It was hard enough working for starvation wages, making bread and cabbage, when you could get it, go too far.

And then there were the children. It was hard watching them grow up badly nourished, and without much hope that things would get better.

They didn't learn anything at school, those who went to school. And their questions couldn't be safely answered.

"Elvittek." ("They took him away.") That was the codeword used when a relative was missing. That had happened a lot during the Stalin years, when his thug Matyas Rakosi was in charge of Hungary. When Imre Nagy was Prime Minister three years ago things had eased up. Then when Stalin had died, it had seemed that things would get better. But then the Russians had kicked Nagy out and brought Rakosi back as Prime Minister. True, he was again removed in July, but Gero was still in, and that was nearly as bad.

Everyone knew change was overdue, and rumors spread fast. There was genuine pleasure about the toppling of the Stalin statue. Radio Budapest was broadcasting news about armed counterrevolution, and warning about reactionaries. "Yeah, real aristocrats like us," one worker said, waving his stumpy hand.

The word spread throughout the district. Janos Magassy kicked himself for having gone to the movies that night, of all nights, and missing the action. There had been a film at the Corvin Movie House that he had wanted to see. When he got out, he was immersed in excited crowds immediately. The Kilian Army Barracks across *Ulloi utca* (Ulloi Street) seemed on special alert. Janos sat at his favorite tavern and sorted out the rumors.

An excited worker caught his attention. Excited, yes, but also cool and focussed. That was someone he had played soccer with from time to time in pickup games. A fellow worker, his name was Imre, Imre Mohacsi. Janos waived him to the empty seat at his table. Imre was full of news. He had been at the Radio Station and he told Janos about it.

"There was firing everywhere," he said, gulping his beer. "The damned AVH started it, when some students tried to negotiate with the radio broadcasters to let them on the air."

Janos asked where the crowd had gotten their weapons. None were in private hands in Hungary. It was illegal. That would get you sent away. *"Elvittek,"* people would then say.

"The army—then special police—were sent to beef up the AVH. They were heavily armed. But I guess that they hate the AVH as much as we do. They gave their weapons to the crowd."

Janos finished his beer and wiped his mouth on his sleeve.

"This isn't going very far without more weapons," he said slowly and deliberately, like the farmer his father had once been. He looked appraisingly at Mohacsi. "I'll help," Imre said. It was a moment of solemn commitment.

As a trusted foreman at the United Lamp Factory, Janos Magassy had access to the keys. That was in case of an emergency with the generators, or in case he had to organize a night shift for some "volunteer" work. Quickly he outlined to Mohacsi what was needed. A truck and a few trusted men, that would do it.

"Get Karoly to help if you can find him," he said. Karoly, a former athlete and circus performer, lived in the neighborhood.

Imre Mohacsi nodded, yes. He had never before been entrusted with such an important mission. He would do it somehow.

Janos Magassy lit a cigarette, yawned and left the cafe, making his way unhurriedly towards the United Lamp Factory. It was time for the submachine guns that the factory actually produced to be put to patriotic use.

CHAPTER THREE

▼

"Mindig A Sarga Ut"

Istvan Szepvaros had been pleased to hear from Imre Mohacsi. Now they were casual, not close friends, but it was always good for a banker to have an inside acquaintance in Parliament. He would of course be attending the reception, and appreciated the invitation. His wife Maria would enjoy the opportunity for an evening amongst Budapest's reconstituting society as well.

The years had been good to Szepvaros. Once he had left the resistance group, there had been no doubt in his mind, none whatsoever. There was chaos in Budapest. The reprisals would soon be underway from the winning communist side, he was sure of that, as he remembered they had been during that terrible day in Republic Square, when the Freedom Fighters had been predominant.

The reality had been that for a brief period the gates had swung wide open, and he could leave Hungary. Szepvaros had seen his opportunity and taken it. Why not? What bound him to Budapest, a shelled wreck of a city in 1956?

Not much, he had told himself. The nightmares would persist of the killings he had seen, he was sure of that. Well, now it would take many years for things to get better in Hungary, if they ever did at all. He didn't have that much time. And what would have been the point, after all, of staying even if it would have been safe to do so? At best, there would have been years of grunt work in a state run financial institution, trying to justify what the political boys did. That was all the Party leadership thought bankers were good for, anyway. Try to fool the West, and catch currency smugglers.

At heart and by training, Szepvaros was a banker. It was not so much the profession of bills and notes, the discounting and rediscounting of commercial paper, or the field of lending that interested him. No, it was currency transactions, the buying and selling of foreign exchange, that had fascinated him.

Istvan had of course in his youth watched the course of Hungary's currency, the forint, which had been pegged at an artificial level by the government, far above its actual value. From time to time, smugglers would come in, in those days in the early 'fifties. They weren't professionals for the most part at all.

The pattern was boringly predictable. They bought forints in Vienna or Munich for hard currency, usually dollars or pounds, and then brought them into Hungary. The point usually was to bring a modest windfall to their relatives or the relatives of friends back in America within the country.

It clearly made a great difference to Uncle Pista in Sopron if he had to declare and exchange dollars for forints at the official rate, or if instead he could receive smuggled forints which had been bought at their true valuation in the West. Szepvaros, as a young bank clerk involved from time to time in the investigation of such cases, had developed a clear idea of what the forint was actually worth. And that was not much.

Let the leadership spout its propaganda about building socialism. Istvan's work hadn't led to any indignation against those who were trying to beat the system and its rigged currency evaluation. They were doing something entirely logical, Istvan thought. The problem was that they were doing it stupidly and getting caught.

No, what struck Istvan Szepvaros was the fact that there was such a disparity in the value of the currencies in the first place. It said a great deal about the relative economies of, say, the Federal Republic of Germany and the German Democratic Republic that the West German mark was one of the soundest currencies, while that of East Germany, itself an economic model by Warsaw Pact standards, needed propping up.

The only intelligent course of action was to leave.

For Istvan Szepvaros, the opportunity came in the turmoil of the 1956 Revolution. He had a good fighting record. He would be welcomed abroad. When the end became clear, his destination was also obvious. He went to the Federal Republic of Germany.

As a refugee, Szepvaros had travelled well. His German was excellent, and so were his work habits. Life as a refugee was actually reasonably brief, all things considered. It was not long before he became a citizen of the Federal Republic. He was, after all, a professional man, and a banker at that.

His willingness to learn overcame any initial professional shortcomings from the point of view of his employers. As a consequence his progress was steady. His career shifts sometimes involved moving from city to city, or between branches of his bank, as he progressed through various bank specialities before settling in, as he could have told his superiors, into foreign exchange matters.

Istvan had kept one habit from his youth, a love of films, and went to see them frequently. Indeed, in a reflexive moment, he had once convinced himself that it was an American film, "The Wizard Of Oz," that had gotten him interested in money and banking in the first place. It was in the darkened Corvin Movie House in Pest just before the war that he first saw Dorothy and her friends skipping off to Oz, singing as they did so "Follow The Yellow Brick Road," or as the Hungarian version had it,

"Mindig A Sarga Ut." And why not follow it, if the yellow bricks turned out to be real gold?

It had been a careful decision to come back to Hungary. Maria had been pleased. There was little except habit to hold them back. Their children, after all, were all out of the nest, married and with lives of their own. In addition, Maria liked to travel, and knew that they would cut a very wide social circuit in Budapest. Herself the granddaughter of emigrants from a very different period, Maria had some nostalgia for the Hungary that she had never seen. In Germany they lived very well indeed. But in Hungary, with Istvan installed as head of their bank, they would live at the highest level, on German salaries. It was in the end too much to resist.

Differences in nuance between returning emigres and those of the same generation who had not left Hungary amused Istvan. Hungarian clothes, even when fashionable, were not of the best material. Differences in medical and particularly dental care were easy to spot. People here seemed older before their time. Language usages were amusing, he found. As a hobby he enjoyed picking up slang that eluded him at first. Habits of behavior were more interesting. Many who had stayed had a certain habit of deference that emigres often seemed to lack. Was that an old world habit, lost in modern Germany, or a way of deflecting criticism or currying favor in a former police state?

Perhaps it was just the difference in money. Often things came to that. He was aware of the caricature of the returning Hungarian as a sort of boob throwing money at local relatives to be accepted. Like most caricatures Istvan thought that one had a slice of truth, but an unflattering truth that cut both ways.

But mostly, Istvan was interested in his work. He decided to establish the bank with modern principles. That meant first cleaning out the old office that in the last days of the communist regime had been permitted a marginal operation. He began by firing everybody and bringing in a new, competent management team, one that he could trust.

Then, Istvan concentrated on ferreting out the best investment opportunities possible. Foreign exchange was just a part of his responsibilities now. More broadly, he had the determining say in whether an entire range of investment opportunities, from a new shopping mall to light industry, would receive the prestige of their bank's backing. If so, more and more it was not even necessary for the bank to provide a major share of funding for a new project. His financial approval now meant leveraging for other investors as well, multiplying the bank's influence many times beyond their actual loan portfolio.

After a while, knowledgeable investors began to refer to Istvan Szepvaros as "the other German Ambassador." He didn't mind that a bit. Besides, his Mercedes was suitable to his position (and a higher series car than that of the Ambassador), and so was his home on Castle Hill in Buda, and his summer villa on Lake Balaton, south-west of Budapest.

"Who was that calling, dear?"

"Imre Mohacsi. You remember, the Deputy in Parliament. We had luncheon in Szeged with him and his wife Magda last year."

"Yes, I remember them. Nice couple. Such penetrating, flashing eyes he has. You knew him in 1956, you said."

"Briefly. For a little while we were in the same resistance group in Pest, before the ammunition began to run out and the position was overrun."

"What's going on now?"

"You'll like it. There is going to be a gala reception in Parliament later this week. Imre thought it might amuse us to attend. They're sending round an invitation in the morning."

"He called personally about that? How odd."

"Well, there was something else. It seems that somebody else is in town from 1956, who will also be at the reception. Janos Magassy. So we'll be having a sort of reunion it seems."

"Janos Magassy? You haven't mentioned him in years. But then, you never talk about those days."

"Best forgotten. No sense living in the past. Still, it will be interesting to see those people once again. And you'll have the opportunity to wear your new red dress."

She was pleased, and smiled at the suggestion. "Come in for dinner. Cook's night off, so I've put something together. Your favorites, *wiener-schnitzel*, roast potatoes and a fresh salad. Then, of course, chocolate cake for dessert."

He smiled and followed her to the dining room.

*   *   *

Attila Nemzeti grumbled at the telephone as he hung it up. He didn't like weekend calls usually. They often meant trouble, and politicians looking over his shoulders. And for an official in the Ministry of Justice, the first thing he understood, but the last thing he could countenance, was a friendly call from a politician. This one seemed different, though. A reception at Parliament could be amusing after all. It would certainly please Margit.

Imre Mohacsi was, of course, in rather a different category from his usual political caller. They did see each other from time to time, but were hardly social intimates.

So Janos Magassy had returned. It was a long time since he had even thought of that name, and what it had meant over forty years ago. He wondered if they would even recognize each other now.

Attila's mind went back to those days. They had been running out of ammunition, and he had left again, after it was plain that Csaba would not be returning. Then Imre had gone out, and also had not returned. It wasn't until much later that he heard the full account about Imre having been wounded, but he had suspected something of the sort.

Down the alley and into the street, towards the police station, which was now deserted, Attila had gone. Occasional tracer bullets and grenades had guided his way. This time he had been lucky. He found another armed group, with more ammunition than defenders. "Take some," they had said, and he had loaded as much ammunition as he could carry back. Then he had made it, and he and Janos and Eva had used it for another day of sporadic defense of their area. That much at least he remembered, or thought he did. Finally they had been overrun.

Or at least that is what must have happened. He had awakened, when? He still didn't have a clear idea of what day it had been. Eva and Janos were both gone. Dead Freedom Fighters were all over the area. Some had been dead, he shuddered to remember, for some time.

For a moment, there had been silence. Then the throbbing of his head had started, and he had again lost consciousness. When night came, he reawakened, and with great presence of mind, got slowly to his feet, and found that he could walk. His head hurt terribly, from some sort of glancing wound, that had masked his face with blood. It probably looked worse than it actually was. Anyone looking through the resistance pocket clearly would have chalked him up as already dead. They would be coming around soon to pick up the bodies. He had to get out of there.

Attila had bound his head as best he could with a large pocket handkerchief. Fanciful stories from novels about escapes through the sewer system came to him, but he didn't know where the entrances might be, and he feared disease or drowning, or the rats. Only one alternative remained.

Like the little boy he had been many years before when a forgetful bus driver had forgotten to wake him up and let him off at his home, Attila singlemindedly walked home, through the debris, through the confused mopping up operations, across town, over towards the Margaret Bridge, and down to the island where he lived with his mother. He had collapsed on his own doorstep.

Attila had been a law student, and had already passed his examinations to practice. Leaving Hungary simply wasn't an option for him. He was never a good language student, for one thing, and for another, this was home. He thought that some people, the British certainly, seemed to be able to travel well. That probably came from being an island people to begin with. But Hungary was different, with its unique language and culture. Living elsewhere was living in exile, no matter how pleasant it might otherwise be. He had even heard that Cardinal Mindszenty had become, over the years, an unwilling refugee at the American Embassy, for much the same reason. That seemed logical.

Attila's immediate problem was making a living. He pleaded his head wound and amnesia whenever untidy questions were posed, and nothing could quite be proved against him. Then he made a living, for years, as best he could, as a day laborer, or sometimes with his violin, filling in with a concert orchestra, or even at a restaurant, when somebody was needed to fill a vacancy. His mother had her small retirement income, and their expenses were minimal. For years, survival was all that mattered, and that seemed assured. They were better off than most people.

Attila knew that his own survival, both during his walk home, and afterwards, was due as much to luck as anything else. Very gradually, a step at a time, he reinserted himself into the professional world. He joined a local organization of the Hungarian Socialist Workers (Communist) Party, after it became clear to him that the days of terror were in the past.

That was one of the many arguments that Attila had had with himself, whether to join the Party. It was a hard decision for a Freedom Fighter to make. Of course, the other Party members could not know that. It would still almost certainly be grounds for his arrest. No, his argument was whether this was morally justified.

He told himself that it was. After all, in the larger scheme of things, the Russians were not going away, and the Americans were not going to help, despite what those broadcasts had implied. No, Hungary was stuck geographically where she had always been, between greater, grasping neighbors. The question was always one of survival. The moral question, it seemed to him, was whether to try to change things from the inside. As a Party member, perhaps he could work to make things better.

People often forgot that 1956 had started as an anti Soviet movement. Many idealistic communist youths were involved. Perhaps that had even been his own motivation. He just couldn't remember. It had, for a while, seemed possible to believe that Imre Nagy could change the nature of Hungarian communism, and make it live up to the promises of a better life for all. If that prospect had been lost to the Russian guns, perhaps the survivors could still do what they could to make things better in Hungary. That might yet validate the sacrifices.

As time went on it became clear that the Hungarian Government would go rather far to avoid another uprising. The trick was to expand the limits of their official toleration, without going too far. Stretching those limits from the inside gave Attila the meaning and excuse for getting on with his life, and his profession.

He discovered that he had not lost the knack for logical argument, and was able to use that for the benefit of Party members who had been wronged in some way, either at their place of employment, or even by the Party itself. Attila became known as fair and reasonable He also had a more valuable knack than either quality. He was very persuasive.

At length, he was able to leave his casual employment and take a very junior position at the Ministry of Justice. Perhaps they reasoned that someone as well-spoken as Attila should not be available to defendants, but should work instead for the state. In any event, his work at the Ministry of Justice began. The first job was beneath his age and skills, really a paralegal job one might say.

It was not too long before Attila Nemzeti, in and around the courts, and particularly the peoples' courts, began to be sought out for advice and lines of argument that might work with the judges. He got along well with those on the bench, many of whom, despite their bluster, needed some reassuring for they clearly understood their lack of qualifications to hear cases. And so, very gradually, he was switched into a junior advocacy position, and then became a member of the Ministry's prosecution team.

Throughout the remainder of the communist era, Nemzeti did his job well. He received just enough advancement to be respectable, but not enough to mark him as a policymaking official. He was known as a compromiser, not a zealot. That is probably what saved him when the regime came crashing down.

"Remembering the old days?" Margit smiled at her husband. It was nearly dinner time, and they were going out to a family restaurant, a tavern really, in their Pest neighborhood. There the beer was fresh and good, the music soulful and unobtrusive, and the food plentiful and cheap. He helped Margit on with her coat. Even though it was May, the weather could change rapidly.

They sat at their table and enjoyed their dinner. Attila returned to her question. "The call was from the Deputy, Imre Mohacsi," he said. "There will be a reception at Parliament later this week, and you and I are to be invited. It should be rather a grand event, from what I gather. Lots of diplomats and journalists and all that. Why not wear that pretty new dress? It's a chance to show it off. It suits you very well."

Margit was pleased. Since their only child, a daughter, had married and now lived in another part of the city, they had lots of time together, but did not often go out. She looked forward to the reception already. It would be rather a treat.

"Did I hear you two discussing someone else?"

"Yes, someone from the old days." From long habit, even now and even to his wife, Attila referred to the 1956 Revolution as "the old days," never directly. "It may be something of a reunion, it seems." He let it go at that. So did Margit.

*   *   *

Janos Magassy was in a good mood. The conversation with Ambassador Kovatch had been productive, and it was always worthwhile to talk with Imre Mohacsi. It seemed strange to him to be able to walk the streets of his native country without looking over his shoulder. For so long, of course, he had not been able to return at all. Nor would he have done so even if by some miracle he had received a Hungarian visa.

The problem then had been the old one, of a communist government at war with itself. Some wanted to snatch the returnees and try them for their part in 1956. In fact, that had been the Kadar policy in the first few years after 1956. Some Freedom Fighters had been lured back, and they had been, despite solemn promises to the contrary, tried and imprisoned for long sentences. Some were even sentenced to death.

Other officials argued that this policy of retribution was insane. Hungary was in desperate need of western currency, hard money with which to purchase needed goods, if any modernization was ever to take place. Without increasing the standard of living, who could promise that the Hungarian powder keg might not explode once again? Gradually, a compromise was worked out. The prosecutions stopped, and a list of Freedom Fighters was kept, of persons who were simply barred from receiving visas.

That helped for a while. But still, people were afraid for their safety. Part of the reason was a legal difficulty. Hungary refused to let its citizens divest themselves of their citizenship, except through a convoluted procedure that few understood and fewer tried to follow. That meant that a returning tourist who had become a Canadian citizen would still be treated as a Hungarian and be subject to military service.

Sorting all this out took time. The United States took the lead finally, in a Consular Convention that was negotiated and approved some fifteen years after the 1956 Revolution. The Hungarian authorities agreed in essence that dual nationals who were returning as tourists would be treated as American citizens, not as Hungarians.

In the eyes of many Hungarian-Americans, that made it safe to return. But for Janos Magassy, whose name remained on the refusal book whose existence was always solemnly denied, it was many years before he could return safely to Hungary.

In lingering reflective moments, Magassy thought that there might be something specific about the Hungarian character that made contentment impossible. He should now, he supposed, feel a sense of accomplishment, if not exhilaration.

They had fought against impossible odds, after all, he and his friends in 1956. And what they had done for many, many years had seemed to be pointless, except for their personal honor. That mattered greatly. But their sacrifices hadn't seemed to achieve any lasting result.

Magassy had worked out a theory about this. Hungary, after all, was a small nation surrounded on both sides by larger, predatory neighbors. In the long run they weren't going to win, fighting either the Russians or the German speakers. Hungary had, after all, done that so often in the past. Sometimes they had even fought both at the same time, as was the case with Lajos Kossuth's 1849 Revolution.

If they couldn't win, the honor was in fighting regardless. In miniature, this was the theme of Ferenc Molnar's *A Pal Utcai Fiuk* (*The Boys Of Pal Street)*. The boys in Molnar's novel had banded together to protect their territory, but finally, despite their heroics and their sticking together, had lost their little park to bulldozers and modernization. Just like our group, the Friends of Barat Street, we protected our territory and did our best, Magassy knew.

In Hungary trying meant a great deal, and success was not to be expected, but a sort of bonus if it did happen. Americans on the other hand tended to judge you by whether you had succeeded or not. They had the luxury of expecting success.

That made Hungarians very different from Americans. Magassy had to smile when he considered just how obsessed Americans were with winning. How indignant Americans always seemed to get when they discovered that the rules were rigged in the first place, as seemed to be the case for example with American politics at all levels. Hungarians expected that, and that is one reason why they considered Americans to be naive about so many things.

Well, for many years, Magassy and his emigre Freedom Fighter friends had only had the honor of their participation in the 1956 Revolution to fall back on. The communists were still in power in Hungary. True, over the years the terror had largely ceased, but it had been replaced, friends who had taken trips home to Hungary said, by an insidious self-policing on the part of the people. They no longer stood up and braved the regime, as they had done in 1956.

For Magassy, that behavior was a form of slavery. But then, he also knew that he could afford to think that. He, after all, was living in the United States and like any American, his main problem seemed to be how to pay for goods that a Hungarian could never have in the first place.

So it was with fascination mixed with disillusionment that he had heard of the fall of communism in Hungary, the lifting of travel barriers, and after a transition period, multi-party elections, and the election of a democratic government. This was the validation that he had hoped for, for so many years.

And then, the euphoria hadn't lasted. It couldn't have, after all. Too much was expected too soon by an impatient people who had suffered too long. They were like an animal liberated from a cage which was disoriented and unprepared for freedom.

The economy hadn't taken off immediately. Inflation had been a serious problem. Janos wryly recalled that in the communist days of the NEM thirty years ago, the government deficit would have been covered by artfully disguised loans from the American Government, some of which would have been siphoned off by the Russians. That was the province of bankers and politicians. But now, the free market prevailed, and it was not free, and people now understood that their pensions bought just a small percentage of what they had in the communist days. Their savings were gone.

Democracy hadn't solved all of the old problems. It had even brought some new and unwelcome ones, including a sharp increase in crime, and the worries of inflation. What made it worse was that now, everyone could see in shop windows all of the goods that they couldn't afford to buy. Hungary seemed a society adrift.

But in one major respect, Hungary was freed. The guilt they caused in the West in 1956 had borne fruit, with NATO membership and national freedom at last. Perhaps they had won after all.

Magassy had felt much older as he returned to Hungary. What sort of world was this where youngsters offered him a seat on the streetcar? He shook his head in wry amusement.

He had returned to Hungary with a project.

He remembered November 1, 1956, All Souls Day, when they had held a burial service for their friends, at Barat Street. Eva had suggested a memorial. It was worth doing. By celebrating them, perhaps he could recapture something of that spirit, something of the desperate, purely Hungarian willingness to fight against all odds for the principle of freedom.

A memorial statue. That would consume his energies for a while. Let Hungarian teenagers remember people their own age fighting as free men and women against desperate odds, and take heart for their own futures, and for their country's future.

It made Janos Magassy feel almost young again.

And it would give him the opportunity to meet again with the survivors of his group, and take their measure, one by one.

He reviewed the weekend once again. The meeting with Ambassador Kovatch had, he thought, been worthwhile. Kovatch was a businessman, and didn't seem motivated by the same causes as Magassy, but he was of the same generation, and might help. He looked forward to talking with that fellow Cutler at the American Embassy. The telephone call with Imre Mohacsi had gone very well indeed. He would cut short his trip to Sarospatak after all and return for the reception at Parliament.

The phone rang in his hotel room. That was unexpected, and so was the voice that he now heard, after so many years. Yes, a late evening drink in Obuda would be fine. He knew the place. *"A Viszontlatasra"* ("See you there later.")

*   *   *   *   *   *   *   *   *   *

The Second Day—October 24, 1956

It had been a long night, but an exhilarating one. Had all that fighting at the Radio Station really happened? Eva had awakened with the sun, and now found herself making morning coffee. She turned to Csaba and kissed him awake.

"What a mess this place is!"

"Don't blame me," he answered with a grin. "I'm just a worker in a friend's apartment, not a fancy student like you!"

She tossed a pillow at him. "Here, drink some coffee."

He did. "Turn on the radio," he said. "Let's find out what is going on." She found the radio on the dresser and turned it on. It was a simple AM set, tuned to Radio Budapest.

Some static began the transmission. Then there was an angry account of the news, blaming yesterday's fighting on "fascist, reactionary elements." "Sounds like us, all right!" Csaba grinned. Then a curfew until eight o'clock in the morning was announced. "Fat chance!" Csaba snorted.

Then the radio crackled again. The announcer cleared his throat. His nervousness was obvious. "Attention! Attention! The Central Committee of the Hungarian Workers Party met today."

"Already?" Csaba mused. "Then they know they're in trouble."

A list of Politburo members followed. Gero was still in as First Secretary. "A bad sign," Csaba said. Eva nodded agreement. She was becoming "political" in spite of herself.

Then came the Central Committee's "recommendation" to the Presidium, that Imre Nagy be made Prime Minister. To make sure that listeners understood what was happening, the announcer repeated the news plainly. "Attention! Attention! We repeat the announcement. Imre Nagy has become Prime Minister of Hungary."

Csaba and Eva looked at each other in astonishment. Had they won already? True, Nagy was boxed in, but he was in office as head of the government. Now he could resume the New Course he had started in 1953. Things were bound to get better.

Csaba snapped off the radio. It was time to celebrate.

"This early?" Eva smiled.

"This early!" Csaba repeated. He led her back to bed. "It's a miracle when Radio Budapest puts me in the mood to make love. Later we'll go out and see what's going on. But that can wait."

*   *   *

Attila heard the rumblings first. "Tanks!" Then he wondered to Istvan, "I wonder whose tanks they are…ours or theirs?"

"We'll see soon enough," Istvan said. "There's only one way to know for sure. They can't be too far away. Let's try to get closer to them."

They went to the corner of Dozsa Gyorgy Street where Stalin Avenue broadened and branched out, and saw three tanks slowly advancing, from several blocks away. They were Russian T-34s.

Attila saw a Russian noncom standing at the lead tank's hatch. "Probably brought in from the countryside. That must have taken a while. Those tanks aren't very fast. They must have been called in last night. When we see three, there are dozens more coming."

They could hear small arms fire in the distance. Then an explosion, then several more. People started pouring out into the streets. There was an excited babble of voices and rumors. "General strike! The workers have called a general strike! Nobody is going to work today!" yelled a passerby.

"So now the whole city is a potential army," Attila said. "Let's hope the Russians don't call in their infantry. Against tanks we still have a chance!"

*   *   *

Janos Magassy had heard the tanks several hours earlier. He had brought the truckload of weapons and ammunition to a Barat Street storefront near the Corvin Movie House. There Janos, Imre and their friend

Karoly, a circus acrobat until he had fallen after mixing highwire stunts with beer, had unloaded the cargo.

As Janos had told Karoly, "It's a great location. Corvin Square commands an approach to the Kilian Barracks, and we can stop the Russians getting to *Corvin Koz* (Corvin Circle) from the other side. There are a lot of streets and alleyways all over the quarter. Just right for bottling up tanks."

They were joined by two wiry, thin teenagers. They wanted to fight and seemed unafraid. They were brothers, who called each other Pista and Red. Pista said that they had had some military training as members of *DISZ*, the Communist Youth Organization.

"I'll look after them, said Karoly. "We'll need everybody." Then he held an impromptu class, with bottles scrounged from the shop's storeroom, and gasoline siphoned from a nearby station.

He filled a bottle with gasoline, then stuffed a rag into the neck with a flourish. "This is now a Molotov cocktail," he announced. "Light the soaked wick, count to three, then throw!"

"What do we aim for?" Pista wanted to know.

Here Janos stepped in. "Nothing until I give the word. This will be in groups of three. First person aims for the tank's tracks. When the tank is stopped, second person aims for the rear of the tank, the ventilation pipe. Third person will blast them with a submachine gun as the crew tries to exit the hatch."

They nodded appreciatively. Janos remembered the chants he had heard last night all over Budapest. *"Ruszkik haza!"* ("Russians go home!"). Now they will wish that they had.

*   *   *

Csaba flipped on the radio once again. There were calls to stop fighting. An amnesty for those laying down arms was mentioned again and again. The deadline kept being extended.

"Let's find out what's going on!" he said. Eva dressed and left the building with him. They headed down the narrow street towards the Kilian Barracks. Then they stopped. A fight was in progress, somewhere near. Slipping around a sidestreet, they saw Hungarian soldiers fight off Russian tanks. So far the Russians had not attacked in force, and the defense was holding its own.

Across the street groups of youngsters near Corvin Circle, cartridge belts strapped around their waists, brandished weapons that looked too big for them. A girl closed her eyes before firing. Down the boulevard people were putting up barricades. Eva wondered whether this was going on all over the city.

Csaba read her thoughts. "Let's find out!" he said.

CHAPTER FOUR

▼

SABRE PRACTICE

Robbie picked up his Ford from the garage near his townhouse and began the leisurely drive to the Embassy. He was not rushed, and his route varied, a reflex that owed as much to curiosity about what was going on around him as it did to his security training. Sometimes he took the bus rather than his car, the better to study other commuters and get a jump on reading the daily Hungarian press before he got to the office.

Vary your routes, they had said at the Foreign Service Institute's security seminars. Don't be predictable. That makes things too easy for…whom, exactly? In Bordeaux there had been the Basque ETA terrorists. That had been left far behind now. He went down Castle Hill, circled *Moszkva ter* (Moscow Square), and headed for the Margaret Bridge, to the north.

The more direct route would have taken him through the tunnel under Castle Hill, an emergency hospital during the war, then across Clark Adam *ter* (Clark Adam Square) and the Chain Bridge. That route then led to Roosevelt *ter* (Roosevelt Square, named after Teddy, not FDR, Robbie remembered), past *Szechenyi rakpart* (Szechenyi Quai) and the imposing building on the Pest side of the Danube which contained Embassy apartments, and then to Freedom Square after a turn or two.

Robbie turned instead north from Moscow Square to the *Margit korut* (Margaret Boulevard) which led to Margaret Bridge. He made a mental note to have luncheon or a pizza soon at the Marxim Restaurant near Moscow Square, whose decoration satirized the communist period with gloomy black and white posters of Rakosi and Party exhortations from that period. It was always packed, Robbie had heard. That was a healthy sign. When an American politician was ridiculed on Dave Letterman, his credibility usually was dissolved in laughter, the universal political solvent. The naming of a pizza for the *AVH* might perform a similar cleansing function here, Robbie thought. Besides it was a good place to wear jeans, hang out, have a pizza and hear what the younger generation was saying.

Robbie crossed the Margaret Bridge, with a glance towards Margaret Island to his left. He had tried the thermal baths there one Sunday and enjoyed the experience. Budapest had been known since Roman times for its hot springs, which is probably why the Romans had located a garrison here. There were still thermal baths around from the Turkish period.

Robbie's father had told him that at the Gellert Hotel on the Buda side of the Danube, there was an extensive thermal bath and pool complex that even featured artificial waves. That would be fun to take his father to, if his parents ever visited him in Budapest. What kept him away?

Robbie turned onto *Szent Istvan korut* (St. Stephen Boulevard), the beginnings of the Pest theater district, and from St. Stephen Boulevard cut onto *Bajcsy Zsilinsky ut* (Avenue) at *Nyugati ter* (Western Square). After six blocks he took a right onto Freedom Square and parked the Ford in his reserved parking space near the Embassy. Robbie was an early arrival, but of course DCM Arnold Johnson was already there. Always worried about the Ambassador and his own chances of getting an Embassy, Johnson was both gatekeeper and problem solver. Except for an occasional social appearance, he seemed to live at his office.

Robbie bounded up the entrance steps and exchanged hellos with the Marine Guard and the receptionist. He saw that Gunnery Sergeant Lemuel Shiflett had made some notations about John Magassy, the Sunday visitor, in the duty log book that was kept at the desk. The visitor's name, local address and the action taken had all been scrupulously entered into the log book. That was about it. Robbie decided against another cup of coffee at the snackbar. He walked past the consular section and the budget and fiscal office to the elevator, and took it up to his office.

The American Embassy took two sides of a hollow square. The other two had, Robbie supposed, commercial purposes now. In the past, they had been stacked wall to wall with *AVH* secret policemen, who tried to pry Embassy secrets with their parabolic microphones, and took picture after picture of Cardinal Mindszenty as His Eminence took his daily late afternoon walk in the central courtyard, attended by an Embassy Hungarian speaking duty officer. Now that era was over, marked just by a plaque in the Ambassador's office commemorating the fact that Cardinal Mindszenty had lived there from 1956 to 1972.

The third floor had some of the Embassy's substantive offices, along its high ceilinged, nineteenth century corridors. The Ambassador and DCM Johnson had the corner offices fronting Freedom Square, and Robbie shared an adjoining suite on the corridor with Economic and Commercial Officer Julia Broadbent. Across from them were offices occupied by the Defense Attache, Army Colonel Joshua Tidings, when he was in Budapest.

Robbie thought of his father again. When he had been stationed here, the Legation had counted barely a dozen Americans. Now there were over one hundred Americans assigned to the spreading Embassy, not counting Hungarian local staff, and everyone couldn't begin to fit into offices in the Embassy building. There just wasn't enough space. The Information Service and USAID, for example, were housed in the new Bank Building at the southern corner of Freedom Square, where Robbie sometimes went for the inexpensive buffet lunch.

There would be the usual Monday morning staff meeting at ten thirty. That left enough time to read through the weekend cables and the unclassified clippings file which the Information Service had assembled, and to glance through the Hungarian press, marking selected articles for detailed attention when he had the time.

With Ambassador Eleanor Horton on home leave back in Oklahoma, the pressure was off his translating ability, since the substantive staff virtually all had had language training. Some, like Deputy Chief of Mission (DCM) Johnson, the second in command, were even back for a second tour of duty. Horton, on the other hand, was a political appointee who had been a major fundraiser for the White House in the last election. Hungarian had not been a qualification for her appointment.

Perhaps, Robbie thought, that might change in the future. He hoped so. He had to admit, though, that she was focussed and understood the country after a year better than he would have imagined. But then, even for professionals it always took just about a year in a new assignment abroad to understand the country of assignment, or to lose preconceptions based on a previous tour of duty in the same country. At that point, the generalities seemed to coalesce, and current political and social realities came into balance. At least that was the case for substantive officers of good judgment, and Robbie had to admit that Ambassador Horton had that quality.

Before that year passed, analysis always seemed rather one dimensional, with each new impression about the country assuming too much importance, crowding out the previous month's insight or discovery. The stories were legendary in the foreign affairs community around Washington about new appointees seeking to justify their place in a largely career service who had made fools of themselves by sending in first person telegrams, reporting their views too soon. These "I believe" messages usually were superficial, often exaggerated the importance of the country of assignment or the wisdom of its leader, and sometimes, like a loud tie on a bad suit, just called further attention to the inadequacies of the sender.

It was the job of a good DCM to stop such cables from being sent. And Arnie Johnson was a good DCM. To make matters even better, Ambassador Horton knew what she didn't know, and that was a rare quality indeed. The same could not be said for her husband Sam. Thank heavens he was also back in Oklahoma, out of everybody's hair, or whatever else he could reach.

*   *   *

DCM Johnson opened the staff meeting with a brief rundown of pending matters. Groans met his announcement that there would be an inspection of the post in six weeks. Most of what was said was already known to the Embassy officers. The meeting was focussed on the attendance of a visiting Deputy Assistant Secretary of State (or DAS) for European Affairs, new to his job and the region, and in Budapest on a familiarization trip to American diplomatic missions in the region. He reported that Ambassador Horton had stopped in at the Department of State before proceeding to Oklahoma.

The DAS said that Ambassador Horton seemed to have touched all of the right bases. Her courtesy call on the Secretary, and her talk with the Assistant Secretary for European Affairs had both gone well. She had smoked out the fact that a major CODEL, or Congressional group, would visit Budapest in the fall. She had also had lunch on Capitol Hill, met on NATO business with ranking officials at the Pentagon, and talked with her counterpart, the Hungarian Ambassador in Washington.

Colonel Tidings next discussed the latest Hungarian defense budget, and how Hungarian military doctrine dovetailed with NATO requirements. Hungarian support for American and NATO efforts in Bosnia in 1996-1997, then in Yugoslavia, and in the ongoing terrorism crisis had given emphasis to Hungary's claim to be a modern nation. If Dad could only hear this, Robbie thought.

The views of Julia Broadbent on the economic and commercial side were equally upbeat. American investment in Hungary was now the largest source of foreign investment in Hungary, with reinvestment of dollars now increasingly important. She and her staff were very busy with visiting American businessmen looking for local representation. It was all getting to be a bit much to handle, really. Perhaps a trade fair would be a good idea, she said hopefully towards the DAS.

Andras Novotny held forth for the Information Service, now folded into the State Department, but universally still called "USIS." Cultural events were no longer funded, and the stream of USIS-sponsored visitors in both directions had become a trickle. On the bright side, the Hungarian press, which in recent years had become heavily foreign owned, appeared to be thriving. There were many newspapers competing for attention, and Hungary's tradition as a nation of newspaper readers was continuing.

Robbie summarized the shifting internal political scene. He traced a clear pattern of power shifting with each national election. Perhaps for their own safety, the voters seemed to prefer change to continuity in power. "And with their history, who could blame them?" Robbie concluded.

In 1990, with the collapse of communism and the emergence of multi-party democracy, parties of the center and right, including the Democratic Forum, FIDESZ, the Smallholders and the Christian Democrats, had won 88% of the seats in Parliament, and the government which had then taken power had been Hungary's first noncommunist government in decades.

Then in 1994 a lethal mix of inflation and economic austerity had caused a sea change in the political landscape. True, the former Communists had changed their dogma, and even the name of their party to the Socialist Party. But with the 1994 elections they held a clear majority of 208 of the 386 seats in Parliament. Together with the Alliance of Free Democrats which held 70 seats and had allied itself with the Socialists, a new coalition had ruled.

The pendulum had shifted once again in the 1998 elections. Inflation and rising crime had become issues of broad concern, and the ruling coalition had taken the blame. In 2002, the Socialists were once again in power. Hungary was still feeling its way, but a new dynamic, including increased foreign investment and NATO membership, were signs of forward movement.

"So that brings us up to the 2006 elections," Robbie added. "Just 50 years from 1956, and Hungary now has a new political tradition of democratic government. The Freedom Fighters would have been pleased, I think."

The DAS asked about the 1956 Hungarian Revolution. Was that still on people's minds, and did it affect our relations?

In answer Robbie mentioned the Saturday incident in Eger. Not that the old issue of the radios was currently on the front burner, he said. His own view had always been that the 1956 Hungarian Revolution had been an explosion against tyranny. What the radios may or may not have said was perhaps part of the mix, but neither the stimulus nor the reason for the explosion.

Robbie couldn't help adding that the 1956 Revolution here was one of the finest moments of the century. More than any other event, it had fore-shadowed the end of the communist system. "Secretary Albright used to say that for many Americans, the defining moment in foreign affirs was Viet-Nam. For her, the defining moment was Munich, meaning of course the West's capitulation to Hitler in the 'thirties. I guess for me, the defining moment is Budapest in 1956. It's hard even now to imagine such courage. As Kissinger said, the Hungarian uprising was a forerunner of the bankruptcy of their system. The communists lost credibility everywhere. We owe them a lot."

There was silence in the room, which was a sealed room within a room, designed in Cold War days to be impenetrable for listening devices. Robbie went on. "It's quite a heritage, but basically, this country, aside from lip service, hasn't quite figured out what to do about 1956. Of course, those who were imprisoned and murdered have now been reburied and are martyrs.

"But what about those who were on the other side then? It wasn't so very long ago, after all. And what about those many people, a number of whom are now American citizens, who lost relatives then?" The DAS was asking for further comment.

Robbie continued and summed up. "We haven't heard the last echoes of 1956. Who did what, and when, will be questions asked for a long time, either in the open or not. The Hungarian Government has sealed its records from the period. That is understandable. Some, even Freedom Fighters, say that is the better course, and will in the long run make healing come sooner. This is the background and we should be aware of it."

DCM Arnie Johnson asked a question "Suppose the books were opened on the period. Would there be prosecutions?"

Robbie grimaced in thought. "One problem is the statute of limitations. Hungarian lawyers say that after 25 years, prosecutions may not be held. At least that is the case for murder. So nothing could be done on murder charges more than forty years later. Several years ago there were some trials held on lower level charges, which had longer statutes of limitations. At the time they were very controversial, resulting in short sentences that nobody thought adequate for the actual offenses, and even then the appeals went on for a long time. Some of those cases have been reopened. And recently the prosecution switched ground, and tried some former border guards at Mosonmagyarovar on grounds of crimes against humanity, a charge that doesn't have a statute of limtations. We'll see how that plays out on appeal."

The DAS raised another point. "If it doesn't stand up, how about the Parliament just passing a law extending the statute of limitations for murder?"

Robbie went on, "A few years ago, that was tried, and didn't get very far. As a practical matter, of course, the Socialist majority in Parliament just wouldn't permit it. They had the votes to block anything then. I don't think the issue will be reopened now. People generally want to move on."

He thought for a minute. "Besides, I'm not a lawyer, but Hungarian lawyers also tell me that they would have a problem with a law that basically changed the statute of limitations retroactively. That's an *ex post facto* law, and our own legal system wouldn't allow it, I'm sure." The visiting DAS summed up. "So what we have now is a situation where the government itself has all the files and information. Will they ever open their files?"

"Since this concerns the way the Hungarians are treating people who were their own citizens at the time, I don't think so. Neither I think does the Hungarian-American community. But Randy Davis would know more about that."

Consul Randy Davis spoke up. "These issues come up sometimes in my shop. The Hungarian-American tourists that I see, and I see a lot of them, are aware of all this. They see good things about Hungary, and they are hopeful about the future, but some of them want the books opened on 1956."

He went on. "Some former Freedom Fighters, now American citizens, have even petitioned the Hungarian Government to declassify their own files from the period, something like an American citizen raising a Freedom Of Information Act issue with our own government. But so far, the Hungarian Government hasn't allowed this to happen. They cite the old standby, 'intelligence sources and methods,' to deny even opening the files of the period just that far, to the individuals directly concerned.

"In particular, one of my visitors last week, a John Magassy from New Jersey, got quite heated over all this. He even went so far as to say that there were two ways to handle the past…in the courts, or in the streets. It sounded ominous."

Robbie looked up in interest. "The Marine Guard called yesterday afternoon to say that Magassy was at the Embassy. He left a package for me. He may be coming in next week. He has in mind a project for a memorial to the 1956 Revolution. He wanted to brief me and the Ambassador about it. Sounded interesting."

"No," Randy continued, "I don't think you'll be seeing him after all. I had a call from the Consular Division of the Foreign Ministry just before staff meeting. Magassy was found murdered in Obuda early this morning. The papers will probably have it this afternoon."

Robbie was stunned. There had not been any note of danger or particular urgency in the request to see him, as relayed by the Marine Guard. It was probably just a case of robbery that had gone wrong, and that was Consul Randy Davis's responsibility. Surely the dead tourist's communication to him had been coincidental.

Still, one couldn't be sure. Robbie felt that he owed it to Magassy's memory to keep a close eye on whatever developed. Randy Davis promised to keep the DCM and Robbie both closely advised of further developments, and on that solemn note, the staff meeting ended.

*   *   *

Robbie was familiar with Obuda, the oldest section of Budapest, just north of Buda with its Castle Hill, where he lived. Buda and Obuda on one side of the Danube had joined Pest on the other side to form modern Budapest as the nineteenth century ended. Most people knew Obuda now only for its superb restaurants, just enough off the tourist beaten track so that a good table wasn't hard to find. Aside from that, the area gave a rather down at the heels impression. It would make a great movie set for a film about Paris in the 'forties, and in fact had done so more than once.

For Robbie, however, the area had a different association entirely. This was where twice a week he took fencing lessons.

His weapon, for the reason that it had been a weapon, was the sabre. At Brown he had been good enough to make the fencing team, and then to win most of his intercollegiate matches. The sport, if that was the proper word for it, was exhausting, like karate or wrestling. It also was a welcome change for a young diplomat who was beginning to suspect that diplomacy held more bureaucracy than he wanted.

Robbie thought that more than either the foil or the epee, the other two fencing specialties, skill with the sabre demanded strength, coordination, and a touch of savage imagination. It was from a different era, and he liked that. He also liked the Hungarian connection. A Kisfaludy-Strobl statue on Castle Hill of a *huszar* brandishing a sabre reminded him that *huszars* were Hungarian, and that the sabre had been their favored weapon.

The Obuda Fencing Club continued this tradition. It was on a side street off Florian *ter* (square). Robbie's fencing coach from Brown had told him about the Obuda Fencing Club and its legendary coaches, and a trial session, at which Robbie had had to prove his skill, had secured him a place as the only American allowed to practice there. Hungary had won far more Olympic medals in fencing than her size would indicate. The rigorous training that men and women received at the Obuda Fencing Club in all three weapons, beginning at a very young age, helped explain that.

Robbie parked his car off Florian Square and walked to the fencing club. It was late afternoon, and he always thought that a Monday session was just the thing to sweat off any extra pounds that substantial Hungarian cooking might have added to his spare frame over the weekend. This was really a self-imposed practice workout. The weekly session with his fencing master would come later in the week.

He entered the club and proceeded to the locker room, then quickly changed into comfortable shoes and sweat pants, with a long sleeved sweatshirt. He took his mask, sabre and fencing jacket from his locker, but would not put them on until his exercises were over, if indeed he put them on at all. That depended upon whether after exercising he got in some practice fencing. Usually he did, and he preferred to do so, but that depended upon another sabreur being present who also wanted the workout. For his weekly session with the fencing master, of course, he would wear full fencing attire, not the informal sweatshirt and pants that he wore at exercise sessions.

Exercising, he knew from personal experience, was vitally important to avoid painful injury. The muscles had to be carefully stretched and toned.

He would do the same exercises at his session later in the week before meeting the fencing master on the *piste*, or fencing strip, but spend somewhat less time at them, depending upon how he felt. The fencing master assumed that his students were adults and ready for their lessons. That meant being in top physical condition.

Robbie entered the practice hall. On the walls, there were fading photographs of past national and international champions. Unlike the weekend, when Robbie occasionally came to make up a session, Monday was a slow day. Only four of the *pistes* were occupied. At the exercise area half a dozen men and women were doing their exercises. Robbie recognized one other sabreur. They nodded to each other. He looked familiar. Perhaps there would be the chance for some practice on the *piste* after all.

Robbie leaned on the mat and lowered himself to the ground. First, a few situps, for stretching the torso. Then he tucked his right foot under his left thigh and, in a sitting position, stretched to touch his left foot. Ten of these, and then he reversed, tucking in his left foot, and stretched his back thigh to reach the extended right foot. Then he stood, circling his arms forward, then backward. Finally, he stood leaning forward, with his right foot anchoring his balance flat on the ground, and leaned forward to stretch his calf muscles. This was repeated on the other side.

He was beginning to work up a sweat. Still, that wasn't enough. He raised himself into a standing position, and stood on his toes. Then he walked over to the wall and took hold of a support bar. This part was something like ballet. He held onto the bar, and slowly lifted his right leg, then lowered it, and repeated the exercise with his left. Then he jogged around the large exercise hall's track at the edge of the room four times, varying his speed but keeping a steady pace.

Finally, returning to the mat, Robbie practiced several lunges without his sabre. After a few neck rolls he felt ready. With a nod to the other sabreur, who had finished his own exercises a few minutes earlier, Robbie put on his fencing jacket and mask. Then sabre in hand he joined the other sabreur on the *piste*. They formally bowed to each other.

They each assumed the *en garde* position, moving into a slight crouch, back straight, facing each other, perfectly balanced with bended knees, back arm slightly raised, back foot at a right angle to the leading foot. They held their sabres forward, but not so far forward that the opponent could accurately tell the entire reach. That was important. Don't show your hand in bridge. Don't let your opponent know your full reach in fencing.

His opponent lunged first. It was an easy lunge, easily parried, and that was the point, as they began. Lunge and parry, lunge and parry, parry and *riposte*, the men practiced the basic defensive and offensive maneuvers.

Straightforward lunges formed the basic attack, the attacker quickly stepping forward, thrusting the arm and weapon, making a cutting attack as the front foot descended, back arm extended for balance. Balance remained the key. If the lunge was too aggressive, the attacker left himself in a vulnerable position for a parry and *riposte*, or counterattack.

The parry, the basic defensive maneuver, was exercised in two basic triangles. They were even numbered. In prime and second, the defender guarded against an attack moving upwards, towards the torso or flank. In tierce or quarte the defender guarded against a downward attack towards the same areas.

Either defense began as the defender first brought his sabre upwards to quinte to guard against an attack to the head. The defender would then lower the blade and raise it again as necessary to ward off the actual attack which could come with the attacker's blade sweeping either up or down.

The first attack came sweeping upwards. Robbie had raised his forearm and the sabre to the basic defensive quint position, his grip hand at forehead level, and the blade held just over head level. That would block a cut to the head.

Then as he saw the direction of the lunge he sharply lowered the blade by pivoting his forearm to block his opponent's upward thrust. Held near his torso, that would protect him from an under cut to the belly. If the attack were diverted towards his flank, it took a split second to lower the hand to chest level, sweeping the blade with it across his front, and deflecting the attacker's sabre. That is where the lunge in fact came, and Robbie brushed it aside.

Next it was Robbie's turn to attack, and he did so. His opponent quickly took the basic parry position. Robbie's lunge was not to the head, but a sweeping cut downwards to the body. The defense was a sudden lowering of the sabre grip to belt level on the flank. The sabre could be swept across the defender's front if necessary to guard against an attack from above towards the torso.

Back and forth the lunges and parries went in turn. With the sabre, points could be made with cuts from the point or with the blade, and each maneuver had its own rhythm. Gradually the two men practiced serial lunges forward the entire length of the fourteen metre *piste*. The lunges and parries continued, faster and defter. Sometimes the attacker feinted an attack at the head, and cut to the torso or flank instead.

Robbie enjoyed this part of sabre fencing. There was a joint movement and shared rhythm to it, a concentrated and coordinated game of hand and eye. To defend, you had to anticipate, to know where the sudden attack was coming. If you were wrong, you had to change your parry immediately. While you were doing that, the opponent might be executing a feint, a thrust in one direction that ended as a cut somewhere else. For example, a lunge towards the head might end as a cut to the body. You had to be prepared for that, and at the same time, be prepared to use your opponent's own momentum against him.

Practice sessions like this one were useful but limited. They stressed offense or defense primarily. The attacker would attack in sequence the entire length of the *piste*. Robbie and his opponent executed their maneuvers with skill. Then, they would switch roles, and the attacker would assume the defense. The movement became crisper, more rapid and sure as they went on. In a real match, offense and defense changed quickly, and the moves seemed to interconnect. If your lunge didn't result in a hit, you wouldn't necessarily have the luxury of another one. You could find yourself facing a quick, furious counterattack.

Others stopped to watch, as their movement became more swift and forceful. At a final series of attacks. Robbie's opponent lunged just a trifle too far, putting himself off balance. Robbie seized his opportunity with a counterattack called *prise de fer*, or taking of the blade, an elegant maneuver which used his opponent's own force against him, like judo. His opponent lunged upwards. Robbie engaged his blade with a circular parry which moved his opponent's blade out of line, and not in position to block his own quick lunge.

That successful lunge ended the practice session somewhat theatrically. with even a sprinkling of enthusiastic applause from several of the younger spectators. Robbie bowed to his opponent and left the *piste*.

The shower felt good. Under the soapy suds, two other men in the men's shower stalls who had just finished their own practice session were talking excitedly. They continued, oblivious to the American who had just joined them.

"Yes, they found him just a block from the club. Imagine the publicity we'll get. Bad enough that we have to have a murder committed almost on our doorstep, and they say an American at that. But this one had the police all over the place most of the morning. Bizarre."

"Imagine, in this day and age, a corpse found with a sabre halfway through his neck. What a mess. It must have been a horrible way to die. I expect the police will be talking to all of us before long."

Robbie toweled himself dry, dressed, left the Fencing Club and drove to his apartment. It looked as though he might once again find himself at the center of a murder investigation. He rather looked forward to it.

* * * * * * * * * *

The Third Day—October 25, 1956

Throughout the night Csaba and Eva had helped erect barricades on boulevards leading towards the Kilian Barracks. This was Budapest's internal network of boulevards, linking Pest in an arc like a drawn bow leading away from the Danube north of the Parliament, then arching at midpoint at *Boraros ter* (Boraros Square) before curving back towards the Danube.

It was exhausting work, but exhilarating as well. The barricades would make a concerted attack much harder. Citizens could then isolate approaching tanks one by one. The Hungarian soldiers stationed at the Kilian Barracks seemed determined to resist. There had already been some isolated firefights with Russian tanks, the Kilian soldiers armed with their antitank guns. And then, clank, clank, clank came the noise of approaching tanks, not far away. Csaba could see them slowly approaching, lumbering like some prehistoric monsters. There were five of them.

"They're Hungarian!" he shouted.

It was true. The Defense Ministry must have spent some time wondering what to do, before sending out a trusted unit. The lead tank stopped not far from the civilians who were putting up the street barricade. The work was far from complete. The tank could still have crushed this improvised defense.

The small and thinning crowd didn't know what to do. The tank's hatch opened, and a slim officer peered out. Then he emerged from the tank. He was a colonel, and he was simply too tall, Csaba thought, to have fit comfortably into that tank.

He walked straight towards them.

"My name is Pal Maleter," he said. "I'm Csaba Kovacs," Csaba said. There were no handshakes. This is weird, Eva thought. So formal, but surreal. This must be what modern painting is like.

Colonel Maleter asked Csaba who he was and why he was resisting the Russians, Hungary's allies. "I'm a factory worker," Csaba answered. "We don't get enough to eat. For me it's not too bad, but most of my friends have families. We hear the food goes to the Soviet Union."

Maleter nodded. That encouraged Csaba to keep talking.

"Yesterday, no, it was Tuesday, we were at the radio station. We tried to get them to broadcast this." He pulled out his wallet. There was the list of sixteen demands, including decent living conditions and Russian withdrawal from Hungary. It was folded, Colonel Maleter noticed, beside Csaba's membership card in the Hungarian Workers Party. Csaba gave the list of demands to Maleter, who perused the paper. They didn't seem unreasonable. He looked again at Csaba and Eva.

Csaba went on. "Then they fired at us, the *AVH*. So we fired back. Now the Russians have joined in. That is why we are building these barricades. It's for Hungary."

Colonel Maleter nodded. He seemed to understand.

Then Maleter did something unexpected. He gave a brisk military salute to Csaba before remounting the tank and leading his tank formation into the Kilian Barracks.

*　　　　*　　　　*

Attila Nemzeti was exhilarated. He was also exhausted. He couldn't remember when he had last slept a full night, although he had found a bench for a few hours' snooze. Nobody was working, and of course there were no classes to attend.

Sometime during the long night his new friend Istvan Szepvaros had muttered something about going home, and had left. Attila had barely noticed. But this was too stimulating, and Attila didn't want to miss a moment of what was going to happen. So he continued to follow the crowds.

He had heard wild rumors from all over Budapest. The Russians were moving. They were leaving Hungary. Their tanks were already in the city. The West was getting reports through their journalists in Budapest. The United Nations would take notice. Perhaps. Attila remembered the broadcasts that he had heard sometimes. There was a lot of jamming, but Radio Free Europe still came through. In the past the Hungarian language broadcasts had more than hinted at American military help.

We'll see, he thought.

Everyone wanted change. The mood of this crowd now forming was determined, and optimistic. Some people carried flags, with the three stripes in traditional Hungarian colors—red, green and white, with a hole in the center where the communist symbol had been torn out. There were a few crude signs, but not many. "Russians out" and "Gero out" seemed to be the main sentiments.

That would be something, Attila mused. If the Russians could somehow be persuaded to leave, this situation was still salvageable. Add to that, if Gero were replaced as First Secretary of the Hungarian Workers Party, then Hungary could find her own way, like Yugoslavia and Poland. It was possible.

As the daylight sun began to warm their faces, the crowd numbering thousands and thousands reached Kossuth Square. There were Russian tanks there, but the Russians seemed baffled. Some Russian speaking Hungarians fraternized with the Russian soldiers. "We are not your enemy," they said to each other. In this autumn sunshine hope was possible, hope for change, peaceful change even now.

AVH men with automatic weapons lined the rooftops of the vast open square. The huge crowd poured into the square, until it seemed that no more people could fit. Attila edged towards the front of the crowd as best he could, in order to hear more clearly what might be said. Then he thought he heard gunfire, or a muffled explosion.

Then, suddenly, the shooting started, from machine guns on the roofs which edged the open square. It seemed to begin from the roof of the Agriculture Ministry, on the corner of Kossuth Square. The firing into the unarmed crowd was a massacre. Screams and shouts and the panic of those trying to escape the onslaught of bullets were all that Attila could hear. He ducked his head and turning around, made for the nearest sidewalk.

It took an agonizingly long time, while the firing continued all around him, it seemed. There must have been hundreds shot. Everyone was a target for the random bullets, and there was no cover in the open square. Never again would anyone who had seen this believe what their government said to them. The outside world would hear of this. Then surely they would help.

Attila and a few dozen others had the same idea. They made their way away from Parliament Square along Bajzsy Zsilinsky Street towards the

American Legation on Freedom Square not far away. A Hungarian speaking officer came out from the Legation and, visibly shaken, talked with the crowd.

"I'll report this to Washington immediately," he said, before turning sadly and retreating into the Legation building. The crowd had pleaded for help, many of them sharing Attila's tears of frustration and rage. So now the Americans knew. Was this their promised help?

Fatigue overcame him. Attila drifted back to his home on Margaret Island where he lived with his mother, in her apartment at the hotel where she worked. Frantic with worry, she was relieved to see him.

Attila ate a sandwich and flipped on the radio. Reports were confused, as though nobody quite knew what the line should be, and so the facts were being manipulated to suit whatever side might win in the future.

The one bit of interesting radio news was that Gero had been replaced as First Secretary of the Hungarian Workers Party by Janos Kadar. Attila remembered that Kadar had had something to do with the purge trials a few years back. Then he had been imprisoned himself. Bit of a chameleon. Well, at least he wasn't part of the Gero-Rakosi crowd as far as Attila could recall.

Soon Kadar himself was on the radio, urging that Hungary and the Soviet Union negotiate their differences peacefully.

Who could argue with that?

Attila flipped off the radio switch and went to bed.

CHAPTER FIVE

▼

THE BARAT STREET FRIENDS

Robbie decided to take Uncle Seth's advice and research the Hungarian Revolution at its authoritative source. That would also give him needed background on John Magassy. He took a taxi from the Embassy to the 1956 Research Institute. The driver let him off at the corner of Erzsebet Boulevard and Dohany Street, a busy intersection, but not a fashionable one.

Perhaps it used to be. There on the corner, with scaffolding still masking some of the exterior as it was being slowly restored, was the New York Restaurant and Coffee House. He was meeting Arpad Novotny for luncheon there a few hours later, after his research at the Institute.

Robbie looked forward to it. Arpad was good company, and could fill him in on Hungarian issues he might otherwise miss. The New York (then called the Hungaria) was a legend of elegant, prewar Budapest. So much so that its interior had turned up in a series of full-page ads in the New York *Times* indicating a lush standard of living if you—what was it?—used the right after-shave lotion or credit card or something.

He walked up Dohany Street barely half a block and, on the left, found number 74, the 1956 Research Institute. No need to ring the bell. The mailman was just leaving, and the front door was open. Robbie walked into the spare open courtyard and up the stairs to the right. The 1956 Institute was on the third floor. A pleasant receptionist greeted Robbie and called the staffer, a serious young darkhaired woman named Zsuzsa who had been assigned to help Robbie for the morning.

She began with a general overview of the Institute, its creation and mission, and then gave him a briefing on available publications. Some difference, Robbie thought, from the officially condemned "counter-revolution" of the Janos Kadar days, to officially permitted research center now.

Robbie's main interest was in the Oral History section of the research center. Zsuzsa showed him the way and told him how things worked.

"Oral histories are divided into three types," she began, gesturing to the shelf where they were stored. They are 'open, researchable, or closed.'"

"What does 'researchable' mean?"

"That means that you can read what the interviewed person had to say, but cannot cite it without special permission. 'Open' means just that. So, unfortunately, does 'closed,' although from time to time people change their minds, and give us permission to let people read their interviews."

"Is there an index of the interviews?"

"Of course. Perhaps more important, we have computerized mentions of individuals, and cross-referenced them to the interview in which the person was mentioned."

"Sounds very helpful." Robbie wanted to encourage her flow, not stop it.

"Yes, it is. If you have the name of someone you want to know about, it's entirely possible that a list of interviews would turn up a blank. We have a lot of interviews and are getting more, but don't pretend that the archives are complete. On the other hand, those giving interviews mention people. So that if you were looking for, say, a Janos Kovacs—mentioning the generic John Smith in Hungarian—you could look him up in the computer and see if anybody had mentioned him, even if he hadn't given us a personal taped interview."

She showed him the shelves full of interviews, and gave him an index. "Who are you looking for, Mr. Cutler?"

"Janos Magassy, Eva Molnar, and four others. I only have their first names. Istvan, Csaba, Imre and Attila. They were all part of the same group."

Her eyes widened. "That's really quite a coincidence. We had another diplomatic visitor just yesterday. I think he was asking for exactly the same files. Let's see. She consulted her pocket notebook. The other four would be Istvan Szepvaros, Imre Mohacsi, Attila Nemzeti, and Csaba somebody. Who was it? Oh yes, here it is. Csaba Kovacs."

Robbie tried to be offhand. "That's right, I think. Who was asking?"

"It was the Australian Ambassador, Alexander Kovatch."

Robbie made a mental note to follow up on this. If Julie was going to give him the come on, perhaps a bit of pleasure and business might be in order.

"What did you find?"

"I've got some notes here. Yes, here it is. Of the six people mentioned, two had filed interviews with us. They were Istvan Szepvaros and Imre Mohacsi."

"Where are they now, do you know? Are they still alive?"

"Certainly. As a matter of fact, they both live in Budapest now. Mohacsi is a member of Parliament from someplace in the provinces." Robbie winced. He should have known that. "Oh, THAT Mohacsi," he said. Nice try.

She continued. "Istvan Szepvaros, on the other hand, is not a Hungarian citizen anymore. He left in November 1956 and went to West Germany. He became a banker, a rather prominent one. Now he's back in Budapest as head of the branch office of his German bank. People think of him in the German community as sort of a second Ambassador. Quite high-powered, really."

"Interesting. Are their interviews open?"

"Yes. I'll get them. Then would you like me to translate?"

It was a nice point. In other words, "How good is your Hungarian, anyway?" Robbie accepted with pleasure. "Not THAT good" was the implicit answer to her unspoken question.

She found the two folders and brought them to him.

Then she added a comment. "This killing of Janos Magassy has upset us all," she said. "You know, he had made an appointment later this week to come in and record his own oral interview. We had tried to get it earlier, in the United States, but he had replied that he would rather come in and talk with us personally. Too bad, really, because as the leader of a group of Freedom Fighters his recollections would have been very helpful."

"Yes, 'The Friends,' they called themselves. I wonder why," Robbie mused.

"I thought it was clever. It's a play on words. Barat of course means 'friend' in Hungarian, as you know, and they were on Barat Street. So, put it together: 'A Barat Utcai Baratok' (*The Barat Street Friends*). Maybe they were thinking of the Molnar novel, 'A Pal Utcai Fiuk' (*The Paul Street Boys),* as well."

"Perhaps. Let's see what Mr. Mohacsi had to say."

Zsuzsa skimmed through the account for him. It was not long, and it was melancholy, a remembrance of youth and defeated hope. Sometimes the author forgot the right sequence of events, and then went back and tried to fill them in.

The group had begun to form at the earliest part of the uprising. He and Janos Magassy and a man named Karoly had found arms at the United Lamp Factory on October 23rd, 1956, when the revolution had broken out. The next day, following desultory street fighting, they had been joined by some kids, Pista and Red. Then the group and its location had coalesced, at a deserted ground floor storefront in Barat Street.

There was a clear tactical purpose in their location, Mohacsi wrote. The Kilian Barracks, the Hungarian Army stronghold on Ulloi Avenue that was defended by Colonel Pal Maleter, was across the street from the Corvin Movie House, which stood inside Corvin Circle. Mohacsi also wrote that he had heard that there were tunnels under Ulloi Avenue connecting the Kilian Barracks with Corvin Circle. This was despite its name a hollow square whose outer buildings fronted both Ulloi Avenue and Jozsef Boulevard. And so this region was a direct part of the main ring boulevard which joined Pest in a semicircle beginning and ending at the Danube River to the west.

Two side streets, Kisfaludy and Prater, led from the Corvin area. Barat Street, a few hundred yards away, lay within the welter of streets that could protect the Corvin defenders from the north. Any group controlling that region could either stop an attack from the rear aimed at the Corvin Circle, or could if necessary fall back there with warning of an attack. Either way, it was an important area, worth holding at all costs.

Mohacsi's account also listed Csaba Kovacs and Eva Molnar, Attila Nemzeti and Istvan Szepvaros, and three more youngsters whose full names he did not know, Magda, Laszlo and Jozsef.

"That is fairly common," Zsuzsa explained. "Often just first names were given. For that matter, we know some of the Freedom Fighters only by their nicknames, even now." The group, apparently, was well led by Janos Magassy, who insisted on rigorous patrolling of their own perimeter, to prevent surprise assaults. Mohacsi credited the group with at least six tank kills, including one of the newer T-54 tanks, with a mounted machine gun part of its firepower.

"Pretty damned impressive for a bunch of kids," Robbie said.

"Yes. Their specialty was the Molotov cocktail. They made them with bottles filled with gasoline, and stuffed rags for wicks. They would get as close to the tanks as possible. And then light the wicks, hoping to hit a vulnerable part of the tank, like an air intake valve, or the tracks. Sometimes, when the turret was open, they could even lodge a hand-grenade down the turret itself."

"How about casualties?"

"Yes, one by one. Mohacsi seems to have been most upset by the death of Magda. She was a young teenager, a real daredevil it seems. She was full of high spirits, and inspired them all."

"What happened to her?"

"It was when they attacked several tanks, in the semi-darkness before dawn. That was on November 4, when the Russians, violating the cease-fire, invaded Budapest for the second time. The tanks then were mostly T-54s, and a turret machine gun cut poor Magda to pieces. Karoly and Laszlo were killed too."

Silence. Zsuzsa went on. "After that November 4 assault, the group held out for another few days, protecting the Corvin flank as long as they could. People were killed and wounded, one by one. Mohacsi says that he wasn't sure for long afterwards who had survived and who had not, but he does try to account for those he believes did survive. His stated purpose in the interview is for the Institute to try and contact them, to get their stories as well."

"Interesting. Whom had he located?"

"Well, this tape was made four or five years ago. Finally, he ran across Janos Magassy in the United States. Attila Nemzeti is here now in Budapest, at the Justice Ministry. He had heard that Istvan Szepvaros made it out to Germany. Poor Eva Molnar had served a penal sentence, and her mental balance was affected. He has never seen her, but hears that she went back to her hometown in Transylvania, in Romania, following her release from prison. The others he assumes died in the uprising, or in the reprisals that followed."

"And has the Institute tried to contact the others?"

"I can't go into that in any detail. From some, we didn't hear anything. But Istvan Szepvaros came in and did his interview, and as I mentioned, Janos Magassy was all set to come in later this week to give us his account."

"Tell me something about 1956, the street fighting I mean. Was it continuous?"

"Oh, no. There were three rather distinct phases. The revolution began on October 23rd. It was directed primarily against the secret police, the hated *AVH*. The Russians came into Budapest from their bases in the countryside. The street fighting lasted through the 28th, at which time the new Prime Minister, Imre Nagy, announced a ceasefire. At that point, essentially the revolutionaries had won."

"Then what happened?"

"There was a period of consolidation, the second phase really. The Freedom Fighters were supposed to become a new National Guard under General Bela Kiraly. It was also during this period that the Russians tried to infiltrate into the Freedom Fighters' ranks. They were growing anyway, because as usual everybody wanted to be on the winning side."

"I take it that the Russian dawn attack on November 4 began the third and final phase?"

"Yes, that's right. And this was of course a planned invasion in force. I get the impression reading through the oral interviews that the Freedom Fighters did their best with streetfighting tactics, which had been so successful in the first phase of the fighting. Now, however, the Russians were supporting their tanks with infantry. That made matters entirely different, and in the end it was hopeless."

"What happened then?"

"Then came the really ugly part. The Russians and the *AVH*, who had crawled out from their ratholes once again, rounded up people in the streets and sent them away. Virtually nobody ever ccme back. The Janos Kadar regime put out its own lying White Book about the 'Counterrevolution,' and people kept quiet about their participation. They had to. It took years and years for some balance to come back, and the terror to stop. We really weren't able to face the past honestly until after the Iron Curtain came down. Some can't even now," she added softly, almost under her breath.

"What about the oral interview with Istvan Szepvaros?"

"It's quite straightforward, and gives an impression almost of modesty. He talks about meeting one of the group members, Attila Nemzeti, as early as October 23rd, the first day of the outbreak, in Heroes' Square, and spending some time with him. Then they lost contact until October 30th. That was the assault in Republic Square against Budapest Communist Party Headquarters in which, by the way, Imre Mohacsi says that several members of his group actually participated."

"I've heard about that day."

"Yes, most people would say that there was great provocation, but that still, a number of *AVH* were killed ruthlessly, lynched in fact. The pictures were flashed around the world, and probably had something to do with the loss of support internationally. From the socialist countries, I mean."

"And there was the Suez invasion."

"Yes. The timing of that couldn't have been worse. There is a record of Prime Minister Imre Nagy at a cabinet meeting finding out about the French, British and Israeli bombings at Suez, which he realized must have meant no Western help could possibly come for Hungary. 'Damn them!' he said. At *least* that."

"He had good reason. Some historians today even think that the Suez invasion was even moved up a few days when the Budapest uprising began to use that for cover, so to speak. That's a pretty cynical calculation if it's true. So when did Szepvaros join the group at Barat Street?"

"He ran across his friend Attila Nemzeti on Republic Square on October 30th, and went back to Barat Street with him. After that, his account is basically the same as Imre Mohacsi's, except of course when they had different orders. Sometimes one would be running liaison with the Corvin stronghold, while the other would be walking a perimeter defense in the other direction, for example. He agrees that they all held out for a few days after the November 4 invasion."

"Does he remember specific military assaults?"

"Yes, in some detail. He remembers being with Magda and Imre doing reconnaissance before dawn on November 4 quite vividly. That is when Imre was wounded, and Istvan Szepvaros helped get him back to Barat Street when the fighting eased. They had located the Russian tanks and infantry coming into their sector, and had sent Magda back to warn the others, and bring up their fighting group. It was on her return that Magda was killed."

"What does he say about the other survivors? Also Mohacsi, for that matter, what does he say?"

"Their impressions were pretty similar. Janos Magassy struck them both as a natural leader, and an intelligent commander. They also both liked Eva Molnar, in almost a protective sort of way. She comes across in their accounts as intelligent and pretty—no, beautiful— and educated. She was a university art student, you know. Aside from that, you can easily pick up from either account that Csaba Kovacs and Eva Molnar were a couple. Married in all but name, although they hadn't even met until October 23rd, and Csaba was a worker while Eva was a student.

"Aside from that," Zsuzsa continued, "Istvan was closer to Attila Nemzeti than anyone else. That seems natural, since they had been together off and on from the beginning. Imre had a very high regard for Csaba Kovacs, and seemed to regard him as almost a substitute leader for Janos Magassy. That doesn't come across in Istvan Szepvaros's interview."

"That's all extremely helpful." For what? he almost asked himself. "Now let's check the cross-index and see if any of the six are mentioned elsewhere."

"You're really thorough. Not many people think to do that."

They found one mention of Csaba Kovacs and looked it up. It was from a florist not far from Ulloi Avenue. He had once come in to ask about flowers. It wasn't for a funeral arrangement, like everybody else did in those days. He was young and in love and wanted some for his girlfriend. She hadn't caught the girl's name, but he had given his, and said they were together at Barat Street. He had had enough money for a few flowers.

"That doesn't seem worth mentioning, really," Robbie said.

"There's more. When the fighting was over, the florist barricaded her shop for a week, but she could still see from an upstairs window what was going on. She distinctly saw a wounded, pale Csaba Kovacs being loaded with others onto a truck and driven away. She made the Sign of the Cross for him."

For the remaining five members of the Friends, they then disregarded cross-references back to the interviews with Imre Mohacsi and Istvan Szepvaros that they had already read. Those aside, the only other person of the six with fresh mentions in the cross-index was Eva Molnar. She was mentioned three times. They were in luck once again. Two of the three interviews were in the open category. The third, by a judge who had been on the People's Court that had handed down her sentence, was closed.

One of the two witnesses had been a fellow prisoner, when Eva was serving her sentence for counterrevolutionary activities. She had received ten years, serving six before being amnestied. Eva was mentioned in a list of fellow prisoners, along with the detail that she was given hard physical labor to do, and even the other prisoners found that harsh.

The other mention was from a prison guard. No prisoner had many visitors, because even close family members were afraid of being picked up by the Kadar regime and charged with disloyalty. But Eva Molnar had had one loyal visitor, her cousin from Transylvania, a man who wasn't quite right in the head. He had tried to bring her food from time to time, and that wasn't allowed, but sometimes the guard slipped a parcel through anyway. Guards are human too, he had defensively added.

It was rather sad, really. The prison guard wasn't sure whether Eva and her visitor ever met in prison. Probably they did later, when things eased up after the guard was transferred. He hoped so.

Robbie wondered about the judge's sealed interview. He asked to be informed if it was ever unsealed.

Robbie decided next to visit the sites of the street fighting, and then visit the cemetery where the heroes of the struggle, including Defense Minister Pal Maleter and Prime Minister Imre Nagy, had been buried following their secret show trials and official murders. Why not do it that very afternoon? Perhaps Zsuzsa could join him, and show the way.

Her flashing eyes shone. Yes, she could do that. Robbie agreed to meet her at the New York after his lunch with Arpad Novotny. She was meeting a boyfriend to fight about some principle of great importance, she said, and would arrange the taxi. "It's better if I do that. Even diplomats can't afford what some taxis with fast meters charge these days!"

Robbie walked the half-block back to the New York through the Erzsebet Boulevard entrance.

Novotny already had a table in the recessed restaurant section, the *Mely Viz* ("Deep Water"). It was Central European luxury defined, rich with high ceilings, chandeliers and gold flaked wall mirrors that showed off the diners and their surroundings. Robbie thought that his Dad would want to hear about this luncheon. If the New York had been open at all during his own assignment at the American Legation in 1956, it had not looked like this. Probably it had not looked so elegant since the turn of the century, when Molnar and other writers haunted the dining room and upstairs coffee shop sections, writing through the days and evenings.

As they were ordering, a rather fat older man came down the steps and greeted Arpad Novotny with a breezy "Long time, no see, Arpad. How are things at the Embassy?"

Novotny did not rise or introduce the newcomer to Robbie, and he barely nodded an acknowledgement of the man's greeting.

"What on earth was that all about, Arpad?"

"He's a columnist, Johnny Szilva. You've probably seen his columns from time to time. He's been covering Hungary for many years, but I knew him in Saigon. That's where we had our falling-out."

"What happened?"

"It was the South Vietnamese presidential election in 1967. Very important as far as we were concerned, and on the level. Well, Szilva got it into his head that the election had been rigged, and he wrote a column saying so—before the election was held. He even had the nerve to show it to me. Said he was going on vacation at election time anyway, which was a month away, so he was going to leave this column with his bureau, to run after the election."

"What a dishonest bastard!

"You've got that right. Anyway, the election was held. What actually happened wasn't at all what Szilva had written. Thieu did win, but it was rather close. So his column wouldn't do after all. So what did Szilva do? He kept all of the earlier column about Thieu being a tyrant, and the election being rigged, and so on. He then just added a couple of paragraphs saying that the final elections results showed that Thieu wasn't a very EFFICIENT tyrant!"

"Anybody catch him on that?"

"Nobody cared, and I couldn't prove it. Just my word against his. Anyway, don't trust what he writes, and don't go out of your way to give him background material. Even in his profession, I wouldn't trust him— and that's saying a lot!"

Robbie told Arpad about his morning at the 1956 Institute.

"They're good people, reliable and scholarly," was his friend's assessment. Robbie brought up the issue of American official encouragement of the 1956 Hungarian Revolution. "I've heard that from a number of people."

"Unfortunately, it's true," Arpad said. "It was also fairly low-level for the most part, at Radio Free Europe, given in Hungarian by emigres who were not well supervised. Very mischievous, and it was believed. People then as now believed what they wanted to believe. I'd say it was stretching it to say that this was official U.S policy even then, but the fact that such broadcasts were made—and they were—was a real black eye for American credibility."

"Not to mention, costing Hungarian lives."

"Exactly. However," Arpad added, "it's going too far to say that the broadcasts caused the outbreak here. They didn't. Stalinism and its local Hungarian subsidiary did. But they did lead many people to expect support once they did rise up. To that extent, it was to say the least irresponsible."

He begged off accompanying Robbie for the afternoon, pleading the press of work at the Embassy.

They finished their luncheon of *porkolt* ("what you Wasps call 'goulash'") with slices of chocolate Dobos cake and extra orders of whipped cream. The coffee was superb, worth an extra cup.

"Another luncheon like this one, and I'll end up like Johnny Szilva," Robbie grinned as they went to the exit. Meals like this were sufficient reason some days for living overseas.

Zsuzsa was waiting outside with their taxi. First they drove to the cemetery, while she filled him in on what happened after the 1956 Hungarian Revolution.

"You know of course, that Prime Minister Imre Nagy and members of his government had taken refuge at the Yugoslavian Embassy facing Heroes' Square, just as Cardinal Mindszenty took refuge at the American Legation?"

He nodded yes.

"After a couple of weeks the Kadar Government said they could come out and go freely to their homes. They had a safe conduct and assurances of safe treatment. The bus picked them up, but it never arrived at their homes. They all just kind of disappeared. Later we learned what happened. There was a secret trial in Romania, where they were taken. Then, a year and a half after they had been picked up, the official announcement was made of their trials and death sentences, 'with no appeals allowed.' By that time, they were already dead."

"Why were they buried out here?"

"The cemetery, Rakoskereszturi Public Cemetery, was conveniently just across the street from Gyujto Prison, where the executions took place."

The taxi drove past the flower sellers and through the cemetery gates. After a while, the cemetery seemed to end, and fields begin. Still the taxi drove on.

"So this political cemetery was really at the back of the beyond," Robbie said.

"In Hungarian, we would say 'behind the back of God.'"

At the far end of the cemetery on the left was Section 298. Zsuzsa and Robbie got out and walked through it. There were hundreds of graves there, of people who had been executed after the communists had first come to power. Judging from the dates, the terror had continued for years. Then they walked to the adjoining Section 301. As with Section 298, a placard indicated the location of individual graves. These were the graves of those who had been killed by the communists after the 1956 Revolution.

They walked over to the grave of Prime Ninister Imre Nagy and then to that of General Pal Maleter. Robbie wished that he had brought some flowers, or a wreath, to lay here or on some unvisited grave. Next time, he promised himself, he would do so.

Zsuzsa explained. "For years, these graves, like those in the neighboring section, were not even marked. Neither could relatives come here. There was nothing. It wasn't until towards the end of the communist regime that this was all dug up, the bodies properly identified, and then the reburials took place. Before that, for years people tried to get the graves at least acknowledged. Even your President Carter, who had given back to Janos Kadar the Holy Crown of St. Stephen, wrote a letter to the Hungarian Government. They didn't even acknowledge his letter."

They walked back to the waiting taxi.

"So when Section 301 was properly redone and the graves were marked…" Robbie began. She finished the sentence for him. "That's when we really knew that communism had come to an end in Hungary."

She continued. "That was an ending. Now I'll show you where the fighting started."

"Why was it so concentrated in the Eighth and Ninth Districts of Budapest?"

"That area commands the southeast approach to the city. That is where the Russians came, both times. Also, it was a working class district, so a lot of the fighters, men and women, came from there."

They took a turn towards the city. Robbie was a little startled to realize that the turnoff was not far from the main road from Ferihegy Airport to Budapest. How many tourists came through every year, he wondered, entirely unaware of what they were passing by?

After twenty minutes they were on Ulloi Avenue, passing a severe, classical building. "It's the Kilian Barracks," Zsuzsa said. "And over there is Corvin Circle." They stopped, and Robbie paid and dismissed the taxi.

"Now you'll get an idea why this was important," she said.

That seemed apparent. There were intersections everywhere. They walked around the area. Here at the corner was the intersection of Jozsef Boulevard with Ulloi Avenue. Jozsef Boulevard continued along the Budapest inner ring. A few blocks away was Erzsebet Boulevard, where the New York Coffee House stood. Branching off on the outer ring beyond Ulloi Avenue was Republic Square, where the people of Budapest had taken their revenge on the AVH on October 30, 1956.

They walked into Corvin Circle by one of the two short passages that connected it to Jozsef Boulevard and Ulloi Avenue. Robbie was surprised and rather pleased to see that the Corvin Movie House was still in operation, located at the center of Corvin Circle. First run American movies were in fact showing there.

Outside the movie house there was a plaque to a Freedom Fighter, a teenaged girl named Ilona Szabo. And then in front of the entrance, sub-machine gun in hand, a statue stood guard of a Freedom Fighter, a kid in his early teens. "Many of them were that young," Zsuzsa replied softly to his unspoken question. "It's nice that they are remembered now."

They left Corvin Circle at Kisfaludy Street, which led west, crossing Prater Street. "Just like the park area in Vienna," Zsuzsa said, "I've been there once." Prater Street still had the marks of fighting on its buildings. And on one side of the street, a memorial plaque had been placed, marking the assaults and many casualties that had taken place there.

Then they wandered down Kisfaludy Street. "If Corvin Circle protected the Kilian Barracks, then where did one protect Corvin Circle?" Robbie wondered aloud.

They found Barat Street, with its little grassy area in the center of a small square, where park benches stood, and several mothers gossiped while their children dozed in baby carriages. It was a peaceful scene. Now, Robbie thought.

Robbie found several storefronts which might have been the headquarters for the Friends. There were no markers, so he couldn't be sure. He'd ask a survivor when they met. That should be fairly soon. He would after all be at the reception at Parliament that very evening. At least he'd be sure to meet Imre Mohacsi there.

For now, it was time to get back to the Embassy and put in a few hours of office work. He thanked Zsuzsa for her help, and they agreed to stay in touch. For one thing, he was still very curious about that sealed oral interview. What had the People's Court judge who had handled Eva Molnar's trial wanted to say?

Perhaps it was a message that could help the living now.

* * * * * * * * * *

The Fourth Day—October 26, 1956

Janos Magassy was exhausted. It seemed that he hadn't slept in days. Odd, he felt exhausted but not tired. It must be the exhilaration that kept him going. It would be good to have a wash or a shave, but the time couldn't be spared. He must be there to guide his kids. As an old man of 26, Janos had responsibilities after all.

Imre Mohacsi had stayed with him from the beginning. He had produced the truck and a few volunteers like Karoly to help load it at the United Lamp Factory. Then he and Karoly had stayed to help out when the fighting spread. The news of the massacre in Kossuth Square outside

Parliament had made this a fight to the finish. There could be no turning back now. In a real sense it was Hungary and Imre Nagy against the *AVH*, the Stalinists in the government and the Party, and the Soviets who propped them up. To hell with them all, Janos thought.

It was clear to Imre and Janos that the Corvin Circle position was critical. Janos had distributed a major share of his weapons and ammunition to the defenders there. In turn, it was imperative to defend the Corvin stronghold against attacks from the rear.

That was the job for Janos and his group.

Throughout the day the Kilian Barracks forces had fought off wave after wave of T-34 Russian assault tanks. Now commanded by Colonel Pal Maleter, who had gone over to the insurgents, the Kilian Barracks was a major Hungarian stronghold.

Thank heavens the Russians were still using the World War II vintage T-34s, Janos thought. The modern T-54 monsters would be another story. There was nothing on the Hungarian side to match them. Except, of course, the courage of the kids.

Again and again Pista and Red, Janos, Karoly and Imre went out to duel with the assault tanks. Their Barat Street corner was perfect. It led into main arteries without being one. Tank access in those narrow streets was a death sentence, and the small band of fighters could scramble in and out of the narrow streets of the area nearly at will.

Unless, of course, the Russians smartened up and sent in infantry, Janos thought. So far, thank God, they hadn't.

Within 48 hours of the start of their fighting, so much had happened that Janos could not remember it all. But there ought to be some record of this. And so he started to take notes, sketchy at first, more detailed when there was a lull.

He started because he kept seeing Pista's brave young face, grinning back at him as he began that last attack. Janos had led every sortie for hours. Then, exhausted and overcome by fatigue, he had called a halt.

Pista went out anyway, with a childish grin. He could have been playing tricks on a schoolmaster.

Pista got halfway across the street when the Russian tank's turret flew open and a soldier's face emerged, his eyes blinking in the light. Then he spotted Pista. Just a kid. The tank gunner started to look away. Then Pista, having turned his back to light the homemade fuse of his Molotov cocktail, started to run towards the tank. He didn't quite make it. The submachine gun fire nearly cut him in half, and his Molotov cocktail, lobbed towards the tank as Pista was hit, exploded on the tank's front track.

The crew quickly dismounted through the turret. "Russian sons of bitches!" Janos screamed as he charged the soldiers, firing his submachine gun. From another corner of the intersection a muscular workman caught the surviving tank crew members in a crossfire, killing them all. It was Karoly.

Karoly picked up Pista's body, killed so recently that it still twitched involuntarily, and crossed the street towards the Barat Street storefront. Karoly half dragged his bad leg. A striking young woman and her young man followed him.

Red came out of the storefront, saw what had happened, and began to cry. "Pista! Pista!" Then to the others, "He was my brother! Which bastard Russians did this?"

"They are already dead," Janos answered. "Karoly killed them all." At that moment Karoly entered the storefront, carrying Pista's body. Csaba Kovacs and Eva Molnar came in with him, and Eva tried to soothe Red. It couldn't be done.

Soon Csaba and Eva were like new recruits. Janos liked them both immediately. She was beautiful, right out of some past image of Hungary that Janos could only imagine. It was a vision that he had once seen in a museum, which he would visit on Sundays sometimes, to see a different world, away from the arms factory. Now she was here.

Csaba was a reliable man, a good worker and a skilled fighter, athletic, a man who took reasonable risks. You trusted him right away. On those spare moments when Janos had to get some sleep, Csaba soon took over. Nobody had to ask. It just seemed natural.

Soon so much had happened that Janos could never have reconstructed what he had written in his little notebook. So much and so little. One after another they destroyed three more Russian T-34 tanks, whose commanders had made the mistake of trying to flush them out. Which sortie succeeded and which failed? Janos couldn't tell any more. He and Csaba, and sometimes Imre, led every sortie for hours. Karoly, his bad leg impeding his movement, provided covering fire as they attacked.

One sortie was forever fixed in his memory. Imre had spotted a tank lumbering their way a few blocks away. "No! Let me go first this time!" Eva had insisted.

And so she had gone first. The tank's turret gun had slowly followed her, its gunner missing the nearly imperceptible sign that she gave as she rounded the corner of the intersection. Before the turret could swing back, Csaba had thrown the Molotov cocktail at the tank's front tracks on the right side.

It was a direct hit.

The explosion began to envelop the tank, and its crew tried to escape through the hatch. As they emerged, Janos and Red mowed them down with semiautomatic fire.

"Another crew blown to hell," Janos said.

"That one's for Pista!" Red replied.

Janos, the old man at twenty-six, liked Csaba. Csaba was twenty, like Imre, and Eva was just eighteen. Karoly at twenty-two was an old man by comparison. Red was twelve at most, but he was so skinny it was hard to know exactly. He looked ten and acted twenty.

Janos overheard Csaba and Eva talking one day. They were intimate strangers, still introducing themselves to each other.

"We're fighting for their future," Janos said to himself.

CHAPTER SIX

▼

A RECEPTION IN PARLIAMENT

Robbie walked the few blocks from the Embassy to the Parliament. It was an early evening reception, so he had stayed at the office an hour or so later than usual, reading everything the Political Section's files contained on Deputy Imre Mohacsi. Then he left the building. The weather was very mild and pleasant. He probably didn't need his light topcoat after all.

It was one of those peaceful, balmy late afternoons when a sense of grace and peace enveloped this historic city on the Danube. It was a perfect tourist's moment. There must have been a number of days like this just before August, 1914, lulling people to sleep. One could almost forget in the perfection of breeze and dappled sunlight the series of cataclysms in this unstable region that had forced so many migrations from Hungary.

He looked forward to seeing friends from the diplomatic community as well as Hungarian political leaders. As he strolled along, Robbie reflected on how much history had taken place in this neighborhood. He remembered the demonstrations that had begun at the statue of Sandor Petofi, the national poet, over near the Danube embankment, and spread, less peaceful as they developed, to the Parliament, the radio station, the secret police headquarters, and elsewhere.

The events of October, 1956 had shocked the complacent world. With Europe divided into power spheres of influence, why was this little nation fighting? It had seemed hopeless, and hadn't made sense to many. That was why Magassy's memorial was worth pursuing, before people forgot, or rewrote history. What had happened here must be celebrated.

The death of Magassy puzzled him. He and Randy Davis had had a brief initial meeting with an official at the Consular Division of the Foreign Ministry. The Hungarians had posed no objection in principle to the Embassy being in informal touch with police investigators, provided of course that official channels were respected and that the police investigators were not hampered in their work. Fair enough.

Robbery was for the time being the working police hypothesis as the motive for the crime. Magassy's wallet had been stolen and the money taken. He had been identified through his hotel room card, which he had been carrying in a jacket pocket. The Consular Division official who had met with Robbie and Randy Davis agreed with them that the sabre was an unlikely murder weapon. Probably Magassy had bought it for a souvenir, and then the mugger had used it when Magassy had resisted, as he surely would have done. The mugger was probably high on coke or ecstasy anyway.

The official showed them photos of the sabre. Robbie saw at once that it was not a fencing sabre. It lacked the blunted, folded back tip that is required in the sport. No, the point of this weapon had even been sharpened. Where had Magassy bought it? That would be good to know for a start. It would also be a good starting point for his talks with the police.

The Parliament was an impressive, ornate gothic structure. It was built as the nineteenth century ended for the elected representatives of a greater Hungary that no longer existed. The Treaty of Trianon that had ended the First World War and created nations from the Austro-Hungarian Empire had made sure of that. Then, of course, those small nations had been left on their own, to face the greater perils of Hitler and Stalin. Robbie thought that the integration of Hungary into NATO was a good sign that the West had learned its lesson from that interwar period, however the Russian bear might growl.

"Implementation of the entry into NATO proceeded in stages," Colonel Joshua Tidings had said in the Monday staff meeting. "It was also managed professionally, and with far more enthusiasm than Hungary's career military had displayed when they were forced to join the Warsaw Pact!"

The cars and limousines began to arrive, and guests entered the Parliament, stopped at the coat check and were then ushered towards an ornate reception room. It was spacious and graceful at the same time, with gilt trimmed wall light sconces pairing large antique mirrors throughout the room. The background decor could have been classical French except for occasional Hungarian references, for example in paintings suggesting the countryside. Robbie surmised that the interior had been done by French artisans, and then Hungarian furnishings had been chosen to complement them.

The welcoming remarks would be mercifully brief, Robbie understood, and then the real diplomatic business could begin. Robbie, like all seasoned diplomats, went to receptions to hold a series of conversations with people whom he expected to see there. Tonight's list, in addition to members of parliament, would include journalists, writers and surely another embassy political officer or two.

As a Hungarian speaker, Robbie knew that he would in turn be on the list of half a dozen other diplomats, who would touch base with him and try to get his assessment of recent events in Hungary before the reception was over.

And then, of course, there was Julie Kovatch's scarf to be returned.

There she was now, standing with her husband. She smiled at Robbie, who walked over to join them. He shook hands with Ambassador Kovatch. "Nice you were both able to join me Saturday evening," Robbie said.

"Our pleasure," Kovatch replied. "Your idea of getting diplomats out of Budapest to learn more about this country is first rate. Shows initiative."

"Well," Robbie replied, "I've always wanted to come here. After all my Dad was at the American Legation in 1956." Kovatch looked at him with renewed interest. "Budapest is attractive, but it just doesn't make any sense to me to stay in the capital all the time. I hope you'll consider joining us for the next excursion. The Lauricettes from the French Embassy will be planning it."

"Thanks. I'll bear it in mind."

Robbie turned to Julie. He almost apologized for not being home when she called on Sunday, but then thought better of it. Perhaps her husband didn't know she had stopped by. Better sanitize matters ever so slightly.

"You left your scarf at my place by mistake. I remembered to bring it for you. It's in my topcoat pocket. I can get it now if you wish."

"Don't bother. You can give it to me when we leave. Sorry to have been a bother."

"No trouble at all. It gave me a good excuse to say hello." Robbie had tried to be gallant, but it sounded lame. He cringed inwardly, but she smiled anyway.

He looked towards the podium. "Well, here is the welcome speech-maker. Let's hope it is brief. They say the refreshments tonight will be excellent, and that's going to be my dinner!"

"Serves you right for being a bachelor," she retorted.

By the time their asides and Robbie's reflections on what they had said, what he wished he might have said, and how what he had said was going over, were mercifully ended, so was the welcoming speech. It was time for refreshments. Ambassador Kovatch spotted someone he wished to meet, and went off to do so, while Robbie and Julie took glasses of wine from the tray being passed by the first of a phalanx of waiters.

"Your husband seems preoccupied this evening," Robbie began, aiming his comment at the figure of the retreating Australian Ambassador.

"Yes. He is really quite shaken up. It must be this Magassy business. You know, Robbie, that Alex had spent Saturday afternoon, when we were in Eger, meeting with Magassy. They had coffee, and Alex was really quite pleased to talk with him."

"That's interesting. Magassy seems to have been making the rounds. I had a note from him too. It was delivered by the Embassy duty officer on Sunday. He wanted to see me, too, after his trip to the provinces. Where was he going? Sarospatak I think."

"He told Alex that he wanted to develop interest for a memorial to the 1956 Freedom Fighters."

Robbie nodded. "Yes, that was in my note as well. Was your husband here in 1956, by the way? He would be the right age."

"He doesn't talk about it much. He did once say that he was too young to take part himself. He seemed to regret that. But yes, he left Hungary then, and came to Australia. No further contact with any relatives here for a long time. His parents died several years ago. I never met them. Not that it matters now. You couldn't find someone who is more Australian now than my husband."

"Is your background Hungarian too, Julie?"

Her eyes sparkled. This was her chance to define herself to this new man, and make an impression. Like an actress with a new audience of one, with warmth and charm she told her practiced tale. "Straight from County Wicklow my people came, part of Ireland's mission to civilize the world! My grandparents both came before the last war. Or rather, Grandmother Mulcahy came first, from Glendalough, and then Himself came from Shillelagh, 'looking for her' as he put it. Whether they even knew each other in Ireland is a matter of whose family mythology you choose to believe. I like to think that they did. So we've been Australians too ever since."

Always leave when interest is high, she thought, and then the chance to escape came, in the person of the dullest drone in the Australian Foreign Service. "Whoops. Mustn't dawdle. Here comes our Administrative Officer. This is my chance to tell him where the roof leaks around the residence. Look me up before you leave, promise?" Robbie's smile trailed after her.

Robbie then spotted Janos Horvath and his wife Ilona, and he thanked them for their hospitality at Eger. "No problem, as you Americans say. We enjoyed ourselves. Now here comes Ferenc Esztergondos, the 'socialist aristocrat.' Is your Hungarian up to it?" Robbie nodded and joined them.

Esztergondos, a tall, imposing man in his late forties, gracefully wore an elegant hand tailored dark blue woolen suit. The material was Dormeuil and his patterned aquamarine tie was Hermes. A gold chain with watch fob spread across his vest. He was the latest offshoot of one of Hungary's great aristocratic landholding families.

Horvath made the introduction and Esztergondos acknowledged it in courtly Hungarian, then switched into British accented English.

"I'm glad to meet you, Mr. Cutler. You have a family diplomatic connection with Hungary, from what I hear. Contrary to what is said, I like Americans. It's just your system that I find troublesome."

This should be interesting, Robbie thought, at the very least an anecdote to tell at the next Embassy staff meeting. "Why is that, Mr. Esztergondos? And may I ask why you became a socialist? One would have thought that your family history would have led you in a different political direction."

Esztergondos smiled. "It is a matter of taste and direction. If Jefferson had been right, and time meant the elevation of popular tastes, I would be a strong believer in democracy. But exactly the opposite seems to have happened. I've seen your country. Your streets are unsafe. You lack any sense of the common good. Your music is execrable, and indeed intended to be such. Your films celebrate noise and vulgarity."

Now he was on a roll. "Your most successful politicians are driven by polls, not by any sense of what should be done. Those elected leaders who do have an education misuse it to construct elaborate excuses for their behavior. I need not cite examples. In short, Aristotle's reservations regarding democracy seen richly realized in practice. Shall I continue?"

"What is the record of socialism?"

"If you mean communism, it is dismal, the worst, a record of persecution. I could not be active in politics then. There was no possibility of orderly change, and that is a necessary thing. Without it, any system descends into tyranny. That is what happened here, of course. What interests me about socialism is that it does not assume that the people know best. They do not. They must be guided."

He continued. "That is what my family has done in this country for generations. The result in the past you hear whenever you go to a concert, for those were the very artists that my family supported. In your country, on the other hand, the arts are under attack. Are they, in your quaint expression, 'UnAmerican activities?'"

Robbie didn't want this to be one of those conversations when his best retorts occurred to him hours later. He took up the challenge.

"Judged by any standard, American democracy has produced greater opportunities than any other nation or system of government, past or present. True, we do not always elect the best people. Some would say that those who are our natural governors do not even enter politics. Those who do are often glib and crude, however intelligent they may be. They remake themselves as they enter the mainstream of opportunity. The miracle is that we still have so many political leaders who are first rate, by any reasonable measure.

"And consider the alternative," he continued. "In most countries still, class dictates opportunity, and more often than not, stifles it. In our own country Abraham Lincoln, I think, remains our best answer to arguments against democracy."

He paused for the argument to have its effect, and gestured towards his listeners. "Meanwhile we have the freedom, and the leisure created by economic opportunity, to be wise or foolish. No government should dictate that. It is our investors that are here now, helping create new opportunities for a more prosperous Hungary. Surely you don't disagree with that, Mr. Deputy?"

"Of course not. And Lincoln is your best argument, even if your own leaders profane his memory. Will more Abraham Lincolns be produced? I sincerely hope so. If not, that glib young historian, Francis Fujiyama, who wrote that history had ended with the production of democracy had it all wrong. Mediocrity is not the hope of mankind. Excellence is, or should be. That is the difference."

"You have said nothing that any generation of elected American leaders who care more about their country than about themselves would not cleanse and cure. That is an inevitable cycle, just as the freedom of Hungary was inevitable."

Might as well nail the argument down. "And by the way, the arts will continue to thrive in the United States, public funding or not. But I think that public funding will survive. At the grass roots level that you seem to decry, the people want it preserved, and have said so to their elected representatives."

Esztergondos smiled. "I'll bet that you are a fencer, Mr. Cutler. I've quite enjoyed our little talk. You have the art of making your points without losing control, and with it, the argument. Perhaps we can continue our discussion at a later date, possibly at my estate in Sarospatak."

An idea came to Robbie. "Actually, Mr. Esztergondos, several of us have put together a small group of diplomats, a dozen or so, who like to learn more about Hungary outside of Budapest. Would it be possible to arrange a future Saturday excursion in Sarospatak with your help? Your colleague Janos Horvath just hosted us last weekend in Eger.

"A good idea. I'd enjoy that. Have whoever makes contact do so with my parliamentary secretary. That might be rather interesting, to show you something of traditional Hungary."

"I'd look forward to that very much," Robbie said with a smile as the conversation ended. They nodded rather formally, and Robbie continued his talk with Janos and Ilona Horvath as Esztergondos left to consult with party leaders.

"You did well not to antagonize him, Robbie," Horvath said. "He has ability, and he could yet be a friend of your country. Despite all that he says, I am not entirely convinced. There is something that doesn't ring quite true, something of the jaded suitor, perhaps. You do well to keep the channels of communication open." Robbie made a mental note to mention the conversation to Charles Lauricette from the French Embassy.

Then the Horvaths and Robbie ambled over to join Imre Mohacsi from the Smallholders Party, who was just finishing a conversation with Australian Ambassador Kovatch.

Horvath introduced Robbie to Mohacsi. "We are gastronomic allies, actually," he said. "My town produces the red wines that go so well with the food from his region. Imre comes from Szeged, the finest agricultural region of our country. That's another area that your group should visit soon."

"I'm honored to meet you, Mr. Mohacsi. Yes, I would very much like to know more about Szeged. One knows the paprika and of course the apricot brandy, but that must be just an introduction."

"It would be. What is the group that Janos mentioned?" Robbie told Mohacsi about the Goulash and Touring Club. "So far, we've visited Eger, thanks to Mr. Horvath. Your colleague Ferenc Esztergondos has just invited us to make arrangements to visit Sarospatak."

Mohacsi grumbled. "He is hardly my colleague, except in the broadest sense of the term. I am more at ease with your diplomatic colleague here, Ambassador Kovatch."

The Ambassador nodded in agreement. "Robbie Cutler and I share an interest in 1956, Mr. Mohacsi. That is when I left Hungary, and I am told, Mr. Cutler's father was assigned to the American Legation then."

"Yes," Robbie said. "And we both had recent contact with a former Freedom Fighter who just died, John Magassy. His writing mentioned you, Mr. Mohacsi, as well as the memorial that he had hoped to undertake. It sounded like a fine idea."

"I'm sorry not to have had the opportunity to hear his views on that," shrugged Mohacsi. "Janos was a fine man, and from time to time over the years we had had some contact."

"He was, I'm told, a member of your own Freedom Fighter group."

"Rather say that we were members of his group," Mohacsi replied. "He was our leader. His memorial idea was typical. Show what is fine, he thought, and people will emulate courageous behavior. I wish I could believe that, as Janos did. Still, what counts is what one did. That doesn't change. We have that to remember."

"I'd like to believe that," Horvath put in. "People do forget. And what happened in the past changes all the time, in the light of circumstances. That is why memorials are needed."

"That's right." Kovatch shook his head in vigorous agreement. "All the more reason to know as precisely as possible what took place in 1956, for example. Is there any possibility that the government will open its files?"

"I believe not, Mohacsi replied. "As you know, some of us, led by my colleague Janos Horvath here, tried to mandate by law that the files at least be opened, or that some prosecutions be considered, but the effort got nowhere. It seems to be a dead letter now." Horvath nodded in agreement, then he and Ilona excused themselves to talk with a constituent.

"All the more reason for the memorial. Are there any more members of your Freedom Fighter group still in Budapest?"

Mohacsi turned to Robbie. "Interestingly enough, that is just what the Ambassador and I were talking about. As far as I know, with Magassy's death, there are just three of us still alive. The other two are also here, in fact at my invitation.

"Magassy had been in contact with me as well, you see, last weekend. It must have been shortly before his murder, and he was also supposed to be here tonight at my invitation. I thought to surprise him with this reunion. He didn't know that Attila Nemzeti and Istvan Szepvaros would also be here. There they are now, with their wives. Let's say hello to them."

As they walked over, joined by Julie Kovatch, who had been chatting with Magda Mohacsi, Mohacsi explained that he had seen each of the other two men from time to time. Nemzeti he had occasionally kept tabs on over the years. He had also seen Szepvaros once or twice since his return from Germany to head his bank. It struck Robbie that this evening was probably the first time that the three men had seen each other in over forty years. The emotion was palpable.

Robbie noticed the women first. They stood beaming with pride as their husbands formally embraced. Then Attila Nemzeti introduced his wife Margit, and Istvan Szepvaros introduced his wife Maria. Julie Kovatch and Magda Mohacsi introduced themselves to save time. So did Robbie.

He couldn't help making some comparisons. Clearly the wealthy Maria Szepvaros was the most elegantly dressed, if the hardest to read. She seemed to Robbie to need the reassurance of comparisons favorable to herself. His first impression was that Magda Mohacsi was the most genuine and likable of the ladies, rather straightforward and pleasant. He liked her on sight.

The cleverest one was Margit Nemzeti. He couldn't tell whether that glint in her eye was intelligence or shrewdness, but the knowledge that her newest dress as a ranking bureaucrat's wife did not pass muster, as compared with the designer gown of Maria Szepvaros, seemed clear enough. Then she gave an almost imperceptible shrug, dismissing the thought. If Attila did not notice, and he would not, it made no difference.

Meanwhile Julie Kovatch revelled in her youth and status as the most beguiling of the lot, a bit too much so, Robbie thought. He began to miss Sylvie Marceau. Christmas holidays were a long time away. He must call her again very soon.

Then he looked at the old Freedom Fighters. They all seemed genuinely glad to see each other again. They said "You remember this" and "I remember that." It would be hard to separate real memory from the suggestion of it after all these years, Robbie realized. He learned that Istvan Szepvaros was now a German citizen, and the head of a prominent German investment bank in Budapest. Attila Nemzeti was with the Ministry of Justice.

The men began to talk about Janos Magassy.

"He was absolutely loyal and to be counted on," Mohacsi was saying. "A born leader. I always thought that he might have made a career soldier, in a different time. He looked forward to seeing each of us. He didn't want what we did to be forgotten."

"Janos Magassy is one of the few persons that I do remember clearly from that time," put in Nemzeti. "My head wound made all of that hard to sort out, but I do remember Magassy. I was one of the youngest, after all. Probably I looked younger than I actually was, you know. Anyway Janos is the one who told me that if things ever became hopeless, that I should go home. I was always grateful to him for that. It was like a kind of absolution. If he suggested something, I'd be for it. Who knows more about his idea for a memorial?"

Ambassador Kovatch sketched what he had been told by Magassy of his concept of a sculptured memorial. He seemed to have taken up the idea with some enthusiasm. Kovatch also seemed transfixed by the reactions of the three men to the idea of the memorial. He needn't have been. They were all in agreement. As a common thread they each seemed initially reluctant to have their own faces put on the memorial, but Kovatch seemed to insist that the memorial be as true to life as possible. That made sense.

"Yes, we must continue his idea," Szepvaros agreed. "What a crime that he is not with us tonight. I did not know him as well as you both did, but he was a good man, and his idea is worth backing. Maybe I can help with the underwriting along with some of my investment experience here, if you aren't averse to money being raised in that way."

"A very practical idea," Kovatch said. They promised to keep in touch with each other as the idea progressed. Robbie agreed to write to leaders of the Freedom Fighters Federation in the United States, to keep them informed of developments. He also made a mental note to keep his father informed as well. Surely that would please him.

It was time for his bachelor's dinner. Robbie found the refreshment table, and helped himself to a plate of spicy Hungarian food, and a glass of chilled white wine from the Lake Balaton region. He saw Ilona Horvath and Marie Lauricette from the French Embassy, and waited for them as they went through the buffet line. They chattered in French, Ilona's foreign language.

"Such spicy food," Marie teased. "Are you sure that it is good for you?"

"I take that as a challenge," Ilona answered for him. "All Hungarian food isn't spicy, although I like that too. Some day you must try some of our more refined dishes, like the *sandre*."

"That's a good French fish," Marie smiled.

"Not at all. We call it the *fogas*, or when young the *sullo*, and it is really Hungarian."

"Whoever is right, I like the idea," Robbie said. "We don't have that in the States. I had it once in a restaurant in Burgundy. Very pricey, and the finest fish I've ever had. They call it 'pike/perch' in English, and it has a subtle, nutlike flavor somewhere between the two. So that is a Hungarian dish?"

"Lots of things are Hungarian, if you look closely enough." This was from Iliu Monescu of the Romanian Embassy, who had just joined them, along with Charles Lauricette. "Remember what they said in Hollywood a few years ago. A producer even had a sign on his desk, 'It is not enough to be Hungarian!'"

Ilona smiled at the Romanian, and that pleased Robbie. The traditional hatred between Hungary and Romania went back for centuries. Perhaps, step by personal step, that could be overcome. He hoped so

"*Salut,* Charles!" Robbie told him about his conversation with Ferenc Esztergondos. "If your planning for our next excursion into the Hungarian countryside hasn't gone too far, perhaps we ought to take him up on the idea of visiting Sarospatak."

"Nothing that can't be altered. I had just made a few preliminary inquiries. But you're right, Robbie. It does make a certain sense to visit a city where we already have a political level contact who can open the doors."

"He said to be in touch with his parliamentary secretary, and mention our conversation at this reception."

"Good idea. I'll do that."

Some music began to be played by an ensemble on the stage where the speaker had made his remarks earlier. The guests drew closer to hear the music, and Robbie found himself standing next to his friends from Bordeaux, Spanish Ambassador Eduardo Dos Campos and his elegant wife Elena. Liszt, Bartok, whatever the classical school, it always seemed to Robbie that Hungarian themes were distinctive. He said so to Dos Campos.

"I don't know what it is, Dos Campos mused, "But there is something in the music that reminds me of the haunting music of our neighbors in Portugal, the *fado*. There is sometimes a minor key, although not invariably so. The tempo is repeated, insistent and dramatic. It is unique and rather haunted. I've always liked Hungarian themes, but I cannot say that I find them relaxing. Beautiful and haunting yes, but not relaxing."

"I hadn't heard it put quite that way," Robbie said, but it brings to mind that Hungarian writing, what I'm capable of reading, is filled with the same sense of drama and uniqueness. Look at the national poem. the *'Talpra Magyar'* of Sandor Petofi. It as stirring as the *Marseillaise*. But it is not nearly as well known."

An annoyed "shush" stopped their conversation, and they listened with pleasure as the music continued for half an hour. When it ended, the applause was spontaneous and genuine.

Robbie and Dos Campos resumed their conversation

"What were you talking with those Hungarian deputies about?" Dos Campos wanted to know.

"Most of them were not politicians, as it turns out. They are former Freedom Fighters. We were talking about the death on Sunday, or rather the murder, of John Magassy. It seems that they all knew him back in 1956. All except for your colleague Ambassador Kovatch, I think," Robbie answered.

"Puzzling business," Dos Campos said. Then he smiled. "I sense that you are becoming just a bit bored with diplomatic life, Robbie, and are looking for another mystery to solve."

Robbie smiled in reply. Dos Campos continued.

"Actually, Kovatch is a closed book. He says all of the right things, with no genuineness at all. Not that genuineness is a diplomatic virtue, of course, but at least one often gets a sense of pleasure from occasions like this, and from talking with people. Kovatch does not. He goes through the motions. He has a different agenda. I cannot read him with any accuracy."

Then he abruptly changed the subject. "Just what do you make of this Magassy business, Robbie? Any theories?"

Robbie began, "Nothing much at present. Robbery is the official working motive, but a sabre is hardly a mugger's weapon. There is not much to go on as yet. But you're right, Eduardo. I am intrigued. Since Magassy was a prominent Hungarian-American, my continued interest is justified, provided that I don't step on anybody's toes in the process. Let me know if you hear anything."

The reception was ending, and the guests started to take their leave. Dos Campos thought for a moment about adding a footnote of warning to his injudicious remarks about his colleague, Ambassador Kovatch. But it was too late. There, ahead of him, Robbie Cutler was retrieving his topcoat. They saw him turn and with an ingratiating smile give a small wrapped parcel to Julie Kovatch.

Elena said to her husband, "I know what you are thinking, and it is probably true. He's a nice young fellow, Eduardo, but let's let him make his own mistakes. He'll learn soon enough."

* * * * * * * * * *

The Fifth Day—October 27, 1956

The funeral service for Pista was brief and reverent. Janos conducted it and said a few gruff words. Eva had gathered some flowers, nobody could imagine where. They buried him in the little green park near the corner of Barat Street, just before dawn. Only Red was missing. It was too dangerous to wait for him to return, so after some hesitation they went ahead.

That was when their name was chosen.

Csaba had heard of other groups. Some, like the Angels, had names taken from their leaders. Janos wouldn't hear of it. "Here we are on Barat Street," he said. "Why don't we call ourselves the Friends? That way others will know us and where we operate." They agreed, and the Friends they became.

"Very Quaker," was Csaba's verdict. "Shows our peaceful intentions."

Eva enjoyed his sense of irony. If only he had had a chance for the education his mind deserved!

There wasn't much time to linger, and there were other concerns as well. Nobody had eaten anything for days. Imre volunteered to go in search for food. Perhaps somebody at the Corvin would know where there was food. Janos Magassy agreed, and gave him a note to the Corvin leadership.

Imre walked down Barat Street, and made a turn on Prater Street. That rather broad street led past a school and some apartment buildings. Now it also featured a captured artillery field gun. He turned left on Kisfaludy Street and then, after a short half block, found himself at Corvin Circle.

There were guards posted about, younger than himself. Imre was glad they had heard of the group on Barat Street. Might as well start by talking with whoever was in charge.

A skinny teenager led him through the hollow circular courtyard surrounding the movie house. On the Kisfaludy Street side there was an extra guard. This, Imre saw, was the gasoline storage cistern. They seemed to be well supplied, with bottles stacked nearby for rapid filling and manufacture of Molotov cocktails.

Beyond the Corvin Movie House on the other side Imre saw two passageway exits, one to Ulloi Avenue and the other to Jozsef Boulevard. There were five story buildings fronting both streets, and from the intermittent firing noises, they were well defended. The building on Ulloi Avenue faced the Kilian Barracks, and the building on Jozsef Boulevard looked across that boulevard at an intersection.

That intersection of Ulloi and Jozsef streets formed an angle favorable for the defenders. Like the boulevards of Paris, they had been formed to ease an army's path. But that was before the days of modern artillery and Molotov cocktails, Imre realized. The buildings were also just right for the front-line defense of Corvin Circle. Within that hollow courtyard, the defenders could rush to whichever point might need them most.

Imre was ushered into the presence of Antal, a muscular, authoritative man in his mid-twenties. Except for his moustache, that could be Janos, Imre thought. The man read his note, and acknowledged that their weapons had come from Janos Magassy.

"We had wondered what had become of him."

"Janos formed his own group in Barat Street, behind you, to protect that flank. I'm one. We call ourselves the Friends." Antal smiled. "There have already been several attempts to outflank you. So far we've taken out several Russian tanks." Antal stood and shook Imre's hand. "Why are you here now?"

"A couple of things." Imre thought fast. "We had a casualty yesterday. A boy died. Had he been just wounded, we wouldn't have known what to do. Could you help?"

"We have several doctors here. They have joined us. Some first aid, perhaps, but they have no supplies. That is the situation now. If things calm down, or get better, perhaps they could get some more. But not now."

Antal's face darkened. "Every day we lose a few more. Always the youngest and most daring. Last night we went to a military hospital, a Hungarian Army hospital, can you imagine it? They said they couldn't treat any civilians. Our kids died, both of them." His arms fluttered open in sadness and disbelief.

He was silent for a moment. Then he cleared his voice. "What else? Janos supplied us when we began, with those weapons from the United Lamp Factory. How are you doing? Do you need any supplies?"

"Not really, not yet. But we're hungry."

"So are we. There's a bakery up the street, along the boulevard. If they are open, we'll get some bread. How many are you in your group?" He paused.

Imre pictured the Friends one by one, Eva, Csaba, Janos, Karoly, Red and himself. "There are just six of us now."

As they got up to leave, the radio burst into sound. Radio Budapest was giving the morning news. Antal and Imre listened carefully. It was the announcement of Imre Nagy's government. It contained several prominent former politicians, people who were not members of the Hungarian Workers (Communist) Party.

"Interesting," Antal said. "What's your reading of that?"

"They only do what they think they have to do," Imre said. "I recognize the names, Tildy and Kovacs. Tildy is a spent force, and Kovacs was a good man before he was broken. This isn't much of a change. Still, it IS a change. They are beginning to understand what the country is doing."

"You think like a politician," Antal said.

"In a free Hungary, that would be interesting," Imre replied. "Let's see if Imre Nagy can get us there. He's still under wraps and doesn't have a free hand, I think."

They left the Corvin stronghold and went up Jozsef Boulevard. There was a long line in front of a bakery, which miraculously was open. Antal and Imre went to the front of the line, their weapons giving them status.

The baker was friendly, but guarded. He understood that food was desperately needed by the Corvin defenders. "How much do you need? Hmmm," he said after Antal's reply. "That's my entire morning's production."

He shrugged his shoulders. "Your problem isn't with me, my friends," he said, pointing to the line of desperate people who were waiting to buy bread. "Talk to them. They've been waiting for hours."

They went outside, and Antal did so. He pleaded for the bread, and said why. The disappointed civilians stared at the ragged Freedom Fighters and agreed. They would come back again the next day.

Antal went back to Corvin Circle to bring back several others to carry the bread. Imre took his share immediately for the Friends. Two round loaves each. He could just carry the twelve. As he rounded the corner he saw an old lady who had been at the end of the line. She seemed confused, and was helped to cross the street by a young man who had also been in line to buy bread. She stopped and looked at Imre.

"You are all so brave," she said, looking at them both. "I wish I could be too. I used to be young once. Now there is nobody at home except my little granddaughter, and we've had no bread for days." She looked hopefully at Imre.

"Here you are, Grandmother," Imre said, handing her two loaves. "We're all fighting for each other."

The other fellow looked at Imre and made up his mind. "I want to join you. I'm sure you can't use a law student, but I was pretty handy with guns in my Young Communist field trips."

"So was I," Imre said. "Come back and meet our group. What's your name?"

"I'm Attila Nemzeti."

"Next time, try to do better than one loaf each," was Janos Magassy's gruff greeting upon their return to Barat Street. "There are more of us now."

Red had returned with three friends nearly as young as himself, Magda, Laszlo and Jozsef. "They knew Pista," Red explained.

"Welcome," Janos said.

He gave each a loaf of bread.

CHAPTER SEVEN

▼

ON GUARD!

Luncheon with Julie Kovatch was a treat that, Robbie told himself, hurt nobody. It was pleasant, and he could find out something about Kovatch himself at the same time. And what was the harm in two friends getting to know each other better?

Her husband didn't seem to mind at all. In fact, he encouraged his wife's "little excursions," as he called them. That puzzled Robbie. Who was keeping tabs on whom?

Robbie admired Julie's taste in clothes. Today she wore a mahogany brown warm weather suit, with a coordinated long sleeved silk blouse in lime green. Their table seemed to Robbie to be the center of attention at the restaurant. Perhaps that was because Julie's Irish eyes were sparkling.

Julie was intrigued that Robbie had mentioned Sylvie Marceau. "Why is he playing that card now?" she wondered. Julie already knew about Sylvie from Elena Dos Campos. She wondered whether Robbie had in turn mentioned her in his letters to Sylvie. Of course not.

Robbie looked at the menu. He was glad that he had mentioned Sylvie to Julie. He had argued with himself whether he was at fault for not also mentioning Julie in his letters to Sylvie. What, after all, was there to say? Going into all that might even imply feelings for Julie. It could only cause needless concern, and it really wasn't Sylvie's business. Or was it?

He would of course make all that clear to Evalyn when the time came. He greatly missed his sister's kidding, affectionate tone, and her ability to size people up precisely but not in an unkind way. They used to have luncheon when her work at the publishing house occasionally took her to Washington for a book promotion tour. Evalyn approved of Sylvie. But this was not Evalyn sitting across the table. It was Julie.

Today was typically pleasant at the *Szaz Eves* ("Hundred Years"). Said to be the oldest restaurant in Pest, it was on the Danube side of *Vaci Utca* (Vaci Street), the quarter's leading shopping street.

The menu was elaborate and expensive by Hungarian standards, but a bargain for the Western visitor. Robbie ordered the *sullo*, or pike/perch. Since Ilona Horvath had mentioned it at the reception a few weeks earlier, *sullo* had become a favorite dish. A chilled bottle of 1990 Chablis *Les Vaillons* would be a perfect match for the fish, perhaps bringing a compliment from Julie.

They had a booth to themselves, with a view that swept the restaurant and its fascinating kaleidoscope of earnest waiters in vests of red and green Hungarian folk designs presenting dishes with appropriate flourish. Robbie savored his appetizer of broiled wild mushrooms on toast points, while Julie enjoyed a traditional hot weather specialty, cold cherry soup.

Robbie didn't miss the "My name is George. I'll be your waiter for luncheon" nonsense. These waiters were professionals. They knew their craft. Robbie supposed that their grandfathers had served with averted glances in the private rooms that had flourished at the grand restaurants in Budapest and Vienna in those days.

The chablis was excellent. They had talked about extending luncheon sometime with perhaps a museum visit. Regrettably there wasn't enough time today. The onset of summer had brought the usual crush of visitors to both embassies, and Robbie even had a fencing session at the end of a busy afternoon. He hadn't deliberately intended that, not really. It had just popped onto his schedule. "So conscience doth make cowards of us all," he remembered. He was angry with himself for a moment.

Robbie's ritual inquiry about her husband led to an uncharacteristic pout. "He seems more preoccupied than ever," she replied. "Almost driven. I must confess I don't understand it. Alex has always been conscientious, but this is getting a little excessive. Almost obsessive," she added, puzzled. Clearly she alone was used to being the object of any obsessive interest.

"I hope he's still planning to join us for the trip to Sarospatak this Saturday."

"He says he has cleared his schedule to be able to come."

"What is going on…visitors from Canberra?"

"No," she frowned. "That's not it. He seems preoccupied, ever since that Magassy business last month. That shook him up. He's been following up with talks with some of the people that we met that night at the reception. You know, that banker, for example, and the Deputy from Szeged."

That sounded reasonable on the face of it, and Robbie said so reassuringly. Any new diplomat liked to pursue fresh contacts to see what light they might shed on the local scene. Purely routine. It was all part of embassy reporting, and keeping in touch. Ambassadors were no different in that regard.

Robbie wondered to himself how this fit into the pattern that began with Kovatch's researches at the 1956 Institute. He filed away as a warning note Julie's concerns. She thought she was conveying the tantrum of a slighted wife, after all.

"What do you hear about the Magassy case?" She seemed genuinely interested.

That question, Robbie was certain, was from her husband. So there was going to be a *quid pro quo* in this luncheon game after all. For a moment he felt badly for Julie. Perhaps it was a twinge of conscience. What would Evalyn say to all this?

"Nothing much to date. I'll be talking with our Consul this afternoon about it. Since the Ambassador's return she has been called a couple of times by the Freedom Fighters Association, and that gives the case domestic political heft. The last I heard there were no new leads, and robbery was still the motive the police were chasing.

"If you find out anything, let us know on Saturday, will you? Alex met with him that last weekend, and so of course he is taking a personal interest in this." What a terrible spy she would have made, Robbie thought. Bored, she was blurting out her instructions without knowing it. Well, she had done her duty, and now she could relax.

Luncheon was superb. The fish was so good that they ate in silence, its rich, nutlike flavor set off perfectly by the crisp chablis. Now Robbie was annoyed with himself for arranging his fencing lesson that very day. It would have been much more pleasant to linger over luncheon, with another glass or two of chilled wine. A double expresso and a shared slice of *Linzer Torte* with whipped cream ended the meal.

Julie did not get up to leave just yet. "Do you really have to go back to the Embassy so quickly, Robbie? I thought perhaps you could join me for an hour of touring about, say to digest your luncheon. Better than dozing off at your desk, I'm sure."

He wasn't going to do it, she guessed. Don't press the point, not yet. It was better to leave with a smile now.

He noticed her smile. It was beguiling, one of her nicest features. That was surely a gift from the old country, from County Wicklow. It framed her auburn hair and hazel eyes.

Had she been there, Evalyn might have said to her brother that now that the moment of temptation had passed, he was permitting himself to look at Julie closely. She would also have guessed that, having really seen Julie for the first time as the luncheon ended, that would be the image Robbie would indelibly remember until their next private luncheon.

Robbie pleaded his schedule in an apologetic tone, and then temporized. He said it was clear for the following week. Why didn't they have luncheon and then go off to see the Hungarian Crown of St. Stephen and regalia? For some reason, he had never done that. Neither, Julie replied, had she.

"I'll look forward to that, Robbie," she said with a quickened smile. He was relieved. He had done the right thing, and she had not minded after all. Her smile reassured him. It made him feel less like an intruder in an ancient land whose laws were a mystery to him, and more sure of himself. With a last sip of chablis, and a quick brush of her hand on the back of his forearm, she was gone.

Robbie was glad to have returned to his office on time. A message was waiting for him to report to the Ambassador. He did so without breaking stride. It was just down the hall from his own office. He greeted her secretary, who waived him in.

Robbie liked the Ambassador's corner office, where Cardinal Mindszenty had lived for nearly two decades. He actually thought that Randy Davis's office directly beneath it had been even more striking, with its theatrical little balcony. At least before it had been chopped up and filled with computers that had been the case. Consul Davis was now exiled to a smaller adjoining room.

Consular work fascinated him. So much human interest came to the Consular Section each day. Robbie preferred his political work, but he also missed the consular problems that he had faced in Bordeaux and in Singapore. Solving them was like detection.

In the end, the lure of political analysis had been too strong, and he had chosen it as his specialty. That's where the career ambassadors came from, after all. Robbie enjoyed figuring out the shifts of public opinion and policy response, before they were apparent. During his last visit home, his father had warned him about just that. "It's dangerous to be right too soon in the Foreign Service. People resent it." His words could be carved on New Hampshire granite.

Ambassador Eleanor Horton was not pleased. Consul Randy Davis had just told her that there was nothing new to report on the Magassy case.

The police were investigating, and that was about it. And to her way of thinking, that wasn't good enough. Now she had summoned Robbie to her office. She showed him copies of the preliminary police reports that had been given to Davis. Included was correspondence to her from Magassy's family, two United States Senators, the Governor of his state, and a cable from the Assistant Secretary of State for Consular Affairs.

"Take a look at this file, Robbie. I'm beginning to think that you should be a special action officer on the Magassy murder case. Its dimensions go far beyond the consular routine.

Robbie understood that meant not to get in Randy Davis's way, but to proceed on his own and do what he could. He confirmed that understanding with Ambassador Horton.

"I know something about your background, Robbie," she went on. "You have a facility, no, a gift, for solving problems."

So she was aware of his cases in Bordeaux and Singapore. Well, they were mentioned in his files, and the Bordeaux terrorist case had after all attracted some public attention.

She elaborated a bit. "John Magassy was a fine man. Now, perhaps he was just murdered in some common, garden variety robbery, as the police seem to think. Frankly, it seems to me that they are just lowering public expectations to position themselves for whatever happens."

That was an unexpected thought. Lowering expectations before a breakthrough was a diplomatic tactic. It had its mirror image, the leaking of good news just before a negotiation failed, so that the other side would be blamed. One could chart the endless history of fruitless intercommunal talks on the Cyprus issue by that tactic alone.

However, hearing that said by Ambassador Eleanor Horton raised her several notches in his estimation. She had, he remembered, been a prosecuting attorney before her marriage and subsequent political fundraising activities.

Perhaps her skills as a prosecutor and his love of detection would make a sort of partnership possible in this Magassy business. He liked the idea.

It stretched the boundaries. He had been afraid that as a new diplomat, she would be too cautious. He tested the waters.

"With your approval, Madame Ambassador, I'll spend some time out of the office on this. I've found in the past that there are usually a number of threads that need to be unraveled before the truth begins to appear. And of course it may all come to nothing.

"The odds are that Magassy, like most victims of violent crime, just happened to be in the wrong place at the wrong time," he continued. "I'll look forward to finding out. But I may need your personal backing from time to time as I proceed. It can become very hard going. If there is anything to this case, it certainly will."

Fair enough, she thought, nodding agreement. He is interested enough to proceed, and in fact rather likes the idea. But he doesn't want to be hung out to dry if the going gets difficult.

"How will you start?"

Robbie pondered this for a moment. "I'll be in touch with the Budapest police, of course. They already expect that. But now a higher profile will be needed. I won't get in their way. For one thing, I have no access to their laboratories and networks. I always work with the police, not against them."

He thought for a moment. "It would help me a great deal if you would let the Foreign Ministry know of my assignment. That would help me in my dealings with local police authorities." He didn't have to add that formal notification from Ambassador Horton would make it far harder for the Hungarians to shut him out if the going got rough. She nodded her understanding.

"I'll make a call to the Chief of the American desk, Ambassador Fekete, this afternoon. He'll pass the word."

Robbie continued. "The motivations for murder are what most interest me. So I will start looking at things from the killer's point of view."

That startled her. He went on.

"Of course, I won't know the killer's point of view for a while. The only way to find it out, it seems to me, is to know more about John Magassy and his trip here. You've heard about the memorial that he wanted to build, to commemorate the Freedom Fighters?"

"Yes. It struck me as a fine idea."

"I liked it too. But quite possibly Magassy may have been up to more than he let on. Either that, or his return had somehow endangered someone. Maybe Magassy himself didn't know he had done that. So to answer your question, my trail begins with Magassy himself. I've already been to the 1956 Institute."

She rose and extended her hand to seal their bargain. "I'm glad that you are here, Robbie. You have the makings of a fine Political Officer. You gauge the wind perfectly. You have that in common with Seth Cutler, a member of your family, I think."

Robbie took her hand, and smiled in agreement. "He is my great uncle."

"Please give him my very best regards when you talk with him next. He may remember me as Eleanor Giddings. He arranged my scholarship in one of the early years, after he directed that his school admit young women as students."

It was a nice admission, and one that he was sure Uncle Seth would savor. So the good that people do does live on, after all. At least in Uncle Seth's case, that appeared to be true.

*　　　　　*　　　　　*

Robbie returned to his office. He took the preliminary police report, the cable and correspondence that Ambassador Horton had given him, and read them carefully. Then he took out from his files the materials that Magassy had left for him, and began to make some notes.

Robbie permitted himself a smile of pleasure. He had always been attracted by detection, ever since that robbery case in Providence when he had been a student at Brown. He knew, after two Foreign Service assignments, that diplomats saw all sorts of reports, political, intelligence, and sometimes investigatory.

That full range of information available to a diplomat exceeded what the police might have access to. That is what had enabled him to help solve several cases earlier, that counterfeiting ring in Singapore, and then the terrorist ETA scheme in Bordeaux. Well, for the first time, his talent along those lines had been recognized, and in her own way, Ambassador Horton had even assigned him to help clear up the Magassy murder case. It was a satisfying moment.

Now to work. Robbie put aside his other projects, and tried to put himself in John Magassy's position, returning to Budapest for the first time. What would his priorities be here? He would give Ambassador Horton's call to Ambassador Fekete a day or two to percolate through the system, and then he would call on the Budapest police. Meanwhile, there was a lot of material on hand to study, and several hours to go before his fencing lesson. Immersed in his thoughts, he forgot entirely about Julie Kovatch.

First he turned to the report from Police Inspector Imre Racz that had been forwarded to the Embassy with a routine cover note from the Foreign Ministry. Racz was from Central Budapest Police Headquarters. Robbie frowned. First problem. Why wasn't the report from Obuda, where the murder had taken place? Obuda was the third of Budapest's twenty-two districts. Robbie knew that the city's police organization mirrored the city's districts. He made a note to look into the jurisdiction issue. Robbie liked to solve the small problems first, if he could. That built a surer foundation for tackling the larger ones.

The police report was brief and ugly. John Magassy had died from a massive invasive sabre wound which had gone halfway through his neck. Robbie couldn't tell from the technical Hungarian used whether he had bled to death or died of shock or severed major vessels. It didn't seem very important at this point. There were also slashing wounds on his forearms. Of course, Robbie thought. He was trying to protect himself.

But why use a sabre at all for the killing?

There was a photograph of the sabre enclosed with the preliminary police report. To Robbie's practiced eye it looked like a good modern copy of an early nineteenth century cavalry sabre, well balanced, somewhat heavier than his own sabre, blade slightly curved. The original would have been used from the saddle as a hacking weapon, the horseman sweeping the sabre downwards and hoping the force of the blow would disengage the weapon after the attack.

Killing in the heat of battle was one thing. To use the sabre as this killer had done was macabre. Again and again Robbie wondered why such a cumbersome weapon would be used at all. Why did the killer do that? And then having used it, why did he leave it at the scene of the murder? Probably it would be too difficult to hide. Robbie's notes for his first talk with Inspector Racz were becoming extensive.

Robbie next read the letters. They reflected the real esteem in which John Magassy had been held. The ones from Governor Stratton and Senator Bosworth were predictable, full of shock and demands that the Hungarian authorities be pressed to solve the crime, and bring the perpetrator to justice as soon as possible. They were, however, not staff products. Clearly Magassy had known these eminent men, and been valued by them. Their shock and loss were genuine, even if their letters were formulaic.

The letter from Senator James Abernathy was similar, but more focussed and personal. It was not a staff product. The letter referred to Magassy's valued service to the nation. What did he mean by that? That seemed to go beyond Magassy's status as a distinguished citizen. Senator Abernathy closed by referring to his trip to Budapest, planned for that fall. He said that he would be monitoring the Embassy's efforts regarding the Magassy murder case at that time.

No wonder Ambassador Horton wanted him to concentrate on the case. From the Senate stationery used, Senator Abernathy was a ranking member of the Senate Intelligence Committee, an important man, someone who wanted to understand things.

Robbie pictured the Intelligence Committee's hearing room in the Hart Senate Office Building, specially engineered so that the most secret disclosures could safely be made there, without fear of electronic eavesdropping. Robbie wondered about Magassy's connection with Abernathy. Perhaps Uncle Seth, with his extensive intelligence connections, could shed some light on that aspect of things.

The letter from Magassy's family was sad and rather endearing. His wife recounted how often her husband had talked of returning to Hungary, when it had not been safe, he had thought, to do so. Now look what had happened. Robbie began to draft in his mind a careful letter to Mrs. Magassy that would have to take the place of a personal interview.

It would be important to know whether her husband had talked with her in detail about his plans for this trip. Perhaps he had left with her some clue, some valuable information of which she herself was unaware, that Robbie might ferret out. Robbie was beginning to suspect that a further agenda for the trip might have existed, but it would be premature to speculate beyond his suspicion. In Robbie's experience, building speculation on speculation was fine for detective fiction, but terrible in practice. He would simply have to find out what Mrs. Magassy might be able to add, without realizing that her contribution might even be important. But that could wait for a few weeks.

For now, she was surely still in emotional shock from having arranged the details of his funeral. Magassy's body had been shipped back in a sealed coffin two weeks after his death, at the family's instructions. There had been no further police need to keep the body in Hungary.

The cable to Ambassador Horton from the Assistant Secretary of State for Consular Affairs was a personal one, marked not for further distribution within the Embassy. That meant that only the Ambassador, and probably DCM Arnie Johnson, had seen it in addition to the communications center folks down the hall.

He was complimented that she let him see it. It was Ambassador Horton's way of laying her cards on the table. The Assistant Secretary had specifically suggested to Ambassador Horton that she assign Robbie to this case, mentioning his work in Bordeaux. Maybe we need a new Foreign Service area of specialization, "diplomatic detective," he thought with a grin.

Magassy's cover note to him was reread next. There seemed to be nothing there. He wondered what Magassy would have been up to in Sarospatak. Perhaps he would find out this weekend. He read once again the draft plans for the Freedom Fighter Memorial, and again liked the idea. Tomorrow he would walk over to the neighborhood in Pest where their armed resistance unit had operated. Might as well get a close second look on the ground. Sometimes memories were distorted or failed, and it was always good to have a personal impression.

Then he turned to the article that Magassy had written about their heroic two weeks. It was not possible to read the article without emotion. It was almost in the form of a battle diary, day by day. One no sooner met participants in the Freedom Fight than they died. Their spirits rose in inverse proportion to their privations. Robbie wondered whether Guadalcanal had been something like that, or perhaps Lexington and Concord.

For a time, this group of youngsters, all of whom were teenagers or early twenties it seemed, scored remarkable successes. The older boys and young men knew how to operate semiautomatic Russian weapons from their compulsory military training. As time went on they taught the two young women, Eva and Magda, how to load and fire the weapons too. A lot of time was spent foraging for food, or for ammunition and supplies to make Molotov cocktails, their tank destroyers.

Magassy was the leader of this unit. It had been a compelling choice, if indeed any formal choice had ever been made. He had supplied the weapons from the United Lamp Factory in the first place. Also Magassy was from this area of Pest and knew it well, while the others came on the scene haphazardly. He was also at least a year or two older than the others and was even called "the old man." Robbie had to grin at that. Magassy was probably twenty five or six years old at the time, younger than Robbie himself now.

Day by day their little group fell, one by one. When the news came of Russian treachery and reinvasion, they must have known that their military uprising could not win. The Americans, rumors to the contrary notwithstanding, were not going to come. Then Radio Budapest ceased broadcasting. The outside world was sealed off.

Magassy had described their last days in detail. Robbie again noted that, with the exception of Eva Molnar and himself, Magassy had not used their last names, just first names or nicknames. Well, Magassy was in safety in the United States. He was writing in 1978, when the prisons had emptied. That meant that Eva Molnar had either died, or having been released from prison, no longer faced any reasonable danger. He wondered which was the case, and how Magassy knew he could safely use her name.

The ten others mentioned were named Imre, Karoly, Pista, Red, Magda, Jozsef, Laszlo, Attila, lstvan and Csaba. Clearly Imre, Istvan and Attila were the men that he had met at the reception. They were, for all Magassy had known when the article was written some twenty years earlier, still subject to possible official retribution. And so he had not used their full names. Zsuzsa's identifications at the 1956 Institute had been helpful.

Let's see. Imre was of course the Deputy, Imre Mohacsi. Istvan was the banker, Istvan Szepvaros, while Attila was of course the Ministry of Justice official, Attila Nemzeti. The others were killed fighting the Russians, except for Eva Molnar and for Csaba and Jozsef, who seemed to have disappeared.

Eva, Robbie knew, had been captured and imprisoned. What had happened to the others? He wondered if this was what Ambassador Kovatch was trying to find out. Kovatch had met with Magassy the day before the murder. It was therefore likely that he also had been given a copy of Magassy's article.

Magassy's account gave the order of their leaving Barat Street. He wrote that as ammunition and supplies ran out, they left one by one on foraging missions. Attila left first, then Istvan, and when he did not return, Csaba. Attila had returned with some supplies just after Imre left.

As time ran out, Magassy had urged Eva to leave, and she had finally done so. She was going, he supposed, to the American Legation. She had talked about knowing someone there.

Good God, Robbie thought. And I sent this column home!

Then Attila had been fatally hit by shrapnel. Magassy, the last person left, had bade farewell to his dead comrades and vacated their position. He had done all anyone could.

It struck Robbie that if Attila was indeed Attila Nemzeti, that Magassy had not then been aware that he had survived the uprising. Nemzeti must have regained conscientiousness after Magassy's own departure, and then somehow made it to safety.

That revelation would have been quite a shock to Magassy, if he had ever lived to realize it.

Robbie wondered if Magassy's hotel had retained the log of his telephone calls. He added that point to the list of matters to raise with the Budapest police.

*   *   *

The fencing room was full of spirited competitors. Unlike the more relaxed practice sessions, a lesson with the fencing master was an event requiring both physical suppleness and mental agility. A failure on either count meant a quick and public humiliation. Odd how fencing still retained that aspect of its origins, Robbie thought. One fought for exercise but at some elemental level, also for pride and survival.

His physical exercises moved from an easy, almost languid pace to an overdrive of exertion. Then Robbie adjusted his mask over his fencing uniform with protective chest underguard and took his place on the *piste* opposite the fencing master, Istvan Szolte. They bowed, Szolte slightly and

Robbie more deeply, before assuming the on guard position. Rather Japanese, Robbie thought.

The lesson did not begin slowly. Szolte lunged forward quickly and skillfully, perfectly balanced, able to recover at a moment's notice and either continue the attack, or shift as necessary to a defensive parry. His cut to Robbie's head landed in tandem with his front foot slapping the ground. The thrust was not haphazard. Its suddenness was designed to exert control and put Robbie on the defensive mentally. The noise of his foot was a planned distraction. The lunge downwards towards Robbie's head was also deliberate and meant to intimidate.

Robbie instinctively dropped his point and brought his sabre sweeping upwards under Szolte's sabre in a circular motion, and parried the thrust in quint defensive position. His sword hand was just above his head on the right side, and the sabre point on a parallel line shielding his head. Szolte's sabre was knocked upwards. The fencing master barked out something in colloquial Hungarian that had not been taught by the polite language experts at the Foreign Service Institute. Moving from defense to offense, Robbie stepped forward with an immediate *riposte*, swinging over and cir-cling Szolte's sabre with a quick lunge, which forced the fencing master backwards. It was a textbook maneuver, readily parried. The initial thrust by Szolte seemed to have triggered some sort of adrenalin rush for Robbie. This was not the cautious diplomat that his colleagues would have recog-nized. Another instinct was at work.

Robbie continued attacking with a sharp series of lunges which Szolte did not interrupt with a *riposte* and counter offensive, as he might have done. Instead, for four lunges he let the offensive play its course with appropriate parries, always controlled and measured according to the direction of the attack. Too tightly held, or too loosely, his own sabre could be knocked out of line and a renewed thrust made. All was controlled force and suppleness.

They arrived at the end of the *piste* and changed roles. It was like any practice session, but far more vigorous. Thrust and parry, thrust and parry, the movements and time roared past. Robbie was fully worked up now, moving easily. It was a sort of deadly ballet in miniature. Other sabreurs waiting for their lessons watched intently.

Robbie sensed that they were being watched and, still smarting from Szolte's initial thrust, decided it was time to attack. He lunged briefly at Szolte's head, but as Szolte rotated his sabre in quinte defensive position, Robbie abandoned that thrust as a feint, immediately rotating his forearm and blade downwards for an attack instead at Szolte's flank.

Szolte dropped his forearm and sweeping the sabre across his flank, parried Robbie's thrust in quarte. He replied with his own riposte which nearly caught Robbie overextended and off balance. It was a close call.

Now, fatigue was beginning to set in. Robbie wondered how the older man could continue at this pace, and then realized that the very thought was hazardous, a serious mistake, and a concession he should not have made. It was time for a supreme effort. Nothing less would do. It should be a cut to the head. Szolte lunged upwards and Robbie caught his opponent's sabre with a parry in prime, his forearm raised and the sabre point towards the ground. Then he suddenly rotated his forearm back downwards, raising the sabre blade into tierce and taking Szolte's sabre with him, the momentum of Robbie's movements taking Szolte's weapon out of line and just a fraction beyond his usual exquisite control. Immediately Robbie cut through the open defense to Szolte's head and scored.

There was an audible gasp from those watching. The sabreurs murmured appreciatively. It was not every day that they were treated to an exhibition of the master being caught by a *prise de fer*, or taking of the blade. That was something to talk about later, over their glasses of wine that evening.

The fencing lesson was winding down. A further series of lunges on each side would probably do it. Robbie now sensed that Szolte was really beginning to tire, his motions becoming less precise. Robbie had won. Why press the point? With the final series of lunges from his fencing master,

Robbie's responses became cautious, textbook, conservative, as Szolte's lunges covered less and space.

Robbie realized his mistake too late. Szolte gave a short lunge, then dropping lightly where the lunge had taken him to the on guard position, straightened out briskly and kicked his toes off from the floor a second time. He shoved off with momentum from his powerful legs like the Olympic broad jumper he had once been.

In midair, his heels first nearly meeting and in perfect control, Szolte immediately extended his arms and legs fully in mid-lunge. He didn't seem tired in the slightest, and this lunge carried him much farther than any he had previously made.

It was a *ballestra*, a feint and extended lunge, and it had been expertly delivered, scoring through Robbie's improvised defenses. The maneuver seemed inspired by a cavalryman's combat lunge from horseback, the sabre sweep begun from the saddle and delivered as the horse jumped to clear an obstacle, irresistibly gaining space, power and momentum, overwhelming any defense.

The watching sabreurs applauded. Raising his mask, so did the exhausted Robbie.

*   *   *

Minouette was gracious, all things considered.

There had been so many receptions and diplomatic gatherings recently that Robbie had abandoned the animal to her own devices for days on end. This evening, however, he had been only too glad to come back to his townhouse after the fencing lesson, heat up some dinner, and spend the evening listening to music and absentmindedly patting Minouette.

The seal point Siamese arched her back with pleasure. Not allowed to go out, she didn't miss the world beyond the door and windows, provided that her own world was inviolate. As to that world, she was no democrat, but a born autocrat. Odd smells bothered her. So did knocks on the door at unexpected moments.

Robbie felt that really, he had been neglecting the poor animal. She had been waiting for him at the door on his return. She always seemed to know when it was his step approaching the doorway. That was worth an extra pat or two. Robbie then found her catnip pull toy. Minouette pounced on it, pleased at the extra attention. Robbie often didn't think to go beyond the patting and feeding stage. She was a playful creature really.

As he patted Minouette, Robbie glanced at his cane collection. He hadn't really given it a thoughtful look in weeks. Let's see. He counted seven canes or walking sticks. He could hardly remember which had been purchased first.

There, of course, was the sharp tipped Basque *makhila* that Commissioner Moineau had just sent him from Bordeaux, along with his sword cane. There was also his Malacca cane, the pride of his collection, which he had purchased in Malaysia. Lightweight and trim, it had been part of a gentleman's uniform in the last century. Oh yes, there was an Abercrombie and Fitch black ebony evening cane with a hidden flask, and a pilgrim's staff from Rocamadour in central France.

His English nobbed blackthorn stick was also there, a weapon really, that he had not had an easy time taking on the plane at London's Heathrow Airport. He had had to confide the stick to an attendant for the duration of the flight. And there was the silver-tipped cane that he had bought at the flea market in Budapest during his first trip here, when he was a student at Brown. He remembered the bargaining process with pleasure.

Surely now it was time to add another cane or walking stick to the collection. He really must prowl around the antique shops here on Castle Hill when he got the free time to do so. They had many interesting things, possibly even sabres.

He patted Minouette absentmindedly while he mused at his canes. A cane with an antler handle would be a good buy, and a genuine Central European addition to his collection.

Drat! There was that clattering facsimile machine. Minouette couldn't seem to get used to it, not least because Robbie could always be counted on to abandon patting her and pay attention to that noisy machine, whatever it was. Probably not even worth the waste of good urine to mark it.

Robbie had stopped off at the townhouse a few hours previously, before leaving again for his fencing lesson, to pick up his freshly laundered fencing uniform and also to send a FAX to Uncle Seth to his home in Rockport, Massachusetts. That had been carefully marked out in code, according to the book code that they had devised.

Each used the same English language edition of Montaigne's *Essays* for reference. Words, lines, pages, in that order, formed the basis for their little code. Each had its own number, which was in turn inverted. The third word on the fourteenth line of page eighty five, for example, was 304158. Pages, of course, could also go to three numbers. In that case, the fifteenth word on line twelve of page one hundred twenty nine became 5121921 After encoding a message the groups were then put in reverse order, so that the last group became the first group of the message, and so on.

It took a little doing. One had to supply punctuation, for example, and no modern words or geographic references were found in the Renaissance writer's work. But by and large, the code worked well, private and unbreakable. It was unlikely that any third party would stumble across the exact book that was used. It would be easier to tap into his e-mail, Robbie supposed.

Robbie had begun his own message with greetings from Ambassador Horton. Then he had referred to his earlier inquiry about 1956 and possible American encouragement, to which as yet there had been no reply. Probably Uncle Seth hadn't yet had the opportunity to take his planned trip to Washington.

Briefly Robbie then had summarized what was known about Magassy's return trip and murder. He cited Magassy's connection with official Washington, using "intelligence" and "senator" in ways that probably would have perplexed Montaigne. He also mentioned those persons that he had met at the reception in Parliament whom Magassy had mentioned in his article, including Ambassador Kovatch. Conveying that information required some ingenuity, since Australia had not been in Montaigne's lexicon.

For good measure, he had also FAXed a clear copy of Magassy's article. Might as well put Uncle Seth completely in the picture. It was worth a try even though Uncle Seth had often said that detection was not his specialty. Intelligence was. Robbie sometimes wondered where the line was between the two.

The acknowledgement was a short one. Robbie poured himself a glass of fiery, clear Hungarian *baracks palinka*, or apricot brandy. He glanced at the groups, and then reached for a pad of paper and a pen, and then for his copy of Montaigne.

"Regret broken wrist delayed my trip to visit with friends. Leaving tomorrow. Murder case most interesting. Have heard rumors more involved than simple robbery. Exercise caution. Suggest first discussion politician. Back in ten days. Regards to Ambassador."

So Uncle Seth's first impression matched his own. There was potentially more to this than a garden variety crime. He had also read Magassy's article, and was encouraging Robbie to begin to interview the surviving members of Magassy's group. That suited Robbie's own inclination. He would brief Ambassador Horton generally on the full reply when it came. It would be enough for her now to know that Washington's intelligence community was being unofficially trolled for advice and help. That would reward her for her confidence in him.

Robbie made a mental note to begin his informal soundings the next morning. He would start as Uncle Seth had suggested by talking with Imre Mohacsi. After all, Mohacsi had invited the others to meet with Magassy. That made Mohacsi a logical starting point for Robbie, as he in turn surveyed what Magassy might have hoped to find.

Robbie shuddered a bit and hoped that the parallel stopped there.

* * * * * * * * * *

The Sixth Day—October 28, 1956

The patrols went on all night, in three hour shifts beginning at nine o'clock. Experienced fighters went out with new Friends. First Csaba went out with Attila, Red and Jozsef. When they returned, it was Karoly, Eva and Laszlo. Then Janos, Imre and Magda had their turn. At six o'clock there was coffee and the remaining bread for breakfast, with a bit of paprika and lard which Magda had somehow scrounged the previous afternoon with her angelic look.

The patrols were Janos's idea. It was better to be prepared for what might come, rather than wait and listen for the tanks. There were so many rumors now. One had to hold firmly to some truths, to what one could see and hear.

Imre and Janos weighed what was known, and what surmised. The Russians seemed off-guard. Their attacks had not terrorized the Hungarian population. Instead, the exact opposite seemed to have happened. The people were energized, and resistance groups were getting more volunteers to replace those who had died.

Meanwhile Attila chimed in with rumors that ranking members of the Soviet Politburo had been in Budapest assessing the situation. The attitude of Imre Nagy's government seemed to be shifting towards the Freedom Fighters. Ceasefires were being locally arranged while the overall situation sorted itself out. And nobody wanted to be the last casualty before a ceasefire took effect.

As the dawn had broken, the noise of fighting from the avenues near Corvin Circle was heard. Another tank destroyed. "Maybe the Russians were trying to get the best position before any ceasefire," Janos muttered. He and Attila decided to survey the Corvin area.

Much of it was a shambles, with more extensive damage than had taken place on the Barat Street side. The acrid smells of sweat and gunpowder were everywhere and permeated everything. There were blackened tank and truck hulks, and extensive damage to the buildings fronting Ulloi and

Jozsef Streets. Those positions could still be held, but this was a vivid sign of Russian firepower. Here and there were unburied corpses, hurriedly covered with lime. If they were Freedom Fighters, bouquets of flowers covered the bodies.

Along the boulevards civilians were putting up barricades. Attila thought this was what it must have been like during the revolutions in France. The romance of that thought faded with the bloated corpses on every street, and the sad sight of people looking for lost relatives, calling beloved names again and again. Often those calls ended abruptly in a piercing shriek, a cry that Attila knew he would hear again and again in the night. Sometimes they ended on a note of joy as a relative was found, still alive now, safe for the time being.

Shop windows were smashed, but there had been no civil disorder, and no looting. None at all. In some stores, Freedom Fighters had drawn up rough inventories of the goods, and left them for the shop owners, touching nothing. Sometimes, when something was needed and had been taken from a shop, money had been openly left in a box with a note, a name and address. There were also donations to pay for windows broken in the fighting.

Several captured 76 millimeter artillery pieces were to be seen in front of Prater Street and also Corvin Circle. They had the traditional Hungarian national emblem traced on them. Janos laughed to see that one also had the ironic sign, "Held Over," from the Corvin Movie House, draped along its shield in front.

"Uncle Janos," came Magda's musical voice from Kisfaludy Street, just behind them. What a sweet child. She was thirteen if she was a day. She seemed to be everywhere at once. "Uncle Janos, come over here! You ought to talk with this man. He's Russian!"

It was true. The Corvin group had captured several Russian soldiers. Their tactic was to jump on the turret of an isolated tank, then threaten to drop hand grenades through the hatch unless the crew surrendered. Several had done so.

Here was one of the soldiers, with two Corvin Freedom Fighters, working to build a barricade on Kisfaludy Street. From his easy manner he had been a prisoner for several days.

The Russian spoke just a little Hungarian, but Magda had paid attention in her compulsory Russian classes at school, and she translated. "He has heard that there will be a ceasefire, she said. "But he won't go back. He'd rather be killed here and now. He wants to help the Hungarian side. That's what he is doing now."

Janos was struck by the irony of it all. "For years, we hear hints and promises that the Americans will come and help us, and then, the only military help we get is from a Russian soldier." He started to laugh. "Sorry, Ivan, I'm not laughing at you. You're welcome here. You and as many others as will help us."

Magda translated. The Russian saw the grim humor and ventured a smile. "Tell them not to make me go back," he said. "You have my word on that," Janos answered.

At six o'clock that evening the Barat Street group heard startling news on Radio Budapest. It was an announcement by Prime Minister Imre Nagy. The entire group gathered close to hear every word, as Eva turned up the volume knob on the set.

This was not the same confused Imre Nagy who had spoken from the Parliament just five days earlier. Now he seemed his own man. He said the fighting had been justified, and he condemned the old ways. The hated *AVH*, he said, would be disbanded.

The Prime Minister announced a ceasefire. and the immediate withdrawal of Russian troops from Budapest. There would be no punishment for anyone who had taken up arms.

And there was more. There would be equality in relations between Hungary and the Soviet Union from now on, and real democracy in the factories, with workers' councils rather than unrealistic production norms issued from above. Workers would be full participants, not just ordered about. Socialism would be given a chance here, after all.

For a moment, there was stunned silence in the room. It was so hard to believe that they had won, against overpowering military forces. No people had ever done that before.

Now everything would be different.

"You know," I'm actually beginning to believe what they say on the radio now," Csaba said to Eva. "That must be a good sign."

"I'm sure it is," she agreed.

CHAPTER EIGHT

▼

Sub Rosa

Robbie's meeting with Imre Mohacsi was quickly arranged. The Smallholders Party Deputy emerged from his inner office and waved cordially to Robbie while he ushered out an important constituent. Then he brought Robbie into his office and they sat down. Their chairs flanked a low table that was filled with magazines and newspapers from Szeged and its surrounding region.

The telephone intercom buzzed, and Mohacsi took the phone. "Sorry," he said to Robbie. "Got to take this one. The party whip is calling." Then he launched into a rapid conversation in colloquial parliamentary Hungarian, as coffee was brought in by an aide. Robbie glanced around the office.

It was not so very different from his own Congressman's Capitol Hill office back in Washington. Here and there were autographed pictures of Hungarian government and sports figures. There were agricultural awards and pictures of Mohacsi's family. Robbie was intrigued to notice a framed citation from the World Federation of Hungarian Freedom Fighters. It was prominently displayed and cited Mohacsi by name.

That gave Robbie the opening he sought. When Mohacsi finished his call, Robbie tentatively began his probes. He pointed to the Freedom Fighter document and asked Mohacsi about it. The Deputy smiled with some pride. "Yes, several years ago, we had a little ceremony. The visitors gave me this certificate. I am proud to be able to display it here."

"What was it like in those days?"

"We were exhilarated, scared, sometimes cold and always hungry. Some people, by the way, thought that you Americans were coming to help us. I never believed it. If there had been any such possibility, it disappeared with the Suez crisis."

Robbie was curious to know how the armed resistance had begun. How had the word spread?

"It was like a live wire of electric current. Everyone was fed up with the way that things were going, and nobody wanted to return to Stalinism. We all had our stories of injustice and tyranny. And we hated the Russians. This was our way of protesting. When the chance came, we took it. As to why I ended up at the resistance unit with Magassy and the others, he and I had been friends earlier. I helped him get the arms from the United Lamp Factory at the beginning."

"Did you know the other people there?"

"At first, aside from Janos and Karoly, not a soul. As the days passed we all bonded of course—I think that's the right term—but the truth is, people came and went. Rumors spread like wildfire. We foraged for supplies. And we went out and fought the tanks. That was our specialty, as it turned out."

Robbie was fascinated. "Did you get a tank yourself?"

"Actually, we always worked in teams, distracting the gunners, dodging alongside and throwing the Molotov cocktails. To answer your question, yes, we got several Russian tanks."

"Who helped you?"

"Different people at different times. We were all kids, you understand. The first battle was on the 25th, I think. Janos Magassy, Pista and I darted out and got our first tank. Then Magassy, Karoly and me. Eva helped too.

The third time, I don't know if we got a tank or not. It seemed to go off its tracks as it went around the corner. I'm not sure. We heard an explosion a few minutes later, so my guess always was that another group in the next block had finished them off. That sometimes happened."

"One of our problems was the lack of direct communications with other groups. We sure could have used some walkie-talkies, but either they weren't Soviet equipment or we didn't capture any. Even if we had, I don't think anybody could have changed the preset frequencies. Communications were a real problem, all of the time."

"Sounds to me," Robbie said, "like you could have used fax machines and cellular phones!"

Mohacsi smiled. "They would have helped the comunications a lot. But we needed food, help and ammunition even more." He thought for a moment. "But I've heard it said that with photographs and television cameras, what we did became known throughout the world very quickly. It was the first television revolution. Now we are used to seeing timely news, news as it happens. But this was the first time."

"Yes," Robbie agreed. "That's why it made such an impact, particularly in the West. The communists lost their credibility, and never quite recovered, I think. After that they still had the power, but no longer the moral force that they had seemed to have. Hungary was the opening wedge. Then came other rebellions, the writings of Solzhenitsyn, the Solidarity movement in Poland, an entire epic of fighting for freedom. But Hungary in 1956 set the first example." He was pensive for a moment. "What happened when the Russians reinvaded on the 4th?"

"That was the saddest time. Istvan and I went out with two kids, Laszlo and Magda. I never knew their last names. They were blasted by Russian semiautomatic fire. They got Karoly too, poor Karoly with his gimpy leg. Istvan and I took out at least a squad of the bastards. Then Csaba and I avenged them. We came at three tanks in an enfilade attack and blew the bastards up with Molotov cocktails. Even Attila 'the lawyer' joined the attack!"

Even now, he savored the memory.

"Was Magassy your leader?"

"Sure. He was a year or two older, had a good tactical sense, and had supplied the weapons. He knew everybody, and we all liked him."

Robbie mentioned the memorial that Magassy had been planning. "Yes, he mentioned that to me over the phone. We had kept in contact in recent years, you know. I had even seen him in my parliamentary trips to Washington a few times. I got to go first as a member of the token opposition, and then as a member of the majority. Janos didn't seem to change much over the years. Always that determination and sense of mission."

"I gather he wanted to see the other survivors from your group."

"Yes. The idea was to interest us all in the memorial. He may even have wanted to go farther than that, and try to reconstruct actual faces, like your Iwo Jima Memorial in Washington. That intrigued me. Anyway, he called. Then I was in touch with Attila Nemzeti and Istvan Szepvaros. I thought that would have been pleasant for Janos, to see them both once again at the reception. But he was killed first."

"That's what puzzles us. He was of course a prominent man, and it's hard to believe that the motive was robbery."

"Nobody believes that. What can I do to help?"

Robbie decided to trust the man, at least for now. He was the sort of man, gruff and friendly, that one would trust. He showed Mohacsi the newspaper clipping that Magassy had brought to the Embassy. Mohacsi read through it silently.

Robbie let him do so. "Magassy didn't use the last names, except for Eva Molnar."

"Yes. He was kind of sweet on Eva. Actually we all were. She was a captivating young woman who belonged in a different Hungary, not a wartorn hellhole. Why did he use her full name? Hard to say. Let's see. The article was written in 1978. Things had changed here then, and of course Kadar wanted the Crown of St. Stephen back. My guess is that Janos knew either that Eva was dead, or that she had served whatever sentence had been imposed on her. Either way, they couldn't hurt her anymore. Who knows? Perhaps giving her name was even a kind of protection."

"The other names seem obvious now, after the reception," Robbie said, like a lawyer in court nailing down proofs for the jury. "You are Imre of course, and Attila must be Attila Nemzeti. Istvan is Istvan Szepvaros." Mohacsi nodded his agreement. "You also mentioned a Csaba. What happened to him?"

"Yes, Csaba Kovacs. Eva's lover. They were always together. What happened to him, I don't know. He left before I did, and I never saw him again. Good fellow, dependable. I liked him. Solid. A good fighter."

Mohacsi looked at Magassy's article again, then seemed to focus on it more closely. Had he noticed something that Robbie missed? "May I make a copy of this?" "Of course."

Mohacsi was searching the past. Not that it makes any difference now, but I'm going to try to recall those days with the help of this article. I'm not sure that Janos got everything quite right. For example, he has Attila Nemzeti coming and going at odd times, returning after I left. I could swear that I saw him return before I left. It probably doesn't make any difference, but it's better to be accurate."

He rubbed his chin. "Like the others, and at Magassy's express order—so I guess you could say in that sense he was in command—I went out looking for ammunition. All I got was a second wound in the arm that put me out of commission. So I never made it back to the others. At that point, I think that just Attila Nemzeti, Eva Molnar and Janos himself were left from our combat group. I never heard what happened to the others then. Maybe we'll never hear the full story for sure."

A buzzer rang. It was time for a floor vote, and Mohacsi had to leave. He thanked Robbie for coming. Their meeting was not really ended. The unstated premise was that they would continue their conversation later. Robbie hoped that Mohacsi would be an ally as his researches continued. He would hate to have him as an enemy.

He thought about 1956 as he walked a few blocks to Marko Street. It had been the most feared address in Budapest. It still housed a prison complex and criminal prosecution offices.

*   *   *

The office bustled with activity. Scruffy and forbidding on the exterior, it was a busy place, and its corridors could not mask the sweat of fear. This was the main prosecution center for Budapest. Robbie's contact, an urbane lawyer named Jozsef Munkas, told him since the end of communism prosecutors were now responsible to the Parliament, not to the executive branch.

Murder of an important foreigner was enough of a rarity for the city's top criminal investigator, Inspector Imre Racz, to have been assigned to head the Magassy investigation by his chief. Robbie shook hands with Racz and sized him up quickly.

Inspector Racz, a late thirtyish professional, dark and solidly built, greeted Robbie with a reserved, not unfriendly welcome. Racz was considered a comer in police circles, and had had a few months of training with the F.B.I. in detection methods.

The point was to show a new type of policeman to the West, one who was totally professional and unconnected with the political repression of the past. Racz in turn saw Robbie's visit as a means of repaying the favor of his American seminar and extending his American connections. They sipped hot strong coffee and reviewed the case.

"Ordinarily, we'd meet in my office on *Deak ter* (Deak Square)," he began. "But things are as usual rather frantic over there now."

"Deak Square?" Robbie wondered aloud. That was central headquarters for police investigations. "I wondered about that when I saw your preliminary report. I thought you might be from the Third District, where Magassy was killed."

Racz grinned. "No mystery to that They have the crucial responsibility of securing the murder scene. But investigating a murder is a headquarters responsibility." That made sense. He didn't have to add that as time went on, and the case was developed, he would also work closely with the prosecutor. Might as well start now, with Robbie's visit.

Racz readily admitted that the case had puzzling aspects. He was willing to share what he knew, and was intrigued by Robbie's interest. He understood that Magassy Janos had been a prominent American citizen. "Please extend my personal condolences, and those of my chief, to Mrs. Magassy and the family. The murderer will be caught. Please tell them that."

Inspector Racz was checking what was known of Magassy's movements since his arrival in Hungary, and investigative teams were retracing his steps as they came to light. This was the essential grunt work of police methodology, interviewing and reinterviewing people who saw or might have seen the victim, step by step, day by day, hour by hour.

Robbie asked about Magassy's phone calls. He had had several during his hotel stay. One was to Deputy Imre Mohacsi. Magassy had received a call from a public phone in Gyula, a small city in Eastern Hungary near the Romanian border. There was also a call to the Australian Embassy, which had been returned, and one to the American Embassy, which had not been. The night he died, someone had called from a public phone in Budapest.

"Yes," Robbie said. "He came to our Embassy over a weekend and left a package for me. We were to have met following his return from a visit to Sarospatak the following week." Robbie mentioned Magassy's project to raise funds and build a memorial to the 1956 Freedom Fighters, a fact that Racz put down in his little notebook, without comment.

Robbie asked about the sabre.

"Ah yes, that was an odd bit of business. Of course there were no fingerprints. Wiped clean."

Robbie said he had seen the photograph of the murder weapon. "It didn't look like a very antique sabre to me."

"You are quite right. It is a modern copy of a cavalry sabre of the last century. Something to sell to the tourists."

"What time did Magassy die?"

"It was about midnight. A policeman found him in an alley about six o'clock in the morning. The body was cool to the touch, and *rigor mortis* had begun. It was a mess. Blood everywhere. The saber slash to the neck almost severed half of it. The mortician did a heroic job, frankly, sewing enough of him together to send a presentable body back for burial."

"Was there just one wound?"

"No. There were several preliminary slashes on Magassy's forearms, through his coat. Evidently he had thrust his arms forward to block the sabre twice before being knocked down for the fatal blow. Horrible business. The patrolman who discovered the body said it was the most vicious crime he had ever seen."

"Do you have a theory of the case yet?"

"Not really." Inspector Racz frowned a bit. "We assume that the assailant was someone that Magassy actually knew. Otherwise, why would he be in such a lonely part of Obuda?" He coughed. "The usual, ahem, tourist lures are elsewhere in the city."

"Was the attack premeditated?"

"That is probably the key to the puzzle. If the murderer had intended to meet Magassy and kill him, why do it with this rather awkward weapon? No. I'll bet money that the murderer met with Magassy not originally intending to kill him, and did so as an act of desperation. That's what this odd weapon tells me."

"What you are saying is that Magassy probably had the sabre with him. Either he had bought it, or had just been given it before he was killed, perhaps by the killer himself."

"Exactly. Anybody setting out to kill him would never have used this weapon. A handgun would have been more the trick, and heaven knows, there are enough of them in Budapest now."

"So the killer had to use what there was on hand."

"Precisely."

Inspector Racz promised to stay in touch with Robbie as developments warranted. It was useful to be able to do so without the usual formal back and forth, due to Robbie's diplomatic status. He supposed that it would be harder talking with the Australian Embassy, to run down those telephone calls, due to the need to get permission through the Foreign Ministry and all that.

"Oh, I don't think you will have any trouble doing that. None at all," Robbie said as their meeting ended.

*   *   *

Charles Lauricette had arranged the Goulash and Touring Club's excursion carefully. It was a longer drive than usual, and so they had decided to spend the day in the region, and not try to drive back to Budapest that afternoon. Instead they would have their dinner in the countryside.

Then Ferenc Esztergondos invited the dozen visitors to be his guests for dinner in Sarospatak. It would be a pleasure to treat them to a real Hungarian provincial experience, he said. They would understand the region even better if they were free from time constraints. They accepted his offer.

First they drove to Tokaj, in three cars. The first included Alexander and Julie Kovatch and their ambassadorial colleagues Eduardo and Elena Dos Campos. The party included Charles and Marie Lauricette, Eleni Papadopoulos from the Greek Embassy, Romanian Consul Iliu Monescu, and Jorge and Ana Angelos from the Brazilian Embassy. Robbie Cutler and USIS Officer Arpad Novotny from the American Embassy completed the group.

This was the world famous Hungarian wine region, with *Tokay* for centuries a serious rival to the finest *Sauternes* or German *Trockenbeerenauslese* as the world's best sweet white wine. It had a serious claim to being the original wine to be processed in the modern way, with "noble rot," or botrytis attacking the grapes one by one in the fall, reducing the liquid in the grape and producing concentrated golden sugar. For centuries court alchemists had conducted experiments trying to extract the "liquid gold" that the wine was literally supposed to contain.

Robbie was struck by the area. It reminded him of Sauternes in the Bordeaux region. The hilly vineyards had good drainage and fine exposure to sunlight. Beyond that, the presence of two rivers, the Bodrog and the Tisza, accounted for the misty autumn weather that shriveled the grapes, causing the *pourriture noble*, or noble rot. That was exactly the situation in Sauternes, with the Garonne and the Ciron, and in Germany with the Mosel and the Rhine.

Somehow, it was discovered here that the process not only resulted in concentrated sweetness, but in a transformed wine of great unctuous richness. Nothing need be added by man except the patience to harvest the grapes and then age them properly. Robbie remembered that at Chateau D'Yquem, many separate daily harvests of individual grapes were held, a process that could take several weeks.

They drove along the little Bodrog River towards Tokaj. Marie Lauricette was enchanted to see large stork nests on the roofs of houses, "just like in Alsace," in the village of Bodrogkeresztur where they stopped for coffee. The waiter told them that the storks always returned, year after year, to precisely the same houses. When new houses were built in the town, for many years the storks would not go near them. They preferred their former homes for their nesting, even though the new ones by law in this protected site were identical to the ones they had replaced!

Charles had arranged a visit and tasting at a property that was now owned by a French wine investment firm. The visitors got out of their cars, stretched a bit, and settled into the conference room for a briefing before the tasting began. There was a video in French and English for the visitors, and it was not designed to sugarcoat the region's problems.

As with other portions of the Hungarian economy, Tokaj had been badly run during the communist period. Now the region was on the mend. The state farm that had enjoyed a monopoly for buying even privately produced grapes during communist days had sold off some property to foreign investors, and handed back more than half of its total acreage to the original private owners. With little reinvestment during the communist period, the equipment now in use in both private hands and cooperative property was sadly in need of modernization or replacement.

In the Warsaw Pact days, quantity was needed, and quality was disregarded. Little attention had been paid to proper methods of agriculture, including preserving the soil and guarding against plant diseases. There was overproduction, and many plants now needed replacement. Those that could be saved needed new wiring of their vines, a tedious job.

Many of the region's famous vineyards were in fact rather rundown. There was now a confusing hodgepodge of small private producers which owned some 80% of the total acreage in cultivation. They emphasized manual labor for their returns. The former state farm still had a small holding. Of the remaining 1000 hectares or 2500 acres under production, about half were farmed by a farmers' cooperative, and the remaining half were owned by foreign investors, like the one the diplomats were now visiting. These were potentially among the best holdings.

Investment and hard work were clearly needed, if Tokaj hoped to regain its former prestige and markets. "We had something of the same problem with Sauternes for a while," Lauricette volunteered. "But with us, the problem was selling a sweet dessert wine to people who wanted instead dry wines and who were preoccupied by diets. That's still a problem. Many people think the great days of sweet wines will always be in the nineteenth century, when nobody counted their calories. That battle isn't over yet, but more and more people are beginning to value our wines. As that happens, the market for Tokay should pick up as well."

Their host poured each a glass of Tokay, and went over the process of its production and fermentation. Unlike other sweet wines, Tokay was produced by adding buckets of rich wine *must* or concentrate to the fermenting wine, to make it ever richer. This was called *puttonyos* or "buckets," for the number added. Usually five was the maximum, and that would be shown on the label.

The knowledgeable tourist who asked for a glass of *"ot puttonyos"* or "five bucket" Tokay wine at the end of his meal in Budapest would receive a real treat as well as respect from the wine steward. That was the richest Tokay wine usually available.

"But the finest and rarest Tokaj is called *Eszencia*," their guide said. "There is no weighted pressing of the grapes at all. Just the juice that comes from the weight of the grapes themselves is used. It is so rich that people used to think that it could revive the very sick back to life. Have a taste."

Even Lauricette had to admit that this wine was excellent. It had sweetness but was not cloying. The wine had "legs," running down the inside of the glass, usually a sign of breed and quality to come. It showed promise. It also seemed to have, to Robbie's taste, something else, that he had not tasted at Sauternes, a kind of fire beyond the sweetness. This part of the taste was not refined or elegant, but it showed character. It seemed to him an essential part of the wine. Something Magyar.

The diplomats spent part of the morning walking through the hillside property. It was a fine June day, not too hot, and the growing season was well underway. The budding had been successful, and row upon row of grapestock stood with its promise of grapes and wine for the harvest, months away.

Robbie walked along the rows with Arpad Novotny. Hungarian on his mother's side, Novotny was pleased to see that some attempts were being made to restore the Tokaj vineyards.

"But what is the reason for those rosebushes at the end of each row, I wonder?"

Robbie's Bordeaux experiences supplied the answer. "They say that plant diseases that attack vineyards are very similar to those that attack rosebushes. If there was a problem, it would show up first on the rosebushes. So it is sort of a warning system. Just like canaries in mines used to be for miners, to warn them of oxygen loss or gases."

Arpad nodded. Then he turned to Monescu. "Do you have vineyards like this in Romania?"

"We have good, everyday wines, but none that are world famous. And I'm glad that these are being looked after at last. I used to wonder a few years ago what the fuss was all about over Tokay wine. It didn't taste all that special. More like mediocre sherry. What we just tasted, however, was quite different. That gives hope for the future."

Arpad said maliciously, "For a Romanian, you're quite open minded."

"It's past time for Romanians and Hungarians to put aside their differences. It's important for us to get along. That's why I said 'hope for the future.' Perhaps with renewed pride and some prosperity, this region will stop being a tinderbox."

Robbie decided that he liked Monescu. Perhaps the younger generation could help build a saner future for the region after all. He thought about confiding in Monescu and decided to do so at an appropriate moment. They walked together to the waiting cars, which would take them to Sarospatak.

It was not possible to say so early what the quality of this vintage would ultimately be. But they would all remember their visit, and more than a few would later buy several bottles of this vintage and save them, the bottles to emerge with the tale of the visit for many years in the future, long after they had left Hungary or perhaps even retired.

*   *   *

The drive to Sarospatak was short, and Ferenc Esztergondos, accompanied by the Mayor and a reporter, welcomed them at his estate. There was also a television newscaster. It would make a good local television story. All had luncheon at the estate.

By common consent Arpad Novotny, as a USIS professional, took over. He made a few flattering on camera comments in Hungarian about the region and their visit to Tokaj, mentioned the fact that the group included the Ambassadors of Australia and Spain, and said that they were looking forward to seeing the sights of Sarospatak.

The city's associations with a national hero, Lajos Kossuth, were mentioned. So was the famous Protestant College, a secondary school founded in the sixteenth century with a national reputation for excellence. "Our Eton or Phillips Exeter," Esztergondos interjected proudly.

But the main sight that awaited them that afternoon was the ancient Rakoczi Castle, the finest early castle remaining in Hungary, its medieval and Renaissance features blending as the ease of the later period masked somewhat the heavy defenses of the earlier one. It had been the seat of the princely Rakoczi family, and as such a rallying point for Hungarian legitimists for centuries against Austrian Hapsburg domination.

Here Prince Ferenc Rakoczi had held a national assembly in the Knights Hall in the early eighteenth century. And here in a vaulted corner room a half century earlier a group of Hungarian noblemen, the Wesselenyi conspiracy, had held a famous meeting to plot against the Hapsburgs. The castle guide with great pride pointed to the ceiling of the vaulted chamber. There was a painted rose, and so it was said that the conspirators were "*sub rosa,*" or "under the rose," and what they would have to say would remain secret.

Their anti Hapsburg conspiracy had ultimately been betrayed, despite the pledge of secrecy. Robbie reflected that betrayal, like loyalty, was an old Hungarian custom, the vice ever seeking to sully the national virtue. Ferenc Wesselenyi and his betrayer, Imre Nagy and Janos Kadar, Janos Magassy and his brave group of Freedom Fighters of Pest and, possibly, a secret police informant? But the story of the vaulted chamber was a lovely legend. As it was being told, Robbie thought that he saw Julie Kovatch smiling in his direction. He couldn't be quite sure.

Esztergondos had planned a rustic dinner at a scenic Sarospatak tavern. He said that he thought they would enjoy "getting out of Budapest" and enjoying some local color. That ingredient was supplied by a spirited gypsy orchestra, with violin players so agile that it was hard to believe they could play so skillfully and so fast.

The entire party took a large wooden table in its own alcove. Robbie and Eleni Papadopoulos sat near Eduardo and Elena Dos Campos and Jorge and Ana Angelos. The other members of the party, at the same table, could only be shouted at when the music was at its loudest. But Robbie noticed Ambassador Kovatch deep in conversation in rapid Hungarian with their host.

"We're making a habit of this," the Greek Consul said.

"A habit of what?"

"Thirteen at dinner once again!"

"Well, It hasn't brought us bad luck so far."

Esztergondos insisted on ordering for them. They began with wine and cups of *gulyas*, real *gulyas*, a soup rather than a stew, containing chunks of pork or beef, peppers, onions and sour cream, with lots of sweet paprika.

"What you call goulash isn't our *gulyas* at all," Esztergondos insisted. "It's a stew. We'd call that *porkolt*."

Next came *fatanyeros*, a Transylvanian mixed grill, with chops and beef and meaty "royal" bacon. It was not fare for the fainthearted. The music continued to fill the tavern's dining hall, which was colorfully decorated with carved and painted designs in wood sconces throughout the room. Something like Pennsylvania Dutch country, but with local meaning and no hex signs, Robbie surmised. At least none that he could read.

At dessert, an epic *Somloi galuska,* a Hungarian version of English trifle with alternating layers of cake, crushed fruit and whipped cream, was served with strong coffee and glasses of fiery apricot brandy. The music resumed in a minor mode and the stuffed dinner guests listened to it. Their host traced the lyrics of regional songs for them.

He struck up a conversation with Eduardo Dos Campos and Jorge Angelos, who had both seemed lost in the music. "This doesn't resemble the Portuguese *fados* at all," Dos Campos said. "It's very different but I like it just as much." Jorge agreed.

There were songs from the Rakoczi uprising. "You probably only know of them through Berlioz's 'Rakoczi March' from *The Damnation Of*

Faust," Esztergondos suggested. There were songs from the village, songs of spinning, of gallantry, love and betrayal. The creative urge that had moved Kodaly and Bartok to save their country's folksongs was very understandable in this context. Robbie doubted that there was a CD in existence that could capture the improvisations they were hearing tonight.

"Yes, there is," Arpad Novotny said. "Marta Sebestyen, and the *'Muzsikas'* group. You may remember her from the movie, *The English Patient*. She did that haunting background music. And her group has carried on the tradition of saving folksongs. They're first rate."

As the music ended Robbie found himself at the other end of the table, talking with Ambassador Kovatch and Elena Dos Campos.

"This must be very familiar music for you, Alexander," Elena was saying.

"Not really. I left Hungary so young that pleasant music isn't one of my memories. Certainly not music this fine."

"You left in 1956, I suppose," she asked.

"Yes. Just afterwards. There didn't seem to be anything left here, any real reason to stay.

"Were you a Freedom Fighter then?"

"No. And I regret it. I had relatives that were, but they are all gone now. I don't even think that I have any family left here. This is like a foreign country to me, but an oddly familiar one. My home is Australia, not Hungary. I suppose you feel that way about England," he said to Robbie.

"A bit. But I feel closer to France than to England actually." A lot closer when, as now, Sylvie Marceau came to mind.

Kovatch asked Robbie about the Magassy case. "Any new developments there, to your knowledge?"

"Well, the police don't consider it a robbery case. Surely it was murder. They haven't come down yet with a theory on whether it was premeditated or not. It may well not have been."

"So, the murder just wasn't planned. It took place because of something that happened between Magassy and his murderer?"

"Something like that, yes. I talked with the police because he was our citizen, and there's lots of interest back home." Might as well establish that. "I'm sure they will want permission to talk with you too, Ambassador Kovatch, as one of the last persons to see Magassy.

"I'm sure of it. No problem, as you Americans say."

Elena asked Kovatch, "What do you think of our host?"

"He's an odd bird, hard to place. He poses as some sort of socialist aristocrat. He'd like us to think of him as a sort of Hungarian liberal democrat with noblesse oblige, but I have trouble with that picture. All things considered I'd rather be on his good side. He's no Adlai Stevenson, that's for sure."

"Why do you say that?"

"He has too much to hide. I wonder if we will ever know what is really on his mind."

Or on yours for that matter, Robbie thought to himself.

*   *   *

They returned late to Budapest. Some last minute thought had been given to staying over, but they had decided not to do so. Sunday was a full day, and the car situation made scrambled plans hard to arrange. Robbie rather preferred the idea of keeping his ritual Budapest Sunday. He enjoyed the leisurely dinner, the walk around Castle Hill, and the service at the Coronation Church. Perhaps he could spend an hour poking around the antique shops.

Minouette roused herself on his return and greeted him sleepily. He checked her dishes and put down some fresh water, not from the tap. Then he checked the telephone. No messages.

There was, however, one short FAX. It was in code. So Uncle Seth was getting back to him quickly. The return number was not Uncle Seth's home FAX number. It couldn't be, of course. He would still be on his trip. Yes, the sender area code was Washington. Uncle Seth must have sent it from his hotel.

Robbie retrieved his Montaigne and checked the short message according to their code. It didn't take long.

"Friends confirm Ambassador brother missing freedom fighter." That was all.

Robbie thought carefully for a moment.

So that was it. Csaba, or rather Csaba Kovacs, and Alexander Kovatch, surely once Sandor Kovacs, had been brothers.

That hadn't been self evident. Kovacs was one of the most common surnames in Hungarian, like the name Smith in English. As a matter of fact, *"kovacs"* even meant smith! It was surely the intelligence community, which was responsible in official Washington for biographic information on foreign officials, that had established the relationship. Uncle Seth had pulled in another old favor. Ambassador Horton would be pleased.

That relationship gave his diplomatic colleague a powerful motive for detection. It did not however explain why he was hiding his identity. There was no reason to keep that a secret, or was there? Robbie wondered what else Kovatch might be up to, *sub rosa*.

* * * * * * * * * *

The Seventh Day—October 29, 1956

They talked together for some time after Imre Nagy's broadcast. Was the Revolution over? Had they really won?

"It's up to each one of you," Janos had said. "I think—no, I hope—that the fighting is all over. But who can be really sure? Anyone who wants to leave can do so now, honorably. Meanwhile, I think we should use whatever breathing space we've got to make this place more defensible."

He paused. "Also, anybody who wants to go home for a while to check on their families should do so right now. He didn't have to add that there might not be another chance later.

Nobody opted out. But Janos had touched on a sore point. What bothered everyone was that nobody knew what had happened to their families. It was hard enough to figure out what was going on just a few blocks away.

How far had the fighting extended in Budapest? Were the bridges over the Danube still in operation, or had they been blown up? Was there only armed resistance here in Budapest, or had the fighting spread throughout Hungary, as some new radio stations were reporting?

Did the West even understand what was going on? After their promises, what would their reaction be now?

Laszlo said he would try to find out what was going on. He'd go home in the countryside, check on things and return in a day or so. That was fine. He was a serious young man and, as Imre pointed out, hadn't seen any fighting yet.

"That's what you think!" Magda blurted out. "We were the last ones left, Laszlo, Jozsef and me, when Red found us. Everyone else in our other group had been killed. I bet Laszlo has shot more Russians than you have!"

The dark-haired girl was quivering with indignation. Csaba thought that at her age, maybe 13, Magda should have been talking about movies and boys, not insurrection and killing. Looking closer, past the girl's red eyes and agitated manner, one could see the beginnings of womanhood.

What a place to grow up, Csaba thought.

Csaba had a talk with Janos after the Nagy radio broadcast. It did look like there would be at least a lull in the fighting. It might even stop entirely. The Government was trying to sort things out, and was now clearly on their side. This was an important new phase of the struggle, a consolidation.

Csaba wanted to see his family, which was normal enough. He wanted to tell them about Eva. For her, home was a Hungarian village across the border in the Transylvanian region of Romania. She couldn't go home. Csaba wouldn't let her risk that. But he did want to see his own family and reestablish contact. That was understandable. Csaba wouldn't be gone long, and Eva would be safe at Barat Street.

"Just bring us some food, Janos commanded. "1'll do my best," was Csaba's parting shot as he slowly vanished into the city. Eva walked with him as far as Ulloi Avenue. There they kissed goodbye, a lingering embrace in case it became the memory of how much they shared and how little they had.

Janos would send out the usual patrols that night. No use being taken by surprise. But now was the opportunity to make their Barat Street headquarters more defensible. They set about doing just that.

Their four-story corner building had storefronts on the ground floor, and apartments above that. Janos and the Friends had been operating out of a storefront, sleeping in a back room, which the absent owner had used for the same purpose. Now they found a vacant apartment on the fourth floor, which gave a good line of sight along the street and the intersection.

Perfect, Janos thought, for observation, and for rest during off-duty time. Janos, Red and Eva hauled bedding up to the apartment, which also had a working kitchen and wonder of wonders, a bathroom with shower.

Best of all from the defense standpoint, the staircase beside the apartment led directly to the rooftop. There they could hurl Molotov cocktails at any tank within their reach. They had just six left, and Janos assigned the firebrand Magda and Jozsef to make some more under Karoly's supervision, scrounging bottles where they could, and gasoline at Corvin Circle or a nearby gasoline station.

Weapons and ammunition were a problem. They had three submachine guns, and enough ammunition for a day or two. That was all. Perhaps he should have kept more from the United Lamp Factory after all. No matter. Janos assigned Imre and Attila to try to get some more, perhaps at the Corvin stronghold.

The storefront itself was a problem. Janos tried to think it through, weighing the options. Broken glass from the window would be a real hazard in case of fighting. So perhaps he should break the glass now, sweep up the shards, then pile up furniture and make a rough barricade of the storefront. That would make it more defensible, for a while anyway.

He thought it over again. After a few days of nice fall weather, now it was getting colder as well, sapping their energies. If the storefront glass was gone it would be much colder at nights. Some might get sick. That's all they needed!

Janos postponed his decision for a day or so. They could still hunt for bags to stuff with dirt, in case he later decided on the barricade option.

Meanwhile Csaba walked towards the Danube embankment. and looked over the river. This bridge was still intact. He would have to cross it to reach his family. What if he was then cut off from Eva? He hesitated, staring at the other side of the river for a long time. Then he turned back.

Late that afternoon, Csaba was back at Barat Street. "I couldn't get through," he said. "Too much action still possible, too many Russians. I don't know what is going on. Everyone is nervous as hell. There's a rumor that they may start blowing up the bridges, like the Nazis did. Most of the telephones don't work. There are burned out tanks just about everywhere. Nobody is working. This has spread all over the city at least."

He grinned "But I did find this." Csaba opened his ragged topcoat, and four loaves of bread fell out. By some miracle, the bakeries were open again. Also there were some canned goods, marked in Russian for export only from Hungary. Then from some deep inner pocket, with a theatrical flourish worthy of Harry Houdini, he produced two dressed chickens! "Tonight we feast!"

They all stared at the food in wonder.

"Where did you get all these canned vegetables?" Eva wanted to know, picking up a can. None of them had ever seen these canned goods before, and yet it was all Hungarian produce, fruits and vegetables They looked to be of fine quality.

"I found them at food storage depots," Csaba explained. "With the cease-fire, their managers suddenly turned patriotic. Usually these Hungarian goods are never seen here at all. They just go to our Soviet comrades."

"That's just what Gero said they were NOT doing," Eva exploded. "They've been feeding the Russians with our own Hungarian food, while our people have gone without!"

Csaba laughed. "It's time we fed our own people first. That's why I liberated these chickens too. I found them in a state poultry shop whose manager is now for the Revolution."

"Well, next time you are liberating something, don't forget the lard and paprika!"

Eva found some in their empty fourth-floor apartment kitchen. The stove burned wood or coal, and fortunately the vent through the wall worked. They were lucky. It might after all have been one of those "improved" smelly gas stoves that some of the newer apartments had.

It was nice to cook a meal, Eva thought. Nice to have a normal thing to do.

Sent out to find what they could, Karoly and Magda returned in an hour with wine and beer. Everyone smiled in anticipation. For a long time afterwards the Friends of Barat Street would remember their feast on the night of Monday, October 29th.

CHAPTER NINE

▼

NIGHTMARES

Robbie glanced around the bank's private reception room. The opulence of the room made him uneasy, all the more so since it was an understated opulence. This setting, he supposed, would be reassuring to wealthy clients. It had the opposite effect on Robbie. He was not used to wealth. It intimidated him.

He was announced precisely on time for the appointment, and Istvan Szepvaros came to the door of his private office to wave him in. Coffee was a good idea at that time of the morning, and it was soundlessly provided. The two men were then left alone.

Robbie had rehearsed a number of scenarios for this meeting. None had seemed quite right. He had even boned up on banking and economic issues with Embassy Economic and Commercial Officer Julia Broadbent before the meeting. Then he realized that Szepvaros would understand that he would not be a usual contact for a political officer. It would be artificial to try, and the effort would perhaps just invite suspicion. Odd, he had felt so at ease with Mohacsi. What was the problem here?

Best to play it straight, he decided.

"Thank you for seeing me, Mr. Szepvaros. I was interested in your remarks at the reception a while back. We were speaking of John Magassy and his plans for a Freedom Fighters Memorial."

"Yes. We were all shocked about Janos's death. Have the police made any progress in finding the murderer?"

"I'm told the case is under active investigation. They have their theories."

"Had you talked with him, Mr. Cutler?"

"I'm afraid not. He had stopped by the Embassy and left me a note, and some materials to study regarding his plans for the memorial. We were to have met after his return to Budapest from the countryside."

Szepvaros seemed to mull this over for a moment as he leaned over the ebony table to put fresh cream in his coffee. Robbie did the same and sipped the coffee. It was delicious, and he said so.

"A Hungarian custom. Coffee, some brandy, some chocolates. Even in the dark communist days these items were available here. Very inferior quality then, of course."

Robbie asked his opinion of Magassy's planned memorial.

"As I may have said at the reception, I think it is a fine idea. Such things should be remembered. What better way to do it than with a realistic memorial at exactly the spot where resistance fighting took place?"

"You spoke of help with the underwriting for the project."

"Did I? Well, I'll stand by that. I cannot imagine that such a project would be very expensive. Low six figures at most. Dollars, I mean. Marks, possibly. There must be Hungarians from all over the world who would want to contribute, and that should be encouraged."

Robbie said that he was thinking of writing to the Hungarian Freedom Fighters Association that Magassy had headed in the United States to see if they would be interested in helping advance the project. "I don't know what their financial picture is, but they must have a fundraising capability under American law, tax exemption and all that. It might be useful if I could tell them of your professional help in getting underway here."

Szepvaros nodded his agreement. "For planning purposes, why not? I think the undertaking should be chartered under Hungarian law. That way we would be able to raise funds, and meet expenses, most of which would probably accrue here anyway. I know about those legalities."

He smiled. "It provides rather a Hollywood ending, as a matter of fact. Imagine forming a corporation in Hungary, a capitalist concept if there ever was one, in order to process charitable contributions for a memorial to those who tried to overthrow the communist regime!"

Robbie relaxed. "I'm writing to Mrs. Magassy as well. She will, I think, also be very pleased to learn of your interest in helping realize her husband's project. She will surely then pave the way with the Freedom Fighters Federation."

Szepvaros smirked. "Yes. Also, this project will be a sufficient excuse for them to have meetings. There is nothing we Hungarians like better than to have meetings. The more disputatious, the better, I'm afraid. You had better sit in on ours, to lend an atmosphere of calm. We'd value your help. I'm sure that Mohacsi and Nemzeti would want to be involved."

He paused, stirring his coffee. "Perhaps Ambassador Kovatch as well. He also seemed enthusiastic about the idea."

Robbie smiled in agreement. He cast around for something to say, to bridge over to what he had in mind.

The silence was broken by Szepvaros. "There were two other members of our group, Csaba Kovacs and Eva Molnar. I sometimes wonder what happened to them."

Robbie made no reply. He opened his briefcase and gave a document to Szepvaros. "Perhaps this will help. It is an article that Magassy wrote about your group nearly twenty years ago. I thought you might like to have a copy."

Szepvaros read it with interest. "Yes, that brings back those days. What bravery. For a while we thought we were immortal. I'm sure that you've figured out who these people actually were. Janos only mentioned first names in the article, except for Eva. Well, that was a different time when he wrote the article."

Robbie let him muse about the article for a while. "Did you see much fighting yourself?"

"Yes, enough to last a lifetime. The vengeance was swift and it was horrible. I mean what we took out on the Secret Police, the *AVH*. You've probably seen the recent symposium results on what happened then. They say that the Russians were prepared for a while to back off, but the Chinese convinced them to stand firm, citing what was done to the *AVH* in Republic Square. There may be something to that. More coffee?" He read silently.

Robbie declined. "Is Magassy's account an accurate one?"

"So far as I can judge, it is. He does telescope things a great deal. He is writing mainly about the final moments, after all. Before his narrative begins, there were comings and goings also. And he probably should have said something more about those six who died. What he does set down seems accurate."

He paused and focussed his memory. "I did leave after Nemzeti, at Magassy's express direction. But soon the enclave was cut off, or so it seemed. It was not possible to find supplies, and suicide has never appealed to me."

"Did you ever see any of the group again, at that time, I mean?"

"I thought I saw Csaba Kovacs, but I could have been mistaken. I was in hiding, and he seemed to have been taken into custody."

"Then you are not sure what happened to him?"

"No. And I've wondered about Eva too, how she survived imprisonment. Odd that Magassy gives her whole name. He must have thought she was safe from further harm, I suppose."

Robbie let that pass. "You mentioned Hollywood. I suppose all this would make a good film."

"I doubt it. Well, such a film would probably be an artistic success, done properly, but a financial disaster. People don't want much truth at the movies. They get uncomfortable."

"You are fond of films?"

"Very much so. I used to find them a good escape and an interesting reflection of culture. Just before the war, for example, was such a fine period for Hollywood. England too. So many films that became classics were made then. And that was in the teeth of what was going on around us, the uncertainty and the hard times.

"The songs were memorable. Everyone had the Depression and the threat of war, but yet there was Judy Garland singing 'Over The Rainbow.' It was quite remarkable. In Hungary, it was *'Szomoru Vasarnap,'* or 'Gloomy Sunday,' equally popular I might add. You never hear it anymore. Too bad. It is just the proper accompaniment for our national addiction to suicide."

Robbie added, "In France on the other hand it was *'Madame la Marquise,'* a delightful cabaret song about everything going to hell, told with wit and style."

"Yes, but with no hope. That suited the French of the period. You see why I like films, and songs too. They can tell you a lot."

The buzzer rang to announce the banker's next appointment. "This has been very interesting, Mr. Cutler. I'll look into these legal matters and call a little meeting of the four or five of us. You see, I enjoy holding meetings too. And thank you for giving me a copy of Janos's reflections. That was really most kind."

*   *   *

Lucille Cutler was never quite sure whether she should wake her husband up when his nightmares returned. But this was a particularly bad one, and he was shouting something that she could not understand. He sat up suddenly and then, turning himself around, struggled with the bedcovers. He nearly fell headfirst from the bed.

Lucille decided that he couldn't be any worse off awake. She held him close and, heart pounding, he regained consciousness.

"What on earth was it, Trip?"

Trip Cutler took a long moment to realize where he was, and that he had been dreaming. For a moment he understood, and then it all began to slip away.

"I don't know," he said miserably. "Sometimes I think I'm back in Budapest at the Legation. The Revolution is in full swing. People are coming to me for help, and I lock the door instead. I hear voices calling to me, and then the tanks roll into the Square."

"What an awful nightmare. You've had it before?"

"It seems familiar. Yes. There is a terrible sense of dread, as if I know what is going to happen next."

"What does happen?"

"In my dream, I never know. But the dream could be real."

"What do you mean?" She had asked, but she was afraid of his answer. She wanted to move, to go to the kitchen and make some coffee, to do something, anything, as the first rays of dawn streaked through the blinds, but she was nailed to the spot.

"Back then, when I was at the Legation, I was ordered by the Minister to lock the doors. We had taken in Cardinal Mindszenty, and others hoped we would take them as well. But we couldn't do it. We really couldn't. I understand that. Asylum is not an Embassy function." He paused and was silent.

She said nothing. Better to let him continue when he could.

"I went out one morning. It was the first time that I had left the Legation in days. Already there were lines of desperate people outside our door. They wanted food or help or medical supplies. Anything. We had nothing left to give. Some people started to disperse. Then I heard the tanks rumbling. There was panic. The people who had been waiting started to run across the square in front of the Legation."

He was silent for a long moment. She almost encouraged him to continue, but couldn't even decide if she wanted to hear what he was going to say next. What poured out was a far more personal version of the antiseptic story she had heard earlier, when the clipping had arrived from Robbie. Now the emotional dam seemed to burst.

"There was a young woman coming across the square. She was Hungarian and she was beautiful. I recognized her. She had called on me a few weeks earlier, asking about possibilities to come to the United States. She wanted to study fine arts. Now she looked tired and her hair was unkempt. It made little difference. I recognized her anyway. She personally called to me, and I recognized her voice. I turned towards her. She was the only person coming towards the Legation as the troops poured into the square. She called again, and again. Then she was cut off, and I couldn't see her anymore."

"How awful. But you couldn't have saved her, you know."

"I keep telling myself that, but that doesn't seem to help."

"What happened to her?"

"That's just it. I don't know. Prison, probably."

"It was that clipping that Robbie sent that set this off, wasn't it? Was that the girl? What was her name…Eva?"

"Yes. She was Eva Molnar."

"Look through your records in the morning, Trip. This is probably something that Robbie could look into and settle once and for all. Evalyn could help when she gets to Budapest. She sees things that Robbie does not, where people are involved. Now go back to sleep."

Chastened, he did so. But Lucille stayed awake through the early morning hours, reflecting on lost love and illusion, the problems of fighting a ghost, and most hurtful and irritating of all because it was so personal, the name of her own daughter.

*   *   *

Robbie settled in at his desk to tackle the afternoon's reading and report writing. The state of the Hungarian economy, always an Embassy favorite, was a draft report that he and Julia Broadbent were negotiating, to predictable arguments. She saw the report as her prerogative. He wanted to analyze the poltical overtones. What he had written was not entirely hopeful, and she was sure that his gloss would discourage investment, and become something of a self fulfilling prophecy. It became a circular argument, one that DCM Arnie Johnson would have to sort out before the report was sent to Washington.

There were rumors of a pending shakeup in the Socialist Party. There were always such rumors. Sometimes they were even based in fact. Robbie had spent too much time in Washington to report what might be somebody's disinformation. Here was a more interesting item in the press. Their host in Sarospatak, Ferenc Esztergondos, had given an interview that stressed building up grassroots support for his party, with credible, well financed candidates everywhere when elections were next held. That was worth noting. What was he up to?

That morning, after his return to the Embassy, Robbie had written again to Mrs. John Magassy, and to the Hungarian Freedom Fighters Federation. His letter to the Federation informed them that there was interest, from former members of Magassy's own group of Freedom Fighters, in continuing Magassy's plans for a suitable memorial. He offered to serve as a contact point for them at the Embassy, and asked whether the Federation had or would now take a position in favor of the project. Best to let it go at that, to give them the ball and see what happened.

His letter to Mrs. Magassy was circumspect. He expressed his condolences. Then he wrote that there was some thought of continuing her late husband's project for a Freedom Fighters Memorial. In that connection it would be helpful to know his list of contacts for his visit to Hungary, if she were aware of any. That might help in continuing the project.

Robbie wrote that he had met three other members of her husband's group, Imre Mohacsi, Istvan Szepvaros, and Attila Nemzeti. He then asked whether her husband had ever talked about the two other members of his group that were mentioned in his article, Csaba Kovacs and Eva

Molnar. If so, had he made any plans to see either of them during his trip? Might as well assume they were alive and see what turned up, if anything.

Luncheon at a nearby restaurant with Iliu Monescu from the Romanian Embassy was a welcome chance to compare notes. Robbie did that from time to time with other diplomats whose judgment he trusted. The Romanian Consul was charmed by the restaurant, which fit his slim wallet and voracious appetite. Just off Freedom Square, it was the restaurant of a well regarded culinary arts school. The food was good, hearty and plentiful, and sold for little more than the cost of the ingredients.

"There seems to be a better state of relations between your country and Budapest these days." Robbie began. "How is the treaty working out?"

"We think that it was the right thing to do, although not everybody agrees. It guaranteed the boundaries between Hungary and Romania, a very sore point in Hungary, for many Hungarians always regarded Transylvania as their territory. In my country, a number of people thought it bent over backwards to recognize the rights of ethnic Hungarians. When the treaty between Hungary and Romania was finally signed in September, 1996, it satisfied nobody. But it was exactly what was needed. Now we can look to the future, not to the past."

Robbie mulled that over. If true, this really was an epic event, settling one of the worst, constant sources of bitterness in this region of Europe. Transylvania, known only for its associations to Dracula at Hallowe'en in the United States, was regarded by Hungarians as part of their homeland. When the rest of Hungary had been gobbled up by the Hapsburgs and the Turks, for centuries only Hungarian Transylvania had remained independent. On the map, it was far to the east. But to many Hungarians it was their heartland, like Kansas for Americans.

"Is that where you are from?"

"No. I'm a city boy, from Bucharest."

"What is it like, being a Romanian diplomat in Hungary these days?"

"I have nothing to compare it to. But I find people friendly, if a little reserved. I'm too young to represent the past, after all."

"What did you make of our trip to Sarospatak last weekend?"

"I thoroughly enjoyed it. That Esztergondos is a man to watch, but I wouldn't trust him."

"Neither would I. By the way, Iliu, we didn't pick the next destination and responsible person to arrange it. I have an idea, and it's not that far from Romania. Would you mind organizing the next outing for our group? We should skip July and August. There will probably be too many tourists anyway. But perhaps at the very beginning of September we could plan a trip. I was thinking of Gyula."

"Yes, I know it. Fascinating place, very little known. If we are lucky, the outdoor theater festival in the old castle will still be going on. I'll check that out and get back to you."

"Iliu, one other thing, a personal matter." Robbie leaned towards Monescu and shared his wish to try to locate Eva Molnar. He gave Monescu a copy of John Magassy's article, and said that he wanted to try to locate her, if she were still living. She was said to have been from somewhere near Cluj (the Hungarian Kolozsvar). It would be valuable to contact her in connection with Magassy's projected memorial. Perhaps she wouldn't want to be disturbed. If Monescu could help locate her, discreetly of course, Robbie would want to talk with her about the plans for the memorial.

Monescu said that he would help. He gathered there was more to this than he was being told.

Robbie now had a further reason for his request. A letter from his sister Evalyn recounting her recent weekend stayover with their parents had given Robbie a more personal incentive for locating Eva Molnar, if she were still alive. Evalyn seemed convinced that the Molnar woman had been important to their father. He would want to know what had happened to her. Robbie determined to try to find out.

*   *   *

Istvan Szepvaros and his wife Maria greeted Ambassador and Mrs. Kovatch warmly. That was not feigned. They had been rather taken by the mismatched diplomatic couple at the reception at Parliament. "He is so driven, not a diplomat at all, and she is rather nice for a trophy wife," is the way Maria had put it. When the Australian Embassy had called for an appointment a week or so later, Szepvaros had suggested dinner instead. Pleased, Kovatch had accepted, and the date had been set with a minimum of back and forth.

There were several other couples invited, but there would of course also be the opportunity for a talk. There always was, in the dinner party dance card, Kovatch had learned. He sometimes missed the straightforward business dealings he was more used to in Australia. There, you could size up somebody at arms length and pretty fast, with plain speaking, a track record you could check, and a firm handshake. This was far more difficult. Along the way, as he had said more than once, he seemed to have become more Australian than Hungarian. But he was up to this game.

He'd better be. He looked across the room. There was Julie chatting amiably with other guests. She had given up looking for someone, that was clear. But she had been looking for someone. It was a hopeful expectation, not an obsession. Well, let her pursue her little interests while he looked into things. For now, the distraction could even prove helpful. There would be time enough to handle young Robbie Cutler later, if that needed doing.

The other guests included another couple from the bank, Deputy Imre Mohacsi and his wife Magda, and the Spanish Ambassador and Mrs. Dos Campos. Julie thought them a tiresome lot of persons from Alex's generation. Were the next twenty years going to be passed in terminal boredom?

Elena Dos Campos sat with her on a small couch as the *hors d'oeuvres* and glasses of champagne were passed. Despite her husband's advice, Elena thought that if there were some way to warn this rather nice young woman, or Robbie, she would be tempted to do so. The moment passed with the call to dinner.

Elena's dinner partner was Imre Mohacsi, and she was charmed by his self- possession. He could discuss the political scene and make it interesting rather than tedious, and he knew how to involve his audience. She didn't quite know how it started, but after a while, the conversation switched to the events of 1956. The table hushed while memories surfaced.

Mohacsi was reminiscing. "Yes, Istvan and I were part of the same group, if you can call a collection of people who were thrown together at different times a group. Still, we share the same memories of our lost comrades."

Kovatch spoke up, from his end of the table. "I have an article that John Magassy wrote about that time, about the last days." Both Szepvaros and Mohacsi said they had seen it as well. Szepvaros mentioned that Robbie Cutler from the American Embassy had given him a copy that very morning Odd, Kovatch thought in passing, what was Cutler doing, mixing in this?

"I only regret that Magassy didn't live to see his idea of a memorial completed. That's what young Cutler was calling on me about," Szepvaros said. "There is American interest in going forward with the memorial. I said that I'd help."

At that point Magda Mohacsi shifted the topic of conversation. She had seen a determined look on Kovatch's face, and she had endured enough conversations about 1956 to know that they could suddenly turn sour and ruin an evening. Maria Szepvaros looked at her with a relieved smile. Let the men continue their talk after dinner if that is what they want.

They did. After dinner Mohacsi, Szepvaros and Kovatch, with Eduardo Dos Campos and the German banker as interested listeners, went back to the Magassy article and those days so long ago in Pest.

"Actually, Janos wasn't quite accurate in everything he wrote," Mohacsi said. "It's probably a minor matter, but the comings and goings may not be exactly right. I distinctly remember that Attila Nemzeti returned emptyhanded from his attempt to find ammunition before I left on the same errand."

"I wouldn't know about that," Szepvaros added. "That was after I left, at Janos's orders. 'Come back with some ammunition if you can,' he had said, and not just to me. 'If that's not possible, then use your own best judgment. If it's all over, save yourself if possible.' I've always regretted doing that, but those were our last orders from Magassy."

Kovatch turned red in the face. "What happened to the others?" he wanted to know.

"Csaba Kovacs left before I did, and I never saw him again," Mohacsi replied. "Aside from Attila Nemzeti, at the end that just left Eva Molnar and Janos Magassy. I heard that Eva was tried by a People's Court and sent to prison, poor soul."

Kovatch persisted. "I heard a rumor once, in Austria, that Csaba Kovacs was betrayed. What do you think of that?"

Imre Mohacsi frowned as he considered that. "If that happened, it was after he left our group. We never saw him again. A decent fellow. I liked him."

Kovatch again, like a persistent prosecuting attorney, asked "If there was no betrayal, then who killed Janos Magassy?"

Nobody had an answer to that.

*   *   *

Ambassador Kovatch sat in his study after their return, mulling his thoughts over a glass of single vineyard cognac. Julie had gone up to bed. He tried to sort out what he knew and what he did not know, about what had happened so long ago.

Janos Magassy had told him personally that members of the resistance group had been free to save themselves, if they could not find supplies or ammunition. Magassy had had no reason to sugar coat what he had said then. Now that was confirmed by Istvan Szepvaros, and Imre Mohacsi had not contradicted him. That seemed to remove any idea of a coordinated betrayal. There would have been no reason for three of the four survivors to agree on that point if it had not been true.

On the other hand, there had been no concerted effort to find Csaba either. That fact alone meant that there was every reason to proceed with retribution on an individual scale. They all were prospering now, in one way or another, and Csaba had disappeared. If there was a traitor, all the more reason to increase the pressure and force his quarry out into the open.

Then he could deal with him finally.

More probing was needed. One inconsistency had surfaced that very evening, come to think of it, the timing of Attila Nemzeti's return to the group. Magassy had written that Nemzeti had returned after Mohacsi had left, not before. Mohacsi's version was different. Who was right? He would ask Nemzeti, of course. Perhaps more inconsistencies would slowly emerge.

Then there was something else that Mohacsi had said, something about "a collection of people who were thrown together at different times" not being a group. He had assumed that they could all vouch for each other. Perhaps that wasn't the case after all. All of that had to be carefully sorted out. Perhaps Magassy had put together the puzzle wrong, or in a misleading way. He would have to decipher it with great precision.

What exactly had happened to his brother Csaba remained a mystery to be solved. He would have to speak soon with Nemzeti to find out what he knew, and privately with both Mohacsi and Szepvaros after all. Maybe that was why Szepvaros had changed his appointment request to a more public, dinner party. Had he wanted to avoid just such a conversation? He would see. Meanwhile his other plans could proceed.

*   *   *

Istvan Szepvaros drank his apricot brandy and thought over the evening. He had thought, with Janos Magassy dead, that his problems were over. Now it seemed that there were two more investigations going on, both led by amateurs.

He could almost understand Robbie Cutler. There was something in his bearing that said that he liked the chase. Szepvaros hadn't believed his diplomatic story about the Magassy memorial fund for a moment. It was true, but it was also Cutler's excuse to nose around, a cover story. Well, there was nothing he could find out.

This Ambassador Kovatch was something else again. He seemed to be taking a personal interest in what happened in 1956, beyond what one could expect from an emigre who had, after all, missed the action.

Or had he?

Of course, that was it. He must be related to Csaba Kovacs. Probably he was Csaba's younger brother. That would explain his dogged interest. Szepvaros sipped his drink. Well, if Kovatch wants to play Count of Monte Cristo, let him try to do so. It shouldn't be too hard to put him off the scent. He thought again, and took another, longer sip of apricot brandy. It was excellent, full of fire and fruit essence.

He thought further. A new plan began to take shape. Why put him off the scent? Perhaps instead I can help Kovatch along and even supply him the Magassy killer. Then let him handle that situation if he really wants vengeance. Properly arranged, that should take care of Robbie Cutler as well.

He swirled his apricot brandy in the glass, and smiled. The stakes had been raised. He almost looked forward to it.

*   *   *

Robbie's message from Uncle Seth was in their usual code. Evidently Uncle Seth had returned from his trip to Washington, where he had done some scouting around. Robbie reached for his Montaigne, took the message from the FAX machine, and started to decode it.

"Revolution was encouraged at low levels by emigrants here. Some moral responsibility appears certain. That however not your problem. Recent murder victim a friend who was attempting discover truth about his group. Watch Ambassador closely. He may attempt vengeance. Killer may strike again if threatened. Senator will be briefed before his trip."

Uncle Seth had raised a number of matters. Yes, Radio Free Europe had stirred up false hope at the time of the 1956 Hungarian Revolution. Let the historians quibble about whether the broadcasts were authorized, and at what level. They had been playing with brave Hungarian lives.

More to the point now, he noted that Janos Magassy had been an intelligence source, or "friend." Probably he had confided in someone at Langley regarding one of his goals in returning to Budapest. Clearly he had suspected treachery of some sort.

Perhaps that was why he had been murdered.

If he developed more information, Uncle Seth would send it through Senator Abernathy. Robbie wondered if he could wait that long. He had the uneasy feeling that events were slipping away from him.

A killer was out there, an extremely cold blooded one at that, on his own territory. The trick was to find him in time. Robbie was certain that the pieces of the puzzle would point towards that killer, if he could just assemble them properly. Might as well start tomorrow by dissecting what Magassy had actually written, and separating those words from what he had assumed that Magassy had meant.

*   *   *   *   *   *   *   *   *   *

The Eighth Day—October 30, 1956

Tuesday began on a humorous note. Imre and Attila had left at dawn, and at noon they returned, laden down with several pistols, a rifle, a sack full of hand grenades, and enough ammunition for a prolonged siege.

"It wasn't hard," Attila explained, laughing heartily. "Imre and I put on official looking armbands, and we made a sign, 'Weapons Turn-in Here.' We also had a receipt book, an official-looking stamp, and a table to sit behind."

Janos decided not to pry too far into where they had obtained that stamp. He didn't have to. "Easy," Attila volunteered, "I know where identity cards used to be made."

"Fine upstanding lawyer you're going to be!" Janos replied.

"How did you get people to give you weapons?"

"It wasn't hard at all. With all of those confusing government announcements, including some about weapons being turned in, people thought that we had the authority to take them. The receipts we gave helped. By the way," he added mischievously, "when are you going to turn in our own weapons?"

Janos was cautious. "I'm too busy to listen to every news broadcast. All I know is that with weapons we've won. We can still defend ourselves if we have to. Once we lose them, we've lost that capability. I want to wait a bit longer and make sure. Certainly I'm not turning them in to clowns like you two!"

But events were moving too fast not to keep informed. About one-thirty they heard the news on Radio Budapest that Imre Nagy had formed a coalition government, a real one. The days of one-party government were over, kaput. Russian armed forces were being officially asked to leave Hungary. This news provoked an explosion of applause around the room.

"Ruszkik Haza!" ("Russians Go Home!") they all shouted. Magda even did an impromptu Russian peasant dance, scooting out the door to emphasize the point, as Jozsef and Red clapped.

Almost as an afterthought, the announcer said that Peter Kos had been dismissed as Hungary's Ambassador to the United Nations. There would be a new appointment.

"That's interesting," Imre said. "I've heard that Kos isn't even a Hungarian citizen! So his dismissal has meaning. It probably signals that Imre Nagy will try to involve the United Nations, and that he wants a real Hungarian in New York."

"Then this isn't over, not by a long shot," Janos concluded. "Well, you two stick around for a few hours. Jozsef, show them what we've done already. Rest for a bit, then try to promote some sandbags for the store-front. I'll go out now with Karoly and Eva and patrol our neighborhood for a few hours. Csaba, I want you, Red and Magda to reconnoiter this afternoon. Stop by the Corvin headquarters, then branch out a bit. Find out what's going on. We'll all meet back here by five."

An hour later Magda came racing back to Barat Street. She was out of breath and excited. "There's fighting in Republic Square." The words tumbled out almost unintelligibly. "Stay here and tell the others," Attila said. "I'll check on this."

Attila set out immediately for Republic Square, several blocks east of the Corvin area. He could hear the firing before he arrived. Republic Square was jammed with people, none of them standing. A fellow wearing press credentials huddling in a doorway filled Attila in.

"Some Freedom Fighters had come to the Budapest Communist Party Headquarters here. They told those inside to give themselves up. While that was going on, a food truck pulled up with supplies for the *AVH* men inside. Some housewives tried to get some of the food, and a sort of free for all started.

Attila thanked the man, who said his name was Johnny Szilva. He was an American, he said, working for Reuters. "Come and see us on Barat Street," Attila said automatically.

"I'll do that."

Then the *AVH* men inside the building opened fire. It was another massacre, not as bad as the one last week in Parliament Square, but bad enough. Szilva said he had his story and left.

People huddled behind barricades and armored vehicles. Attila was too far away to get a close look at the building, but obviously now it was under siege. Half an hour passed.

Attila crept forward, barricade by barricade. One by one he saw three people he knew.

There was that fellow Istvan Szepvaros, whom he had seen at Heroes' Square the first night of the Revolution—was it really only one week ago? He was crouched behind a nearby barricade, looking intently across the square at the Budapest Communist Party Headquarters building.

Attila bent over and, running low, joined him behind the barricade. From here, they had a fairly clear view of what was going on.

A group of Freedom Fighters was trying to force its way into the building. Csaba was with them. Gunfire rained down on them, but not from an angle that could be effective. The attackers were in an alcove near the front entrance. Suddenly they raced over to the door and began to batter it in with rifle stocks.

"Watch out, Csaba!" Attila yelled instinctively.

Just as the grenades fell Attila recognized another one of the attackers, not more than a boy. It was Red.

Attila leapt to his feet and screamed again. "Get the hell out of there, Red!" It was too late. The explosions of the grenades coincided with the splintering of the front door of Party Headquarters. After a moment the dazed surviving Freedom Fighters raced in, joined by others who had lost friends and relatives to the hated *AVH*.

The *AVH* men started to come out, their hands in the air. Other members of the crowd surged into the building in search of anyone who might be hiding.

It was bloody chaos. Attila was sickened by what followed. There was no legality, socialist or otherwise. The *AVH* men were shot if they were lucky. Otherwise they were lynched by the crowd. Press photographers were also at the scene taking pictures.

Attila knew that was a bad sign.

What happens if those pictures get shown around the world?

Then he had an even more chilling thought.

Who are all these photographers taking pictures anyway? Not all of them were from the press, the Western press anyway. Those that were wore some kind of identification, like that fellow Janos Szilva had done. Who are all the others? Maybe they are gathering evidence, the law student thought, some indication of who was here. Best to stay the hell out of their way.

He'd warn the others once he got back to Barat Street.

Attila paused. Istvan Szepvaros was stunned, seemingly unable to move as he watched what was happening. He was staring open-mouthed at the Freedom Fighters and the *AVH* men being killed, his expression unreadable.

"Come on, Istvan!" Attila said. "We've got to get the hell out of here. There's nothing that you and I can do now. I'll take you to where you'll be safe for a while." Attila grabbed Istvan's arm and shoved him forward.

As they left the square the two men turned for a final look. An *AVH* paybook had been found. It was ten times the normal worker's wages. When that *AVH* man was shot they propped him up and pinned the open paybook to his coat and then just left it there, soaked with his own blood

Sickened, Attila was about to leave when he heard a great shushing noise. It came from people across the square, near the stormed Party Headquarters

Despite themselves, Attila and Istvan recrossed the square.

By some miracle, faint shouting had been heard from under the ground. Soon, careful digging began. The shouting grew fainter. Everyone was shushed and a gun was fired, in the hopes that whoever was underground would hear the signal and shout again. A fainter signal was heard, then nothing. The realization spread that prisoners had been placed in underground cells, and just left there when the *AVH* men had deserted the building. The digging continued, as crying men tried to reach the prisoners in their abandoned underground cells in time. But the noises from below ground gradually were heard no more.

"The filthy bastards," someone said. "I wish they were still alive, so that we could lynch them all over again. Once isn't enough for people who would do this to other Hungarians."

Attila shook his head in agreement. Then, half leading a stumbling Istvan, he made his way back to Barat Street.

CHAPTER TEN

▼

PARRIES

Attila Nemzeti had preferred an informal meeting with Robbie Cutler, coffee in the neighborhood instead of an office visit. That would save questions if others at the Ministry of Justice ever wanted to know why they had met. After all it was a personal meeting, connected surely with the Magassy memorial sculpture project. And if their meeting was observed, so much the better to have it take place in a public coffee house.

Gerbeaud's in Pest is still probably the most ostentatiously public of all of Budapest's many coffee houses. It had long since reverted to its original name, although some still called it Vorosmarty's. It anchors a large square adjacent to the British Embassy, just a stroll from Vaci Street, still the most fashionable Budapest shopping district.

They ordered coffee and pastries and took an outside table. The waiter followed them with the order and glasses of chilled water. The morning was glorious, sunny with a pleasant breeze, just enough to be refreshing without blowing the newspapers.

Robbie gave Nemzeti a Hungarian translation of Magassy's article. The lawyer's English was halting. He could understand and make himself understood, if you made allowances for the grammar. Robbie's Hungarian was about the same. They switched carefully back and forth between the two languages. Robbie sipped his coffee and waited while Nemzeti read the article.

"This brings back so many memories," Nemzeti said. Robbie had to wait a full five minutes for more comment.

"Those were desperate days. Most of those who rebelled the hardest were disillusioned young people. We had believed their promises, you see. Young people do. They had said that a better life was coming, one worth our sacrifices. Then we heard about Khruschev's denunciation of Stalin. That was electrifying. And here in Hungary, the tyrant Rakosi was gone. They lied to us. We resisted, as the Poles had done. Imre Nagy promised a new path for Hungary. It was worth fighting for, when fighting became necessary. But the cost was so high…"

His voice trailed off. It was all jumbled together. Robbie felt like an eavesdropper overhearing a private sadness.

"I've talked with others in your group. Imre Mohacsi remembers the specifics of some of your street combat. He recalls your role in destroying a tank, for example."

"Yes. We did that together. I hope he remembered Magda, too. Who could have imagined such a graceful slip of a girl taking a man's part? Nobody could have done more."

"What about Istvan Szepvaros?"

"He came in late, after I ran across him in Republic Square. But he was very effective, particularly with small arms. That seemed to be his specialty. He helped us destroy a tank."

"I was struck by the fact that Magassy only mentions one full name, and that is Eva Molnar."

"Yes. Well, you have to remember when this was written. He couldn't be sure what any survivors might be doing. As it turned out, his caution did me a real favor. I was then, as I am now, in the Justice Ministry. Had it become known that I had been an active Freedom Fighter, even in 1978 it would have been very difficult for me."

"What happened when the fighting ended?"

"I had been wounded, you know. Shrapnel. It still bothers me sometimes. I guess I had been left for dead. Anyway, I woke up and it was cold and I was bleeding and hungry. I just walked home. That seemed the only thing to do. I hid out for quite a while. My wound finally healed and following a great deal of rest, I was able to start working again. One thing led to another, nothing particularly heroic."

"How did you end up at the Ministry of Justice?"

"I had studied law. The point was to resume a career that hadn't really even begun. I started in a small way, with union work, representing people in grievances."

"I wouldn't have thought that was possible under the communists."

"Oh yes, in small ways, probably as a safety valve. I can see that now. But gradually, I built something of a reputation. People trusted me, and the Party, which I had joined, thought that it would be better to have me inside the Ministry of Justice than outside."

This time it was Robbie's turn to be silent.

"To answer the question that you didn't ask, yes, I did join the Party. At that point, there seemed no alternative. I thought that the system would never change. I was in good company with that belief, you know. I can't think of many prominent Americans, on the right or left, who thought it would change, either."

He sipped his coffee. "You see, I thought that the best thing that I could do would be to try to change things from within."

He savored his coffee cake with enjoyment, a small and rare self-indulgence, and basked in the late morning sun for a moment. For one of the few times in his life, aside from Uncle Seth, Robbie felt that he was in the presence of a man who had lived what he preached, and who had done so with courage and grace. Robbie hoped that Nemzeti was what he seemed.

"What do you make of Magassy's article? I gather he was in charge of the group."

"Yes, there is no doubt about that. He was strong and decisive and capable. We all joined the group at different times. I myself wasn't there for the first few days. But our fight was an epic. I once heard that Magassy had replaced another man who had been killed the first week, but that was just another rumor perhaps. The entire truth now cannot be written. I'm not even sure that it could be reconstructed."

"Was Magassy correct in what he did write?"

"Let me see." He read the article through again slowly. More coffee was ordered and served. Lost in thought, Nemzeti sipped his coffee without realizing it was a fresh cup. It was too hot, and needed sugar. That brought him back to the present. He frowned slightly, pursed his lips, and went on.

"There are several details that I remember differently," he said at last.

"For example?"

"He isn't quite right about me. Actually I came and went several times. The search for provisions and for more ammunition was quite desperate then. I left once and returned the following day, for example, while Imre Mohacsi was still there. Then he left, and I left once again to look for supplies. This time, I found some and again returned."

He paused. "You'll see from Magassy's account that I was wounded by shrapnel after I returned the second time." He frowned. "He then writes that he and Eva were the last ones left." He put down the paper and stared at Robbie. "By that, clearly he was assuming that I had died!"

He shook his head in disbelief and looked back at the article. "I regained consciousness after he and Eva left."

"So you were the last one to leave after all?"

"That's what I can't remember."

*　　　　*　　　　*

Robbie went early to the restaurant for his luncheon with Julie Kovatch and tried to sort things out. What was known and what was not known seemed to be somewhat elastic. It depended upon whose recollections you had heard. Still, some bore out what each other had had to say.

All spoke of John Magassy as their leader. Imre Mohacsi remembered Attila Nemzeti as an active fighter. Nemzeti said the same about Istvan Szepvaros, and had emphasized his part in destroying a tank. Everyone seemed to have fought the Russians, if current memories were reliable. There was no treachery after all, Robbie thought. Perhaps this would lead nowhere.

Inconsistencies included Nemzeti's comings and goings, but it was a confused period. Nemzeti was surely the best source on that. He probably had left and returned more than once. There was no reason to expect greater precision. Nobody had a clear idea of what had happened to Csaba Kovacs, but Istvan Szepvaros had said that he thought he had seen him "taken into custody."

It was too bad that Magassy had not survived to attend the reception. He would surely have been astonished to see Attila Nemzeti once more, having thought he had died with the others in 1956. And then there was the mystery of Eva Molnar. He hoped that Iliu Monescu would be able to shed some light on her current whereabouts, if she were still alive.

Julie Kovatch entered the restaurant. She seemed a bit preoccupied, or rather, she was preoccupied until she spotted Robbie. Then a nice, warming smile emerged. She looked like a young girl at her first and most important dance. Robbie rose to greet her and kissed her cheek affectionately.

"Can't stay today, Robbie," she said. "I called the Embassy, but you had already left."

"Yes. I had an appointment downtown, and came here directly after it was over. Something come up?"

"Yes. Alex is putting in a command performance. We have a visiting Minister who has dropped in on us at a moment's notice. He didn't like his schedule in Vienna, so left Austria early. I had to arrange today's luncheon in record time. Say, why don't you join us? It's about time I reciprocated anyway, and I'm sure that you would enjoy it. Alex wouldn't mind."

Robbie raised an eyebrow as she continued. "As a matter of fact, he suggested something of the sort. And you'll help me out with the seating. We'll have to postpone our excursion to see the Crown of St. Stephen for another afternoon, of course."

Robbie hesitated. There really was a lot he could be doing back at his own office, but nothing that wouldn't wait.

"I'd be glad to come. Who else will be there?"

She looked relieved. "Mostly a dreary lot of businessmen. Some politicians—Ferenc Esztergondos will be there. So will the Spanish Ambassador and Mrs. Dos Campos. You enjoy their company, as I remember."

Robbie took a taxi with her to the hotel restaurant where their luncheon would be served in a private dining room. He met the visiting Australian dignitary. As usual, Alexander Kovatch's face was a frozen mask that he could not read. Deputy Ferenc Esztergondos greeted him with rather elaborate civility, before buttonholing the visiting cabinet minister.

Elena Dos Campos greeted him. "Glad to see you again, Robbie. Are you still looking into this Magassy business? It was quite the subject of conversation last night."

She went on, gauging his reaction. "I thought you might be interested. Istvan Szepvaros gave a dinner, and our host and Julie were there, also Imre Mohacsi. They talked just a bit about what happened in 1956. Magassy's visit seems to have stmulated a fair amount of local memories."

"What was said?"

"Well, I didn't hear most of it. The men continued their talk after dinner by themselves. But I did think of you in connection with one thing that was said at dinner, by Imre Mohacsi I think."

"What was that, Elena?"

"I forget exactly how the conversation had started. But at some point, someone asked Mohacsi about his resistance group. He rather deflected that term. He said something about not 'calling a collection of individuals a group,' I think. It seemed rather an odd way to put things."

Robbie's eyes narrowed. It was a new way of looking at things. "Thank you very much, Elena. Very perceptive of you to have picked that up. It may well be relevant. I'll talk with Mohacsi again to see what he had in mind."

There was Kovatch at the head of the table, sharing the honors with his visiting cabinet officer. Both were enjoying a story by Esztergondos. They seemed delighted with each other's company. Robbie could just catch snatches of their conversation as the courses succeeded each other, but it was clear that Esztergondos was making an impression. He seemed to mix anecdotes about the old Hungary, with exaggerated references to his importance as a political figure in leading the new one. All predictable. Why then did it give Robbie an uneasy feeling?

Julie at the other end of the table gave Robbie a "thanks for helping with all this" silent smile. He pitched in, engaging the attention of an officious aide from the Australian Foreign Ministry. Robbie was asked for his own view of the current Hungarian political scene, and gave it. Then tongue in cheek he recited the old observation that Hungarian national politics often was the reverse of the fortunes of the national soccer club. If they were doing well, then the country itself probably was going to hell.

"Same with us in lots of ways," the Australian replied. "What do you make of this fellow Esztergondos?"

That was a tough one to answer diplomatically. The fact of his invitation here meant that Ambassador Kovatch was showing him off. Robbie decided to parry the question. "Personally, he is a charmer. He hosted a group of us recently in Sarospatak. His family, of course, has been eminent in this country's history for centuries. But it is an odd mix, his becoming a Socialist. Some of them are the former communists, after all.

"He clearly sees himself as a national leader. But he carries a lot of baggage. I wouldn't take him at face value. Better check him out very thoroughly."

"There may not be time, but thanks for the perspective."

The aide might be tightlipped and humorless, but he was a professional. He could judge the situation, and what had been suggested rather than said.

*   *   *

Istvan Szepvaros surveyed the legal documents with a practiced eye. The Freedom Fighters Memorial Fund Association would be legally created, and then could collect and disperse funds under Hungarian law. The draftsmanship was exacting. Space remained to insert the names of the chartering officers. Well, that would surely cause no problem. He thought of Mohacsi, Nemzeti and himself. Later they could amend it by adding prominent members of the Hungarian emigre community.

He spotted a correction or two, and then asked that copies be made. Then there would be the matter of getting the officers together to agree, and to decide on the next course to take. Szepvaros tentatively selected a date several weeks away, then he thought again, and decided that a more festive occasion would be appropriate.

Well, why not? He called Maria and she agreed. They would inaugurate the plan not at his bank office, but instead at their vacation home overlooking Lake Balaton, on the more expensive northern shore, not far from Tihany Peninsula, with its thousand year old Benedictine Abbey. They sometimes entertained business visitors there. Nothing like a genuine touch of the Millennium to impress Americans.

The invitations could go out that afternoon. He would write each person a personal note. Might as well include Alexander Kovatch, and let him decide whether his official position would be a bar to his participation. That might take some sorting out between Kovatch and the Australian authorities in Canberra. Surely some sort of observer status could then be settled on.

The same would be true, of course, for Robbie Cutler from the American Embassy. Cutler would be invaluable once the fund got underway. The American Hungarian community was an important one. Szepvaros supposed that they would do their own funding at home. Most emigre associations did.

However, to avoid duplication at some point they would surely transfer funds, and in return they should also participate in the inevitable decision making. Everyone would then have a point of view on the sort of sculpture to be commissioned, for example. He would be flexible on that, just the indispensable facilitator in the background.

Szepvaros was enjoying himself. This is what he did best, he knew, organizing the legal and financial arrangements for wealth to be properly used. The officers for the new fund would of course meet from time to time, and decide just how their funds should be invested. A good return on their principal would surely follow. The funds coming from overseas would be part of his bank's overall pattern. Very helpful, all around.

Szepvaros then turned to subtler business at hand. The new foundation would give him the excuse to monitor any possible developments. Beyond that, like the skilled chess player he was, he pondered the pros and cons of his own probable next moves.

Surely the fact that Kovatch had not declared his own relationship to Csaba Kovacs meant something. Szepvaros was convinced of that. Kovatch must be assessing them all, one by one. It was not yet clear to him if Kovatch was entirely rational. One could be addled by a quest for revenge after all.

Suppose that Kovatch wanted just to find out once and for all what had happened to his brother? That was understandable. It needn't pose any threat, not properly handled.

But suppose, on the other hand, that Kovatch wanted to do something about it, go to the police, for example?

No, that would be Cutler's way of thinking. And Ambassador Dos Campos had just told him at their dinner that Cutler was something of an accomplished amateur sleuth, judging from what he had done in Bordeaux, helping the police round up ETA terrorists. Cutler would take the legal way.

Kovatch might do that, but Szepvaros thought it more likely that he would not. It probably would come down in the end to a certain fastidiousness. Kovatch seemed cold blooded enough for killing, but when it really came down to it, he might recoil. Of course, better not let things proceed that far.

He left his office and walked along the banks of the Danube, lost in thought. It was a beautiful afternoon. Here and there one could still see signs of the shelling from 1956, but over time, even those marks would fade or fall to urban renewal.

He tried to think what Kovatch would do next, what steps he might take. Of course. If he were going to play Count of Monte Cristo, he would want to take revenge on the survivors. Well, there were just the three of them now, excepting Eva Molnar. She was either dead or as good as dead, and could pose no threat. He had made very discreet inquiries. She was alive, but her long prison sentence had upset her mental balance.

Szepvaros weighed the possibilities, one by one.

Mohacsi the politician. He almost seemed beyond the reach of revenge. He was a popular politician, and his background was rather admirable. He could only be threatened at the polls. Perhaps that was it! That could explain Kovatch's playing up to Esztergondos, an appealing ploy for a diplomatic amateur.

Szepvaros the banker. That brought to mind the original Count of Monte Cristo. Kovatch would love to catch him in some sort of financial irregularity, or even create one. That would ruin his reputation as a banker Well, there was no way that Kovatch could trace his foreign deposits, the source of his branch's investment seed money. The rest was irreproachable Hungarian funds, earned in the new capitalist system. Rather patriotic, really. No, he was in the clear.

That left Nemzeti, the legal bureaucrat. He would make a fine scapegoat, if it came to that. He had, after all, been the only member of the resistance group to join the Party. That would be held against him. Then his shrapnel wound had addled his memory, so that he couldn't reliably recall everything that had happened. Turned around, that could also indicate that he was hiding something. At least Kovatch could be led to believe that to be the case, if need be.

Yes, all things considered, Kovatch would bear close watching. It was all quite manageable.

Szepvaros stopped and watched the young people on their benches by the Danube and the pensioners at their regular tables at the coffee houses. Here and there early summer tourists, guidebooks in hand, were gawking at the sights of Pest.

He ambled away from the river and through the theater district. Crossing the boulevard, he realized that he was in *Jozsefvaros*, the Eighth District, near the neighborhood of their resistance group.

He was suddenly curious to see it once again. It had been so many years. Could it have been on this corner that he saw Csaba Kovacs being led away?

Szepvaros found the little side street that led into Prater Street. He tried to remember Freedom Fighters darting back and forth from side streets where the tanks could not maneuver, into the boulevard where so much fighting had taken place.

He walked down the side street, made a turn, and then saw the corner building. Yes, there it was, with shell marks still over the facade. That is where the Friends had held out.

Now it was an apartment building once again. Szepvaros crossed the street and surveyed the building appraisingly. Yes, Magassy's idea could be realized. The building's facade was plain. The memorial could be erected as a sort of frieze on the building itself.

Perhaps alternatively the memorial might be placed in that little park over there, where he remembered Pista and Red had been buried. Either location would do very nicely. They could all talk about that as the memorial fund advanced, and they developed a clearer idea of the steps to be taken. Surely Mohacsi could help with the politics of it all, with the mayor's office and the city councillors.

Szepvaros was pleased that he had taken a look at the site. So would the other members of the chartering group who would join Maria and him on the Balaton in a few weeks' time.

He stopped by the Corvin Movie House. Except for two Freedom Fighter statues in front of the building, it looked much the same. He decided that there was just enough time to see a matinee before returning to close the bank for the day.

*   *   *

Attila Nemzeti had also left the offce somewhat early, and was relaxing with his wife Margit before dinner. "I had a visit from that young American diplomat this morning."

"So you said. What did he want to know?"

"He has taken an interest in 1956, and what happened then. He seems to have read rather closely what he could find on the period. He even gave me a copy of an article that Janos Magassy had written about our resistance group."

"Sounds like a normal interest to me."

"Well, nothing is normal about it anymore. Behind every question is the memory of what happened to Janos. I just can't believe that I'll never see him again. We went through so much then."

"Yes, but those days are more than forty years in the past.

"Literally, yes. But I still replay them often. It's hard to realize, but I never knew that Magassy had thought me dead all of these years."

"A natural thing for him to think. You had a bad head wound and were unconscious when he left. That cannot be a surprise."

"I don't know. I guess I thought that someone else might have mentioned it to him over the years. Istvan Szepvaros, of course, lived in the west all this time, in Germany. And Imre Mohacsi had even seen Magassy several times in Washington when he travelled there. It's an odd feeling, after all."

"Do you think that either of them was somehow involved in Magassy's death?"

"It's hard to think why. No, it must have been a robbery, as the police said."

"Odd robbery, if you ask me. Who would use a sabre?"

"Perhaps it was a souvenir that he had bought, and the robber panicked."

"Sounds rather farfetched. Better to leave such things to the police. Will you get involved in some way, officially I mean, at the Ministry of Justice?"

"Not as a general rule, unless something unusual emerges. The Minister does call a few of us in from time to time in some hard cases. This might be one. It's not possible to say at this early stage. There is no prosecution yet, of course."

"Did Mr. Cutler add anything to what you already knew about the Magassy matter?"

"No, not really. He was fishing for information."

"Well, best not to give him too much."

Attila knew exactly what Margit meant. He had never shared with anyone except her all that he had finally remembered about those last days in 1956. There was no reason to dredge all that up again. After all, nothing he could do at this point would bring Csaba Kovacs back to life.

*   *   *   *   *   *   *   *   *   *

The Ninth Day—October 31, 1956

Laszlo returned from his scouting mission to Barat Street in the morning, just in time to attend the burial for Red, or what was left of Red. Csaba had carried Red's body back from Republic Square, to be buried next to his brother Pista.

Magda remembered a prayer that her grandmother had taught her. It was a grace at meals, but nobody else could think of anything more appropriate. The adults wished they knew a prayer to say, but that was impossible. Let the child speak. Tomorrow would be All Saints Day. They would find flowers for the little Barat Street park area and place them on the graves then. That custom had survived from the old times.

"We must remember," they nodded to each other. "Never forget Pista, or Red." Pause. Not one person moved. A silent addition in their thoughts included those with bowed heads who might soon join the two boys. "Please remember me, too, if it comes to that." Thus their ceremony at the park by the street ended.

Laszlo had heard some news. Not only in Budapest, but around the country there had been fighting The *AVH* had massacred some unarmed civilians near Gyor, by the Austrian frontier. Laszlo confirmed that Russian tanks had left Budapest, but they had not returned to their bases. He had seen them still poised on the outskirts of the city. Also, there were some high-ranking Russians in town talking with Imre Nagy.

The radio added a few details. Apparently now there was even some question whether Hungary would stay in the Warsaw Pact.

"I'm getting nervous," Imre said. "There is only so much that the Soviets will take, after all."

Janos called Attila aside. "Who is this new fellow you've brought with you?"

"His name is Istvan Szepvaros. We've met before, in Heroes' Square on the 23rd. Then I'd seen him a couple of times. Yesterday we ran across each other at Republic Square. He was pretty dazed by what happened there. So was I, for that matter. I told him to come with me."

"Does he want to join us?"

"Ask him."

Janos talked with Istvan. The fellow was a bank worker by trade. Yes, he'd like to join them. But could he be trusted?

There were newcomers now, after the ceasefire. Many were genuine, but some were not. The struggle certainly wasn't over in Janos's estimation. There wasn't any way to check him out. The phones didn't work, and there was no central registry for the revolution in any event. Groups were self-regulating.

Janos knew that some newcomers, suspected of being spies, had simply been shot, if nobody could vouch for them. After all, there were still plenty of traitors around, Hungarian informers who knew the old ways. That's how they lived.

Or maybe a new volunteer was really a Russian intelligence agent. Who could tell for sure? You had to rely on your instincts, and they had to be right the first time.

There were after all patches of Hungarian speaking settlements in Ukraine. Another group on the other side of Ulloi Avenue had caught an infiltrator. His Hungarian had been fine, but he didn't know any slang, did not recognize Hungarian soccer teams, and wouldn't say where he was from in Budapest.

The group commander had shot the man.

He was right to have done so, Janos had thought. True, there was a possible individual tragedy, but letting a spy in would be a death sentence for everyone. That was far worse.

This was a close call, but after all Attila had picked him up, not the reverse, and also could vouch for him, well, sort of. That had to mean something. But mainly, Janos thought there had been enough killing for a while. He thought of Pista and Red.

Now they were ten again. There were the three kids, Laszlo, Magda and Jozsef. There was the couple, Eva and Csaba, Janos often separated them on details. He couldn't stand the thought of one seeing the other die. There was himself, Janos, plus the earliest members, sensible Imre and game Karoly with his bad leg. And now Attila the law student and Istvan the bank worker! Well, ten was the right size for this area, to defend it and if necessary provide advance warning for the Corvin fighters.

In late morning a visitor ambled up. He was wearing a press credential on his overcoat lapel. His shoes looked American.

Attila recognized him. "We talked yesterday in Republic Square. You were there taking notes, I think."

"Yes. I'm Johnny Szilva, Reuters. Remember? You said I could come here." His Hungarian was good, but heavily accented.

Attila remembered and nodded.

"Are you an American?" Janos was curious. He had never met a Hungarian-American, although there were lots of them, of course.

"Yes, from Cleveland. My family came from Miskolc before the war. The First War, I mean."

The group was silent. They were suspicious. Szilva sensed that he had to provide a bit more background before they would tell him anything.

Eva asked first. "How long have you been here?"

"I was sent in to cover the story of this revolution. I've been here for three days, since the ceasefire was announced."

They were all hungry for news. "Do you know what is going on outside Hungary?"

"Yes. We've got a tape open, for now anyway, through to Vienna. I file my stories a couple of times a day, and then they send back updates on what the world's reactions have been."

"And?"

Szilva looked at them. He decided to play it straight. After all, their lives were on the line.

"It's not very good news, I'm afraid. The Western Alliance is falling apart over control of the Suez Canal."

"WHAT??" They were incredulous.

"Yes. Obviously there was a plan arranged by the British, French and Israelis after Nasser nationalized the Canal. The Israeli Air Force attacked a day or so ago. I'm fuzzy on precise dates. So much has happened. Then as planned the British and French joined in. Eisenhower is furious, and there will be hell to pay. It's all you hear about at the United Nations."

"The fools. Their timing couldn't be worse!"

"And the prospects for any American help for us?"

"No chance, not by a long shot. Not now."

"What about the Russians?"

Szilva shrugged. "Well, I'm an American. You'd probably call me a capitalist. At least I'd like to be one! But I wouldn't trust those bastards. I think they're just regrouping, stalling to get ready and set you up."

Imre asked, "Has America done anything to discourage them?"

Szilva looked almost ashamed. "My country is covering its rear end. Secretary of State Dulles gave a speech in Texas a few days ago. He told the Soviets we didn't consider Hungary part of our defense zone. Something like that. He probably thought that would make it easier for Hungary to deal with the Russians, and come to its own defense arrangement."

"Stupid bastard!" It was Istvan Szepvaros, speaking up for the first time. "That's not how you deal with the Russians. That just gives them the green light. We'd better be prepared for some tough times ahead, and soon."

He added mournfully, "We'll end up as Hungary always does, alone, just looking after ourselves."

They stared at him. Nobody disagreed.

CHAPTER ELEVEN

▼

SUNDAY ON THE BALATON

It was time to give a report on the case to Ambassador Horton, and to ask for her help. The two went together. Robbie knew it was harder to be turned down when you had just shown initiative. He waited a few moments in her outer office, admiring the antique Hungarian wall clock that an enterprising Consul had found on the Budapest flea market decades earlier.

"Hi Robbie. Getting much?" That is what passed for clever repartee from Sam Horton, the Ambassador's husband. Sam was probably going out, his allowance in his pocket, for an afternoon of boozing and cruising. Sam neither expected nor deserved a reply, but no, Robbie wasn't getting very much.

He was announced over the intercom and then waved into Ambassador Horton's office. Judging from her demeanor, instead of her husband her last visitor might have been Cary Grant. Or Jack the Ripper, for that matter. Nothing seemed to faze Eleanor Horton. That boded well for what Robbie had to request.

Robbie gave the highlights of his meeting with Inspector Racz, and then briefed her on the plans to continue with Magassy's memorial project. Then he got down to business.

"Madame Ambassador, I think that the murder of John Magassy may be connected with the events of 1956. I also think the chances are quite good that it may never be solved."

Startled, she asked why.

"There is as we know, total silence from the Hungarian Government on intelligence matters relating to the 1956 Revolution. The reason—and I understand it—is to avoid retribution, and dredging up the past."

Ambassador Horton nodded in acknowledgement.

"To solve this murder, though, we must know what happened in 1956. On the face of it, there may be no connection. But it remains possible that an intelligence agent from 1956 killed Magassy."

"What makes you think that?"

"Frankly, the proof isn't solid. But consider these elements. Magassy was the leader of a small resistance group in 1956. He returned to Budapest, for the first time since then, to promote his idea of a sculpture memorial to his group. That means getting them together."

She listened intently. There was nothing there yet to stimulate her dormant instincts as a former prosecuting attorney. But he was getting to something, at her request, and this was his game.

"When I first started researching Magassy and his group, it all seemed to fit together well. His 1978 written account talked about the few survivors, most of whom are still living and here in Budapest, by the way. I've talked with them."

"Who are they?"

"They are rather high powered, and you probably know several of them. There is Deputy Imre Mohacsi, the German banker Istvan Szepvaros, and Attila Nemzeti from the Ministry of Justice."

There was a slight intake of ambassadorial breath. Robbie decided not to mention Eva Molnar for the time being. That could wait until he had found her, if he ever did. He went on.

"Each person has his own version, slightly different in minor respects, of what happened in 1956."

"Are the details important?"

"Probably not at all. What IS important is that their varying memories lead me to believe that I can't rely on Magassy's account, or indeed on anybody's memory. Somebody may be hiding something. For example, there is testimony that each person actively fought the Russians—hardly what a spy would do. I must have further facts. So it's time to plunge beneath the surface, or we may never know who killed John Magassy."

"What do the available official accounts say?"

"I've spent some time at the 1956 Information Center. There is a lot of useful background information there, and it would be helpful to the general historian. The political parties involved—including the Communists—have donated files. One can find daily accounts of the fighting, and a good overview."

"But?"

"But, there is no account of government intelligence agents at the time, and I doubt very much that there ever will be."

"Robbie, let's go back to my question. Why do you think 1956 has anything to do with Magassy's murder?"

"If it does not, there is no problem, and eventually the police will handle it. But I think that 1956 has everything to do with it. It is something that one of the Magassy group said the other night at a dinner, that it was wrong to think of them as a 'group.' What they were, really, was a 'collection of individuals,' thrown together at different times."

"What are you getting at?"

"That means that different people were at Magassy's resistance area at different times. I had been thinking that they all knew each other then. That may not be quite true, and memories tend to fade over time. They know each other now. But unless someone was continually there, in the same spot, day after day, nobody can say with assurance that that person was just part of the Magassy group, or even if he was, that it wasn't for another purpose, like spying for the communists."

"Why was Magassy killed, then?"

"There had been rumors of betrayal. John Magassy knew all of the survivors. His return might somehow have threatened someone who was an intelligence agent then. He may have stumbled onto something. Killing Magassy removed the threat of exposure.

He paused. Should he mention Uncle Seth's message? No. Not yet. Better to wait for the Senator's visit than to play his cards all at once. But he could lay the groundwork carefully.

"The Magassy murder is also, of course, a fresh crime. We are no longer talking about something that happened in 1956, with a 25 year statute of limitations under Hungarian law. We are talking instead about a murder that happened recently."

"So you want the files opened?"

"Yes. I want you to explore this with Ambassador Fekete at the Foreign Ministry. And there is something else. It concerns one of your colleagues."

"Alexander Kovatch?"

Damn. So the news of his luncheons with Julie was getting around.

"Yes. He is part of all this, and I think potentially a dangerous element.

This was news to Eleanor Horton. She leaned forward with a quizzical expression.

"What are you driving at?"

"Ambassador Kovatch is one of the most driven persons I've ever seen. He doesn't relax, ever. He has an agenda of his own. He is a Hungarian emigre, of course. Kovatch escaped from Hungary in 1956 or 1957 and went to Australia."

"Go on."

"I've checked him out. One of the members of Magassy's group of Freedom Fighters who didn't survive, as far as anybody knows, was one

Csaba Kovacs, spelled the Hungarian way. I've been in touch with Uncle Seth, who had a word at Langley. You know their bio people. That's their specialty. He has reported back to me that Ambassador Kovatch is the brother of Csaba Kovacs. He seems to be hiding that fact. I think he may be out for revenge."

"You don't suspect him of the Magassy murder?"

"No. Not at all. I think he is trying to find out what happened to his brother. But what happens if the murderer is on to him? Things could get even nastier. Meanwhile, your colleague is something of a loose cannon."

Ambassador Horton tried to keep up. "What's he been up to?"

"I'm not entirely sure. For one thing, he's been courting Ferenc Esztergondos."

She made a face. "You mean the 'socialist aristocrat?'"

"Exactly. I went to a luncheon that Kovatch just gave for a visiting cabinet minister. He and Esztergondos were thick as thieves. I suspect he is up to something. I don't have the details, but it could be something to do with his brother, or revenge for him. My guess is that he is trying to undermine Imre Mohacsi, in what way I don't know."

Robbie concluded. "I'm taking part, on sort of an observer basis, in a group that one of the three, the banker Istvan Szepvaros, is setting up to make plans to realize Magassy's Freedom Fighter Memorial. If you have no objection I'll continue as liaison with the American Freedom Fighter community."

She nodded agreement.

"At the same time, of course, that will give me the opportunity to watch all of the characters in this little drama. The others, including Ambassador Kovatch, are also taking part. We'll all be getting together at the Balaton this Sunday, as a matter of fact."

Time to play fair. "One other thing," he added. "Magassy may or may not have suspected that there was an intelligence agent in his former group. If he did, that might have put him in deliberate jeopardy as well, forcing his killer's hand."

She let that pass. "What do you make of the sabre?"

"That puzzles me a great deal. It is not a weapon that a killer would use. Handguns are more the style nowadays. Unless, of course, the crime was unplanned and that was the only weapon that the killer had available."

"Robbie, I'll give this careful thought. This probably shouldn't be put in writing to the Foreign Ministry, at least not for the time being. I want you to give me some notes in a sealed envelope, the best case you can make for opening the 1956 files on the Magassy resistance group. I'll take it up privately with Ambassador Fekete."

"Good. You'll have the notes tomorrow morning."

"And Robbie..."

"Yes?"

"Watch yourself with Alex Kovatch. He is, as you say, a determined and a dangerous man. I wouldn't want him as an enemy."

Robbie nodded acknowledgement and left her office.

*   *   *

Robbie checked the mail before putting his notes together. There were three items, beyond the usual forwarded magazine renewal subscription notices. A letter from the Freedom Fighters Association expressed interest in continuing Magassy's idea regarding the Freedom Fighter Memorial. A touching letter from Mrs. Magassy, in stilted handwriting, acknowledged his letter, but gave no details regarding her husband's itinerary. It was all an open book, she thought.

The third letter was from his father. It was sad and rather lyrical. The letter commented on the Eva Molnar that Magassy's article had mentioned. His father wrote that he had met Eva Molnar just a few weeks before the outbreak of the fighting. She was an art student from somewhere near Cluj or Kolozsvar in Transylvania. He wondered if she were still alive.

She had called on him at the Legation. He had no record of where she had lived, either in Kolozsvar or in Budapest. It was at or near the university, of course, but that was over 40 years ago. His father had wondered what had become of her.

That was all, except for a rather poignant post script.

"Uncle Seth tells me that you are looking into the Magassy killing for Ambassador Horton. If you locate Eva during your research, please let me know. We couldn't help our Hungarian friends then, and it has bothered me ever since. I hope you are never in that position. By the way, she would remember me as *'Konzul Elvtars.'* It was something of a joke that we had."

And then a further note. "Mother joins me in sending love. The Red Sox are in second place and surging. We've got our fingers crossed for another World Series at Fenway Park! Love, Dad."

                *   *   *

It was a glorious Sunday for a drive to Lake Balaton, the largest lake in Central Europe, just fifty six miles southwest of Budapest. Lake Balaton was close enough to be a weekend retreat for many who wanted to escape the city. Good fish and game restaurants abounded, although many visitors preferred to simmer their own traditional Hungarian dishes over a fire at their weekend retreats. The expensive homes were on the hilly northern shore, with fine views over the water. The southern shore was more popular and affordable. There the shallower water was somewhat warmer, as well as safer for families with young children.

For a morning of real tourism, though, Robbie decided first to stop at Szekesfehervar, about halfway to Lake Balaton. This was the first royal capital of Hungary, where King Stephen built a cathedral and royal palace at the turn of the first Christian millennium. Over the next five hundred years, twenty seven Hungarian kings were crowned here, until the city was occupied and its castle and cathedral were destroyed during the Turkish occupation. With that threat from the south, Hungary's religious center returned to Esztergom in the Danube Bend north of Budapest, while its seat of royal government settled in Buda.

Robbie thought that nostalgia could be a leading Hungarian product, as he strolled through the open air *Romkert*, or garden of ruins, where the former royal palace and cathedral were etched by building stones on the ground where they had once stood. Nearby, baroque and rococo buildings from the eighteenth century gave color and grace to the area, as Hapsburg stability had replaced Turkish destruction. It was a beautiful region.

The cynical might say that such rich architecture was a fine backdrop for the souvenir shops that also had sprung up, here and there. But Robbie was addicted to postcards, and the habit of sending them to friends and family. He looked at a nearby display and chose a half dozen, buying stamps as well.

Robbie sat down at an outdoor cafe along the historic walking street, ordered coffee and pastry and wrote his cards. The first went to Sylvie Marceau in Paris. It took a while to find just the right wistful note. Then he wrote to Evalyn, to his parents, and to Uncle Seth. He thought for a moment, and then wrote a card to the staff of the Consulate General in Bordeaux, his last post.

That left one card. It annoyed him that he had nobody to send it to. He remembered the old story, from Singapore. Bill Bailey, who maintained to his last that he was the original of "Won't You Come Home, Bill Bailey?," used to pour the occasional Tiger Beer at his bar and tell the story of his internment at Changi Prison during the Japanese occupation. Allowed one card, he had sent it, he maintained, to the Publisher William Randolph Hearst, with the notation "Wish you were here instead of me!"

The next block had shops higher up the scale. No T-shirts here. There were books on Hungarian history, books of photographs and paintings of all sorts, as well as skirts and blouses that were hand embroidered in traditional red and green designs, probably from the *Matyo* region near Sarospatak. Evalyn would enjoy them. He must remember to take her shopping.

There was also an antique shop. Where there was an antique shop, usually there were canes to be found, and this was no exception. The assortment was of good quality but limited in range. There were a number of nobbed walking sticks, just the thing for walking in the hilly region north of Lake Balaton, he supposed.

Ah, there they were, a fine assortment of handmade canes, with antler handles. He found one that was just right for his height, as if he would ever actually use the cane for walking, instead of being part of his collection. What could be more evocative and Central European, he thought as he took the cane to the counter.

Well, that could. In the counter case, there was a fine sabre for sale, slightly curved, with a fitted scabbard. There were in fact several.

Robbie paid for his cane and asked about the sabre.

"We are proud of them. A local artisan makes them. Very good copies they are, too, of what an officer would have worn a century and a half ago. We sell five or six every month."

The clerk took the blade out for his closer inspection, and Robbie brandished the sabre. The weight and balance were excellent. It was expensive, but not unreasonably so. It would have made a formidable weapon. Certainly the exact duplicate that had been used to kill John Magassy was proof of that.

*   *   *

Robbie drove along the Tihany Peninsula with pleasure. It was a national park and the site of Tihany Abbey, whose glorious abbey church, rebuilt in the eighteenth century, traced Hungary's history nearly to the time of St. Stephen. Robbie was pleased by this reference to the first millennium. As a bonus, the Abbey's bells were a pleasant backdrop for the Sunday visitor.

Judging from the cars parked along the driveway, the others had already arrived. There were the official BMW and its driver dozing on the front seat for Ambassador Kovatch, Szepvaros's own late model Mercedes, a Citroen probably owned by Imre Mohacsi, and a relic from the socialist past that somehow had survived the drive from Budapest, that by process of elimination must belong to Attila Nemzeti.

Robbie was pleasantly greeted by Maria Szepvaros. "First a short meeting, then a nice informal Balaton dinner," she promised. He took a drink and joined the others in a comfortable salon with a picture window that overlooked the lake. Istvan Szepvaros stood and shook hands with Robbie, then gave a stage cough that announced that their deliberations were about to begin. He passed around copies of a thin portfolio to each of the other four men.

"I've gone ahead and had our legal people research setting up a legal entity to handle Janos Magassy's memorial project. Their draft is enclosed. It is fairly short and I think self-explanatory. If you agree, it will allow us to raise funds and invest them. The purpose, of course, is to establish the memorial and see it through to completion. We will need officers for form's sake. It shouldn't be onerous. The bank can handle the paperwork. We've all already informally agreed that we want to continue. All this does is to put us in the right legal framework to carry forward what Janos wanted to do."

It all seemed straightforward enough. There was quick agreement that there should be three officers of record, and these would be the three former Freedom Fighters, Szepvaros, Mohacsi and Nemzeti. Kovatch and Cutler, as diplomats, would serve in an informal capacity as liaison to their respective private emigre communities, which were expected to help fund the project.

Mohacsi expressed a particular interest in the sculpture itself. "What form will it take?" He wasn't sure that he wanted something whose meaning the average citizen would have to guess.

Istvan Szepvaros answered him. "This is nothing that we can settle here and now. However I tend to agree with you, Imre. I walked over to our former command post the other day. I even stayed to see a movie at the Corvin," he sheepishly added.

"Later, I had some pictures taken." He passed copies around the room. "You'll all see that the building still stands and that the small park further back in that street is still there. The memorial could be at either location, in the Park or as a sort of frieze on the exterior wall of our building. Either one will require some political connections, of course.

With that broad hint, Mohacsi agreed to explore the political ins and outs of getting construction permits in Budapest, and finding out who was responsible for both the building and the park. The Nemzetis and Magda Mohacsi would solicit artistic suggestions, but they all would be free to explore preliminary ideas for the memorial. When that was done, they could decide the sort of statuary that they preferred. That would be followed by bids for the final project.

It was a good beginning. There was a general feeling of satisfaction and preliminary accomplishment. Kovatch and Cutler would inform their respective emigre associations in Australia and the United States that the legal papers were being filed, and that the group was properly chartered under Hungarian law and could accept contributions.

They agreed to meet again at the call of Istvan Szepvaros in his bank's conference room. Attila Nemzeti suggested that they also meet in Budapest on October 23rd, the anniversary of the beginning of the Revolution in 1956, and hold a dinner in celebration and remembrance. This was acclaimed, details to be worked out later.

Business over, Ambassador Kovatch sat chatting with Attila Nemzeti. "Any progress on the Magassy murder?" Nemzeti gave him an odd look. "I thought you might have some idea, being in the Justice Ministry."

"I haven't heard a thing. But I have had a visit from the police, an Inspector Racz." Here, there was a general murmur of assent. The other men had all talked with Racz. "So have I," said Kovatch, "since I had talked with Magassy that last weekend. I don't think the police have made much progress, judging from Racz's line of questions to me."

"Hard to judge from that, I'd say," ventured Mohacsi. "In my experience the police usually start off with small steps. I wonder if this means we're all under suspicion." Silence.

"I don't see why we should be," said Nemzeti. "I hadn't seen Janos since 1956." Neither had Szepvaros. "A real tragedy, his being murdered just before we all could get together once again. All the more reason to proceed with this memorial project, if you ask me." He finished his drink and took another one from Maria Szepvaros. That made three in a very short time, Robbie realized. Margit Nemzeti must have noticed the same thing. She crossed the room and sat protectively next to her husband.

Robbie sat next to Julie. That was making it harder to watch her husband. He got up and followed his hostess into the kitchen to get a pair of fresh drinks. There Ambassador Kovatch, sitting by the picture window, seemed to be taking the measure of each of the men in turn, first Szepvaros, then Mohacsi, then Nemzeti.

Only Nemzeti seemed nervous. And only their host seemed to notice that nervousness. He smiled at Robbie.

After her husband's fifth drink, Margit Nemzeti had a decision to make. Should she plead a sudden illness and get them out of there, or should she try to brazen it out? She decided on the latter course. Some solid food was what Attila needed at this point. That, and some hot coffee.

She was right about that. His strong sense of bureaucratic propriety began to kick in at just the right moment. He complimented his hostess on her wonderful *halaszle*, homemade fish chowder, and went easy on the Balaton white wine that accompanied it so well. Robbie reflected that the slopes on which those grapes had grown were probably not more than twenty minutes away from the villa. The rough bread was delicious and everyone mopped their soup with it. The next day, after all, it would only be good for pounding nails.

Dessert was also excellent, chocolate *palacsinta*, or pancakes with grated nuts, and warm chocolate sauce with whipped cream. It went well with strong coffee.

After dinner, Nemzeti sat talking with Julie Kovatch, who asked him what it had been like in 1956. She had never really heard, and they all seemed to know. And so he told her, nearly whispering.

"At first it was exhilarating. We were all younger than you are now, my dear. I suppose you know the reasons for the revolt. We were all such idealists in those days. We expected so many changes, that things would get better."

She nodded encouragement for him to continue. "Khruschev had denounced Stalin, and in Hungary, the Rakosi group, our homegrown Stalinists, were out of power. We thought things would get better, and we wanted the Russians out of our country."

He took a short sip of his coffee.

"We got together almost by accident. Then we began to fight, and to find the ammunition to fight with. The Russian tanks couldn't negotiate the narrower streets, and that is where we put our little headquarters. We could get bottles, gasoline rags, and make Molotov cocktails. Sometimes we would raid a police station, or they would come over to us, and that added more arms and ammunition. It was exhilarating. But the cost was terrible. One by one, we started to die."

"What happened to you?"

"I went out for ammunition several times. Then finally I succeeded in finding some. I returned for the last time. Janos Magassy was still there, and so was Eva Molnar at the end. Then I was hit by shrapnel. I could hardly see."

He seemed a bit overcome. Margit gently suggested that it was time to leave. She was probably right. She usually was.

*   *   *

Nemzeti sipped his coffee again and then, excusing himself, got up to take the cup into the kitchen. Istvan Szepvaros walked along with him. He put the matter so gently that replying seemed more an acknowledgement of the undeniable than an admission.

"That must have been very difficult, Attila. You were in shock from your shrapnel wound. It's a wonder you didn't bleed to death then and there. And you had been left for dead by Magassy. That was unforgivable of him. Nobody could blame you for remembering that desertion all these long years."

The ugly accusation hung in the air. And now Magassy was dead, murdered, and they were all suspects.

Nemzeti's response was instinctive. "No, Istvan, you've got it wrong. How could I blame Janos for what happened? He left because he thought I was dead. Nobody could blame him for that. If anybody is to blame for leaving, I am. Sometimes I wish I hadn't done so."

"Then you weren't the last to leave?…Of course not. You couldn't have been. For one thing, I thought I saw Csaba Kovacs in the neighborhood when I was trying to return, before it was cut off. You saw him too, didn't you?"

Pause. It was time to acknowledge a debt that had been too long denied. "Yes. You're right. I wasn't the last to go. Csaba helped me. He must have returned after Eva and Janos had left, and he found me there. He bandaged my wound and cleaned the blood from my face so that I could see. He gave me something to eat and then he told me to go. He said he'd cover my retreat. I somehow made it home. I never saw Csaba again."

It seemed obvious that Nemzeti had never spoken of these matters before. Szepvaros could almost see the topic closing in his mind like the doorway to a secret room locking tightly.

"Have you told this to the police? It might clear you of any suspicion of Janos's murder."

"It isn't any of their business."

"Attila, I think you should never again mention this matter. For your own good, old friend. You can never tell who is listening. For one thing, be very careful about trusting Ambassador Kovatch. I saw you talking with his charming young wife at dinner. But consider his age and name. He just might be related to Csaba Kovacs, after all."

Nemzeti's eyebrows shot up. He sobered up in an instant, caught his wife's arm, made his excuses and left.

*   *   *

Szepvaros said goodbye to his guests as they left.

That silly young American, Robbie Cutler, was the exception to the rule. All of the others had had something elegant to say. Even the usually sullen Kovatch had managed to praise the dinner while they walked along to his car. "Poor Attila," Szepvaros had admitted, when Julie had mentioned her concern over Nemzeti's distress.

"I hope it wasn't anything I said," she ventured.

"No, not at all. He was just remembering the old days, and the man who saved his life at the end, the last man to leave. Csaba was his name. Even the strongest of us can be overcome by such memories." Szepvaros gave Julie a peck on the cheek and shook hands with the impassive Kovatch as the Embassy chauffeur came around to open the door for the Ambassador.

Compared to that, Cutler was a cipher. Well, he was an American after all, boyish and full of advantages, but no real depth. He humored the young man as they walked towards his car. Cutler was recalling their common interest in old movies. Old movies indeed. Yes, he knew scenes by heart, and did play his videos from time to time.

Who wasn't fond of "Gone With The Wind?"

* * * * * * * * * *

The Tenth Day—November 1, 1956

At ten o'clock that morning, All Saints Day was observed in the courtyard at the Corvin Movie House. A priest celebrated mass for the dead. It was the first public religious ceremony that Magda had ever witnessed. The brief ceremony included singing of the National Anthem. Everyone had joined in singing its slow, dignified strain, the exact opposite of what foreigners regarded as characteristic Hungarian exuberance.

Magda had gone with Karoly to find flowers for Pista and Red. Everyone had contributed whatever *forints* they had for a nice bouquet, and Magda and Karoly soon found a florist shop open on an undamaged side street near the ring boulevard. Entering, they had stared at the flowers.

"You are looking for a wreath?" asked the proprietor, a lady with a pleasant smile. She had been up nearly all night. All Saints Day was perhaps her busiest day of the year. Everyone wanted a wreath for their lost ones. That was one custom that hadn't changed even under the communists.

"Yes," Magda answered, trying hard to sort out which flowers were right, and what they could afford. Some had their prices marked, and others did not.

"Did you have in mind something for a grandparent perhaps? This is a formal wreath, very dignified." She pointed towards a wreath that almost made Magda shudder. Magda looked at Karoly, who made a face and shook his head. No.

"Something more cheerful," Magda started to explain.

No that's not right. What could be cheerful about this?

She began again. "You see, our friends Pista and Red were so very young. They died in the fighting, and their graves were just dug in the park on our street. We knew today is All Saints Day. We want something nice for them. We're going to bring the flowers back for the others."

"I understand," the woman said, her ever-present smile now sad and wistful. "You were right to hesitate. None of these is right. You want some pretty flowers, full of color, with perhaps a few ribbons. Give me an hour and I will put their names on the ribbons too. That would be Istvan, and what was the other name?"

"Istvan yes, but we always called him Pista. Yes, we'll all want Pista. His brother was Red." The shopkeeper nodded in understanding as Magda and Karoly left her shop.

They arrived at Corvin Circle as the service was ending. There a lady in her mid-thirties spotted Magda and called her name. "Magda! Is it really you?"

Magda stared at her. Where had she seen her before?

Of course. She was the boys' mother, *Maria Nenyi* (Aunt Maria). She was looking for her sons, Pista and Red. "It's not up to us to tell her," she whispered to Karoly. "I just can't anyway. She should hear it from Janos. You take her to Barat Street, and I'll meet you there with the flowers."

Karoly took the woman's arm. She wondered as he did so what Hungary was this, when young men have become warriors in the streets of Budapest? Magda said that Karoly would take her back to their own head-quarters on Barat Street, where she should talk with Janos Magassy, their chief. Magda added that she would rejoin them shortly.

Slowly, in a daze, the woman allowed the limping Karoly to lead her out of the Corvin stronghold.

In an hour the bouquet was ready. Magda had never seen anything so beautiful. It was a celebration of flowers and life. Ribbons in the Hungarian national colors, white, green and red, embraced the flowers. Magda looked more closely. The woman had actually duplicated the national flag with the ribbons, the revolutionary flag of the Freedom Fighters, with the center missing. But for this wreath, the names Pista and Red crossed at the center. It was magnificent, fit for a head of state.

"It's so beautiful. I've never seen anything so fine. I don't know if we have enough to pay for this," Magda said.

"Keep your money, my dear," the florist answered. "You've already paid enough. Pray to the *Magyar Nagyasszony* (Mother of Hungary) that you don't have to pay any more. This is my contribution. I only wish it could last. But you will remember, I'm sure."

When Magda got back to Barat Street, Janos had finished talking with the mother of Pista and Red. She stood sobbing with the others at the lit-tle park. Magda stepped forward towards the woman, who took hold of one end of the large wreath. Together they placed it in the park. The wreath came with a little metal stand, and so it stood upright. It was beautiful. Nobody could think of anything further to say.

Later that afternoon, Janos, Eva and Csaba sat at an outdoor cafe near the Barat Street corner, talking with Magda about the Corvin service and the floral wreath. The cafe was now open again, in a tentative sort of way. It was a holiday, or perhaps just a day of renewal. Earlier Attila had gone over to the Parliament to find out what the government was doing.

"She said that she wouldn't charge us anything for the flowers. That was her contribution. She only wished it was more permanent," Magda was saying.

"Maybe when this is all over there should be something permanent," Eva had said.

Janos was interested. "That's the art student speaking. What would you have in mind?"

"Some sort of memorial. Perhaps a statue with people, our group, perhaps not. Perhaps a memorial with this magnificent wreath for all to see. I really don't know. It's just an idea."

"It's a very good idea," Csaba said. "But I'd add something military. This is a fight after all, and that's how Pista and Red both died."

Janos was curious. "What did you have in mind? Our weapons aren't exactly artistic material. A Molotov cocktail?"

Csaba grinned. "Of course you are right when you put it that way." He was silent once again.

Eva was intrigued. "Wait a minute. I've got an idea. This all began at the Petofi Statue, after all. Something national and distinctive, something traditional above all, something Hungarian."

Then the idea came to her. "Of course. It has to be a cavalry sabre. Hungary invented the *huszars*, and that's their symbol." She remembered more. Enthusiastic, she went on. "In the 1848 Revolution that's what they did, after all. They put a sabre in place of the Austrian crown on the battle flags."

"Perfect," Janos agreed. "I hope we live to do it."

Attila returned later that afternoon. His usually serious face was even more serious than usual. "I've just come from Parliament," he began. "All around the sidewalks people have lit little votive candles, to mark the victims of the massacre there one week ago today." He shuddered at the memory.

"What's the news? What's going on over there now?"

"There is a lot of coming and going. The Russian Ambassador, Andropov, was leaving in his car when I arrived. Some Western correspondents are there too. I saw Johnny Szilva. He says that the Russian troop movements are continuing—the wrong way. They are coming back INTO Hungary. That's why Imre Nagy was meeting with Andropov, he said. We better turn on the radio and hear what Nagy has to say. Something big seems to be building."

They were just in time for the Prime Minister's broadcast. Imre Nagy announced that Russian troop movements were continuing into Hungary. He had therefore, in the name of the Hungarian nation, removed Hungary from the Warsaw Pact and declared the nation's neutrality. A cable had been sent to the United Nations informing Secretary General Dag Hammarskjold of these events. Imre Nagy then had appealed for help from the United Nations.

Janos added, "Now we must hold out until that help comes."

CHAPTER TWELVE

▼

EVALYN ARRIVES

As August and the summer ended, fine Danubian weather, not too hot and with welcome breezes, announced the reward of an early taste of fall to those who had not been able to take summer vacations from Budapest. And in that same week came the first visitors of the fall season, Robbie's sister Evalyn and United States Senator James Abernathy.

Evalyn arrived first, on Sunday morning. She was delighted by many things and carried her enthusiasm with her, a late twenties enthusiasm that made Robbie see old sights through her fresh and cheerful perspective, and appreciate them anew.

"Two weeks of welcome vacation, Big Brother, and to think I'm spending all of it in Hungary. I've heard so much about Budapest. Now I'm going to see it for myself. But please, no heroics…I remember my last 'vacation,' in Bordeaux!"

Robbie hardly needed reminding about the terrorist car bombing that she had just missed in Bordeaux. He steered her expertly through customs at Ferihegy Airport, and then they drove to his townhouse apartment in

Buda, where Evalyn greeted Minouette and was awarded the guest room on the second floor.

In an hour Evalyn had unpacked, explored Robbie's townhouse, and admired its views over the Danube. Together she and Robbie strolled along the old streets of Castle Hill. They appreciated the Fishermen's Bastion and outside the Matthias Church, Strobl's stunning equestrian statue of St. Stephen.

Then they admired the Baroque architecture of many of the houses in the district. Their gold fronts faced narrow streets, which had been sized for horse drawn coaches. Not all were still in private hands. Some now housed institutes or were government guest houses. Others had been adapted for restaurants, and Evalyn made plans to visit every restaurant and coffee house that she found attractive. She began to take notes, but gave up when she saw that her list could easily last for her entire vacation, and they hadn't even left Castle Hill yet!

Ruszwurm's, however, couldn't wait. They stood in line at this tiny cafe and ordered coffee and *dobostorta*, a rich five layer cake with burnt sugar topping. Their order arrived with the clearing of a small table, set with wire backed chairs like those of a turn of the century ice cream emporium back home. The coffee was rich and the *dobostorta* delicious, topped with extra whipped cream at Robbie's request.

"So what's going on, Robbie? I gather that you are involved in this murder case. John Magassy, wasn't it? And he was head of a group in 1956 that included someone Dad had met, an Eva Molnar. Have I got all that right?"

"You do. Ambassador Horton has given me the go ahead to look into this murder, and I'm making some progress. Not much, but some. It would really help if we could locate Eva Molnar, or find out what happened to her. She may be the key to this business. Perhaps you could help me with that end of it."

"I'd like to very much indeed." Robbie told Evalyn about his fruitless attempts to locate any files on Eva Molnar. "But she was from Kolozsvar, or Cluj, in Romania, and I've asked a Romanian diplomat, Iliu Monescu, to try to locate her if he can. He is their Consul, and you'll like him I think. He's soft-spoken and understated, just like you!"

She laughed and looked for something to toss across the table. Finding nothing appropriate, she went on.

"I gather Dad feels badly about this Molnar woman."

"Yes. I think so. It wasn't up to him, but he knew her, and then he couldn't save her when the Revolution was destroyed by the Red Army. It's probably haunted him for years."

"Then by all means, let's find her."

She continued. "Robbie, what do you hear from Sylvie Marceau?"

"Not as often as I would like. I saw her at Reims on the way to Budapest. That new job in Paris is keeping her occupied. But not so occupied that she's forgotten me. We're spending the New Year together in Vienna."

"She's a nice lady. She passed the Evalyn test. Whether you are quite good enough for her is another story. You'd be really dumb to let her get away, Robbie."

She wasn't a little sister any more. It was nice to hear what he believed but didn't often admit reaffirmed by Evalyn.

"You two aren't engaged, are you?

"No, not exactly."

"Not exactly means not engaged. Why not? Are you seeing anybody else?"

This was getting too close for comfort. Robbie decided to answer the question in a mature, responsible way. He stuck out his tongue at Evalyn and ordered more *dobostorta* and whipped cream. "Not with you looking over my shoulder, I'm not," he finally blurted out.

*   *   *

It was an eventful Monday morning for Attila Nemzeti at the Ministry of Justice. He had been asked to one of those rare private meetings by the Minister, and he believed that it had gone well.

"This is a delicate matter, Attila," the Minister intoned. "You know our policy about releasing the full intelligence files from 1956. We cannot permit that, and the reprisals that might follow. It's a political decision anyway, decided by a ranking Minister in the Prime Minister's office, but I would have a voice in any recommendation to release individual files."

Nemzeti nodded. What was the Minister leading up to?

The Minister continued. "Now we have the problem from a slightly different angle. A foreign diplomatic mission here has requested that a file be opened. It's the matter of the Janos Magassy murder. They say that the files may be important to moving forward with that case. They further argue that the Magassy case is, of course, a current one, not barred by any statute of limitations. What do you think?"

Nemzeti thought coldly and very carefully. Istvan Szepvaros was right. He could read through the Minister's discretion. Clearly Ambassador Alexander Kovatch was trying to get information regarding what had happened to his brother. Raising the Magassy case was just an excuse. The killing didn't really have anything to do either with Kovatch's inquiry, or with 1956 for that matter. Murdered on the street. It does happen, even in Budapest. So opening the files wouldn't help solve it.

But, if files were made public, he could be put at risk. He knew the way that intelligence gathering had worked, the thousands of informers, each adding just a bit here, a morsel of information there. In the files of the former German Democratic Republic, it was said that perhaps a hundred thousand had helped the *Stasi* collect their information. What had happened there, for years, surely had been replicated in Budapest. He had to assume that they knew everything. Or that there was full information now assembled somewhere, just waiting to be used.

And what would that mean? Now that more had been pieced together, the last days of their group were surely memoired somewhere, probably in one of those time bomb files that should never start ticking. If Szepvaros could figure out a motivation for his killing Magassy, who had left him for dead, then so could the police.

Also Kovatch was clearly fishing. If he ever found out that Nemzeti had left his brother Csaba, that might be a death sentence. Who could tell what Kovatch's reaction might be? Attila didn't want to find out. Better, far better, to keep matters under lock and key. And far safer too.

"It's an interesting problem, Minister," he began. "But who can say where this sort of back door into intelligence matters might lead? I know of course about the Magassy case. You should know that in 1956, I actually knew John Magassy. I was part of his group." The Minister remained impassive. "I cannot imagine that our few survivors had anything at all to do with Magassy's murder. I think it is better to keep the files sealed. Let the police come to us directly if they wish to make a more informed request, based on something more solid than sheer speculation. That isn't enough here to create a new precedent as important as this one would be."

The Minister thought it over for a long moment, and then nodded in agreement. He would call in Ambassador Fekete and explain matters. Let Fekete deal with the Americans. Attila Nemzeti went back to his office and breathed deeply. For an innocent man, he surprised himself with a sigh of relief.

He was sure that Margit would be pleased by his handling of the issue.

*   *   *

Robbie was always impatient at the slow pace of official investigations. He understood that this was how they worked, the painstaking gathering of evidence or elimination of leads, and that it took time, a great deal of time. He had thought that after he reported his discovery of the sabre sales outlet to Inspector Imre Racz, that matters would continue at a brisker pace. If anything, they seemed to have slowed down.

Inspector Racz had sent a message that he wanted to see Robbie, so perhaps that meant progress. Robbie hoped so as he entered Racz's office at Deak Square in Pest's Fifth District.

"Jo napot, titkar ur" ("Hello, Mr. Secretary") came Racz's formal greeting. "And many thanks for alerting me about the sabre. We've spent a lot of manhours tracing them."

"Who makes them?"

"A craftsman in Sopron makes them. It is really quite an undertaking, straight out of the sixteenth century. He has his own foundry and produces the blades himself, hammering them to a fine edge. It's like watching something from the late middle ages. Another craftsman does the leather grips, and then this man fits them together. He produces perhaps a dozen a month, and then sells them through a few selected outlets, like the one that you saw at Szekesfehervar."

"So there are other outlets then?"

"Yes. There is one outlet in Debrecen and one in Szeged. He wants to expand, and is looking, he says, for a suitable outlet here in Budapest. But he wants to maintain the craftmanship. He won't compromise on that. And therefore another outlet does him no good at present."

"Have you had any luck tracing his buyers?"

"We're just starting. At Szekesfehervar there are several clerks. It depends upon the time of day, of course. They work in shifts. They have not recognized any members of Magassy's former group, if that's what you mean. Nothing back from Szeged or Debrecen yet."

"I didn't really think that they would recognize anybody. What interests me is the prospect that the killer might try to replace the sabre that he has lost."

"Exactly," Racz agreed.

"Does the artisan ever do any private commissions?"

"Not for years. Anyway, we brought him the murder weapon, and he recognized it as one that he had made. He couldn't say just when. They are all pretty much the same. Too bad they are not numbered or dated. He'll let us know if he is contacted for any private commissions."

All this was interesting, but hardly worth his being called in. Robbie waited a moment while Racz poured some coffee, and then let him begin.

"*Titkar ur,* I'm in a bit of a dilemma here."

Robbie nodded in silent encouragement.

"I'm under orders to be cooperative with you, and that is not an easy thing." He paused again. "We are aware that your Ambassador has officially asked that the 1956 files from the Magassy group be opened. I am sure that you will not be surprised when you learn that her request will probably be denied."

"I'm disappointed, but not really surprised. It was worth a try."

"Well, you have to understand the point of view of the Ministry of Justice. They don't want to open the files. They are probably afraid of what might happen. Look at the German example, the DDR. What a mess. At the very least, consternation, divorces, lawsuits. At worst, who knows…murder? And what good can be served now for all that to see the light of day?"

"Yes. I thought so. People say that opening the files, probably even this little crack, would focus people on the past, not the future. I can understand that."

"So can I," Inspector Racz said. "But that doesn't solve our problem."

Robbie saw that the time had come to be direct. Since it was "our" problem now, perhaps Racz had something in mind. "Where do you think we might go from here?"

"I haven't seen the file, mind you. But I did a little checking based on the article that Janos Magassy had written. I was intrigued by what he said, and what he failed to say." He paused for a longer time, sipping his coffee and thinking hard.

"There is a possibility that this case may never be solved," he finally said. "If it is not, that offends my very profession, particularly when I think we may have the means to proceed."

"What do you mean, Inspector?"

"There may be a witness who could help. I mean Eva Molnar of course. We finally located her, but she refuses to talk with us. She distrusts the police. After what she has been through, who can blame her? She may not even be of sound mind. That seems to be her way of coping with intruders. All I can say is that she might hold the key to this puzzle, or part of it."

"How did you find her?"

"I located her through ordinary police methods. Anybody could do the same with the same access. I did not use the 1956 files, which by the way I am not authorized to see. And so, leaving 1956 aside, I wonder whether you might have better luck in asking her to cooperate with us. It is an unofficial request, of course. Anyway, as you'll see, she is out of our national jurisdiction. As a diplomat, perhaps you'll know what to do."

Robbie was intrigued. "I am highly complimented, and I'll do what I can. Where does she live now?"

Inspector Racz wrote down the address. It was a tiny agricultural village not far from the city of Gyula at the edge of the Great Plain, and just on the Romanian side of its border with Hungary.

*   *   *

If Robbie's ears were ringing during his luncheon with Julie, it was with good reason. His sister Evalyn and Elena Dos Santos, renewing their acquaintance formed in Bordeaux, were at that same moment having luncheon at the *Busulo Juhasz* restaurant in Buda. The "Sorrowful Shepherd" restaurant clearly did not derive its name from its pleasant hilly location, with a fine view overlooking the Danube.

"I'm not really keeping an eye on your brother, you understand. But I do notice things. She doesn't seem happy with her husband and well, you know, the grass is said to be greener. What has happened to that nice French journalist that Robbie knew in Bordeaux, Sylvie Marceau?"

*   *   *

Robbie, meanwhile, fiddled with his *wienerschnitzel* in the little restaurant near the *Varosliget,* or public park north of Heroes Square in Pest. It used to be fashionable, but now the area was down at the heels, and prob-ably could be bought for very little money.

At the turn of the century this had been a fashionable public area, Budapest's Tivoli Gardens, with a carousel so famous that Molnar's *Liliom* celebrated the man who ran it.

Robbie had seen *Liliom* at the Madach Theater recently. It was pure magic. He had even recognized Liliom's teasing speech, which had become the song "If I Loved You" in Rodgers and Hammerstein's "Carousel," their adaptation of Molnar's play.

That seemed to fit where he and Julie were.

Or did it?

He enjoyed her company. Her anxiousness to see him was flattering. He worried about sinking into bureaucratic middle age. She seemed to be proof that he was not doing that.

Alex was away from Budapest for a few weeks. There was an Australian Chiefs of Mission conference back in Canberra. Robbie was intrigued by the possibility. But he realized something very important as they finished luncheon. He did not love this woman. He was fond of her, yes.

There was no magic, no Molnar in their relationship. For just a moment he remembered Sylvie Marceau, sitting beside him in the St. Andre Cathedral in Bordeaux.

Nothing had yet happened that needed to be unraveled, but all was possible, all was near. The possibility to begin came and lingered in the air.

Robbie asked about Alex instead.

Well, if he wants to be reassured about Alex's distance, he'll get it, Julie thought. She replied that since their Sunday afternoon at the Szepvaros villa on Lake Balaton, her husband had been more remote than ever.

"It was when we were leaving. Szepvaros said something about his group. You know, Robbie, the Magassy survivors. He told us that Nemzeti, that funny little fellow at the Ministry of Justice, had not been the last survivor after all.

"It seems that Nemzeti had drunk too much and was babbling that someone named Csaba had reappeared and had saved him. Insisted he leave at the last possible moment. No wonder he always looks like he has just met a ghost. He's haunted."

"And that interested Alex?"

"So much so that he kept dead silence all the way home."

Nemzeti may meet his ghosts sooner than he thinks, Robbie thought. His decision was made. He paid the bill and drove Julie back to her empty residence. There they shared a lingering and affectionate kiss. It did not strike her until much later that it meant goodbye.

*   *   *

Robbie returned to his office. He had a couple of hours free before his visit with Senator Abernathy to the *Nemzeti Muzeum* (National Museum). He had a visit from Iliu Monescu, and then a call from his sister Evalyn.

Evalyn's voice had been a bit arch. She wanted to know what the dinner plans were. Robbie thought the *Matyas Pince* (Matthias Cellar), a folkloric tavern restaurant on the Pest side near the Danube that was popular with tourists, crowded and jolly, would be just the thing.

Iliu Monescu had stopped by the Embassy to compare political notes and share his plans for the trip to Gyula. The outing would be a long drive, but a pleasant one. They could all see a play at the Gyula Castle ruins in the evening if the weather held. During the day, if they wanted, Monescu could also arrange an excursion into neighboring Romania.

"By the way," he confided, "I think we've located the Eva Molnar that you mentioned." He gave Robbie an address. It was the same one that Inspector Racz had furnished earlier. "She lives there with her daughter. She doesn't see many people. You might possibly be the exception."

After Monescu left, Robbie wrote a very careful letter in Hungarian to Eva Molnar. He asked to see her, and gave the date that he and Evalyn would be in Gyula. That seemed incomplete and unsatisfactory. Then he smiled and wrote that he hoped that she would remember his father, the *Konzul Elvtars.*

*   *   *

Senator James Abernathy was a natural story teller. Robbie enjoyed his company, all the more so since he was not saddled with being control officer for the visit. Since the Senator's main interest was NATO integration, Colonel Tidings had drawn that duty. But Abernathy wanted to see the Crown of St. Stephen, and Ambassador Horton understood that this would be Robbie's best opportunity to talk with him about the Magassy case.

The Embassy car let them off at the National Museum. They stopped and glanced at the statues of Garibaldi and the Hungarian poet Arany near the entrance. Robbie said that this was the very spot where Sandor Petofi, reading his poetry, had led the March 15, 1848 demonstration against the Hapsburgs that sparked a national rebellion for freedom.

"It was the original Paul Henreid scene from Rick's *Cafe Americain* in 'Casablanca,'" Robbie said.

"No wonder that the 1956 Revolution began at the Petofi statue near the Danube," Abernathy nodded in agreement.

Abernathy then answered Robbie's question before he could even formulate it properly. He wanted to get it off his chest. "I was the most junior member of the House Committee on International Relations back in the Ninety-Fifth Congress, in 1977," he began. "It was all new to me. We had had the Hungarian crown and regalia since the end of the war, when they had fallen into our hands. The question of returning them was a perennial one. President Carter finally made the decision to give back the Crown of St. Stephen to the Hungarians, and he announced it the day that Congress had adjourned. We were bombarded with letters and telegrams from Hungarian-Americans in our districts. And so a hearing was held. I'll never forget it.

"Whether or not you agreed with Carter's decision, he went about it ass backwards. As I said, he waited until Congress was out of session to announce it. Then word started to leak, so the White House announced it—on November 4. 1977. That was the 21st anniversary to the day of the Red Army's brutal suppression of the 1956 Hungarian Revolution. Nice timing!

"Our Committee, or rather the Subcommittee on Europe and the Middle East, got recalled by Chairman Lee Hamilton on November 9th. It was the first really spontaneous descending on Washington I ever saw. Busloads and busloads of people, most of them mad as hell. 'Why was the Crown of St. Stephen being given back at this time when Janos Kadar, the traitor who brought in the Russians and betrayed the 1956 Revolution, was still head of the Party there?' That was the main question. But there was another one…'Why did you lie to us about your plans?'…For right up until the announcements, there were flat official denials that anything of the sort was underfoot.

"The testimony was compelling. I hadn't known much about the Crown of St. Stephen, one way or another. But I'll never forget that hearing. At the end, it was obvious to me that the entire thing was badly done. I wouldn't go as far as some, to say that the return of the Crown should have awaited a democratic government. Hungary, after all, had almost never had one. But if such progress had been made away from tyranny… and that was the Carter Administration's case…then they should have been up front about it. For another thing, they should have exhibited the Crown and the regalia in Cleveland and Washington or New York under proper guard before they were returned. Then decent Hungarian-Americans could have seen their national treasures here. But that was the Carter Administration's way. No class."

They went up the steps and entered the museum. Then they paid the separate entrance fee to see the Crown exhibit, to the left of the entrance hall. Their tickets were collected and they entered a small darkened room, alone except for a hovering guard.

Abernathy finished his narrative. "The most marvelous thing about those hearings came at the very end. A former Prime Minister, Ferenc Nagy, and Major General Bela Kiraly, who had been Commander in Chief of the National Guard, Freedom Fighters in 1956, both spoke. They favored the Crown's return. The crowd didn't like what they heard, but they listened respectfully.

"It seemed like theater, almost, and those of us up on the dais for the Committee became irrelevant when they spoke. You could almost see the house lights dim. They talked about the need for young Hungarians to know their own heritage, and that just wasn't possible with the Crown in a vault at Fort Knox. I thought then they were right and I still think so, but I was ashamed of how it was done."

Robbie and Senator Abernathy read their guidebooks silently. The Crown of St. Stephen was presented to King Stephen by Pope Sylvester II in the year 1000, its Latin half later united with a Byzantine lower crown. Stephen was crowned as a Christian monarch at Esztergom, and later was canonized. That set Hungary's course as a Western nation, and the Crown of St. Stephen became, over the centuries, the legal personification of the Hungarian nation.

It had fallen into American hands as World War II ended. With it in three separate display areas were the royal sceptre and orb, and Gisella's robe, which by tradition had been woven by Queen Gisella for her husband Stephen's coronation.

They were struck by admiration for Gisella's Robe. Hungarian craftsmanship still could rise to the heights. The damaged cloth had been expertly rewoven and was well displayed. Senator Abernathy grumbled. "Well, anyway, the Carter people were right about one thing. Here, on exhibit, these precious objects do some good. I'm glad to have seen them."

"Too bad we're the only visitors here," Robbie softly added.

The two men lingered by the exhibition cases, out of hearing of the museum guards. "What do you make of the Magassy killing? Ambassador Horton told me that she has assigned you to follow that investigation."

"Yes," Robbie answered. "It depends upon where you start. If the idea is that his murder was somehow linked to what took place in 1956, it would be helpful to see the files from that period. But that isn't going to happen. So we're trying to reconstruct what went on without the files."

"You mean that someone who knew Magassy then might have killed him?"

"Something like that. My working theory is that someone who was pretending to be a member of that group killed Magassy to avoid exposure."

Robbie continued. "Do you know anything else about his plans for this trip, Senator?"

"Well, he briefed me about his plans, and the memorial project in particular. That struck me as a fine idea, by the way. I hope that it can be continued. He was going to contact the surviving members of his group. I remember he was really looking forward to that. There was certainly no sense of any danger as far as he was concerned, although he did want to try to find out—and lay to rest—the persistent rumor that his group had somehow been betrayed. Also he was quite sure that he could contact one missing member, the woman Eva Molnar."

"Did he mention Csaba Kovacs?"

"Odd you should mention him. Magassy said he wanted to find out, once and for all, what had happened to Kovacs. That was why he wanted to gather the group together. Perhaps someone could set his mind at rest. But I didn't have the impression that he had any real hopes of doing so."

"Where does Ambassador Kovatch fit into this?" Senator Abernathy asked. "Your Uncle Seth and I had a chat the last time he was in Washington. He told me that Kovatch was taking a special interest in the Magassy case."

"Yes. As Uncle Seth may have told you, we think that Ambassador Kovatch is the brother of Csaba Kovacs. So does the Agency. Ambassador Kovatch, who emigrated to Australia after 1956 and made a fortune there, seems to be trying to reconstruct what happened in 1956. Possibly he has revenge on his mind."

"Sort of a modern Count of Monte Cristo?"

"I think so. The problem is that he didn't know the original group members personally, which means he can be misdirected."

The Senator pursed his lips. "That may explain something that Australian liaison passed us a while back in Canberra. Kovatch is seeking his government's backing for a number of political candidates in the next elections. He wants secret backing for Esztergondos and a few others. He argues that the winning candidates will be grateful and well disposed towards Australian investment."

"In other words, he wants his government to intervene in the internal politics of a friendly country. He's seen too many CIA movies. Are they taking him seriously?"

"No. He'll probably be recalled after a decent interval."

Robbie mused, "That explains what his revenge would be against one of the group, Deputy Imre Mohacsi. He's trying to target him for defeat in the next elections. I wonder what information he'll have them use." He didn't add that he wondered what Kovatch had in mind for Nemzeti, the next on his list. He suspected that he already knew.

"Odd you should mention Mohacsi," Senator Abernathy said. "I've met him and been rather impressed."

"So have I," Robbie agreed.

"That is why I wondered about his wife Magda. It was an open secret that she and Magassy had met during one of her husband's first trips to Washington. They were smitten with each other. I don't know how far it went, but I can guess. That was one reason why Magassy was so eager to return to Budapest. His wife knew nothing about it."

Swell, Robbie thought. That enlarges the list. Now I've got Mohacsi, the jealous husband. There is Nemzeti, who may or may not have felt betrayed by Magassy in 1956. And then there is Szepvaros, who seems to have joined the group at the last possible moment in 1956. Nobody knows what happened to Csaba Kovacs. He's probably in one of those unmarked Section 301 graves that I saw at the cemetery.

To make matters worse, the Hungarian Government won't open their intelligence files. The one possible remaining eyewitness, Eva Molnar, is said to be a mental case. And to complete this jolly picture I've got Ambassador Kovatch returning in a couple of weeks from Canberra, revenge in mind.

"You know," Senator Abernathy went on, "this is all really quite interesting. There are times when I wish that I had gone into diplomacy."

Sometimes I wish that I had too, Senator, was Robbie's unspoken thought.

*   *   *

Evalyn and Robbie enjoyed the lively gypsy orchestra in the *Matyas Pince*. They interspersed requests with familiar medleys of gypsy and Hungarian favorites, and some well-known operetta songs. Lehar and Liszt were both Hungarian, after all. It was a crowded restaurant, noisy and the food was good.

"How can I be serious with you in a place like this?" Evalyn pouted.

"My strategy exactly, to put you off stride. What's on your mind?"

"Robbie, I had luncheon with Elena Dos Campos, and we talked a bit about you."

"And?"

"And you ought to know that your get togethers with the wife of the Australian Ambassador are making the rounds. You don't really need that problem for your career, Big Brother. Just what's going on?"

"Nothing I can't handle." He was annoyed.

"I thought that you really cared for Sylvie Marceau. Or was that just in Bordeaux?"

That stung. "Evalyn, I can tell the difference between what is real and what is not. Yes, I was attracted to Julie Kovatch. It's flattering to be the center of her attention. No, I am not serious about her. I am about Sylvie." He paused and carefully studied the menu.

That didn't work. They had already ordered. Evalyn smelled that something else was going on. "Robbie, I know you too well. You're not levelling with me. What's up?"

He folded his hands in a mock prayerful attitude. "Saints preserve us from prying Baby Sisters. Yes, something is going on, something worthwhile."

She waited.

"I think that her husband is snooping around trying to investigate what happened in 1956. Uncle Seth tells me that Kovatch and one of Magassy's group, a missing man named Csaba Kovacs, probably were brothers. When Ambassador Kovatch finds out what happened, I wouldn't put revenge past him.

"Meaning murder?"

"Meaning murder. Julie doesn't know it, but she has kept me informed of what her husband knows. That's why I started seeing her in the first place." He looked carefully at his sister. "Well, that's stretching it. The truth is, I'm not exactly proud of myself, but it may be worth it in the long run. In the meantime, I can put up with some negative press."

She nodded for a moment in understanding, then she gave the lecture. "I still think it's a lousy thing to do. Another month and you'd be paying the price. Typical dumb male. It's a good thing I came just when I did!" She shook her head emphatically.

He tried to let it pass. "How is your stuffed cabbage?"

"Superb. I'm glad we weren't brought up on it. I'd be thirty pounds overweight." She thought for a moment. "Robbie, is all this connected with the Magassy murder?"

"It seems to be. There is more to it than Kovatch looking for revenge. My working theory is that Magassy was murdered because he had found out who were the genuine members of his group in 1956, and who was a police informer. There are other possibilities. But there may be one sure way to find out."

"Tell me about it."

"I'm going to need your help on this one, Evalyn. We talked about it earlier. It's a very touchy matter, not only for this case, but it brings back memories for Dad as well."

"Have you located this Molnar woman?"

"Yes, I have. I've written to her. She lives just across the border in Romania. We'll be going near there with my diplomatic touring group shortly, to Gyula. I'd like you to come along and help me talk with Eva Molnar. It may be very important."

"Will she see us?"

"That's an open question. She won't cooperate with the police, and they've asked for my help in talking with her. There is no harm in trying. Your presence may reassure her, frankly."

"I'll do what I can. Why is she so important?"

"She may not be. But if, like Magassy, she can still identify the members of that group, then she may hold the key to solving his murder."

* * * * * * * * * *

The Eleventh Day—November 2, 1956

The day smelled like trouble to Janos. Hell, he could almost see the trouble that was approaching. Still, it was not there yet. It took a while for a modern army to plan and execute a well-coordinated attack maneuver. Clearly the Russians would have learned from their half-assed attempts to terrorize the civilian population earlier.

This time they would forget the Socialist brethren bullshit and attack like an army. It would come soon, Janos thought. Soon, but not quite yet.

He called his group together and told them that today, everyone who wanted to and could, should go home for a family visit. Who knew when it might be possible again? Now was the time. He only insisted that at all times, there had to be three people at Barat Street, two in perimeter patrolling and one at their storefront headquarters.

Eva and Karoly elected to stay. Karoly pointed out that, after all, he had nowhere to go. Eva nodded and said that her home was across the Romanian border, and her family was here now. There was no point in her going back to the university for the day, and she would meet Csaba's family at the proper time, not now. Csaba decided to stay with her, despite her protests.

They agreed to meet again at Barat Street by early evening, while it was still light. It was too dangerous to be out after dark anyway. Despite the weapons turn-in, and the National Guard formation, there were still lots of trigger-happy people on the streets or at their windows.

Jozsef couldn't bring himself to admit that he had nobody to visit. He wished so much that he did have someplace to go. He was an orphan, and there was no point in seeing his aunt again. They had said goodbye anyway after the wreath-laying for his cousins Pista and Red. Going there would just aggravate her pain. He decided to wander down the boulevard towards the Danube. It was a nice day, not too cold.

He started out. The destruction was widespread. It looked like World War Two to his eyes. There were burned-out tanks on all the major streets. After a while, he stopped counting them. Shop windows were broken in many areas, but there had been no looting. That was startling behavior for a needy population. Jozsef felt no urge at all to reach into the unguarded windows and help himself. For a rather practiced shoplifter, that was amazing. Not that he didn't need everything. He did.

What he missed, he realized, was a sense of being normal, like everybody else. That meant being warm and having parents and a place to stay. It also meant getting food regularly, although he knew from experience that that was not a given as far as his friends were concerned either. Still, just imagine having a bowl of rich meat soup and some crusty bread, and even butter. A glass of beer, or maybe even wine from the Balaton would be fine too. Pipedreams.

He could just remember his parents, at one celebration, a wedding ceremony he thought, enjoying a glass of wine together. It had been five years earlier, just before his mother had died of tuberculosis during that freezing winter. Then the *AVH* had come for his father, whose political opinions were said to have been unreliable. *Elvittek.* They took him away. Jozsef had just missed going to the orphanage, when his Aunt Maria had taken him in. He was lucky that she had done so.

There had been some friends at school. In addition to his cousins Pista and Red, he had really looked up to Karoly, in the last form, years older. *Karoly Bacsi* ("Uncle Karoly") was athletic, good at games, and endlessly practiced his soccer moves, both defensive and scoring. Karoly had once told him that soccer would be his way out of Hungary. There was a national team, and they did play in international competition. Maybe if he could make it, the chance would come to defect during a tour of the West.

"Disszidalt" ("He defected"), they would then say. He defected. It was something you heard about in whispers. The punishments were severe, for you and your family, if you were caught. For that matter, even if you made it without being caught what was meted out to your family that stayed behind was bad enough. The authorities counted on that, and it was always impossible to take everyone, even with a small family. Someone was always left behind, like a hostage.

Karoly hadn't made the national team. He was good, actually very good, but not quite good enough. And then, Jozsef had heard that Karoly had tried the circus. Circus people also got passports and travelled, and sometimes were even allowed to visit the West. But then Karoly had fallen, and that was that. He was glad that Karoly was with them. That was like family.

So was Magda, in a way. He wished that he could have summoned the courage to ask her to go on this walk with him. She had been easily the prettiest girl in the class, and the nicest. One week she had been out of school, and he had found that he missed her a lot. When she returned, she told him what happened.

She hadn't really been hurt, she assured him. They had just slapped her around a bit. It had been a nice spring day, and she had worn a pretty scarf, a light-colored silk one that set off her hair beautifully. It was obviously foreign.

In fact it was from Italy. Her mother had gotten it during a trip to Rome, before the war of course. She had died a few years after the war. Remembering her, Magda had worn the scarf for the first time that morning.

She had been seen on a streetcar wearing the scarf. Someone had denounced her for this evidence of Western decadence. The police had told her that it was lucky for her that she was just a child. Still, they cuffed her a bit, and her ears hurt for a long time afterwards. She even had had trouble hearing the judge's lecture when her case came before the People's Court.

"It was a good thing that I couldn't hear the judge. I think they were trying to scare me and break my spirit," she had said to Jozsef. "Just like they are breaking our country."

It was true. Hungary was a nation of fear. People informed on each other. They took refuge in drink. They went sullenly to work, did the minimum required, and then went home and argued. And everywhere they were surrounded by symbols of the proud Austro-Hungarian Empire, stones shouting that today was a lie.

That is why, after school, parents very cautiously would ask their children what they had learned that day. When the children were old enough. they would be told the truth about their country and its history. It was dangerous, but it helped to keep just alive a spark of freedom. As Petofi had written, one day they would be slaves no longer.

Jozsef lingered before the darkened building on the corner of the ring boulevard, not far from Parliament Square. He decided to have a cigarette and rest from his long walk. He really had walked farther then he had intended, lost in his thoughts.

There was a sudden gust of wind off the river, and his match went out. He stepped into an alcove to try again.

It was a quiet moment, with nobody else on the street. He lit his cigarette and took a deep drag, filling his lungs with the cheap tobacco smoke. Then he coughed in surprise.

Coming out of a side door of the building just a few feet away was a man who looked familiar. He was surrounded by four harsh-looking *AVH* men whose flap overcoat pockets couldn't conceal the fact that they were armed.

There was no place to hide.

"Get that kid! He knows me!" A quick scuffle, grabbing hands, and pistol butts smashing into his head. That was all that Jozsef knew before the darkness fell.

Chapter Thirteen

▼

Ladies' Choice

The phone call from Sylvie Marceau was an unexpected delight. Evalyn took the call, and with a pleased expression handed the phone to her brother.

"*Bonjour, Mon Cheri. T'as envie de te promener un peu?*" Her voice was like silver bells. Robbie thought that he never heard such welcome music.

"Sylvie, where are you? Of course I'd like to take a trip. What's on your mind?"

"A new assignment, not exactly in Hungary, but next door. President Chirac is taking a state visit to Prague, and my television station chose me to cover the visit. So I'm going this time, with a cameraman. It's this next weekend. Can you come and meet me?"

Robbie didn't even look at his sister. "Of course. It's our Labor Day weekend, a holiday at the Embassy. Can we make it a long weekend? How long will you be in Prague?"

"Just Saturday and Sunday morning, for the official portion of the visit. I'll arrive Friday noon. Have to be back Sunday night, so my curfew is the press plane early Sunday evening."

"Leave Friday night and Sunday for me to plan. Have you got your hotel reservation?"

"It's being made by the station. I'll tell them to make it a double, with a great view."

"I'll call you in a day with my plans. *Je t'aime.*"

Evalyn grinned when Robbie told her his plans. "Say hi for me, Robbie, if you can remember anything once you see Sylvie."

*   *   *

It was a glorious weekend throughout Central Europe, one of nature's periodic dispensations for the cruelties of the region. Imre Mohacsi congratulated himself for having decided to go home to Szeged for the weekend. Everyone knew Szeged from their purchases of paprika, but that was about all. His adopted town had been forgotten by the world, he sometimes thought.

Not that Szeged didn't have its own attractions, besides the paprika. It was a university town with a rich past, although come to think of it, when Szent-Gyorgy won the Nobel Prize for his work here in isolating Vitamin C before the Second World War, it had been paprika, not oranges, that the scientist had analyzed.

Now the *art nouveau* town, largely rebuilt after epic flooding in the nineteenth century, was at its most appealing. Clearly the promise of Emperor Franz Joseph then that the town would be rebuilt, more attractive than ever *("Szeged szebb lesz, mint volt")* had been realized. Mohacsi particularly enjoyed strolling through *Klauzal ter* (Klauzal Square), admiring its neo-classical buildings. When the Tisza River stayed within its boundaries, life here was pleasant indeed.

Tucked into the edge of the Hungarian Great Plain on the nation's southern frontier, Szeged suited Mohacsi perfectly. Last night's dinner in the garden at the Fisherman's Inn on the Tisza River with some key local supporters had been delightful. Mohacsi could see why the restaurant had been a favorite haunt of Edward, Prince of Wales at the end of the nine-teenth century.

Magda was particularly enchanting throughout dinner. Sometimes, when Imre was preoccupied with his official political responsibilities, time had seemed to go by without any savor, like a speeding calendar flipping its pages. Accomplishment was measured by small bargains made, kept and lost. And then, some grey hairs began to appear, and what had been the profit and loss? He couldn't remember. When he couldn't remember, it was time to reassess his priorities.

He had accomplished a lot, Imre thought, but had only enjoyed life with and through Magda. The prospect of a cabinet ministry did appeal to him, he had to confess it. But he would never be Prime Minister. And he was beginning to doubt whether any further advance that took him away from his city and his wife could possibly be worth the effort.

He had discovered the cache of letters quite by accident, really. It was one of those utterly stupid things. Rising late that Saturday morning, he had cut himself shaving. No styptic pencil. He then had checked his wife's cabinet to see if she had any antiseptic. The letters were there below the cabinet in a small storage area. She must have been looking at them, for the package was untied, and that is how Imre noticed the ribbon just jut-ting forth under some boxes of paper tissue.

They were not numerous, but they were to the point. It was obvious that they referred to the past. They also showed the writer, Janos Magassy, as the supplicant. Clearly his attentions were no longer timely or welcome, judging from their pleading tone, and the repeated references to earlier let-ters not having been answered.

The latest had been written a few weeks before his trip to Hungary. Magassy had asked to see her once again. It had been several years since their last trip to Washington. He said that he would be in touch with her husband shortly after arriving in Budapest. Then they could take matters from there. If that were indeed the case, then Magassy had probably been killed before he had been able to plan a more private meeting.

Unusual for him, Mohacsi lit a prebreakfast cigarette, and tried to decide what to do. The choices seemed fairly clear. So did the fact that his wife had not seemed terribly upset when the news of Magassy's death had reached them. The emotions of the past were clearly spent, whatever they had been. He replaced the small packet of letters in the cupboard, exactly as he had found them. He finished the cigarette and stubbed it out.

He went downstairs and joined Magda at the breakfast table. He looked straight at her for the first time in ages, and smiled. She was his only audience, indeed the only one that ever really counted. "How about a special evening out tonight, Magda? Just the two of us. We haven't done that in years, it seems. Wear that fine new dress that suits you so very well. We might as well take advantage of this glorious weather. We should do that much more often, don't you think?"

*   *   *

Julie Kovatch was furious. The receptionist at the American Embassy confirmed what Elena Dos Santos had already told her, that Robbie had left Budapest He was spending the weekend in Prague. The receptionist hadn't known of course what Elena had mischievously added, that Robbie's quick trip to Prague was to see that old girlfriend from Bordeaux. He had mentioned her name to her once, in an offhand sort of way. Sylvie Marceau, that was it. That was the same person that Elena had mentioned. And Elena had known them both in Bordeaux. "Quite a couple," she had said.

Well, what did she expect? They had no understanding. They had had luncheon a few times. He had seemed interested, but it hadn't gone any farther than that. If only Alex were more attentive! It was ridiculous to be discarded under these circumstances before their relationship had even properly begun. It was almost funny, in a way. Still, Robbie should have said something. She blamed him for that.

Everything was such a muddle.

And this Magassy business seemed to cut across everything. Her husband Alex seemed rather preoccupied by it. So, come to think of it, had Robbie. And then, at the opera just the other evening, when she had been included in the Szepvaros box, even that German banker had pumped her just a little about the case.

Well, they had all been in it together in the past, she supposed. It was almost with a sense of malicious delight that she played with Szepvaros's innocent sounding questions. Yes, Alex had been interested in the Magassy case. She assumed that it was because he had been intrigued by the memorial. That had sounded like a very good idea. Worthwhile, he had said.

"The curious thing," she added, "was that Robbie Cutler had been almost as interested as Alex in all of these details. It seemed to go beyond the question of the memorial. Come to think of it, he had been more than intrigued by whatever interested Alex. Just the other day, it was that business about someone named Csaba being the last survivor of their Freedom Fighter group."

He had raised an eyebrow.

"You remember, Mr. Szepvaros, you had said something about that to us as Alex and I were leaving your villa at the Balaton. It got Alex's attention, and that's putting it mildly. When I mentioned it to Robbie Cutler the other day, he seemed quite interested as well, although he hid his interest more smoothly than Alex ever could have done."

Julie had no idea what her host's smile meant. She hoped that it meant that Cutler would have an uncomfortable moment or two. Serve him right if someone else solved his precious little investigation, while he was off in Prague with what's-her-name!

*   *   *

Attila Nemzeti was walking with Margit in the *Varosliget* in Budapest. On such a fine Saturday morning the crowds were full of good humor, and treats were liberally bought from vendors by attentive young escorts. They might be wearing the latest jeans and T-shirts showing western rock groups and slogans, but the gesture showed something else, something more Central European. It was Liliom showing off on a glorious day.

Attila and Margit strolled past the little bridge that led to the *Vajdahunyad*, the replica of the Janos Hunyadi Castle in Hunedoara, Transylvania. Like so many other monuments around Budapest, on both sides of the Danube, the castle replica had been started towards the end of the nineteenth century. It was built for an international fair to mark the millennium of the migration of Hungarian tribes here, Arpad's arrival in 895.

That castle had been a good idea, really, Attila always thought. With Transylvania lost to Romania, at least we have a replica in Budapest of the Hunyadi dynasty's most famous castle. It was King Matyas "The Just" Hunyadi who had elevated Buda to a capital on a par with any in Europe, at a time when the populations of England and Hungary had been roughly equal. From the Matthias Church or *Matyastemplom* to the *Matyas Pince* Restaurant, memories of Hungary's legendary king, who mingled with his people in disguise, could still be found.

Attila suddenly remembered that even the name Corvin had its connection with King Matyas. *Corvinus* was Latin for raven, and there was a raven in the Hunyadi family crest, the legendary raven that had brought hope to an imprisoned king.

How appropriate, Attila thought.

Not far away in the park was Gundel's Restaurant, now restored to its precommunist glory. Attila could not afford to take his wife there, on a bureaucrat's salary. But he planned to do so anyway, when he could. It was first rate, his Minister had said, world class. They sat on a bench and enjoyed the sunshine.

"What's bothering you, Attila?" She could always read his moods, clear as a mirror.

"No hiding anything from you, that's for sure! We had a question the other day, about opening up the 1956 intelligence files. I got called in. It goes to a Minister Without Portfolio in the Prime Minister's office, but we have some input."

"Does that happen very often?"

"No. It is rare indeed. What made this one so unusual is that it is linked to the Magassy murder."

"What is the connection?"

"Somebody seems to think that there may be something in the files to explain what happened to Magassy, an intelligence connection of some sort."

"Who was asking about it?"

"They didn't say. But I think that Szepvaros was right. It must have been the Australian Ambassador, Kovatch, trying to find out happened to his brother."

"Have you seen the file?"

"No. I am not authorized to see it. Neither is my own Minister, for that matter. We were concerned with the precedent. Anyway, we advised against opening the file."

"And that troubles you, Attila?"

"Somewhat, yes. As I said, I don't know what is in the file. It could be a lot of garbage. Probably is. In my experience, that is what most intelligence files contain anyway, a lot of unsubstantiated rumor, some allegations to curry favor, and not much if anything that is usable, at least from a legal point of view. It would have set a very bad precedent."

"That's what they've found out in the old DDR, I gather."

"Yes, exactly. I wouldn't be surprised if intelligence files in the western democracies were similar. They have to be handled very carefully, and taken with shovels of salt."

"So why are you upset about this?"

"It's my conscience. I suppose that I'm concerned that Kovatch could have found out that I was the last to see Csaba. It must be in the records somewhere. Possibly they caught Csaba at the end, since he's never turned up, and interrogated him. Who knows? Or the police investigating Janos

Magassy's murder might have found a motive for me to kill him, since he had left me there wounded. It's all pretty farfetched, but there it is."

"What you are saying is that you wish that you had given different advice to the Minister?"

"No, really I'm not. As an outsider, I would have given exactly the same advice. I really don't think that these files should ever see the light of day. Just, well, it's complicated morally, given my personal involvement in all this. Which, by the way, I mentioned to the Minister."

"That's why the believers have their confessions, I suppose."

"Exactly."

They sat on the bench in silence for a few moments. The Vajdahunyad Castle formed a splendid backdrop. Just beyond it, the lake rippled a bit in the breeze. That is where Attila and Margit joined hundreds of other skaters for an afternoon's skating several times each winter, when the lake froze over.

"Attila?"

"Yes, Margit?"

"Why do you suppose that Kovatch is asking for those files?"

"To take his vengeance, I suppose."

"You mean to say that his revenge includes suicide?"

He was puzzled. "What do you mean?"

"I would think that associating his own name with such a request would be the very last thing that he would do. Are you absolutely sure that Kovatch did that?"

Attila thought for a moment, trying to recall exactly what they had been told. His memory was now much better, through constant effort.

"No, come to think of it. You're quite right. I assumed that it was Kovatch. What we were actually told was that the request was a diplomatic one."

"So it wasn't explicitly said, that the Australians had asked?"

"No, it was not," he said slowly, deliberately. "I just assumed that."

"Who else might be interested?"

"The Americans, obviously. We've seen that their political attache, Robbie Cutler, has been following the Magassy case. That seems quite natural, after all. Magassy was a prominent American citizen. They would want his murder solved."

"Tell me the truth, Attila. If you had thought that the Americans were asking rather than Kovatch, would your advice to the Minister have been the same?"

He did not hesitate. "Without question, yes."

"Are you absolutely clear on that?"

"Yes."

"Then I think you may want to have a little talk with Cutler. He may turn out to be your best ally."

"Oh." He looked at Margit with love and appreciation. "We really should plan to have dinner at Gundel's soon. Why should the nicest treats in Budapest always be reserved for the tourists? And you deserve it, my dear."

*   *   *

The weather was perfect for the short flight to Prague, and before he knew it, Robbie had landed and hailed an airport cab for the Hotel Inter Continental Praha, perfectly located on the Vlatava River in downtown Prague.

It hadn't been difficult to get this Friday afternoon off, and Evalyn had assured him that her plans for the weekend would keep her busy. If anything, she seemed pleased that he was meeting Sylvie. Evalyn would crown a shopping weekend with a Saturday Danube Bend dinner cruise that left from the banks of the Danube in Budapest. She was looking forward to it.

Robbie had thought to wire flowers for the room, and he had brought some 1988 Taittinger *Comtes de Champagne* to toast their reunion. Sylvie was waiting for him in their room on an upper floor of the Inter Continental. She opened the door, and he dropped his bags and stared at her. It was as though they had not been separated for nearly a year, since their farewell in Reims when Robbie had left to drive into Budapest, and Sylvie had returned to her television reporter job in Paris.

Stunningly dressed, at least to begin with, the exquisite Sylvie held him at arms length and inspected her property. "You haven't gained any weight on that famous Hungarian food. That's good. No new girl friends either, I trust?" she teased. Then they kissed and spent a memorable afternoon. Taittinger makes a nice chaser for her kisses, he thought. Nice that he remembers my favorite champagne, she thought. And that was all the thinking that either did until it was time to dress for dinner.

"Any preferences, *Ma Cherie?*"

"Actually, I thought something very informal," she said. "I know that you will have planned something nice for Sunday. You may surprise me with that. I'll surprise you now for tomorrow night. The official party had two extra press tickets for the opera at the Estate Theater. Would that please you? They're doing Mozart, I think. I'm not sure which one."

"Perfect. I've been reading about it." Robbie's guide book on the plane had featured the historic Tyl Theater, now renamed the Estate, where Mozart had given the premier performance of *Don Giovanni*. "Any preferences for tonight?"

"Yes. I want to go to a real Czech beer hall. The most famous one in Prague is called *U Fleku*. We can walk there and see something of the city too."

Their walk through the old and surprisingly undamaged city was a delight. They first strolled through the Old Town Square, arriving just in time to admire the Town Hall Clock Tower and its intricate mechanism, with medieval history including the threatening Turkish figure appearing before their eyes in a series of lifesize figures that had made their hourly rounds for five centuries.

They walked over the fourteenth century Charles Bridge spanning the Vltava River. Flanked by baroque statues, it seemed to invite snapshots. On the far bank the narrow old twisting streets of the Hradcany Castle district delighted them. Robbie had no difficulty imagining Franz Kafka in residence in his cramped little house in the district. Their walk ended at a scenic promenade overlooking the Vltava River.

Looking around the square on the castle side Robbie saw a fashionable restaurant and decided to keep it in mind should Sylvie's busy schedule tracking the visit of President Chirac permit. Then he hailed a cab to take them to the *U Fleku* beer hall. They crossed the Vlatva River, turned right and entered Kremencova Street.

This was the biggest beer hall that Robbie had seen since Munich. It was noisy and atmospheric. They found a table easily and ordered pork with bread dumplings, and dark Lezak beer. It was heavy and delicious. Robbie smiled at Sylvie. She was fun to be with, and as at home in this beer hall as she had been at the elegant wine estates they had visited together in Bordeaux. The energetic band played some crowd pleasing music that they didn't recognize, but Sylvie and Robbie hummed along anyway.

"Has Budapest turned out as you wanted?" she asked.

"It's a beautiful city, something like Prague, and I like the people. I'm getting outside of Budapest, too, to explore the countryside, and there is a lot to see. Yes, I'm pleased. You'd like it. I'm glad to be there. But it's too far from Paris."

She smiled at that. "And what are you up to? You must be involved in something. Your postcard hinted at that. You don't write as much as you used to do, by the way. I think that means that you are caught up in something. Am I right? What is it?"

"No fooling you, is there? Yes. There has been a murder, and our Ambassador has asked me to keep on top of the police investigation."

"Keep on top of it, or help them along?"

"The one while I'm doing the other, I suppose."

"Tell me about it."

He did, in some detail. Her journalistic instincts were aroused. She wanted to know more about the characters involved. The refusal of the Hungarian Government to open its intelligence files on the 1956 Revolution intrigued her. She wanted to know where in the city the fighting had taken place. He described the location and flavor of the Corvin region in southeast Budapest.

"How curious. Just like our *Faubourg St. Antoine* in Paris."

"What do you mean?"

"The quarter of Budapest you are talking about seems to correspond exactly to the part of Paris that was called that."

"What happened there?"

"Nothing much…only the siege of the Bastille in 1789."

By the end of dinner, several beers later, Robbie knew just how much he had missed her, and how much he also appreciated her interest in his cases. They seemed to have a love for detection in common, both historical and present.

       *   *   *

On Saturday afternoon the young woman walked down *Tancsics Mihaly utca* (Tansics Mihaly Street) in Buda's Castle Hill District towards the Matthias Church, gripping her large handbag as she walked. From time to time, she stopped to admire the yellow Baroque architecture of the houses. Architecture had always been one of her interests. It was an anomaly that the rich profited from this art. In a more justly organized society, that would not be so. Neighboring *Fortuna utca* (Fortuna Street) was also one of her favorites.

She crossed the street and walked towards Robbie Cutler's townhouse. Yes, that was the address. Just as she neared the townhouse, the front door opened. Bad luck. A young woman dressed for an informal evening emerged from the townhouse, looked at her closely for a moment, and then hailed a taxi. The pedestrian continued her walk without hesitation. Who was this young woman in the American diplomat's house? That complicated things. No matter. The package could be delivered the following day, suitably rewrapped of course.

       *   *   *

The visit of President Chirac to Prague was a busman's holiday for Robbie. He rather enjoyed watching the preparations for the visit from the viewpoint of the media, having once taken part in an official visit of the Secretary of State to Singapore. He was fascinated by the meticulous care with whch Syivie practiced where she would stand, if she had the good luck to get a personal interview with either Chirac or another ranking member of the French official party.

Once she even asked him to stand in for Chirac as they adjusted the camera angle, its filter and focus.

"Why me? Just because I'm around and don't charge union scale?"

"No, silly. You are about his build, coloring and size."

Suddenly an idea came to Robbie. He wondered whether the Hungarian police had thought of it. Perhaps not. He could hardly wait to try out his idea back in Budapest. It was a long shot, but it was worth trying.

*   *   *

The dinner cruise had been delightful, and the dance orchestra had added to the fun. Evalyn had really enjoyed herself, and stayed out later than she had planned. First there was the cruise along the Danube Bend, and then some of Robbie's Embassy friends had talked her into a late night of pub crawling in Budapest. It hadn't taken a great deal of persuasion. Well, why not kick up one's heels a bit while on vacation? Robbie would-n't object. That's what vacations are for, after all.

Finally as the dawn was breaking, the French Consul dropped her off at the townhouse, chivalrously waiting until she was safely inside before driv-ing away. No need to get up too early the next morning. Evalyn patted Minouette and talked to her for a few minutes to make up for her absence. Then she filled the cat's bowl to bribe her into a sound sleep, and herself went to bed. This diplomatic life was really quite pleasant, she decided.

*   *   *

The next morning Robbie and Sylvie packed into his rented Ford and drove out of Prague. The official side of the previous evening had been longer than they had thought. It meant grabbing sandwiches while the dignitaries dined. "Sure you prefer this end of official visits?" Robbie asked.

"I'm not at all sure of that," Sylvie said with a pout. It was a becoming pout, though. They had managed to get to the opera on Saturday evening, although they missed the first act of *Cosi Fan Tutti*. But now it was time for a pleasant drive.

Robbie's surprise was a day's excursion to Karlovy Vary, or Carlsbad, perhaps the most famous spa in Central Europe. In its heyday it had greeted kings, czars, emperors, writers, all the famous persons of the day. Some ninety miles west of Prague, Karlovy Vary was, with Marianske Lazne or Marienbad, one of the delights of the Czech Republic.

They took the northern route 6 instead of the southern route through Plzen. "We drank enough Friday night," Robbie recalled. Still, one day it would be fun to visit that brewing capital. Robbie had long thought that until microbrews became the rage back home, genuine Pilsener Urquell from Plzen was the finest beer made anywhere. You didn't have to spend a fortune for excellence. Pilsener Urquell proved that.

Sylvie was delighted with Karlovy Vary, "as long as I don't have to drink any bad tasting mineral water or bathe in mud," she had insisted. Like Bath in England there were fashionable shops and arcades. Little by little, the hotels and restaurants were beginning to reclaim their former splendor. Some were succeeding. The setting was green and pleasant, with rolling hills and forests, on the edge of the German border.

Their restaurant had an atmosphere of bearing and ease, perfect for an elegant luncheon. The waiters were unobtrusive, anticipating their wishes. Nobody wearing an apron wished them a nice day or mentioned his first name. There were helpful suggestions on the menu, with some light wines to match. Here being a waiter or a wine steward was a profession with its gradations and its own well-earned dignity.

At the beginning of their luncheon Robbie asked about desserts, and ordered a Baked Alaska. After the spritzers, the trout *amandine* and the loin of veal, the Baked Alaska was carried in triumph to their table by the head waiter, and lighted. The presentation was superb. So was the dessert. To their delight, the cake layer was clearly freshly made for their order. Sylvie smiled with pure pleasure. It was delicious.

She didn't dare ask what he was thinking, gauging rightly that he would take his own time and either recognize the moment, or not. The days when differences in religion, or the demands of a career, had seemed so terribly important, were now secondary. She wanted to spend the rest of her life with this delightful, courteous anachronism of a man.

Robbie turned to her with an open smile. "I don't know how this is done, really. I hardly care. All I know is that this is a moment that I'll remember always. And I don't mean the luncheon. You are so lovely. Will you marry me, Sylvie?"

She didn't even pretend to think it over. "Of course, *Mon Cheri*," she answered. Robbie kissed her. Without being asked, the wine steward appeared with a bottle of vintage Pol Roger champagne and poured them each a glass.

*   *   *

Evalyn's plan to bribe Minouette into sleeping late that Sunday through overfeeding hadn't worked. There the animal was, talking and licking Evalyn's face and acting for all the world like a dog that wants to go for a walk.

Minouette jumped on top of the *armoire* and meowed. Well, Siamese were talkers. Evalyn conceded defeat and got out of bed, stretched, reached over to pat Minouette, and looked out her window at the street below. It was just time for the early mass at the Matthias Church, but not many people were up yet.

Robbie had said that she would enjoy the service, and their father had mentioned it too. Now that Minouette had gotten her up, Evalyn resolved to go to a later service. She thought she heard the doorbell. Evalyn peered out the window again.

Just crossing the street, a little past the townhouse, was a young woman pushing a baby carriage. She got to the other side of the narrow street, and instinctively looked back. Evalyn, just hidden in the shadow of her window, distinctly saw her.

Puzzled, she went downstairs and carefully opened the door. As she had half suspected, a package was there, addressed to Robbie by hand. It was a routine package with American Embassy identification on the upper left hand corner. She gingerly brought it inside and put it on the kitchen table. It had a slight greasy stain. Whether the stain had come from the inside of the package she could not tell.

Evalyn went to the telephone and called the Embassy. After a number of rings, the phone was answered by the Marine guard. She identified herself.

"Gunnery Sergeant Lemuel Shiflett, Ma'am!"

Marine guards were friends. At every Embassy where her family had served when she and Robbie were children, Marine guards had been good company, and given them more of a sense of security than their numbers probably allowed. Also they always said nice things about their Mother's Thanksgiving Dinner, although turkey was the one thing their Belgian mother made badly. Marine guards were to be trusted.

"Gunny, a package has just been delivered here for Robbie. As you know, he is in Prague for the weekend. The person who brought it did not stay. She just rang the doorbell. I brought it inside. It's on the kitchen table, and seems to be leaking very slightly."

"Does it have any markings?"

"Yes, that's the curious thing. It has Embassy markings, and is hand addressed to my brother. The heavy outer envelope seems genuine enough. Did you send it over with the duty driver?"

"No, Ma'am. It didn't come from me. I'll check the book." He put the phone down for a moment. "No, it wasn't sent over yesterday, either. Nothing was sent. We wouldn't do that anyway without calling you."

She had remembered the procedures correctly. "I thought not. Gunny, I think I got a look at the person who delivered it. I saw her yesterday too, just outside the door. I'm sure it was the same person. Just one difference."

"What's that, Ma'am?"

"Between yesterday and today, either she has put on thirty pounds, or she has suddenly become eight months pregnant!"

His reaction was immediate. "Don't go near that package, Ma'am. I'm calling the police right now to send their bomb squad. I'll also send over the Duty Officer immediately. It's Consul Randy Davis this week. Have you met him?"

"Yes." She knew that if needed the Gunnery Sergeant would have given her Davis's description.

"Thanks so much, Gunny," she added. "It's always reassuring to know that the Marines have the situation in hand."

Gunny couldn't resist. "*Semper Fi*, Ma'am!" he said.

*   *   *   *   *   *   *   *   *   *

The Twelfth Day—November 3, 1956

The Friends gathered around the radio at noon and listened. Another government shakeup had taken place. The headline news was that General Pal Maleter had been made Defense Minister.

"We are getting ready," Imre ventured. "The other ranking officers have just gotten out of prison, or have not been hardened by combat. Maleter has been. We'll need that experience."

"Sure," Istvan said. "Don't forget though that the Russians are getting ready too. If they can't live with our being neutral, then trouble will be here soon. And this time, they'll do it right."

Janos Magassy looked around the room. Everyone seemed ready. They had all come back, except Jozsef. Well, who could blame him, Janos thought. Just a kid, and his cousins had been killed. Probably he and his

Aunt Maria had settled all that during her visit here on All Saints Day. No sense trying to talk them out of it. They had all suffered enough.

Rumors continued throughout the day. The Russians now had Ferihegy, the Budapest airport. That meant that United Nations forces couldn't land even if they had the spine to try it. The Russians were said to be pouring in from the east and were even, following a pincers movement, cutting off the border with Austria.

Optimists pointed to the negotiations going on with Russian Generals Stepanov and Chekhanen in rooms at the Parliament building. Heading the negotiation for the Hungarian side was Defense Minister Maleter. The Russians were said to have agreed to withdraw their armed forces. What was under discussion now was the timing for that withdrawal.

In the evening Csaba and Eva asked to be left alone, and withdrew to the apartment. They listened to the apartment radio for a while. The news was upsetting. Nothing concrete, but nervewracking all the same. Why was Maleter going to a dinner hosted by the Russians at their headquarters? Couldn't he see the trap?

Eva turned off the radio. She started to cry. "Now we're all alone," she said. "Nobody is ever going to help us. It's going to end for us the way it always has. Just us, and nobody to help."

Csaba held her in his arms and tried without success to kiss away her tears. His own were not far behind. The endless strain, the fighting, the worry about superior force, his concern about Eva and what would happen to her, it was too much to stand.

"We've done what we had to do, what is right," he said. "Maybe that will last. I'm only sorry that we had to meet when we did. We should have met in another time, in a different Hungary, a happier time, when we could have been together."

It was a very long speech for Csaba.

She kissed him silent. "Anytime with you is precious, my darling. I love you so. Promise you won't forget me, ever."

"How could I? Of course not. If they separate us, I'll find you. I'll always be with you, and love you forever."

She smiled at him. "You'll always be with me," she murmured. "Now everything will be all right."

She promised to take care of him forever. Our love will be our answer to this insane world, she decided. The thought sustained her through the long and sleepless night.

CHAPTER FOURTEEN

---▼---

Prise de Fer

Evalyn's call to the Inter Continental in Prague had been just too late to catch her brother. Robbie had already checked out for the return flight to Budapest. Sylvie was still there.

She had thought twice about upsetting Sylvie with her news. There was just no point in her worrying from afar. As it happened, Sylvie was too thrilled with her own news to pick up on Evalyn's nervousness.

"I really should leave this to Robbie," Sylvie said. "But since you have called, you'll be the first to know. Robbie proposed marriage today, and I said yes."

Evalyn was genuinely pleased. She had met and liked Sylvie in Bordeaux, and thought her a good match for her brother. Besides, it was clearly time for him to settle down, if moving to a new overseas location every few years could be called settling down! She congratulated Sylvie with real warmth. Her own news could wait.

Consul Randy Davis had made the arrangements with the police, and stayed with her until Robbie arrived from Ferihegy Airport. As soon as

Robbie had stashed his bags they drove together to see Inspector Racz, accompanied now by a security detail.

Evalyn and Robbie sat with Inspector Racz at Police Headquarters in Deak Square going over pictures from the known terrorist file. It was late Sunday evening.

"Do you see a connection between this attack and the Magassy murder?" Racz asked. "We do, for planning purposes anyway."

"Yes. Well, probably yes. It came sooner than I thought it might," Robbie replied. "We must be getting closer than we thought."

Evalyn's description was first programmed into the central police computer records, and then crossreferenced with national police files. There was no direct fit, although a few Hungarian woman criminals were tentative matches. None checked out. The available pictures of the possibles were not close matches.

"The woman is not Hungarian. Either that, or we are dealing with a new criminal, one that we haven't seen before." Racz frowned. "Let's open up the inquiry," he said to the computer technician. "Who have we got from the Russian Mafia active here now?"

Again the computer profiles did not match central records.

They tried something else. An artist's sketch from Evalyn's description might help, Racz suggested. One was made. It wasn't quite right. Evalyn thought there might be some danger that she would settle for an image that was something like the girl, but not really. If she looked long enough at what the police artist had produced, she might really begin to think that was what she had seen. But if it wasn't, how would that help anybody?

"Please excuse me," she said. "Maybe I can do this. After all, I saw her twice." Evalyn was a competent draftsman, and she produced several sketches, of the woman both as she had first seen her, and then "pregnant" on the second day. Evalyn fussed a bit, and then pronounced herself satisfied with the likeness.

Racz wrote up the woman's method to accompany the sketches, and then computer photos were sent to the FBI, INTERPOL, and other agencies with international connections. For good measure, Robbie had a copy messengered to Consul Randy Davis, for checking with the Department of State's Tipoff, or counter-terrorist retrieval files.

An hour later, as Evalyn was finishing her written statement, and Racz's orders for their protection had been approved by his superiors, the first answer came, from the French *Surete Nationale* in Paris. Confirmation from Tipoff in Washington came soon afterwards, with the notation that the suspect had never been known to apply for an American visa.

"The sketch and *modus operandi* match Eliane Ouberrou AKA 'La Baionnette' DOB March 18, 1965, Bayonne France. Professional assassin. Suspected as teenager of running revolvers to Belfast for Basque terrorists. Implicated Baader-Meinhof Gang killings in Germany early 'eighties. Since then selected contract work for IRA Provos, Middle East groups. Unconfirmed reports she now affiliated with Russian and Ukrainian Mafia. This is her first sighting in nearly four years. Very attractive, appears younger than her age. Commands going rate for top assassins."

It was hard to associate Bayonne, the residential city neighboring Biarritz, with the bayonet, but that was where the ugly weapon had been invented. Now *La Baionnette* was after Robbie. Evalyn had had a very close call, and they were grateful for their personal police protection.

"I don't expect that she will try again," Racz said. "Now that she has been spotted, she will be miles away from here, I'm sure. She is probably not even in Central Europe any more. They'll send someone else now, and reassign her. She won't fail them a second time."

"Why use a woman at all?" Robbie asked.

"For one thing, the Mafia is what you Americans call an equal opportunity employer, and there is big money to be made, for a skilled criminal without a conscience who is expert with weapons. Small arms or letter bombs can be managed by either a man or a woman. Sheer physical strength is not important."

He thought for a minute, and continued. "Plus, there is something else. We are not really conditioned yet to women being violent criminals,

despite your films. Women, particularly with such props as a baby carriage, are practically invisible. They are seen, but seen as innocent features
of the urban landscape. That gives them a real advantage as terrorists."

Robbie remembered his father's story of a female Viet Cong assassin in
Saigon in the early 'seventies. Young, lithe and attractive, she rode on the
back of a Vespa during the late evening hours just before curfew, hailing
lonely GIs. Admiring servicemen never got a more intimate look, and her
motorcycle escape was always immediate. The rumor was that she had
killed at least a dozen men at close range.

He shivered. Robbie didn't want a closer acquaintance with *La
Baionnette*. He hoped that Inspector Racz was right that she was probably
long gone by now. He also hoped that nobody more skillful would take
her place.

*   *   *

Attila Nemzeti was welcoming if rather formal. In retrospect, Robbie's
only surprise was that the meeting was taking place in Nemzeti's office at
the Ministry of Justice.

"Thank you for coming in, Mr. Cutler. I know that you have been
interested in the Magassy case. I am even now told that you have been
looking into it, on behalf of the American Embassy."

Robbie nodded in encouragement.

"I know also that the intelligence files from the period which might
pertain to this matter have been sealed, and that they will not be made
available."

"Yes. We did formally request them." Robbie decided to leave it at that
and see where Nemzeti was headed.

"That being the case, I think the best policy is to tell you exactly what I
remember from that time. Perhaps it may assist you in gathering the facts
of the case."

"That would help me a great deal, Mr. Nemzeti. I am grateful to you."

"I am not a trained investigator myself, you understand. But I have seen enough criminal prosecutions to realize that the more facts are made plain, the better the chance to arrive eventually at the underlying truth."

Robbie again nodded his agreement and encouragement.

"Actually I haven't been officially asked about any of this before, and so there is nothing I need correct. But I did want you to have the full picture, as I understand it."

"It concerns Csaba Kovacs, I suppose."

"Yes, exactly. How could you guess?"

Robbie didn't answer. "What was the final sequence of events that you can remember at the resistance pocket?"

"I was hit by shrapnel fire towards the end. When I awakened, I was alone. Janos Magassy had left. My wife and I have talked this over, and we don't like the interpretation that could be placed on this, Mr. Cutler. I did not and could not blame Janos for leaving. He is after all the one who several times had urged me to leave. I succeeded in finding some ammunition on the second try, and returned. Janos and Eva were still there. He was telling her to go."

"When I was hit I was unconscious for some time. When I awoke, I found them both gone, but that Csaba Kovacs had returned. He was the last person there, not me. Clearly Janos's memorial ought to attest to that."

"Why did you leave then?"

"Csaba insisted. I was useless as a fighter. I could barely see. But it was just possible, with the bleeding stopped, that I might be able to make it home. Csaba mopped me up and insisted that I leave. I did. Now I'm concerned about how others might read that action."

"Mr. Nemzeti, allow a much younger man to say that you did exactly the right thing, both then, and in telling me about what happened right now. You have brought us all closer to the truth. You may also have helped us avoid a further tragedy."

Nemzeti did not care to ask Robbie what that further tragedy might have been.

*　　　*　　　*

Robbie went to the fencing club in Obuda automatically. He was blind to the distractions of the route, which usually would have delighted him. Dr. Samuel Johnson was quite right when he had said that facing death composes a man's thoughts remarkably. That seemed to be the case with *La Baionnette*. All Robbie could think about was the Magassy case and its various ramifications. He had had his routine fencing session earlier in the week. Perhaps meeting the fencing master now would help him concentrate his thoughts, and form a plan of action.

Robbie arrived at the fencing club, and quickly put on his fencing garb. Today was his lesson with the master, and he looked forward to it. He exercised strenuously while waiting for the master to finish a lesson.

They faced each other on the *piste*, saluted formally, and Robbie began a series of attacks down the *piste*.

The list of suspects seemed to be growing, he thought.

The master blocked Robbie's lunge in tierce. Robbie recovered automatically and continued his attack. Everyone still living that he had met from Magassy's 1956 group seemed to have a motivation for murder, he thought. It was not even possible to exclude Eva Molnar, until he had talked with her personally. Perhaps she was also still embittered by events then. It was not possible to say, or to dismiss her.

The master switched to the attack and nearly caught Robbie off balance. Imre Mohacsi, on the face of it, Robbie thought, was the least likely suspect. But that was only true if what took place in 1956 was the reason for Magassy's murder. Perhaps it was not. If Senator Abernathy's information was correct, Mohacsi may after all have been infuriated by his wife's infidelities with Magassy. In that case, he might be dealing with a very clever feint. Robbie nearly was sucked in by the master's own deceptive maneuver, but recovered just in time to meet the sabre sweeping downward, blocking it in quarte.

Robbie's thoughts went next to Attila Nemzeti. He was to be sure an appealing man, and from all that Robbie could gather, genuinely heroic. He was all the more heroic in that he had repeatedly returned to danger, placing himself in jeopardy even though he was hardly of the John Wayne mold. Heroic enough to commit murder to save himself, if he must?

Clearly there was far more to Nemzeti than met the eye. Perhaps his conversation with Robbie had itself been a clever feint, designed to use the Hungarian Government's decision not to release the intelligence files as cover to color Robbie's view of what they really contained.

Robbie almost hoped not, then caught himself. It was not very smart to start playing favorites in a murder investigation. You could end up being sucked in by a suspect's manipulative skills. Robbie was hit by the fencing master's sweeping lunge, just a split second before his guard could be shifted.

They started again and bowed. Then, Robbie thought, there was Istvan Szepvaros, smooth, successful, and in many ways personally the least appealing. That might be because of his money, who knows? It looked like he was setting up Kovatch, but how could Robbie be sure of that? That might also be a feint, designed to mislead Kovatch, and Robbie too for that matter. Perhaps Szepvaros was just plain scared, and wanted Kovatch to be the lightning rod should the Magassy murderer strike again. A normal enough reaction for a scoundrel, Robbie thought.

The master lunged. Robbie leaned with the lunge, twirled around the master's sabre and caught him on the outstretched wrist with a *prise de fer.*

They started once again at the middle of the piste, bowing formally. Robbie knew Kovatch to be an interesting customer, rough hewn and self made, and made also, Robbie mused, to be manipulated by someone more skilled and cynical than he was.

Well, there was surely one way to find out.

The fencing lesson continued. The hall grew silent except for the vibrant sound of sabre on sabre, and the scuffing sounds made by the rapid advances and defensive retreats of Robbie and the fencing master as each sought an opening, an advantage. Then the master lunged a bit short and, catching himself, suddenly extended himself further in the *ballestra*... This time Robbie was waiting for him just beyond the conclusion of the extended lunge. He caught the master a bit off balance in another *prise de fer* and scored once again. The two men bowed and took off their masks.

"For an American, you have remarkable powers to think ahead," the master said. "Give me a little more time, and I could prepare you for our national team."

Robbie absently acknowledged the rare compliment. But his mind was somewhere else. As he had hoped, an end game strategy had just suggested itself to him.

*   *   *

He returned to the Embassy. There was an excited message from Zsuzsa at the 1956 Research Institute on his voice mail. The People's Court judge who had handed down Eva Molnar's sentence in 1957 had finally agreed to open her interview. Robbie was invited to come in and read what she had had to say.

"This will interest you. Mr. Cutler. You really should come and read it." Robbie said he would do so as soon as he could. This would be useful background if he got to talk with Eva Molnar. Who knows, perhaps it would be solace for his father's demons, as well.

Someone, perhaps Julia Broadbent, had dropped on his desk a letter addressed to him from Romania that had been delivered by regular mail to the front desk downstairs. It was in a delicate hand, the letters artistically formed. The person who wrote this could earn some money addressing fancy invitations, Robbie thought. Then he remembered.

It was from Eva Molnar.

She would be glad to see Robbie and Evalyn at her home, agreeing to the suggested date and time. She expressed some mild curiosity to meet the children of the *Konzul Elvtars*. If he were still living, she asked Robbie to remember her to his father. With a formal Hungarian ending (where did she learn that in a communist school system, Robbie wondered), the short letter gracefully ended.

It was time for a talk with Ambassador Alexander Kovatch.

*   *   *

Kovatch had just returned from Canberra, driving into Hungary from Vienna. As he had suspected, as a diplomat he was waived through the border at Hegheshalom. No fuss was made concerning the Beretta 93 R that he had tucked into his luggage in the trunk of the Embassy car. The luggage was not searched nor was it even scanned, as would have been the case at Ferihegy Airport. And so the handgun was not even found, let alone questioned.

Meeting with Kovatch was a tricky business. Robbie had cleared it with Ambassador Horton, an essential precaution. He had to make absolutely sure that his back was covered. Still, Robbie was walking on eggs when the receptionist showed him into the Ambassador's study.

There were no preliminaries. The conversation might be roundabout, but it would not be time consuming.

"Thank you for seeing me, Mr. Ambassador. I trust everything went well in Canberra?"

"Yes, thank you. I may have even drummed up some preliminary interest in Magassy's memorial project. We'll see how it goes."

"I came to bring you up to date on some developments in the Magassy case, Mr. Ambassador." Kovatch's craggy eyebrows lifted in surprise. He waited for Robbie to continue. Robbie paused, assessing carefully just how far to go.

"As you may be aware (Robbie was sure that he was not), I've been monitoring the case with the approval of Ambassador Horton. She is aware of this meeting."

Kovatch blinked in surprise. There might be more to this young Cutler fellow than he had supposed. Fascinated, the Ambassador let him continue.

"At first, I was mainly concerned by the fact that a prominent American citizen had been murdered. Then, gradually, the situation became more complicated."

"What do you mean?"

"It seems probable that the murder was somehow related to what had happened in 1956. I've been to the 1956 Research Institute, as you have been as well."

Kovatch nodded.

"They are helpful, but they cannot trace individual records from 1956. And, of course, the intelligence records from the period are still sealed by the Hungarian Government. Ambassador Horton tried to get them opened for the Magassy murder investigstion, but the official response was a denial."

This was news to Kovatch. What came next was a splash of cold water.

"Mr. Ambassador, I am aware that Csaba Kovacs, a member of the Magassy group in 1956, was your brother. You have a powerful motivation to find out what happened to him, and I understand that you also have been making inquiries."

Kovatch did not deny it. He also did not deny his relationship to Csaba Kovacs. What was this interview leading to? He had the clear impression that it had veered out of his hands. This Cutler was onto something.

"The Magassy killing is made more difficult by the fact that we have no access to the official records, of course. But it is by no means impossible. I want you to help me solve it."

"How can I help?"

Robbie gave him the address of the store in Debrecen and explained what he wanted done.

Stunned, Kovatch agreed. "Will this help find the killer?"

"In my experience," Robbie said, "a determined killer rarely stops at one killing. There may be another one, as he seeks to divert attention and cover his tracks. I am trying to prevent it. The more artful trick for a clever murderer, of course, would be to get someone else to do his killing for him."

That hit Kovatch right between the eyes. He paled.

Robbie continued in another vein, as though he were mining a new subject. Slowly he began, underlining every word. "I have a personal interest in this, of course. This last weekend, a Mafia contract killer left a package bomb at my townhouse."

Fascinated, Kovatch listened closely. This was a league far beyond his homemade plans for vengeance.

Robbie went on. "Fortunately my sister Evalyn, who was home at the time, was raised in the Foreign Service. She remembered her security training. The Hungarian police believe the assassin, who has been tentatively identified, is a professional contract killer for the Russian or Ukrainian Mafia.

At that, Kovatch went white. "All of this has been kept out of the press," Robbie added. "So you see, I have a personal interest in solving this case, as cleanly as possible. And so do the Hungarian police, and my government at a high level."

"I'll do what I can to help," Kovatch said.

Robbie assumed a more conversational tone. "By the way, Mr. Ambassador, I'm afraid I owe you an apology. Recently, with your permission, I have enjoyed the company of your wife at luncheon. Julie is a charming and lovely woman. But now I hear that our luncheons have caused some gossip. They must therefore not be continued. That's one of the disadvantages of a small capital, I'm told. People with little to do gossip and cause trouble. I'm sorry if any of this has offended you."

Kovatch, surprised again, was magnanimous. They parted on a more friendly basis than either would have thought possible.

*   *   *

The man from St. Petersburg enjoyed his return trip to Budapest. He had served here years earlier, while a major in the Soviet Army, in the Warsaw Pact days. But then he had only seen Budapest briefly, while on his way to the Taszar Army Base near Kaposvar in western Hungary.

How times had changed. Now the Russians were out, the Warsaw Pact no longer existed and neither did the Soviet Union, and a Russian officer could starve for all anybody cared. Better to try one's luck with the real leaders in Moscow.

He had learned enough street Hungarian to talk his way around Kaposvar years ago. Enough of it came back so that he could get around now in Budapest. This was a contract job, his first outside of Russia. His specialty since leaving the army had been working the docks at St. Petersburg, making sure that his bosses' control remained firm. The pay was good, and he knew his business.

In this line of work failure was not an option. He had never heard of a contract not being fulfilled. His own score now stood at eleven killings. Some might call that regrettable. He was just doing what he had been trained to do. Let others worry about cleaning up.

He had received the assignment three days previously, and had been pleased. It was a sign that he was being noticed. And the chance to come to Hungary was a decided plus. The advance money was good. Provided that he didn't call attention to himself, he could enjoy something of Budapest for a day or two while planning the killing. Afterwards he would disappear over the border to the south. Slovenia, probably.

His weapon was a standard AK 47, an old friend from his army days. He could have field-stripped the weapon in his sleep. It disassembled and packed easily with a folding metal stock. The 30 rounds of 7.62 mm ammunition fitting the loaded magazine would be more than sufficient for the job.

He took a day to get used to the weapon, which had been waiting for him in Budapest. That was a nice touch, preventing any possible problem at the border. His contact had even made arrangements for an afternoon of firing practice at a range outside the city. Within half an hour at the range, having fired several hundred shots in different postures, he was familiar with this weapon and comfortable with its recoil and trajectories.

Now it was time for a light luncheon. Nothing too heavy before business. And he looked the part. When the lightweight weapon had been disassembled and packed into a fitted briefcase, he could have been any midlevel businessman with some files to ponder.

Weapons, a target, Budapest. It was like the good old days.

*   *   *

Robbie knew that his father would be pleased to hear that he had located Eva Molnar, and that he and Evalyn would actually be meeting her shortly. He called the townhouse. Evalyn was out, shopping at one of the new malls, he supposed. Then he called Massachusetts. It was the end of the working day in Hungary, and about lunchtime at home. He reached his father, who was delighted, particularly since Eva Molnar had sent her regards.

The tone of his voice told Robbie that his father's mind had been eased rather considerably. He would look forward to a report on how the meeting had gone. Robbie drove back to the townhouse in a carefree mood, tired from the fencing lesson, and intrigued with his plan of action. He would go over it in detail with Inspector Imre Racz the following day.

As usual, his car was discreetly preceded and followed by Hungarian security men. The detail had been carefully planned following the initial stopgap security assignment of the previous Sunday. Robbie had to admire their professionalism and training. They were not distracted, the drivers were experts, and, he had been assured, each man (and the two women on the detail) were expert marksmen(women) and crosstrained in at least one martial art at the expert level.

The security detail was not obvious. The first car preceded Robbie's car by a block, the driver having coordinated Robbie's route with him. When it arrived, the security agents would park in the vicinity, while Robbie and the second car arrived. When that happened, the senior security agent already on the scene would give a signal to the security agent stationed inside the townhouse that the door should be opened. Then the agents in the second car would screen Robbie to his door. It worked like clockwork on paper. Now it was being put into practice.

As the lead car arrived, the security agents took note of the few visitors in the residential street. None was dismissed. Any one of them, male or female, young or old, could be an assassin.

Robbie's car approached his townhouse. He parked it and got out of the car. Later, a security agent from the second car would take it to a specially secured garage.

As Robbie neared his door, a man with a weapon emerged from a parked car. The security agents on foot spotted him and yelled something in very colloquial Hungarian. Only Robbie and the Russian assassin failed to understand the command.

It made no difference for Robbie. He was tackled by a security agent and went down just before the shooting started.

It did make a difference to the Russian. His unfired AK 47 clattered to the sidewalk. The burst of bullets from the security guards nearly ripped him in half.

*   *   *   *   *   *   *   *   *   *

The Last Day—November 4, 1956

Eva heard them first. CLANK, CLANKETY, CLANK came the thundering noises. From how far away, nobody was quite sure. It was pitch-dark, and the only thing one could know for certain was that these were Russian tanks. They had returned in force.

Then came the noise of firing. It was small arms fire for the most part, often sporadic but concentrated sometimes. Then would come the piercing heavy wails of cannon and the solid sound of explosions as ordnance hit its mark.

"We know what's going on without even seeing it," Magda said. "They are returning small arms fire with heavier fire, including tanks. Bigger tanks than we had seen before."

She was right, Imre thought. This child, no, this young girl, barely a teenager, ought to be sorting out her life like girls in other countries worrying about normal things for someone her age. Instead she is talking with us like a veteran infantry soldier about ordnance.

They were all up immediately, congregating in the ground floor storefront. Someone made a pot of very strong coffee, and they sipped it from their cups in the cold predawn, while Janos went over their assignments.

Each of the nine remaining Friends had a specific assignment, until relieved by Janos.

First, liaison with Corvin headquarters throughout the fight was vital, for they were sure that fighting would center in their area. That liaison mission would be up to Eva and Attila. They would alternate. One would watch the Barat Street storefront headquarters, while the other monitored developments at Corvin. Then after a while they would change assignments.

It was also essential to patrol their own region, and not just wait defensively for an attack to start. Janos assigned Imre, Magda and Istvan to take the first reconnaissance, adding Laszlo as their runner back to Barat Street as soon as the Russians were spotted anywhere in their sector.

The first assault team for any tanks that penetrated Barat Street or near it would be Janos, Csaba and Karoly. Each weapon was carefully checked, while the assault team quickly added more homemade Molotov cocktails to their arsenal.

Eva flipped on the radio switch for the latest news. It was Radio Budapest. The National Anthem was being played. That was followed by Prime Minister Imre Nagy, who personally announced the Russian invasion. "Our troops are in combat. The government is at its post. I notify the people of our country and the entire world of this fact."

Then Schubert's *"Ave Maria"* was played. The broadcast ended.

"I wonder who the traitor was," said Attila. "The Russians always like to claim that someone invited them in, after all."

His question was soon answered, as a scratchy broadcast from rural Hungary identified Janos Kadar as the Hungarian communist leader who had invited the Soviets back into Hungary to fight the "counterrevolutionaries."

"Some day we'll all meet again, those of us that can still do so," said Eva. "Let's remember that, all of us," Janos said.

He raised his cup. "To our meeting in a free Hungary!"

"To a free Hungary!" they answered. Then there was a ritual clinking of cups, a last sip of coffee, and they filed out to their assignments. Dawn had still not broken over Budapest. As she walked along, Eva could hardly believe her eyes. The invading Russians had not only come along the broad avenues, but were attempting to penetrate streets which intersected with them and with the Corvin area as well. She saw heavy casualties on Kisfaludy Street, but it had held. If it had not, they would already have been cut off and isolated at Barat Street.

She saw two Russian tanks bigger than the ones they had previously used. She also saw fresh new horrors. There were several dozen dead or wounded Freedom Fighters, still bleeding and twisted into angles by their agonies. There was an equal number of Russian casualties. At least they were wearing Russian uniforms, but they didn't look Russian to her. Perhaps these were the Mongol soldiers whose presence in the Hungarian countryside had been rumored earlier.

Eva made herself known at the Corvin headquarters and picked up what information she could. Details of the Russian invasion were extremely sketchy. Clearly this confused room, with people screaming for attention, was not a well-ordered command center. There was no overall map with positions indicated, for one thing. But Eva and those she talked with were very clear about two important points.

First, the self-imposed mission of the Barat Street Friends to protect the Corvin area from its rear was clearly of vital importance. Second, this was not a tank terror mission like the first Russian assault ten days ago had been. This was a full-scale military invasion, with supporting infantry.

An authoritative-sounding Freedom Fighter briefed Eva. "We have to be prepared for anything. And if the time comes to leave our positions here," he said, lowering his voice, "there is a contingency plan to fight on in the hills. General Bela Kiraly will be in charge of our National Guard, including mostly the armed Freedom Fighter units. Make that known to Janos."

Then he added, "Meanwhile, keep us closely informed of what is going on in your sector. It's vitally important."

That struck him as a bit gruff. She was surely as scared as he was. Why add to that? He smiled and said, "You're the newlyweds, aren't you? You and what's-his-name?"

"Csaba." She smiled.

"Well, don't worry too much. You'll celebrate your annivesaries in a free Hungary. I know it!" Eva turned and started carefully back to Barat Street.

Imre, Magda, Laszlo and Istvan threaded their way along Barat Street towards the Danube. This was Magda's neighborhood, and with her whispered comments the other three soon knew these streets too. They went two by two, swiching their order from time to time.

Then Imre dropped, signalling in the early dawn for the others to hit the pavement as well. He started firing. Some fifty yards down the street was a group of soldiers in Russian uniform slowly leading several tanks, how many Imre could not quite make out. But this was clearly a change from their earlier tactics, and much more dangerous.

Imre motioned for Laszlo to join him behind an improvised street barricade.

"Go back and tell them at Barat Street that the tanks are coming," he ordered the boy. "Give them this location. Tell them that Istvan, Magda and I will hold off the infantry, then gradually fall back. They are to meet us half-way, where Barat Street intersects with this one. Tell them to bring lots of Molotov cocktails. We'll try to lure the tanks there, killing as many of the infantry as we can along the way. Now GO! Get out of here!"

It was an unlucky shot. Full of enthusiasm for his important mission, Laszlo had risen to his feet and started to run. The sudden movement attracted attention from the enemy. He was caught by a burst of semiautomatic fire before he had gone very far. It was a scene that Imre would remember with anguish again and again. Why, oh why hadn't he told the kid to keep his head down?

There was no time to mourn. He motioned to Magda to join him. Crouching past Laszlo's still body, she did so. Imre repeated his earlier order, adding to it that she must crouch, keeping to the shadows. She nodded understanding, and was gone.

Playing for time, Imre and Istvan poured steady fire at the invaders. Six Russian soldiers went down, dead or wounded. Imre was hit in the left shoulder. "Don't worry about me. Drop back. You've got to meet the others for the plan to succeed!" he pleaded.

"Not without you!" Istvan shouted back "Get up! I'll help you if you can't make it. But we've got to get out of here. NOW!"

Somehow, clinging to the fading shadows near the buildings, Imre and Istvan managed an orderly retreat despite Imre's wound. The Russians gingerly followed.

They all met at the corner of Barat Street.

Three T-54 tanks lumbered along the street after them, escorted by the surviving Russian infantry, now only a squad. The lead tank's turret was open, and a gunner fired his machine gun at the Freedom Fighters.

It was almost simultaneous. Csaba's expertly launched hand grenade landed right in the open turret. Just before it exploded the gunner squeezed off another round of bullets. He couldn't quite fathom the location of the attackers in the semi-darkness, but his instinct was sound. He caught Magda as she was running to rejoin Imre and Itvan. She was dead before her young body hit the street.

Karoly was whipped into a blind fury. From the sidewalk he charged the second tank with two Molotov cocktails, lit the wick of the first with his cigarette lighter and launched it towards the second tank before the gunner had a clear field of fire.

Then he lit the second homemade bomb and pitched it through the first tank's open turret. Following the earlier grenade, the Molotov cocktail did its job. An explosion was crowned by a secondary roar of flames, as the lead tank was engulfed from the combined effects of the grenade, the Molotov cocktail, and its own ruptured gasoline tank.

Karoly's bad leg failed him. He stumbled, and was engulfed in the rapidly spreading flames. A strangulated cry was all they heard.

Csaba and Attila led the assault on the third tank, which was swinging its turret around to try to locate the attackers.

"Try to finish off the second one while we're doing this," Csaba yelled to Istvan. "And give us lots of covering fire," he yelled back to Imre and Janos.

They made a good team, lithe and athletic, like striking attackers on a soccer field, weaving in and out. Explosions rocked the second and third tanks. In a short while, the attack had been repulsed, and most of the attackers were dead. The survivors had been driven off.

They listened, and there was no sign of any renewed attack. In the distance, there was firing from many locations, from the Danube throughout Pest and even the Buda hills beyond Moscow Square. But their own sector was quiet for the time being.

Janos told Istvan to stay out and patrol for an hour, reporting to him immediately if any Russian movement was detected. "Don't be a hero," Janos added. "Don't take on any Russians by yourself. Just report back to us if you see anything."

Janos went out to find Laszlo. He brought the child's body back to Barat Street. Csaba picked up Magda's body and carried her back to the storefront. No burial would ever be possible for what remained of Karoly. The burial for the two children must await another time. They would join Pista and Red then.

It had been a costly morning for both sides in the Barat Street sector. From their nine, the Friends had sustained one wounded and three dead.

Meanwhile, they had taken out three tanks and their crews, as well as at least two squads of Russian infantry. Janos mused that the Russians could afford comparable losses. If this kept up, the Freedom Fighters would be decimated before many days had passed. If, indeed, days rather than hours were left to them.

When he returned, Csaba had gently put Magda's body down on a couch in the storefront's back room, alongside Laszlo. He covered them as best he could with a tarpaulin, and said a brief prayer.

Eva entered the back room, saw Csaba covered with blood, and screamed.

Csaba shook his head sadly. "It's little Magda," he said, pointing to her covered body. "Laszlo and Karoly got it too," he added. There seemed to be nothing for either to do but to hold each other close for a long moment.

Then Eva remembered. "I've got to tell Janos what I was told at Corvin headquarters," she said. She paused. "There's another thing, Csaba. At Corvin they were releasing some prisoners. They said they didn't want blood on their hands. They led them down Prater Street, disarmed of course, and let them go. I was there when it happened."

"They wouldn't do that unless this was a real emergency. They need every person now for fighting. So this is really it, just as Janos thought."

"Yes, Csaba. But there's something else. They were nearly all Russian soldiers. But there was one Hungarian with them, an interpreter I guess. He saw me just before he ran back to his side. He even spoke."

"What did he say?"

"It was the oddest thing. I don't know why he did it, or whether what he said was true or not. But he saw me and seemed to know who I was. He said, 'You look like a nice girl. I wish we were on the same side.'"

"That's not so odd."

"It wasn't that. Just before he left he added, 'Watch your back very carefully. You have an *AVH* informer in your group.'"

Chapter Fifteen

▼

A Trip To Transylvania

The attempt on his life made CNN's headline international news, with follow-ups throughout New England. Robbie had immediately called his parents to assure them that he and Evalyn were fine. They were not reassured. He then called Uncle Seth.

As he half expected, Uncle Seth talked through his worry by tackling the problem at hand. It was an old OSS habit. One had to do something while waiting for contact from the field.

"It's puzzling. I don't understand this business," he said. "What is the point of an open attack on you, if the records are all sealed and will remain so? It makes no sense at all. But then I never held with Conan Doyle anyway."

"I'm not following you, Uncle Seth."

"Well you remember, Robbie, that Conan Doyle has Sherlock saying repeatedly that if you eliminate the usual, what is left, however fantastic, must be the answer. Well, something like that anyway, if not those exact words."

"Yes, that's well known."

"I've never believed it. The reverse proposition has always made more sense to me. When you are only left with something unusual or fantastic, you may be overlooking something rather simple. In fact, you may be intended to do so."

Robbie thought that over. "Yes. If all the books are sealed anyway, why call attention with a Mafia hit?"

"Exactly. Remember "The Purloined Letter?" Poe had it exactly right."

"Yes," Robbie agreed. "Don't ignore what is in plain sight." He wondered as he hung up the phone what Poe would have advised him to do now.

His next call was to Sylvie in Paris.

She was full of concern and insisted that he leave Budapest.

"No. It was a mistake to leave Bordeaux. After all, I could have drunk much more wine! I'm going to finish here. It isn't so very long, after all."

"How about this famous murder case of yours, *Cheri?*"

"We may have a break on that before long. I certainly hope so. Perhaps I'll settle things by the October 23rd anniversary."

"Will there be a ceremony or something in Budapest?"

"That is when Magassy's group will hold a commemorative dinner. It should be very interesting. Perhaps I'll know more about Magassy's murderer then."

"Then you'll play Hercule Poirot at the dinner?"

"Something like that." He could feel her teasing him, to ease the stress.

"I hope I'm invited. I wouldn't miss it for the world."

So she wasn't intimidated. She was intrigued, and wanted to be in at the end of the chase. They made arrangements that very afternoon for her trip to Budapest.

*   *   *

There were twenty officials around the conference table at Central Police Headquarters when Robbie arrived. Inspector Racz sat halfway down the table, facing an empty chair that was reserved for Robbie. Some men wore uniforms. Robbie recognized only the Customs Service and the Defense Ministry. He was sure that various security services were represented. The mumbled introductions did not entirely clarify the picture.

The meeting was chaired by a senior police official, Commander Varkonyi, who wore civilian clothes. Varkonyi introduced Lieutenant Madach, an officer from the state security investigative branch, the designated briefer. Madach gave a brief overview of what was known about the Russian Mafia assassin who had tried to kill Robbie.

"The gunman was a former KGB officer seconded to the Soviet Army, who had once been stationed here. Perhaps that is why he was assigned to this contract. I mean in Hungary," Madach added with coloring face, as he saw the impression his words had made on Robbie.

"We will of course confer with Russian security police. We are already doing so in fact. But the best defense is exactly what has happened so far—tight security for Mr. Cutler." Madach added the few known details about the assassin's movements, his arrival in Hungary and where he had stayed. His contacts were not known.

"Pity he wasn't taken alive," Racz offered.

"In a way," Madach agreed. "However, all he would have been able to tell us if he had talked at all would have been the identity of the Mafia superior in Russia who had hired him. He would have had no idea whatsoever who had hired the Mafia organization, let alone whether the Mafia was only involved for the attempted killing, or has a broader interest in this matter. And since the Russians are copying from the Sicilians, it is unlikely that he would have told us even that much," Madach said with a shrug. "I think that we must conclude that Mr. Cutler remains in great danger."

"What is the tie-in between this assassin and *La Baionnette*, who tried earlier with the package bomb?" Robbie wanted to know.

"We think that he was sent after she failed and was seen. At least that is the working assumption. We may never know for sure. We'll keep you posted," Madach nodded to Inspector Racz, "if anything new turns up." Then he closed his briefcase.

"Not 'when,' "Robbie mused. "'*If!*'" It was not a comforting distinction.

There was a moment of silence and paper shuffling while Madach left the room.

Commander Varkonyi began to speak. "In an odd way, Mr. Cutler, a number of things are coming together. For months now, the Government of Hungary has been investigating the activities and influence of the Russian Mafia within our country."

He continued. "We are the working group that has been assessing the problem. This is the first known attempted assassination of a foreign official by the Russian Mafia in our country. We wonder whether there may be some connection between your diplomatic inquiries and our own investigation."

"I am honored by your trust, Commander," Robbie began. "My own interest has been, as I am sure Inspector Racz has explained to you, the successful investigation of the murder of a prominent Hungarian-American, Janos Magassy. I assume that the attempts on my life have been somehow connected with my own investigation."

"We assume so as well," Varkonyi replied, nodding towards Racz.

Racz spoke next. "The motivation for Magassy's murder has always been rather puzzling. One school of thought is that Magassy was killed because of something that happened in the 1956 Revolution." He poured a glass of water.

"That may well be the answer. However, it is not a very satisfactory one. There are no prosecutions from those days still permitted under our law. The statute of limitations has expired. So what did the killer really have to fear from any exposure? That is what has puzzled us."

"You are looking for a more contemporary motivation?" Robbie began to see where they were going.

"Yes," Varkonyi answered. "Perhaps in some way the past is the key to understanding this murder. We are only speculating of course. But perhaps someone cared enough about avoiding exposure to murder Janos Magassy and then call in Mafia assassins, not once but twice."

Robbie nodded. "Please fill me in, gentlemen. What is the nature and extent of Russian Mafia activities in Hungary?"

A senior official in civilian clothes who had entered late and sat next to Varkonyi answered. "I am Ambassador Fekete from the Foreign Ministry, Mr Cutler. We are realizing more and more that international crime must be dealt with vigorously. You must be aware of our two treaties on money laundering—we call it *'penzmosas'*—with Ukraine. More effort is necessary.

"The days of military confrontation are over, but there is a new menace now. It is international organized crime. When we talk about the Mafia, people get a colorful image from the Don Corleone movies. There was some truth to that image, perhaps. But it is very much out of date now."

He poured a glass of water and went on.

"Look, for example, at the near collapse of the Soviet Army. The Army and the old KGB are no longer forces for stability as they used to be, whatever you thought of them. Now thousands of former soldiers and security officers are desperate men. Their jobs and reason for being have vanished, and so have their salaries. They are as dangerous, in their way, as the missiles being sold through organized crime syndicate channels."

Varkonyi added a point. "In Hungary, since you specifically asked about their activities here, Mr. Cutler, they seem to have specialized in money laundering and in the transmission of arms illegally sold to third parties. We have little doubt that other types of criminal activities may follow. But for the time being, they must establish safe channels for their money, and I am talking about huge sums in hard currencies."

The man from the Defense Ministry spoke up. "It would be a very tragic matter indeed if Hungary had led the way towards liberalization in this region, experienced the freedom of the abolition of the Warsaw Pact and the occupying Soviet armed forces, joined NATO…and THEN fell prey to a new, vicious and well organized species of international crime!"

"That is where matters stand, Mr. Cutler," Commander Varkonyi concluded. "The Russian Mafia is what we face here. But it is loosely allied, we feel sure, with other strong elements of international crime, including the Sicilian Mafia, the Chinese Triads and their counterparts in the Columbian drug trade and the Japanese mafiosi, or *yakuza*. As a start, we stand ready to do everything possible to help you and Inspector Racz find the murderer of Janos Magassy. But please be aware of the broader criminal interests that may be at work here."

"Tell me about your money-laundering laws," Robbie said. "Have there been any convictions?"

His answer came from a Finance Ministry representative. "Our laws have been on the books for a few years. There are some cases under investigation, but it is very hard to prove. Plus," he coughed, "we have to go about this with real discretion. We want to encourage foreign investment, after all."

"I thought that bank accounts were secret here," Robbie said.

"They are confidential. But we have started protecting ourselves. For one thing, we now require the tracing of deposits from overseas in excess of $50,000. It is a start."

"So you think there may be a connection between organized crime, money laundering, and this Mafia killer?"

Commander Varkonyi answered. "None of us is sure. But we invite American attention and help. And so we thought it important to share our thoughts officially on the possible implications of this case. It may help us work together."

The broader meeting ended with Robbie's promise to bring their concerns to Ambassador Horton's immediate attention. Then a smaller group retreated to Inspector Racz's office, to take up developments in the Magassy case

"I have some news, Inspector," Robbie began. He told a delighted Inspector Racz about the letter from Eva Molnar. He also briefed Racz on his talk with Ambassador Kovatch.

"Well done, Robbie. I suppose I may call you that? We have been very much concerned about Kovatch and what he might have attempted. The other day, he even brought in a Beretta when he crossed the border! It looks like you may have managed to head him off from any drastic action. I surely hope so."

"Just one further thing, Imre," Robbie said. "I very much appreciate the protection that I've received. After all, it has just saved my life. But it had better be very low-key when I go with my sister to see Eva Molnar. She was not easy to see, as you know, and I am very much afraid that she would react very badly to a security presence. Her experiences, after all…"

"I see what you mean. It will be done discreetly, on both sides of the border."

"That's all I would wish. She may just hold the key to what we are all looking for, whether or not she is aware of it. In the meantime, I suppose that you are keeping a close watch on the possible suspects?"

Racz smiled. "If you mean by that an esteemed international banker, a Deputy in the Hungarian Parliament, and an important official in the Ministry of Justice, well, yes we are."

"You are a master of discretion," Robbie replied.

*   *   *

Robbie went directly from Deak Square to the 1956 Research Institute on Dohany Street. An excited Zsuzsa met him. She already had the oral transcript transcribed. It was from the People's Court judge who had sentenced Eva Molnar in 1957.

Robbie started to read it, then asked Zsuzsa to translate it for him, word for word. It was not long. The judge wrote that she had been thinking over those days, in the light of what had happened since. She had been a convinced communist, she wrote. Then in 1989 the graves had been found. She became ashamed of her part in what had happened. It had never occurred to her that the executions would be so shamefully hidden, and the burials so uncivilized. She had thought that socialism respected people.

She remembered the case of Eva Molnar in particular. The evidence was clear. As an attractive woman, Molnar was an easy target for the police to catch. She had seemed in despair at the trial where, she had said, she had nothing to hide. Something about her bearing had compelled respect, the judge recalled.

There was really no case for her, and no reason not to pass sentence of death. The judge had done so a number of times before. But here, there was a new element. The file contained a notation from the Foreign Ministry, that a Mr. Cutler from the American Legation had made an official inquiry in her case.

There was no guidance from the Party. What should the judge do? There was plenty of evidence to hang the woman.

She had decided to pass sentence of ten years hard labor. That would probably be enough to finish off the Molnar woman anyway. It would also save her from criticism if the Party wanted leniency for its own reasons. These things were impossible to gauge.

The judge's testimony ended in a different mode. Now that era was over. She was glad that she had not sentenced the young woman to death. She hoped that somehow Eva Molnar had survived. She thought about that often as she now sat alone in church as her parents had once done. She hoped her judge understood.

Robbie listened in profound and grateful silence. Then he asked a surprised Zsuzsa where the public government records of the period were kept. He wanted the several volume *History of the Counter-Revolution* that Kadar's whitewashers had compiled.

*   *   *

Ambassador Horton greeted Robbie in her office. After this meeting he was going to brief a staff meeting about the latest attempt on his life, at the urging of the Embassy security team. But for now, his meeting with the Ambassador couldn't wait. He heard her concern, read the message from the Assistant Secretary that suggested he leave Budapest, and flatly said that he would not do so. She seemed relieved.

She read Robbie's draft cable to the State Department with interest. This was, after all, the first time that international crime had been raised as an issue for potential cooperation on the bilateral agenda between the United States and Hungary.

There was some precedent, however. For years, there had been exchanges of information between the United States and Hungary on law enforcement matters. Even during the communist years, there had been some cooperation on customs matters, largely aimed at controlling the drug traffic. And now the FBI Academy in Budapest trained Hungarian police in the latest investigative techniques.

Ambassador Horton agreed with Robbie that the topic was ripe for action. Clearly, if international crime was dangerous to this new ally it must be addressed, with serious resources. Surely the problem was not limited to Hungary, either. The approach must be a regional one. The message proposed an initial frank exchange in Budapest between the Foreign Minister and Ambassador Horton. Suggested action would then follow.

She initialled Robbie's cable after marking it for the Secretary of State's personal attention. "Good job, Robbie."

That was her highest praise. Robbie shook his head in thanks. "I hope it gets Seventh Floor interest. The Department keeps concentrating on terrorism and spreading democracy. That's all well and good, as far as it goes. But there are no resources worth talking about for fighting international organized crime. I bet the money the Mafia launders every month would be several times the entire yearly budget for diplomacy that Congress authorizes."

"Perhaps this will finally get some people in Washington thinking about tackling international organized crime, Robbie."

"I hope so. Maybe some official with integrity will attack the international mafia organizations as solidly as Robert Kennedy attacked the mob domestically. It needs to be done."

"How is the Magassy case coming along?"

Robbie filled her in on his talk with Inspector Racz, and said that he had seen Ambassador Kovatch. "The three men known to have survived Magassy's 1956 group are all being shadowed. Each is a suspect. But I increasingly think that we have to go beyond 1956 to understand the killing."

"Why is that, Robbie?"

"It's possible, of course, that there is a personal vendetta going on. That certainly was true as far as Ambassador Kovatch is concerned, but he's on board to be helpful now. I rather think that we are beyond a Dumas script here. What complicates things is that an intelligence spy, much though you and I would detest such a person, was acting for the government in 1956."

"Meaning?"

"Meaning that if someone was a police spy in 1956, the concealment of that fact is probably not a sufficient motive for murder over forty years later."

He paused. "I'm not sure in my own mind about this, Madame Ambassdor, so let me argue with myself."

"Go right ahead."

"We could have our every day murder motive. For example, Deputy Imre Mohacsi's wife had been having a long distance affair with Janos Magassy. Perhaps her husband found out and killed his rival."

This was news to Ambassador Horton. "Go on, Robbie."

"On the other hand, perhaps it is connected after all with 1956. Attila Nemzeti made a rather big point of telling me that he had not, as we had all thought, been the last person to leave the resistance pocket. Ambassador Kovatch's brother had done so. Nemzeti was clearly worried that Kovatch might be after him in order to revenge his brother.

"To make matters a bit more complicated, there is also the reverse scenario. It has been suggested that Nemzeti was furious with Magassy for leaving him for dead, and that he had nurtured a hatred for Magassy all these years. Then, when Magassy returned to Hungary for the first time, Nemzeti killed him."

"Is that plausible?"

"Possible, yes. Plausible, I'm not so very sure. Nemzeti did seek me out to tell me this. And after all he did put himself in danger repeatedly, despite Magassy's telling him to save himself, by returning twice to the group's headquarters. He also said that when he had been wounded by shrapnel, it would have been normal for Magassy to assume that he had been killed."

"But after all he could have been planting his version of what happened, in order to throw you off the track?"

"Exactly."

"And what about our international banker, Istvan Szepvaros?"

"He could bring the matter up to date, if he were the Magassy killer. His overseas banking is an obvious cover for money-laundering. It would also give a motive for hiding the past, if that connection could be proved."

Robbie frowned. "His case is puzzling. Eyewitnesses saw him take a vigorous part in fighting against the Russians. That's not what an *AVH* spy would have done. If he were a spy for the intelligence forces then, that wouldn't convict him of anything today. I need something more. Above all, PROOF!"

"How did your talk with Ambassador Kovatch go?"

"Very well. The fact that I am onto him meant that the Budapest police probably were as well. They even knew, by the way, about the Beretta that he tried to sneak into the country following his recent trip back to Canberra. And telling him that you had authorized my visit was important."

"So he will stand down from playing Count of Monte Cristo?"

"For the time being, yes. I've even enlisted his help, in a strange sort of way. More on that later, if it works out. He will let the law take its course if he sees that is going to happen. If he is not persuaded that will be the case he may just go ahead, even though he knows that his moves are known. He is a very determined man. We mustn't underestimate him."

He mulled things over, summing up. "I think I can piece things together, Madame Ambassador. But it will stand or fall on proof. Can I prove what I think really happened, or not?"

"What's your next step, Robbie?"

"To go and interview a ghost from the past, who may hold the key to sorting this all out."

"Where will you interview your ghost?"

"Why, in Transylvania of course. Where else?"

*   *   *

Iliu Monescu had planned the Saturday excursion carefully. His idea was to explore the Great Plain region lying south of Tokaj, that his colleagues had already seen. This is the *Nagy Alfold*, the famous Hungary of horseback riders, where specialized riding tours are still given, full of folklore at the beyond of Europe.

This traditional Hungary had kept its essential character over the centuries, despite Mongol invasion and Soviet conquest. "If you want to understand Hungary," Trip Cutler once told his family, "then learn about the *Tiszantul*, the region beyond the Tisza River."

First came a pleasant morning's drive from Budapest, with a pit stop for strong coffee and sweet pastries. Then came a memorable luncheon at the Hortobagy Inn, with demonstrations of riding that kept the dozen visitors fascinated. The fresh air, excellent food and colorful costumes of the Great Plain were reminders that Budapest was not the entirety of Hungary.

The Ladoucettes from the French Embassy were enthralled. "It's like the Wild West in the East," Marie commented. Evalyn was clearly having the time of her life. "This must be the Magyar equivalent of *La France Profonde*," she said.

Ambassador Kovatch had come with Julie. He was formally polite, but only seemed to open up when he saw the treasures of the Great Plain. After a while he began to comment on them for Julie, who seemed to revel in her husband's attention. "Not a moment too soon, either," sniffed Elena Dos Campos to her husband. Jorge and Ana Angelos from the Brazilian Embassy, and Greek Consul Eleni Papadopoulos completed the excursion party.

Robbie was pleased that Inspector Imre Racz was as good as his word. His security escort was discreet, noticeable only if you knew to look for it. He and Evalyn enjoyed the excursion even more since they knew that security had been provided.

After luncheon, the party split. The main excursion was to continue to Debrecen, the third largest city in Hungary. Debrecen had been a Protestant center, and was still well known for its university. Hungarian Independence had been proclaimed there against the Hapsburgs in the 1848 War of Independence. There was enough to see, but also, time for shopping as well.

Robbie and Evalyn, however, went on, driving east to cross the border into Romania. They would rejoin the group later in Gyula for dinner. Only Iliu Monescu and Ambassador Kovatch knew their exact destination. For the rest, it was a whimsical American wish to see something of the Transylvania of legend.

They crossed the border into Romania, had a cursory customs check, and then continued north, towards Carei. At that point they veered southeast through glorious mountains to the valley village of Sinmleu-Silvanei and after it their destination, Zalau, lying northwest of Cluj (the Hungarian Kolozsvar), a principal city of the Transylvanian region.

"I can see why the Romanians and Hungarians have been fighting over this region for centuries," Evalyn commented. "Someday I'll come back for an extended visit. If you could somehow screen out the socialist era factories, this would be one of the most beautiful regions in all Europe."

They spent an amusing half hour trying to remember all of the campy old legends about Transylvania, from the movies, and from Dram Stoker's Victorian thriller, *Dracula*. They recalled something about Count Dracula welcoming Jonathan Harker to his castle, with the eerie reminder that "Transylvania is not England." Then there were the opening scenes from the Lon Chaney film, "The Wolf Man," with gypsies and superstitions uniting in a backward, mountainous region.

And yet all that was foreign to the people who actually lived here, in this beautiful, remote and rather wild region. Contested by Magyar and Romanian for centuries, the argument finally seemed to have ended in the recent treaty between the two countries. Perhaps that was the new era emerging, with people such as Iliu Monescu on one side, and Deputy Janos Horvath on the other, who looked forward and tried to move beyond the hatreds of the past.

Here and there were castles perched on mountainsides, with the promise of many more in the interior fastnesses of Transylvania. That would make quite a backpacking trip. The churches were colorful in their stolidity, assertive rather than beautiful, striking rather than graceful, in harmony with the region. Many had been built by German settlers centuries ago, "the Saxons" as Romanians referred to them.

Robbie and Evalyn felt an unspoken eagerness to return at more leisure, and explore the region in depth. They could even see the prototypes for Dracula's Castle, at Brasov and Bran. Robbie told Evalyn that realizing the hard currency to be made, Romanian authorities even in the fading communist days had begun to encourage "Dracula" tourism in the region. Now that took place more frequently. Still, the region remained largely unspoiled. The thoughtful tourist would still be able to find a wholesome meal at low cost, stay at a rustic inn, enjoy a mountain vista, hike and pursue legend or history in one of Europe's largely unspoiled areas.

What legendary tyrants had not accomplished here had almost been done by the real thing. The communist dictator Nicolae Ceausescu, anxious to destroy any Hungarian sentiment in the region, had earmarked it for nearly total "socialist modernization." By that was meant the erection of cheap, polluting factories, and tenements that would quickly become slums. "It reminds me of the Basque country," Robbie told Evalyn. "This is what Franco tried to do there. He wanted to destroy the region. The result was terrorism."

Time had not let either dictator wholly succeed. Here the starved peasants were beginning to regain their sense of self respect and their hospitality. And the scenery was breathtaking, even as the abundant evidence of poverty, in ramshackle housing and unpaved roads, was a marked contrast to the relative prosperity and modernity of eastern Hungary across the border.

It was mid-afternoon as they approached Zalau, and they were right on time. They surveyed the edge of the town as they approached. Few concessions to the beginning millennium's concepts of progress could be seen. Here and there were stores where articles in common use were for sale. There was a tiny, well-tended village church, with fresh flowers at the door, which was kept open for the occasional visitor. For the rest, one story houses lined the streets, clearly sufficient for the needs of the few hundred souls of the vicinity.

Even the scale of existence in this portion of the town suggested that the visitor was an intruder. The town was located in a slight declivity, which separated it from its neighbors, defining its existence while minimizing its scale. There were two or three old cars parked along the main street, which was named in Romanian spelling for a Hungarian hero. Several side streets radiated busily from it towards nowhere in particular, like village girls at a dance with no partners.

The town was not that far from Cluj, but the lack of television antennas implied a far greater distance. The Saturday afternoon turned warm and languid. One or two persons entered and left the store. There were no young people to be seen. Perhaps they were all working in the fields that surrounded the town. Or perhaps they had taken the bus to Cluj for the evening.

It struck Evalyn that the American twentieth century myth of single generation assimilation was proved wrong here. She remembered the stories about Ellis Island, and immigration into the United States in the early years of the century. Stolid European families in odd clothing wondering about the new world, and how they might fit in. And then their children, becoming assimilated to the point where they refused to speak the old language even at home. Evalyn thought that it would take at least a generation for a family from Zalau to get used to Cluj or Bucharest, let alone America.

Abruptly Evalyn and Robbie arrived at their destination, a house that was small even by the standards of Zalau. Robbie parked the car and they walked up to the gate, but there was no need to knock at the door. There was Eva Molnar pruning the rosebushes in her garden.

She saw them as she peered towards the gate from the bushes near her front gate. Evalyn stared at her as, tall and slightly bent but still very graceful, Eva Molnar straightened herself up, adjusted her shawl, peered at her visitors quizzically for a moment or two, and then waved them towards her door, where she met them and ushered them into her home.

"Magda," she cried, and Magda, a woman about Evalyn's age, shortly appeared and joined them.

It was clear without words that Eva Molnar and Magda were mother and daughter. Magda almost seemed older than her mother, for her responses were like obedient, cooed replies, while Eva Molnar had the voice of personal authority and the reserve of one who has seen much. She hid her hands, Robbie noticed. They were alone except for a workman who glanced at them from time to time as he trimmed the hedges that bordered Eva's yard.

The ritual of strong coffee, small glasses of brandy and a plate of pastries was followed. Probably they hadn't done that in six months, Robbie thought. Evalyn looked at her brother with new eyes. He was treating this elderly lady and her daughter as though they were, well, royalty. In their own home, they were.

Robbie thanked Eva Molnar for agreeing to see them. He said that his father sent her his very best wishes. Clearly, she had been much on his mind over the years.

"Yes, from time to time I have remembered the *Konzul Elvtars* as well," she smiled. Then something occurred to her, something that she had written out in her mind. She decided that this was the best time to say it.

"You may tell your father that I never blamed him for what happened. I tried to reach the American Legation. I was just too late. The soldiers pouring across Freedom Square prevented me from getting there. It was not possible for me to reach the Legation, or for your father to reach me. I was always grateful that he was trying to reach me, and especially for the expression on his face, that proved clearly he wanted to help. It helped sustain me through what followed, and the camps."

Robbie replied. "I found out something just yesterday. My father tried to intervene officially at the Foreign Ministry on your behalf. He said that the American Government took an interest in your case, since you had had an appointment at the Legation, and had been prevented by force from keeping it. The People's Court Judge in your case wrote that this intervention was the deciding factor in your being sentenced to a term of years."

He didn't have the courage to add what she understood, that the intervention had spared her from a death sentence.

Eva Molnar smiled. Even at her age, Robbie thought, that smile would be remembered for a very long time.

Robbie translated the conversation for Evalyn, and then translated into Hungarian what Evalyn wanted to say to her. "He always remembered you. He even named me 'Evalyn,' perhaps in remembrance. Since Budapest, our father has suffered from nightmares. I think that hearing of our talk, he will not have them any more."

Evalyn and Eva Molnar smiled and joined hands for a moment.

Robbie said that they had another special purpose in coming. It referred to what had happened in 1956, and just possibly, what had happened recently to their leader, Janos Magassy, who had been murdered in Budapest.

Eva Molnar was shocked. "So that is why we didn't hear from Janos again! We went to Budapest to see him. He had written me about the monument he had planned to build, and asked me for my suggestions. We had talked about it back then in 1956, after Pista and Red were killed. I had wanted to be a sculptor, you know."

She seemed to hide her hands deeper within her sleeves. "I was an art student in 1956. People said that I had some talent. That is before my hands were hurt again and again, in their camps."

She was not the only person to cry over her lost past.

"So you hadn't heard about Magassy?"

"No. We were so pleased to see him again. And I was pleased to bring him my idea for his memorial statue. Great leaders of our people were born here, or fought here, and even died here. The Hunyadis, Petofi, many of them. Petofi even died on the field of honor here against the Russians, probably cut down with a sabre, his back to Hungary. That's what gave me my idea for Janos's memorial in the first place."

"What idea was that?"

"My idea in 1956 had been to use a Hungarian sabre in the memorial. Janos, Csaba and I and poor little Magda had talked about that. It stands for national resistance. Our statue would then be a revolutionary flag, with an inscription and sabre in the middle, where the communist symbols had been torn out."

"So you brought him a sabre?"

"Yes. We found one in Debrecen and brought it to Janos when we saw him. That was my contribution. He liked the concept."

Robbie thought of the errand that he had sent Ambassador Kovatch on that was taking place about then, in Debrecen. It was a well founded hunch, after all. Funny thing about hunches. You either have them, or you do not. For Robbie, they were the key to detection, when you knew all you could know, and it was time to make a leap of faith, great or small. This time, they just might save more than one life.

"So you didn't see Janos Magassy here in Zalau?"

"Oh no, we went to Budapest for that. It was the first time in many years. We didn't stay."

"Have you seen any other members of the 1956 group?"

She did not answer. Robbie gently rephrased the question. "There are now three members of your 1956 group in Budapest, Istvan Szepvaros, Attila Nemzeti, and Imre Mohacsi. Have you seen them recently?"

"No," she nodded. "I was so pleased to tell Janos that Attila had survived. He hadn't realized that. He thought Attila was dead." She stopped talking and looked at Robbie closely.

"It would be good to see them all again," she said.

Robbie gently went on. "Much has changed, and for the better. It is hard to accept, but now the police are on our side, and they are anxious to solve the murder of Janos Magassy. I have also been asked to tell you that the American Ambassador to Hungary, Eleanor Horton, would be honored to welcome you to Budapest, and to have you stay with her as her personal guest."

"A woman is the American Ambassador? How wonderful! What would you like me to do?"

"We are going to have a dinner in a few weeks, on October 23rd, to mark the 1956 Hungarian Revolution. The survivors of your group will be there. I would like you to attend the dinner. It would be a surprise for the others present. You see, it will be a fine reunion. However, the police think that you might also recognize something that others have missed.

"If one of those present was an intelligence spy," Robbie went on, "especially one that was masquerading as a Freedom Fighter, you might know. As a matter of fact, that may be why Janos Magassy was killed. We think that he might have been able to identify and expose the person who killed him. You may have been the last person to see him before the murderer. That is why we are asking for your help."

She didn't hesitate. She nodded understanding of being asked. "I'll be glad to come," she said. "Yes. I'll help you, Mr. Cutler. It is time for justice in Hungary."

*   *   *

They drove back through the rolling hills over to Ciucea, then followed the better road to Oradea and Salonta, making good time. A few miles south of Salonta they crossed the border to Hungary, and found themselves in Gyula.

"I can see you making a mental note, Robbie. What is it?"

"The lack of border formalities there for Romanians. It's what they call 'small border traffic.' Usually the only ones to use that crossing live in the immediate vicinity. They'll have to tighten that up when Hungary joins the European Union in a few years."

"Why is that important?"

"That is where Eva Molnar went across the border undetected into Hungary when she and her companion went to see Janos Magassy."

"You mean Eva Molnar and her daughter Magda."

"She didn't say that."

They drove in silence to the restaurant, keeping their observations to themselves. They arrived shortly before the others. The restaurant was a good choice, rustic with the smell of excellent food coming from several outdoor grills.

"It's not Taillevent in Paris, but they have perhaps the best sausage in the world here in Gyula," Robbie said.

"I'm really looking forward to it. You'll be surprised how often I don't have dinner at Taillevent, Big Brother!"

"OK. Just back me up on what I'm going to tell them!"

Dinner was excellent. Robbie and Evalyn took some kidding about their excursion into Transylvania, so Robbie made up a yarn about searching for the lair of Dracula, in order to secure tourist promotion rights to his castle.

"Careful there, Robbie, you are coming perilously close to disrespect to one of my country's national heroes," Iliu Monescu warned, only half in fun.

"If you mean the famous Vlad the Impaler, he is the very last person I'd ever disrespect," Robbie replied. "Compared to him, Count Dracula looks like a choirboy!" He ducked the roll that Monescu threw at his across the table.

The open air performance at the medieval castle ruins in Gyula was memorable. A pleasant evening breeze added to their enjoyment. The play evoked the early days of the Magyar tribal invasion of the Hungarian Great Plain, perhaps right here.

From Arpad to King Stephen, the tableaux followed in pageantry that could be easily followed, thanks to the foreign language summaries that the ushers had handed out to the theatergoers as they entered the open castle courtyard.

The next day, they drove back to Budapest. Evalyn's vacation was ending. It was time to return to the publishing house. She was sorry not to be on hand for the solution of the Magassy case, but very pleased to be entrusted with telling their father all about their meeting with Eva Molnar.

Also, of course, Sylvie Marceau would be coming before long. "So I'll be leaving you in good hands, Big Brother!" Evalyn said. "With her around, even your famous capacity for getting into trouble has its limits!"

"I'll ALWAYS need my Kid Sister to bail me out!" he assured her. She doubted it, but it was reassuring to hear all the same.

*   *   *   *   *   *   *   *   *   *

Csaba's Journey—November, 1956

Rocking along in the darkness, Csaba tried to wake up fully but could not. Why did his head hurt so? Ohhhhhhh! Throb, throb it went, lights green and blue and then black again. Voices. "What about this one?" "Leave him alone. The body people will be along later. He's gone. No need to waste a bullet finishing him off." Overcoats marching away. Was that cigarette smoke?

Sandor. He had spoken to Sandor. Mama and Dad too, but they had seemed so resigned. "Eva? Who is this Eva?" They didn't understand. Sandor might, but he had to get out. Csaba had to make him understand.

"Listen, Sandor, you've got to get out. It's going to get very, very bad. Leave. Leave today if you can. We're holding out, but it won't be very long. Don't worry about me. I'll either make it or I won't and there is nothing anybody can do. Well, maybe Eva can. I've got to get back to her. Promise me you will leave this country. Promise. PROMISE!!"

There came the lights again. This time, a little yellow too. Was that the sun? There weren't any windows here, just slits. They seemed to be moving. It was like the Tibor Tollas poem he had heard over the radio "They've covered all the windows." It was said that Tollas had written it in his head in the jet darkness of his prison, and had memorized the words.

Csaba remembered Eva's smile and laughter. Mostly he remembered their few moments together, holding her close, in what The Friends called their honeymoon. Well, there hadn't been any marriage, but there had been a honeymoon. Our Lady of Hungary would bless them and sort it out.

CLANK, clank, clank. You could hear them long before you could see them. People came out from their hiding places and talked to each other. He would remember it forever. Clank, clank, clank, the rumbling, rumbling of ominous huge beasts nearing the city.

Csaba tried to think what they could be. "Mama, what's that big animal? Is that a giraffe?" "No, my dear, the giraffe is the tall one. That's a hippopotamus." "Horse of the river," his father had added. Dad was always proud that he had finished school, but he didn't talk about it much.

Was that a hippopotamous then? No, it wouldn't clank. Then why am I losing control? Why are my pants dirty? Mustn't let the others see. Great God! They've brought in the T-54s. The Russians are back. Did they ever really leave? Now they'll get us one by one. The volunteers are leaving us, all of them.

Csaba was very tired.

Were they all dead? That was a new worry. If we are all dead, then where is Eva? She wouldn't leave me alone.

Groans and whispering. I'm not alone after all. Other people are here. Where were they during the fighting?

It had gone on for days. Bam! Bam! Bam! The artillery and tank assaults on the Kilian Barracks could be heard throughout the area. Where was Pal Maleter? The last broadcast, let's see, had him as Defense Minister going to negotiate with the Russians at their military headquarters on Csepel Island.

"This is Radio Budapest! The heroic working peoples have appealed to the Soviet Union to crush the counterrevolutionaries who have sought to overthrow our socialist state." Janos Kadar had returned. He had brought his friends with him. Those who had thought they were on the winning side after Nagy's announcement on the 28th had now melted away. The Friends, those who were still alive, were still there at Barat Street, still fighting, still protecting the main groups on Corvin Circle. Eva had never looked so beautiful. Csaba couldn't keep track anymore. Janos Magassy sent out for supplies from time to time. Everybody went at least once, some more than once. Some bread, some rags, bottles and gasoline, lots of rumors, not much hope.

His head throbbed again. Why does it hurt so? Csaba felt a stiffened bandage on his head, and raised it a bit. The pain was sharp, but now he could see. Throbbing in waves, his head spoke to him and told him to go home and lie down in his own bed, where his Mama would make some broth and that would ease the pain. He should really be more careful in these pickup soccer matches after school. One could get hurt.

A light flashed near him. Someone was lighting a cigarette. It was so sudden that the light's halo lasted for a full minute afterwards. Csaba could only make out that dozens of people were packed together. He was on a kind of bench. They were moving. When the light from the match had flashed, Csaba had seen in the corner a clump of people. One had his mouth grotesquely open. His journey was already finished.

"We moved him to let you lie down," said his neighbor with the cigarette. "After a while the blood stopped, I think. Are you awake now? Do you want a puff?"

Gratefully Csaba took a drag from the cigarette. Dad would not like it. Better finish before he was found out. If only his head wouldn't throb so! "You'd like Eva, Mama. She's a wonderful lady. She'll give you beautiful grandchildren, you'll see."

"In a world like this, is that a blessing?"

Csaba went back down from the Buda hills towards the Danube and tried to decide which bridge to cross. If you picked the wrong one, chances were you'd never live to get to the other side, he thought. On the other hand, walking too far along the river bank to get to a safer bridge wasn't any good either.

In slow motion he walked across the Chain Bridge.

It was a beautiful day, and the ladies had parasols and wide skirts, just like that picture in the National Gallery. Some had the very latest treat, ice cream in a waffle cone. There was Eva in a long dress at the other side of the bridge, near the Art Department of the University, at the Petofi Statue where they had first met. When was that?

It must have been in the early summer. They would meet and then go on to the fair at Margaret Island. There was always the Varosliget Park on the other side of Heroes' Square, but Margaret Island was best. The books said so. Their pictures looked so pretty. Mama why does my head still hurt so much?

Csaba dozed off and the man next to him carefully removed the burning cigarette from his fingers.

It had gone on for days. Who would have thought that they could last so long?

The last sortie was like the others, but this time Eva had stayed out if it. Csaba had insisted. It was far more dangerous. These T-54s had machine guns mounted in their turrets. Still, they could be disabled if you got your gasoline bomb in the right spot to dislodge the tank tracks, and then could follow up at the air intake valves. Then the soldiers, gasping for breath, came out and could be picked off with submachine gun fire.

They weren't Russians. They were from Central Asia. Maybe too many Russians stationed in Hungary had been sympathetic, who knows? Some said that they had heard that these new troops thought they were fighting the British and French imperialists in Egypt. A few even believed that the Danube was the Suez Canal, and had gone looking there for crocodiles!

One by one the buildings in the quarter stirred and were shaken by heavy fire. Gashes would appear across the face of a building like bloody slashes in the face of a farmer who had fallen into his harvesting machinery. Top floors of buildings would begin to crumble.

And then, wondrously, from those same buildings the firing would start once again.

For days it went on. Now there was only propaganda even if one had a radio. The neighboring groups, which had started to be in touch with each other after Nagy's October 28th declaration, had soon lost contact. Once again it was piecemeal, with the pace of the fighting relentless.

Where was Imre Nagy? Where was Pal Maleter? Where was the promised help from the West? Where was Hungary?

There was a lurch and Csaba seemed to waken more fully.

As the reinvasion of Budapest had ground on, day after relentless day, they had fought on in Barat Street.

All except one. That was a face of hatred and treason.

Better to remember Eva and stay sane if he could. He didn't remember how or when he had been hit, or how long he had been unconscious. It must have been when he was returning to Barat Street. All he could remember was her beautiful face, as they talked before he had left to see his family.

"Eva, darling Eva, give me one day. Two if you must. I will come back and we will leave for the border together. But I may not come back. That is always possible. You must leave if I have not come back within two days."

She had not agreed. Never.

"Eva, there is nothing left for you here. You must save what you can." She refused.

"Don't argue, my love. What if you have our child? That must be saved."

She stopped protesting. That was a new thought. She could honor Csaba and their love through their child. She became an automaton, too tired to think or to reason or to argue. But she knew he would be back. Throughout their last night he insisted softly.

"If I do not return, go to the American Legation. You said you knew somebody there. Maybe he can help. We heard that Cardinal Mindszenty was given refuge there. It's a possibility. I want to think you and our child have a chance to live." Finally she gave up and agreed with him. He went to sleep.

Eva cradled his head for hours, weeping softly.

When he returned to Barat Street three days later, she was gone. His head had been roughly bandaged. He remembered the force of an explosion only. He hoped she had made it to the American Legation. There was nobody left. Then he had heard the low moan. It was Attila, face caked with blood, but still alive.

Somehow he had managed to clean up Attila, who told him that only Janos was left when he had passed out. Eva had gone. Csaba sent Attila home. There was nothing more for him to do there. Csaba would stay for a little while in case Eva returned. He would regain some strength, and then go in search of her.

He had passed out. Then he had heard the other voices, seen those overcoats. He passed out again on hearing their cruel words. So he wasn't worth a bullet, was he?

I'll show those slimy traitor bastards.

Later others came. "Here's one who is still moving!"

"Shouldn't we just shoot him?"

"Nah, we've got our quota from this quarter, remember? He won't be in any position to object. Besides, he may be better off where he'll be going. Better than the People's Court anyway."

The familiar voice came from his left. Csaba saw him for a moment as the other man looked away. Two other men picked him up and slung him into the back of a truck like a sack of grain.

There were many other people in the truck, men and women. They drove for a while. Then the truck was unloaded. They were at the railroad station. Which one, he couldn't be too sure. Then he had passed out again, this time for a very long time.

The train had lurched to a halt. Csaba could hear gunfire outside. Inside the train there was dead silence. The silence of the dead? No, not quite. Not yet. The silence of hope.

There was nothing they could do except wait. The doors were locked from the outside. Csaba realized that it would have taken his full strength, and plenty of room, to swing an ax (if he had one) to make an opening in the wall of the car. But there was no room and precious little sunlight through the cracks of the car. No ax and no strength. All they could do was wait.

The firing continued. Then some shouting.

"Unlock those cars, you bastards! You're not taking any more of our people away today. We're putting the Ukraine Express out of business!"

The noise of keys could be heard. The door slid open. Slowly, blinking at the sunlight, the prisoners lowered themselves from the car onto the field adjoining the tracks.

"Don't wait! Don't wait! We're too close to the border. Soon they'll be back in force. Get the hell out of here while you can. SCATTER!!!"

Csaba looked up from the field at the speaker. He was a boy not over 16 with the voice and authority of a man, standing on top of the train car they had just left. Csaba waived weakly.

The boy waived back with a flag of Hungary, the revolutionary flag with the center ripped out. "Long live Hungary!" he shouted defiantly, as the refugees scattered into the forest.

CHAPTER SIXTEEN

▼

Ballestra

The October 23rd memorial dinner had long been planned, at a private upstairs room in a secluded Obuda restaurant near Florian Square. Robbie had reserved places for Eva Molnar and her daughter by saying that Ambassador Horton and her husband were expected. The menu had been chosen and was festive, with fine Hungarian specialties.

Places were marked for Istvan Szepvaros, Imre Mohacsi and Attila Nemzeti and their wives. Ambassador Kovatch, who had become increasingly committed to fundraising for the memorial, would preside, which pleased Julie. At the other end of the table, next to the door, was Robbie Cutler's place. He had been relieved by Julie Kovatch's reaction to the distancing of their friendship. She had chosen to treat it as a nonevent. That would make Sylvie's reception easier, Robbie hoped.

The evening would begin with drinks in the restaurant's private garden. Perhaps a *puszta* cocktail, a touristy concoction with a brandy base, or champagne. They would take advantage of the fine weather before retiring to their private dining room.

Inspector Racz and his men would wait in the hallway outside the private room, in case Eva Molnar, arriving after the cocktails, could make her identification. There was no other exit from the private room except for the other door, which led directly down narrow steps to the kitchen. An armed policeman would be stationed there as well.

During dinner, the drivers would as usual wait downstairs. Eva Molnar had chosen to use her neighbor friend as driver for the evening, rather than accept Ambassador Horton's offer to use her own official car.

It was warm for the season, with a refreshing breeze off the Danube. Robbie and Sylvie arrived first. He had briefed her on the evening and its cast of characters, following her arrival at Ferihegy Airport from Paris the previous afternoon. She looked lovely, with a smile that radiated happiness. They each took a glass of champagne while waiting for the others.

Ambassador Kovatch and Julie were the next to arrive. Julie tensed slightly when she saw Sylvie, a reaction that was not lost on Sylvie, who chose to ignore it. Maybe it would be something to tease him about a few years in the future, but most probably not. Happiness to Sylvie Marceau was not a situation comedy, and serenity certainly was not.

Kovatch and Robbie had a brief private word as their drinks were brought. "I don't know what it means, Robbie, but you were right about the store in Debrecen. They remembered having sold a sabre shortly before Janos was killed. It was to a woman in her late fifties or early sixties, not to a man at all. They remembered her very well. She had a fine, proud way of standing, although she was not well dressed. She had just enough money for the sabre, and could not afford the hand tooled leather scabbard that often was sold with such sabres."

"That's extremely helpful, Ambassador Kovatch. I think we'll meet the lady herself before long. What else did they say about her?"

"She hid her hands, which seemed scarred. There was a younger woman with her, and a man who took charge of the sabre after the shopgirl wrapped it up. He was a neighbor who was driving for them, apparently."

"Here come the others."

Attila Nemzeti and his wife Margit were the next to arrive. They greeted Ambassador and Mrs. Kovatch, and then Robbie introduced his fiancee. "We are complimented that you came all this way to join us for our dinner, *Mademoiselle*," Nemzeti said.

"All the world knows now what you did in 1956. I am proud to be here and meet you," Sylvie replied.

"We were forgotten for many years," Attila reflected.

"But no longer," Julie Kovatch put in. She had metamorphosed back to The Ambassador's Wife very well.

Next came Imre Mohacsi and his wife Magda. They took *puszta* cocktails ("touristy, but we like the taste," was Magda's verdict). She looked wistfully about for something to snack on, but decided not to ask. Just possibly, the dinner itself would be sufficiently filling.

She hoped that they wouldn't be exposed to many tearful speeches after dinner. She could give most of Imre's by heart now. How odd it was that Janos Magassy would not be there tonight.

Janos! At one point, in the fleeting past it now seemed, just looking forward to seeing him would have been food for pleasurable speculation for weeks before the dinner. How sad that it had all ended in such violence, before she had even had the opportunity to see him once again, and in Budapest too. The message that he was coming had reached her too late.

Istvan Szepvaros and Maria were the last to arrive. They strode into the garden, richly dressed and smiling. Szepvaros sent his driver up to the dining room with copies of the latest fundraising estimates, and some sketches of design possibilities for the memorial. Then he and Maria made the brief rounds to say hello. They greeted Sylvie cordially.

Robbie excused himself for a moment, and checked with Inspector Racz at his command post. It had been difficult to manage unobtrusively, but a metal detecting device rigged on the inside of the door leading from the hallway to their private dining room would show if anyone was carrying a concealed weapon. Racz was almost certain that nobody would, but it was always best to be sure.

He rejoined the group in the garden after a few minutes with Racz. The restaurant manager, nervous about the guest count, came and conferred with Robbie.

"No, everything is all right. The other two guests will be joining us in the private room shortly after we are seated, I think. That will make the twelve."

"Very good, *Cutler ur*. We will be serving in ten minutes."

Robbie surveyed the group. This was the opportunity he had planned for, but there was no guarantee that it would work. If it did not, then at least he would have managed to bring Eva Molnar back to her friends after so many years. Janos Magassy would have appreciated that. So, he thought with a smile, would his own father.

They went up the stairs and filed into their private dining room. On the walls was the only decoration that mattered. It was the revolutionary flag of Hungary with the center torn out. How appropriate that the hated communist symbols are now replaced everywhere by the Crown of St. Stephen, Robbie thought. It's a new era. He looked forward to the next hour with pleasure.

*   *   *

The diners found their places, as Robbie explained that the Hortons were delayed and would arrive shortly. Twelve for dinner. Robbie remembered the superstition about thirteen for dinner, and was glad that had been avoided for once.

The waiters entered from the kitchen door side and began to serve the first course. Behind them, a wine steward poured a light, white wine from the Balaton. And then the door from the hallway opened.

Imre Mohacsi was the first to see her. He turned pale, then, coloring, rose to his feet. "Eva!" he said. The others looked up, as Eva and her daughter Magda came towards the table.

Robbie watched their reactions carefully. Eva absorbed Imre Mohacsi's light embrace, and looked around the table. "I thought I would know you all immediately," she began in some confusion. Then it dawned on her that this group also included others, like the wives of her 1956 colleagues.

She recognized Robbie and smiled.

Eva walked over to Attila Nemzeti and put her hand on his shoulder. Overcome with emotion, he did not, perhaps could not, rise to his feet.

"Attila…and Janos thought we had lost you," was all she could say. Nemzeti, choked with emotion, seemed incapable of speech.

Istvan Szepvaros looked stolid, as though he were weighing the situation. Then he came forward. "Eva. It has been so very long, and we were together such a short time. I am Istvan Szepvaros and this is my wife Maria." It was adroitly done. Eva swallowed his name and began to introduce her daughter Magda around the table

"Now this is a real celebration," Szepvaros said. "We have Eva Molnar with us once again, and with your charming daughter as a bonus."

"I am Kovacs Sandor," said Ambassador Kovatch, introducing himself and his wife Julie. "I am sure that you well remember my older brother Csaba, a member of your group."

At that statement several people, including Julie, gasped with surprise. She looked towards Robbie, who nodded in friendly collusion as if to indicate that more had been going on than she had been aware. She began to understand.

"Yes," Eva said. "We all knew your brother. He was an example of our uprising at its finest. He was brave and resourceful."

Attila Nemzeti coughed and began to speak. "Some of you know this, but I am only alive today because of Csaba Kovacs. When I went back to Barat Street for the last time and was wounded, I regained consciousness finally. Eva had left then. So had Janos. Surely he thought I was dead from my shrapnel wound. When I regained consciousness, there was Csaba. He had returned."

"Yes," Ambassador Kovatch said in encouragement. "He had been home, to our apartment, to say goodbye. He hadn't had any luck in finding any supplies. I talked with him then. He decided to return to the fighting."

"I owe him my life," Nemzeti went on. "When I became aware of where I was, Csaba found me. He bandaged my head a bit and stopped the bleeding. Then he told me to leave, and go home. I couldn't defend myself any more, he said, and my staying there would serve no purpose. He urged me to leave, and so I did. He covered for me. In doing so, he may have lost his own chance."

Imre Mohacsi nodded with interest. "So that is what happened," he said. "Csaba left just before I did. I think you, Attila, had already gone then. I never saw him again. What a very brave fellow he was."

Robbie turned to Istvan Szepvaros. "But one person did see Csaba Kovacs again, or at least thought he did. Isn't that right, Mr. Szepvaros?"

"Yes, that's true. I was in hiding. trying to decide what to do, and where safety might lie. I saw, or I thought I saw, Csaba Kovacs in the hands of some military fellows."

"What day was that?" Eva Molnar wanted to know.

"It was towards the very end. I'm sure I don't know now which day it was. Early November, of course."

"That was when I left, towards the end," Eva mused. Everyone listened closely, especially her daughter Magda. It struck Robbie that quite possibly her mother had never spoken of these things with her before.

She continued. "Attila, you had returned. Then a piece of shrapnel hit you. Janos had told me to go. I was the last woman there, and he said that you had just brought back enough ammunition for him to hold off one more assault. So I went."

Nemzeti nodded in agreement.

Robbie listened intently. So did Sylvie, who imagined herself in those circumstances and wondered what she might have done. Thank God she would never know.

"I had the idea of leaving, but I wasn't sure at first where to go. The university quarters didn't seem like a good idea at all. Csaba had remembered that the Americans had granted asylum to Cardinal Mindszenty. I had been to the American Legation on Freedom Square once before. It was a foolish dream, perhaps, but I had wanted to find out about studying art in the United States. I had an acquaintance there, as a matter of fact. It was Mr. Cutler's father. But I arrived just too late. I never made it. The troops cut off the square before I could reach the Legation's front door."

Nobody moved. Each wandered back to that time. She went on.

"I was luckier than some. At least I was not shot outright. Some of our people were, by the way. Later perhaps I'll tell you about that. It was a horrible few days. Finally, they gave me to some Hungarian police, who after a while took me to prison. After a few months there was a trial, if you can call it a trial. They said they had eyewitnesses who had actually seen me fighting, so it was a miracle that I was not sentenced to death."

She smiled at Robbie. "It seems that the American Legation had intervened on my behalf. I got a ten year prison sentence at hard labor instead."

She went on. "Prison life was very hard, and the guards were cruel. My hands were not used to the labor, and I was also beaten. These are not the hands of a sculptor anymore. But again I was lucky. I was serving one of the shorter sentences, and after an amnesty I was let out several years early. You know what happened to many others, the 'trials' and death sentences, and one that was even carried out by hanging when the prisoner reached his eighteenth birthday. I never did understand why Janos Kadar was viewed as such a communist reformer. Perhaps someone can explain it to me one day."

Nobody tried.

"That is when you went home, to Transylvania?" It was Imre Mohacsi's question.

"Yes. That seemed the only thing to do. We had a small house, not even worth confiscating, and it seemed safer there."

"How did you happen to come here tonight?" asked Istvan Szepvaros.

"It was Mr. Cutler who told me about the dinner," she answered. "But I had been in Budapest once before, quite recently. It was here in Obuda, in fact."

Nobody spoke. "I had had a letter from Janos Magassy. He had written from America about his plans for the memorial. How I wish he could be with us here tonight! I looked forward to seeing him. It seemed a miracle that he had survived, and I was pleased that he wanted to see me, and remember what we had all done. And so when he asked to come and see me, I thought it would be an opportunity to try to rejoin the world I once had known, and I came to Budapest to see him."

"And did you see him?" Ambassador Kovatch asked.

"Yes, I did. He said that he looked forward to seeing all of you, too."

"You had a gift for him, I think," Kovatch continued.

"How did you know? Yes, I had brought a sabre with me. It seemed like an appropriate Hungarian symbol of resistance to tyranny. I thought he might find it symbolic when the memorial was planned. It was my contribution."

"How sad and ironic that it was that sabre that was used to murder Janos Magassy," Robbie added. "And now, perhaps, we can begin to put together just how and why that happened."

*   *   *

The waiters left the room by the door leading to the kitchen. The guests hardly were aware of Inspector Imre Racz as he led three men into the room from the door leading to the hallway. Robbie began in a conversational tone.

"The common thread is, of course, the 1956 Revolution and your part in it. That is why Janos Magassy returned. That is why we are here this evening. But that doesn't explain what happened to Magassy. No, for that we must dig deeper."

He took a thoughtful sip of his wine.

"It has always, of course, been possible that the Revolution itself was just a backdrop, and another motive, jealousy perhaps, explained the killing. I'll return to that. But the 1956 connection seemed likely to furnish an answer, if we could just decipher it properly."

"Isn't it obvious that somebody here has something to hide, and that explained it?" Ambassador Kovatch put in.

"Probably everyone has something to hide," Robbie agreed. "That doesn't necessarily furnish grounds for murder, but it certainly muddied the waters for a while."

"First, I looked at the public records. I found the people at the 1956 Research Institute on Dohany Street very competent and helpful. However, there are some gaps. You cannot, at least not yet, punch in a name and come up with a personal history.

"I know," Ambassador Kovatch said ruefully. "I tried that for my brother Csaba shortly after my arrival. It just isn't possible to track a missing person."

Robbie agreed. "Their records are excellent for the general historian, but not for someone who wants to track a single missing person, or for that matter one resistance operating group, such as yours. So we tried to open the official records.

"If we could only have had an investigation with those files fully open, our task would have been easier. We could, for example, have understood who—if anyone—was an intelligence spy in the group," Robbie reflected. "But those files are sealed. My Embassy asked to get them opened, but we couldn't get official permission to do so. And so it has been necessary to reconstruct what happened."

"Janos's article must have been a helpful starting point," Istvan Szepvaros interjected.

"To a certain point, yes," Robbie agreed. "However, he wrote from one perspective. If he didn't see something, or his memory failed him, the record would be wrong. Also, some member of the group might want to change the record. We have several examples of the written record being at variance with other accounts."

"Such as mine," Attila Nemzeti said quietly.

"Exactly," Robbie agreed. Magassy had your comings and goings wrong, and he hadn't realized that you had survived. He was sure that you had been left for dead. That told me that I couldn't rely on his written recollection alone."

"I don't really see how this is getting us anywhere," Imre Mohacsi put in rather testily.

"Oh, but it is a start," Robbie said. "Before returning to Hungary a few months ago for the first time since the Revolution, Janos Magassy had only seen you, and Mrs. Mohacsi, in the United States. He contacted you as soon as he returned to Budapest. And he contacted and then saw Eva Molnar. As far as we know, he did not see Attila Nemzeti or Istvan Szepvaros."

Both men nodded agreement.

"As far as he knew, unless Deputy Mohacsi had mentioned Attila Nemzeti to him when they spoke over the telephone and Mohacsi invited him to the Reception at Parliament, Nemzeti had died over forty years ago."

Imre Mohacsi gave confirmation. "I didn't mention either man, although I did call them both immediately after I spoke with Janos, to invite them to the reception for our reunion."

"Yes, I thought so," Robbie said. "That is how you all knew that Magassy was back in Budapest."

"What about the sabre? That has always puzzled me," Ambassador Kovatch said.

"First, we had to locate where it had been bought, and if possible, who bought it. The police were looking for the killer, and tried photographs with the salespeople at the outlets where these special handcrafted sabres are sold. As I had thought, they got nowhere."

"Why do you say that?" Julie Kovatch wanted to know.

"It was very unlikely that the killer would go stalking Janos Magassy with such an ungainly weapon. Better to use a handgun, or a knife for that matter. No, I think that the killer received an unexpected welcome from Magassy, made an immediate decision, and used Magassy's own sabre to kill him."

"As I said, I had brought it to him," Eva Molnar repeated.

"Yes. There were two possibilities. Magassy might have bought the sabre himself and still, at the end of the day, had it with him when he went out to dinner. That was possible, but very unlikely. He would surely have left such a bulky item in his hotel room. Much more likely was the other possibility, that he had been given the sabre shortly before he met his assailant, and that he had it with him, since he hadn't yet returned to his hotel."

"I gave it to him at dinner that Sunday, the night he died, at a restaurant not far from this one in Obuda," Eva said.

"He didn't say he was expecting.to meet anyone later that evening?"

"No," Eva answered softly, "but he said he had left the name of the Obuda restaurant where we were having dinner at his hotel reception, in case there were messages."

"I thought so," Robbie said. "Now let's get to motives."

"One possibility, as I said, was a motive unrelated to the events of the 1956 Revolution. Jealousy, for example. In that case, the murderer would have known Magassy because of 1956, but that event forms a backdrop only.

"Is it really necessary to go into this?" Magda Mohacsi asked.

"We must examine the possibility," Robbie imperiously answered. Sylvie, fascinated, shivered slightly. This was a side of her fiance that she had not seen before.

"If jealousy were a motive, I said 'if,' then Magassy had only seen you and Deputy Mohacsi of the group prior to his return to Budapest. And if, I say 'if,' your husband had a jealousy motivation, it is highly unlikely that he would seek out Magassy. No, no. Far more likely, he would observe Magassy and you together for clues as to whether his jealousy was justified.

One might even stretch a point and give that as his real motivation for inviting Magassy to the reception. He could then get a pretty good idea of where matters stood, and then decide what steps to take."

Sylvie was transfixed. So was Julie Kovatch.

"So I concluded that it was unlikely that Imre Mohacsi would seek out Magassy to commit murder for such a reason, if such a reason existed. That takes us back once more to 1956 and what happened then," he said, staring at Attila Nemzeti.

"I've already explained what happened then," Nemzeti stammered.

"Yes, and rather convincingly too," Robbie agreed. "You said that you did not hold anything against Janos Magassy for leaving after you were wounded. He must have assumed that you were dead. Also, he had several times urged you to save yourself, as he did others including Eva Molnar, but instead of heeding his warnings you had put yourself in harm's way by returning repeatedly to the headquarters. This was no betrayal."

Attila Nemzeti shook his head. "The saddest part of this for me is that I never got to see Janos again."

"At this point," Robbie continued, "I began to worry about a different matter. I was aware nearly from the outset that Ambassador Kovatch was Csaba Kovacs's brother. It was also evident that he was concealing that fact. 'Why?' I asked myself. The answer came when I saw that you, Mr. Ambassador, were taking a particular interest in the socialist deputy, Ferenc Esztergondos. It began to occur to me that you were concocting a scheme of revenge against the survivors of the group. Perhaps you could funnel some money through Esztergondos into the next cycle of parliamentary elections, for example."

Kovatch said nothing. Everyone understood that meant that Robbie was on the right track.

"If matters had stood there, the problem would have remained a very difficult one. But then, our murderer got too clever by half. He understood who you were, Ambassador Kovatch, and what you were up to, and he decided to help you get revenge. If you realized that your brother Csaba had been left by Attila Nemzeti, for example, that might have pushed you to murder Nemzeti. At the same time, Nemzeti would then have been blamed for Magassy's killing. You would have disposed of Nemzeti, leaving Magassy's real killer in the clear, and you holding the bag. All things considered, you both had a rather narrow escape."

"That leaves me," said Istvan Szepvaros acidly. "All that you have put together is interesting, but hardly proof of anything. I was a loyal member of the 1956 Revolution. and you cannot prove the contrary."

*   *   *

"But I can, you bastard!"

The shout came from near the hallway door.

"You betrayed me, just as you betrayed others. I saw you leading the Russians to our area as I was trying to get away. They sent me to the death camp after you pointed me out. That's what I told Janos Magassy. That's what he threw in your face when you went to see him. And that's why you killed him!"

"Csaba?" Ambassador Kovatch recognized his brother's voice before he saw through the years. "*Csaba!*"

Inspector Imre Racz and his men stepped forward. "I've heard enough," he said, ordering his men to take Istvan Szepvaros into custody. Shaken, Maria Szepvaros left with her husband.

*   *   *

The reunion between Csaba and his brother, and Eva Molnar's reappearance, made it a festive dinner after all. As the waiters resumed service, the questions to Robbie piled up.

"I understood most of this, Robbie, but perhaps you'll go into more details," Julie Kovatch said. "I still don't follow that business about the sabre."

"For another thing," her husband added, "how did you know that Csaba was still alive?"

"And why did you think that Szepvaros was Magassy's killer? What motive did he have, after all this time?" This question was from Sylvie Marceau, ever the investigative journalist.

"As I said," he began, "there were several possibilities. The fact that a sabre was used for the killing meant that the killing was not carefully planned. The killer decided to murder Magassy on the spot. He used what was available. Like that scene in *Gone With The Wind*."

There was a minute of silence. Then Margit Nemzeti said, "I know what you mean. Scarlett O'Hara kills the intruder, the Northern Army soldier. Was that it?"

"Almost. Just after that scene, remember what happens? Melanie Wilkes comes down the staircase *clutching a sabre. That was all that she could find!* That's what gave me the idea. It wasn't the killer's weapon at all. It was Magassy's. That's why it was necessary to find out where he got it."

"But the police were checking that out, surely?" Margit Nemzeti persisted.

"Yes, after I found the outlet in Szekesfehervar. They tried that outlet and the other two, in Debrecen and Szeged, after talking with the craftsman who made the sabres. But they were too limited. They used pictures of Magassy, who might have bought it himself. I thought that was unlikely, but it had to be checked out. They also used pictures of your husband, Mrs. Nemzeti, and of Szepvaros, and Deputy Mohacsi. Nobody remembered selling a sabre to one of those four people. It is a limited production item, so the chances were fair that if we had the right picture, the buyer could have been recognized."

"How did you get around that?" she asked.

"It struck me that if the sabre had been a gift, the logical person to have bought it might have been another member of the group. Only Eva Molnar of the known survivors had not been checked out. The police weren't looking for a woman. And so I asked Ambassador Kovatch to pursue that possibility when we went through Debrecen recently. He did, and a salesperson was struck by his imaginative description. He also, by the way, said that a man was with her when the purchase was made."

"That told me," he went on, "that Eva Molnar and a man had bought the sabre. The same day, my sister and I visited with Eva Molnar and her daughter in Transylvania. Excuse me, I suppose I should have said *Erdely*." Robbie used the Hungarian term for the region.

They smiled. "Eva Molnar received us most graciously. She also said something very important, that she had given the sabre to Janos Magassy to use in the commemorative memorial."

"Why was that important?" Julie wanted to know.

"That meant that Eva, or more exactly her male companion, had not killed Janos Magassy. There was a reason for their giving him the sabre, and no revelation that he could have made that would have made either want to kill him. No, instead, *the motivation for his murder had to be something that they had told him*." Sylvie gasped a bit. Here was Robbie, eliminating suspects that nobody else would even have suspected. Very logical, very Cartesian.

Inspector Racz, quiet until now, spoke up. "Robbie, how did you convince Csaba to come to Budapest?"

"I didn't. I saw him in Transylvania, I thought, but I've never met him or spoken with him. That was part of the problem, after all of the injustice they had seen. They had to trust me."

Ambassador Kovatch spoke up. "I don't see how you traced them. Janos Magassy told me he didn't know where Eva was."

"He lied to you. He wasn't sure who you were, and I'm sure that when he had established contact with Eva, through Freedom Fighter channels, she had asked that he keep the secret."

Eva Molnar nodded her agreement. Robbie continued.

"My first theory was the obvious one, that there was a spy among you from the beginning. Deputy Mohacsi was, I thought, almost telling us that when he spoke of the group as a 'collection of individuals.'" Mohacsi nodded.

"But that didn't quite pan out. You all did know each other. My first solid clue was when Istvan Szepvaros referred to 'those six who died' in a talk with me. I knew about five—Laszlo, Karoly, Magda, Pista and Red. But there were two that were unaccounted for, Jozsef, whom nobody ever talks about, and Csaba Kovacs. That meant he knew something else about who had died."

He looked at Eva Molnar. "It was your colleague, Eva Molnar, who put everything into place. First, she decided to trust me. I think it may have been because she realized that this was her chance to make Csaba safe, once and for all."

"Yes," Eva answered. "If you could find us, then Szepvaros and his new Mafia friends certainly could. We had to expose him to be finally safe."

Inspector Racz asked, "Again, how did you know that Csaba Kovacs was alive?"

Robbie smiled. "Eva Molnar herself told me. When my sister and I visited her and her daughter Magda, she mentioned that they had gone to see Janos Magassy in Budapest. She said that he was surprised to learn from her that Attila Nemzeti was still alive! Now, she had to have learned that from Csaba Kovacs. After all, Eva Molnar had left Barat Street thinking that Nemzeti had died. Nemzeti had just sustained his shrapnel wound. Magassy thought that Nemzeti was dead. Surely she did too. How could she possibly know that he had in fact survived? Only Csaba could have told her that."

"She also cleared up for us the question of the sabre. It had been her idea, shared with Csaba and Janos Magassy in 1956, to have a Hungarian sabre in the memorial. She came to Budapest to give him one."

"Then all of this talk about choosing a theme for the memorial…?" The question came from Magda Mohacsi.

"Camouflage. Janos Magassy wanted to settle, once and for all, if the group had been betrayed. His tragedy was that he had no idea that the informer would kill to protect his secret. That's the case, except for one final detail. Before we get to that, I'm anxious to hear the real story. I'm assuming I was right when I spotted Csaba Kovacs as the gardener near Eva Molnar's home. What really happened in 1956? And how on earth did he ever survive after the Revolution?"

His question was addressed to Eva Moinar, who answered softly. "He had been wounded and left for dead. But Csaba was lucky. He had been given some first aid that had stopped the bleeding. Then came the bad luck. Csaba was rounded up with the others on the street and packed off in a railroad car for a Ukraine prison camp."

There was a collective gasp. Then, unexpectedly, Csaba slowly began to speak. "That was what hurt the most, the betrayal. There was someone with the *AVH* and the Russians. He was looking for me, and pointed me out to them. It was Istvan Szepvaros! He was the traitor who betrayed me. All these years, he must have felt safe, believing me dead."

"But it didn't end that way," he continued. "I was so lucky. I never got to that prison camp after all. Just before we got to the border at Zahony we heard some shots. The train was stopped by Freedom Fighters. They must have put some obstruction on the tracks. I never saw just what they did. All I remember is that the door of the cattle car opened, and I saw sunlight."

"People were shouting for us to get out, get out as quickly as we could. It was hard moving my legs at first, and my head hurt terribly. But I'll never forget that young Freedom Fighter on top of the car, waving our revolutionary Hungarian flag. Never. Those brave kids saved our lives."

"What happened then?" Attila Nemzeti asked for all of them.

"We went in small groups into the woods. I was lucky again. One of the youngsters from the region saw that I couldn't make it by myself. I really needed help. So he stayed with me. First, he brought me some food. Then, he and another man, when it got dark, carried me into their barn. They hid me when the *AVH* came looking for stragglers. Fortunately their search wasn't very thorough. They assumed that everyone on the train would have gotten out of that area. In fact I stayed there for several weeks, until I was strong enough to move on my own."

"Why didn't you go to the border?" Imre Mohacsi asked.

"I did, but not to the border everyone else crossed. Eva and I had talked a lot, and I knew where her village was in Transylvania, across the eastern border in Romania. I thought that if she got away, maybe she would go there. It was hard, but nobody was looking for someone going in the wrong direction. After all, hundreds of thousands of people were going in the other direction, to Austria!"

He poured a glass of wine, and nearly finished it at one long gulp.

"I found her village and her family. They're gone now, but they let me stay with them. Then, gradually, we formed a plan. The Hungarians in the region are resourceful. They've had to be. I was supplied with some fake identification, and slipped back over the Hungarian border to try to find out what had happened to Eva. The border there isn't patrolled now at all. Then, it was all haphazard. and if you were careful you could avoid the border patrols."

"So you came to Budapest?" Robbie, quickly translating for Sylvie, was fascinated.

"Yes. I found Barat Street pretty much destroyed by the fighting. Only a flower seller was there who remembered us. I asked her never to mention that she had seen me again. She didn't know what had happened to Eva, but she did know about the courts that had tried the Freedom Fighters that were caught."

He poured another glass of wine and continued. "I also remembered that we had talked about her going to the American Legation. I guess that didn't work out. We got that idea from a broadcast the last night of the fighting. One of the underground radios broadcast in English, before it signed off. Eva told me that it was the Gettysburg Address of your President Abraham Lincoln. That is why we thought of the American Legation, where Mindszenty went, after all. It was worth a try for Eva."

"How did you find out what happened to Eva?" Imre asked.

"It was very hard. Finally the Kadar regime began to publish lists, the dead, the accused, the trials, and their own white papers, whole books full of lies. It took months—months!—to confirm that she was alive. She had been tried and sentenced. Thank God she hadn't been taken with a gun in her hands. They hanged people for that."

Eva said softly, "There were times when I wished they had taken me with a gun, for that very reason!"

Csaba went on. "As her cousin, with my fake papers, I went back and forth. The Hungarian authorities didn't give me too hard a time, because I was Romanian, or so my papers said. And I developed a routine, of asking for Eva."

"You developed some legitimacy," Attila said. "And like any successful confidence man, you were persistent."

Csaba broke into his old smile. "Exactly. Finally, after a year or more, I found out which prison Eva was in. Then I began to try to visit her. I even sent in some parcels of food. I was sure that the guards confiscated most of it, although I hoped some got through. But mostly, I just wanted them to get used to me. Finally, they did."

"Did you manage to see her?"

"Yes, finally. She was so surprised. She had no idea whatsoever who this 'Cousin Laszlo' was, and she thought I was dead, but she was too clever to betray her surprise. I motioned for silence when they led her into the visiting room."

"I nearly fainted from surprise and happiness," Eva said.

"Quickly I gave her the story. You can all imagine. I said something like 'Dear Eva, you may not even remember me. It's been so long. It's Cousin Laszlo from *Erdely*. The family has been so worried. They asked me to try and see you. Are you all right?'"

"I fell in with it," Eva said. "I couldn't believe what was happening. Here, after all, was a Freedom Fighter, inside a prison, under their very noses. He must have still been high on their wanted list. He had come back for me, after all."

"Just as we promised," Csaba said softly. She nodded. "Then, when I was released, they even formally notified 'Cousin Laszlo' as the responsible party! He came and got me, and we went back home together. Still, despite all this time, we were afraid of the *AVH*. So we pretty much hid, and finally my parents died. The house was ours. There was no reason to leave."

"And your reluctance to talk with officials…even putting it out that your mind was affected?"

"Whose wouldn't have been? But no, Csaba had never been tried. And so we worried that if they caught him, he would be. The only thing to do was to stay hidden. So he did."

"Why did you decide to go to Budapest to see Magassy?"

"We both admired Janos. It was a chance, perhaps our only one, of seeing a more normal life. We had heard that so much had changed but we didn't dare believe it. If Janos had come back, it must be true. And Csaba had to find out about Szepvaros."

"He did tell Magassy about Szepvaros?"

"Yes, exactly."

Robbie took it from there. "After you left Magassy that night, he was murdered. Magassy might have called Szepvaros from the restaurant after Eva and Csaba had left. Either that, or Szepvaros wanted to see if he was in the clear, and decided to see Magassy before the public reception. Either is possible. What surely happened is that at some point as they walked from the restaurant through an alleyway towards the square, Magassy brought up Csaba's terrible accusations."

"That was his death sentence. It surely had never occurred to Magassy that for Istvan Szepvaros, preventing exposure as an intelligence agent over forty years ago was worth killing for even now."

"And why was it?" Ambassador Kovatch wanted to know.

"His motive was concealment. He wanted to protect something that is going on now. He was afraid that if the past yielded up its secrets, his present activities would be investigated. I suspect, Mr. Nemzeti, that your Ministry of Justice had better start a thorough investigation of the financial dealings of Szepvaros's bank here." Inspector Racz nodded agreement.

"I follow you. What do you think we will find?"

"The Russian Mafia connection is the logical possibility. It was the Russian Mafia, according to Inspector Racz here and his people, who tried to assassinate me. Twice. All very professional. Whoever called them in was no amateur out for revenge, but someone who was in league with them. That also was a factor tending to rule out everybody but Szepvaros."

"What would be their connection with Szepvaros?"

"Money laundering on an enormous scale for the Russian Mafia. Szepvaros had either been located and blackmailed, or he had kept his intelligence connections alive, turning that liability into an asset. We know that the Russian Mafia is riddled with old KGB agents. Why shouldn't it work in reverse, with those agents reestablishing their networks with old Warsaw Pact informers throughout the region? A banker, particularly for a respected German bank, would be a natural.

"Further evidence came when the Mafia tried to kill me. Clearly that pointed straight at Szepvaros and at no other suspect. That confirmed the current Mafia connection.

"Until Magassy reappeared, Szepvaros had thought he was quite safe," Robbie continued. "The intelligence files are sealed, and the statute of limitations for what happened during the 1956 Revolution has passed. Then the past began to catch up with him, thanks to all of you. Even Magassy couldn't have known about Szepvaros's real identity. It was only Csaba Kovacs who knew, and Szepvaros was certain that Kovacs was dead."

Imre Mohacsi protested. "But Szepvaros fought with us against the Soviets. I saw him kill them myself!"

"Yes," Robbie admitted. "That was the perplexing part. I think you could make the case that Szepvaros wanted to be a patriot. He did in fact fight them, as several of you have confirmed by eyewitness testimony. You couldn't all have been wrong about that. It puzzled me for a while."

They were silent. Robbie took a glass of wine, then continued.

"It was right there in front of us all the time. You found him, Mr. Nemzeti, in Republic Square the day that *AVH* men were publicly lynched.

I looked up the published records that the Kadar people put out. Janos Szepvaros, a young *AVH* trainee, was one of those killed. He was probably Istvan's brother. Like yourself, Ambassador Kovatch, his real motivation was vengeance for his brother. He saw your brother Csaba there at the assault on Communist Party Headquarters in Republic Square, and connected him with that killing."

There was silence. "He was wrong," Csaba Kovacs said. "I had nothing to do with those deaths. I even tried to stop them. But now we can understand. Perhaps, in time, we can even heal the wounds and begin to forgive."

Ambassador Kovatch summed it up. "I think we should go ahead with Janos Magassy's plans for a 1956 Revolution Memorial." All agreed enthusiastically.

Eva smiled. She had something she wanted to add. "You have all met our daughter Magda. She was named of course for our sweet young fallen colleague." They nodded in remembrance. "You should know that our tradition continues. Magda herself is a Freedom Fighter too!"

"Yes," Csaba proudly added. "You remember several years ago, the campaign that brought down the hated dictator Ceausescu?"

Heads nodded.

"It began in Transylvania. Our daughter was a university student. She took part in demonstrations from the beginning."

Robbie saw Eva Molnar smiling, and Csaba Kovacs, and then he seemed to see them with Janos Magassy and Imre Mohacsi and Attila Nemzeti as youngsters once again, fighting impossible odds for freedom, and finally, after so many long years, winning. The memorial should be built. The world must remember.

Sylvie smiled at Robbie. She understood that Hungary would always be an important part of his life. But for now, all she could think of were the plans for their wedding in Bordeaux and their honeymoon in the Dordogne.

As they left the restaurant a lady selling flowers smiled, gave corsages to the women, and disappeared into the night.

ABOUT THE AUTHOR

▼

William S. Shepard served as Consul and Political Officer at the American Embassy in Budapest. He was made an Honorary Freedom Fighter in 1981, the 25th anniversary of the 1956 Revolution, by the World Federation of Hungarian Freedom Fighters.

0-595-20740-5